CUMBRIA LIBRARIES
D0275610

THE
PLOUGHMEN

THE PLOUGHMEN

A NOVEL

KIM ZUPAN

PICADOR

First published 2014 by Picador
An imprint of Pan Macmillan, a division of Macmillan Publishers Limited
Pan Macmillan, 20 New Wharf Road, London N1 9RR
Basingstoke and Oxford
Associated companies throughout the world
www.panmacmillan.com

ISBN 978-1-4472-4778-4

1 3 5 7 9 8 6 4 2

A CIP catalogue record for this book is available from the British Library.

Printed by CPI Group (UK) Ltd, Croydon, CR0 4YY

To Bill and Virginia Zupan.

And to Janet.

For we are strangers before thee, and sojourners,
as were all our fathers: our days on the earth are as a shadow,
and there is none abiding.

—1 CHRONICLES 29:15

THE PLOUGHMEN

PROLOGUE

The boy got off the bus at the end of the dry lane in the fall of the year, the shelterbelt as he shuffled past shirring with the sound of grasshoppers that wheeled crazily out of the weeds and dusty pale leaves of the Russian olives, blundering into his pants legs, careening off his shirtfront. One day a month he and his schoolmates were released early and encouraged to use the time to perform Corporal Works of Mercy. Val was a serious boy. He shifted his books from hand to hand as he walked toward the far house and began to list them: visit the sick, clothe the naked, bury the dead. What others? The neighbor's black cattle from the bluff looked down, their shapes swimming and wandering eerily in the heat haze. Visit those in prison, that was one. Give drink to those who thirst. To the west he could see his father on the Minneapolis-Moline circling the Schmidt field in a cirrus of dust below thc bluff.

His mother's handwriting was a lustrous script perfected under the scowls and flailing yardsticks of the same forbidding Sisters of Providence who now taught him—the notes left in his lunch box or in the margins of a birthday card or, on the rare occasions she and his father went out, he found on his pillow—keepsakes to be hoarded. There was care in the rendering of the loop and slant of her letters as if, like words chiseled in a temple frieze, they were meant to last a thousand years. On this September day the note stood upright between salt and pepper shakers in the shape of smiling pigs. *Darling—Come alone to the shed.*

He went into his younger sister's room and she lay sleeping under rumpled sheets with her thumb in her mouth. He took an apple from a bowl by the sink and stood at the counter eating it. Through the window across the gravelly lot he could see the shed door standing open. A meadowlark lit atop the lone yard-light pole, warbled, flew. He stood staring after it. In a month it would be gone.

In the yard, dust rose beneath his feet and the day was bright. In town, his friends were playing tag on the green boulevards but his place, he knew, was here. The door to the shed swayed on its hinges groaning and what he could see of the interior was only darkness. A single cloud in the brilliant firmament towed its image across the ground miles away. She would have stopped to watch it go.

For years they'd kept chickens in the metal pole barn, an enterprise she had said was a losing battle, as those that did not simply freeze to death fell victim to fox or skunk and if she was going to be in the business of feeding every predator in the country she'd just go ahead and buy dog food and be done with it. The chickens had been gone a long while, yet when the wind blew and the building shuddered under it, feathers still drifted down from the purlins and collar ties all but invisible high above in the murk of shadow. Now as he stood inside, arms around a rough post, one such filthy snowflake fell in random drift and he could see in the gloom overhead the rope looped twice and tied.

Later he remembered the smell of the chickens there and he imagined them in the dim recesses bobbing their scabrous heads and clawing the gravel with their horrible feet. He remembered these things and that her hand when he finally touched it felt like the wood of the post he gripped so tightly, watching in the dusty fug the slow slow metronomic swaying of her body.

He righted the ladder from where it had fallen, ascended the steps as she had and sawed at the rope for a long time with his pocketknife. With a bespattered grain tarp he covered her where she fell, dust rising from its folds in the stifling air like a sprite, and he touched her leg once to assure himself that she was wooden now, was not his mother but some other thing left in her place.

He stepped into the brilliant doorway, turned briefly. His outsized shadow lay across the floor and across the tarp and leaned aslant on the wall in a scarecrow parody of himself. He considered his work and it was not right. He went once more across the ranchyard to the house, rummaged in a closet in her room. He checked on his sister, swept back a damp curl from her face, laid a hand on her narrow back to feel the timorous swelling of life there and went out again across the gravel to the shed carrying the box. He pulled back the tarp and stood looking down at the naked feet.

Afterward he rearranged thc tarp, tucking it carefully. He leaned the ladder against the wall and smoothed the dirt with his foot where he had knelt and then had walked across the shorn fields and summerfallow toward the cloud of dust with his father inside it. He stopped once to look back at what his life had been and then kept walking.

"It was a mistake," his father said. "That note was for me." If theirs had been a different marriage it might have been an invitation to a tryst but he would have known. He would have known it was not. "She forgot you'd get home early. It was all just an awful goddamn mistake."

The boy didn't hear or didn't believe and he stood staring at the dirty toes of his school shoes. He had been summoned. In the sensuous cursive of his mother's hand he had been given responsibility. He would not relinquish it.

"I don't understand." His father could not stop shaking his head. He made a strangled sound. He hadn't touched her. He hadn't touched the boy. "She hated those slippers." He looked at the boy and the boy looked away. The boy thought, How do you not understand? It was simple: it was for me to do. I was her Valentine.

"It don't make sense," his father said. "She never wore them once."

ONE

As if to fend off a blow he threw up his arms in front of his face and the first bullet went through his thin forearm and through the top half of his right ear and went whirring into the evening like a maddened wasp. The next as he turned to run took him high in the back of the neck and he fell headlong and did not move. The old man went to him and examined the wound critically. He turned the boy over. The bullet had come out below his nose and the old man considered its work, while the boy batted his eyes and took in the sky beyond the killer's bland and placid face—gray clouds of failing winter, a small black leaf, a black kite, at last an enormous wheel of March's starlings, descending with the mere sound of breath.

From where he sat, the old man could see the river, the whitecaps and the pitching gulls indistinguishable, and he could see the tallest buildings of the old smelterworks beyond the coulee's steep flanks and in the east the shadowed Missouri Breaks raggedly diminishing into the hazy blue gloaming of coming spring. He could feel the last of winter in the wind, see it in the color of the river, gray and churning like molten lead.

The soil there was poor and sandy and the grass on those slopes grew sporadically and reminded him of pigs' hair. There were yucca and prickly pear and he could hear like a faint voice in his ear the hiss of blowing soil at the ridge crest. Still a farmer, he thought. He sifted the dirt through his fingers. The slope below was nearly bare and troughed by the melt-off of ten thousand springtimes. Still a goddamn farmer. Seed put down here would most likely just wash away. Scattered about lay cobbles of sandstone, spalls of shale like medieval roof tiles randomly shingling the slanted ground. A gull came near enough that above the wind and the sea-spray hiss he could hear its thin woman-cry. He looked up briefly, then called to the young man below him in the coulee bottom. "Deeper," he said. "You got to make it deeper."

The man looked up and leaned on his shovel handle briefly and then continued to dig.

"Hear me?" he said.

"I hear you." The younger man was sweating and had thrown aside his jacket, its arms twisted among the brittle weeds.

He watched the digger assail the dirt ineffectually, then raised his eyes to the broken landscape below him. He liked this place. He had used it before and that comforted him. It was like a warehouse he knew well and that was there when he needed it, quiet and close to town. The dirt was poor but there were few rocks and the digging was easy. Boys came to this side of the river in the early fall to sight in their rifles for hunting season. The sound of gunfire was not unusual. At the head end of nearly every coulee lay boxes with targets taped to them, and brass shell casings lay about everywhere as though a series of battles had raged down the ravines and over the low divides and sere hills.

Shortly the other man laid aside his shovel and waited and then the two of them rolled the body in and they began covering it over, one with the shovel, the other, the farmer, because he still held the blunt pistol, pushing in the soil with the side of his foot.

The wind swept momentarily down into the raw gulch and the hair on the older man's balding pate stood straight up. The gull circled, calling into the pale blue sky where immane banks of cloud raced toward low mountains in the south, bound to the stratosphere by filaments of distant rain. The older man, whose name was John Gload, stooped to pick up a grain sack which held in its bottom the severed hands and head of the young man whose body they'd just consigned to the thin and unproductive soil of the Missouri River Breaks. Anonymous bones now, among others—John Gload's dark signature on the landscape of the world.

Two hundred years earlier, the wayfarers under Lewis and Clark had portaged over this very ground, trundling their boats in the heat around the impassable falls. Gload, never voluble when he was at work, remembered that bears had once lived here and the thought made him smile.

"Bears," he said. "Grizzly bears, right here."

The younger man looked at him uncomprehendingly.

"Don't give me that look," Gload said. "I'm trying to teach you something. Used to run around here like gophers. Hundred fifty years ago they would of had this asshole dug up and ate before we got over the hill." The older man pointed up the slope where dun cheatgrass sawed about under the March wind, imagined there old silvertips a-totter on their hind legs like lethal storybook ogres, sorting out the scent of them. "Course they might of got us, too." He held the small pistol flat in his palm and considered it. "This goddamn thing wouldn't do nothing but put a little spring in their step while they ripped your head off." Gload surveyed the country round, imagining the hills alive with such beasts. He ran his eyes up and down his thin partner appraisingly. "You wouldn't make more than a bitty turd-pile."

They walked then down along the flat coulee bottom, the younger man with the shovel over his shoulder like an infantryman. They stepped among bluestem and sagebrush, bottle shards glistering in the silt like gemstones, and passed without note the stripped bone cages of the poached and butchered deer of the previous fall.

The younger man who now drove the car was named Sidney White and was called by all who knew him Sid the Kid. Though he had never sat a horse or been among cows he thought himself a cowboy and his fabrication was one of snap-button shirt and tight jeans stogged into a pair of secondhand boots a size and a half too large, the uppers gaudily colored and stamped with flowers and elaborate glyphs and tooled with the initials of the previous owner. He was vain of his lank black hair combed back slick, and so eschewed the addition of a hat to his costumery. John Gload had found him through a series of dismaying defaults and in the end had used him simply because of his youth and apparent good teeth, which the old man judged indicated an abstinence from methamphetamine. This was Sid White's first real score and he was excited.

As they drove, White suggested they turn north on an

intersecting gravel road which would take them in fifteen minutes' time to a house set among the strips of vast wheat farms north of town that had indeed once been a farmhouse but had in recent years been home to an older woman and her three younger charges.

"You know the place? It ain't but ten miles." He wrung the steering wheel, agitated, swung his narrow eyes from the curving river road to John Gload and back again. "I say we cap things off with a little trim."

Gload stared at the river through a verge of leafless willows and the water frothed under the wind. The gulls he so despised hung against the gray crepe of the spring sky like Japanese paper sculpture pinned there.

"No," he said.

"You don't know it?"

"I know it. And no is the answer."

"This here's the turn coming up." Sid White slowed. Perhaps the old man might change his mind. The unmarked road, little more than parallel ruts with a hemstitch of wheat stubble, aspired gently northward and seemed to vanish, gone at this evening hour the frontier between summerfallow earth, summerfallow sky.

Gload sighed and turned to regard the kid's profile, an acne-pitted hawk's face with a profusion of ragged blue-black Indian hair. "We're not going there just so you can remind yourself that you're better than the thing you just put in a hole."

The kid looked at him. "What you talkin' 'bout?"

"That's why you feel like you need to get laid. It's no more than that."

"Bro, that ain't true. I live for that poontang. Anytime, anywhere."

"And don't talk that fake ghetto talk around me. You're no spade."

"Whatever, man."

"Yes. Whatever."

They went past the turn and drove for a time in silence. John Gload brushed at a stain on his trousers. On their left the river had turned the color of wine, the stone bluffs on the far shore in the sudden shadows turned to statuary—dour countenances, creatures seen in dreams.

Sidney White said finally, "Might of done you some good, though. It relieves tension, sex does, and I ain't making it up because I read that somewheres."

"Do I look tense to you?" Gload said. "Do I appear tense?"

The kid glanced over at him and then began to slowly nod his head. His small teeth, revealed in a leer, were brilliant. "Okay," he said. "All right. They got stuff for that. I could hook you up, pard."

The older man appeared not to have heard, an unaccustomed uneasiness at that moment creeping into his limbs. When he was a boy, once, sitting on a bald and rocky hillside in the early dark, a bat came so near he felt the air beside his face move and it left him with a chill of foreboding that had little to do with the October evening. It was a stirring much like that he felt now in the still interior of the car. He looked to see that the windows were rolled up and that the heater's fan was off, and he glanced at the kid to see if it was some trick, some sleight of hand.

White caught the look. Sensing some interest he said, "That's right. Your old lady would be plumb wore out."

He'd been thinking about her even before the kid conjured her image, how in bed her slim leg would be draped across his own as though to maintain a connection even in sleep, as if not touching him even that near was to be utterly apart.

John Gload, as if to pat the kid on the shoulder, raised his left arm from the seat back where it rested and put the short barrel of the gun to the kid's ear. The kid drew in his breath and held it.

"I don't need nothing," Gload said.

"Okay."

"Don't ever talk to me about this kind of shit again. You understand? You don't know nothing about me and never will." The kid nodded very slowly, as if afraid even this vague movement might ignite death in his ear. As an afterthought Gload said, "And none of that bullshit jailyard talk, either."

The kid drove, pouting, until Gload told him to stop. He pulled the car onto the shoulder of the road and sat smoking while Gload got out and began shifting the contents of the trunk behind the raised lid. Then he could hear the hatchet working. He dandled his wrist atop the steering wheel and stared out broodingly at an outlandish sky, long flaming celestial mesas and reefs and the copper half disk of the sun diminishing beyond stagecraft mountains in the west and sucking after it, into that far void, minute birds the color of embers. The chopping sound from the rear of the car went on rhythmically—chunk, chunk, chunk.

In the side-view mirror he watched Gload walk to the rocky shoreline and throw something into the murky chop. The gulls, substantiating from seeming nowhere, began to dive and keen while John Gload waved his arms about like a conjurer. He stooped and threw handfuls of gravel. The kid watched this in the mirror and finally turned in the seat to watch out the window and when Gload came back the kid was smiling.

"You can't never hit nothing with just rocks."

The old man favored the kid briefly with a bland look and settled into his seat without replying. The kid shrugged, levered the car into gear, and drove west on the narrow blacktop, in the windshield the sun a tangerine shard wedged among the distant black peaks.

"A shotgun, now," White said. "That'd get your point acrost."

They went in silence toward the garish sunset and then Gload said, "Pull over at the dam."

"Hell, it'll be dark here pretty quick."

Gload ignored him. "Pull over up here." Sid eased the car into a pullout for utility company vehicles, at the head of a long set of wooden stairs descending to gloom. "Pop the trunk and wait here," Gload said.

The kid watched him go down the stairs with the grain sack. Below, the lights along the great curve of the dam began to flicker on. Presently he saw John Gload appear in the first circle of light and fade and reappear in the next, progressing this way along the concrete catwalk, incorporeal as a phantom.

A fine spray rose above the dam's railings from the torrent roaring through the floodgates and when Gload finally stopped it appeared as a downy luminescent cloud above his head. He stood at the rail and watched the amber water of spring thaw surge through the sluicegates. He turned. Behind him in the curve of the dam, tree limbs wheeled about in a huge scum-covered whirlpool, rising and falling like the arms of drowning giants. Half-inflated plastic grocery bags like men-of-war bobbed in the wrack and there were animals so terribly bloated that they may have been cats or hogs and he could make out the dented prow of a skiff and there was all manner of floatable trash and slim branches fluted by beaver teeth and there were ducks and small waterbirds, their dead eyes gemlike in the glare and everywhere in the slime like a grotesque choir the round sucking mouths of voracious river carp.

Gload turned and strode across the concrete walkway and dropped the sack into a great spout of water and it shot forward and past the brief yellow corona and was gone. On that ancient riverbed were the bones of fish long extinct the size of dolphins and there were the bones of plesiosaurs and mastodons and the disjoined skeletons of luckless Cree and Blackfeet two centuries old. Standing in the dark interstice between the spillway lights, Gload felt connected with history, a part of a greater plan. For all that, he took no chances. He had taken the young man's hands and chopped the teeth from his head and with these now settling on the river bottom the corpse was as nameless as the fossilized bones of preadamite fish.

When he got back to the car, Sid the Kid was asleep sitting up with his hands on the wheel, a cigarette smoldering above his knuckle. Gload stood outside smoking and waiting and then the kid began to yowl and shake his hand and stuck two fingers in his mouth. Gload slid in on the passenger side, shaking his head.

"Take me home," he said. "Tomorrow we go get rid of the stuff."

Amber leaves of the previous fall lay pooled beneath the apple trees, thin and black against the gunmetal sky. A covey of Hungarian partridge scuttled across the weedy lot, articulated like a tiny train, in the window's light the males' ruby throatbands flashing an electric brilliancy amid all the dun color of the wild grass. In that yellowed rectangle he could see Francie pass and repass. The chimney issued bone-white smoke that stood in the strangely still air as rigid and substantial as a church spire. As he watched her, the uneasiness once more fluttered past. He batted the air beside his head as though it were a living thing.

He had walked the half mile up his drive from the county road where he'd had the kid drop him and now he stood among his trees smoking. Though the river was two miles away its smell was on the air and it was faintly perfumed by the sage on the benchlands that lay just to the south.

Once in a drought year a bear had come, shambling down from the Highwood Mountains twenty miles distant, and taken up residence in the grove, eating the fallen bitter little apples and sleeping there unabashed on the ground amid the brittle leaves and rimed grass and leaving like spilled preserves huge piles of his shit everywhere. In the end he took to climbing the trees for the few apples that would not fall and at night from their bed they could hear the small knurred branches crack under his weight with the sound of distant fireworks. Gload had left it alone, seeing in its shape and nature something of himself.

When he'd gone in and poured coffee into his favorite cup and sat at the table, she said, "Do I look any better through a window than I do in person?" She had turned from her work, smiling, swirling ice in the glass she held.

"You won't sing when I'm in the room. I like your singing."

"I could have you run in for spying on a lady like that."

"For a hell of a lot more than that," he said.

From behind the kitchen counter she approached him a little unsteadily and she laid a soft, cool hand alongside John Gload's face. She stared down into his eyes, dark wells wherein such things existed that he could not tell her or anyone. And as if she glimpsed some of what was there she said, "There's some good in you, Johnny. And I might be the only one knows it." Gload's hands lay on either side of his cup and she took her hand from his face and placed it atop one of his. He looked down at them wordlessly. It might have been what he loved most about her, that she seemed to know some things, horrible things, but she forgave him them and this small act—of laying her smooth hand atop his own, which had so recently held the bloodied instruments of his trade—was a sort of absolution.

"I got to leave tomorrow. For a few days."

"I ought to know the pattern by now. So we'll eat a nice dinner and watch the TV and go to bed early."

"That would be nice."

"Am I allowed to ask when you'll be back?"

"Sure you can ask, but I don't know. Three, four days."

"What if one time you don't come back? Me out here all by myself? I couldn't do it. For a few days I'm okay. But even a week is getting to be too hard, Johnny."

"I always come back. Have I never not come back?"

"If you never did come back we wouldn't be talking right now about you coming back."

John Gload extricated his hand from under hers, a quavering translucent bird of a hand, and cupped his own brutal paws over his ears.

"Let's eat," he said. "You're making my head hurt."

They ate a long leisurely meal and Francie for her dessert drank two glasses of port wine in a jam jar and as was their long habit sat at the side door listening to the evening sounds and watching the western sky flame and slowly transubstantiate to an ebony velvet arrayed with shards of quartz. They went to bed and made love on the cool sheets with the windows opened slightly to a cross breeze. Pale skin, pale sheets—beneath him she seemed a being fading from view, the look she wore, so dreamy and distant, as if like a person going down slowly down in a lake, she watched the cruel surface recede with bemused carelessness. Before John Gload's heartbeats subsided Francie was asleep and softly snoring and he lay listening to miller moths battering themselves on the window screen behind his head—small souls seeking the freedom of the greater world. Recently he'd begun to imagine Francie's spirit fluttering among them.

He could not sleep but neither did he want to get out of bed. She would not wake up, he knew, because she slept as deeply as a child, but he hated to be far from her when he knew he was leaving. So he lay in the dark. She slept on her back composed as if by an undertaker, even to her white hands crossed on her small breasts, though one leg stretched out to rest against his. A tether, a lifeline. The wind shifted the thin curtains and rattled the curtain rings on the brass rod that held them and in the neglected orchard beside the house an owl called. Some long time later, with her breathing close at his ear and the curtains like pale spirits hovering at the edge of his sight, he slept. He had been imagining a long-ago field and he rode the plow around and around in that dreamy sunlight.

TWO

It was dark among the trees and when the young man came into a clearing the snow lay deep and untrammeled, lit softly blue from the quarter moon and the stars swarming in the cloudless vault above the peaks. After a while the boles of the ponderosa and lodgepole revealed themselves from the blackness and then soon the lower branches hung with moss like hag's hair, and small birds began to rouse and dart out before them like vanguards. The small stream he followed muttered beneath a thin pane of ice and among the topmost branches of the trees a faint wind was another secret voice and he stopped to listen. He peered ahead to the black rampart of timber. Maybe today, he thought. Maybe it will be today.

It was the first week in April and the deputy sheriff and his dog tracked a young woman separated from her skiing companions during a brief and vicious early spring storm at a forked drainage in the Crazy Mountains. A night and a day and another night had passed and on the following morning Valentine Millimaki on snowshoes set out from the trailhead in frigid darkness.

In the course of his duties with the Copper County Sheriff's Department he spent time investigating rural crimes and he endured his required hours in the old jail building adjacent to the county courthouse, a grim edifice of sandstone blocks hewn by Croatian masons which in its earliest days had held cattle rustlers and horse thieves. But it was work outdoors that he loved, with the three-year-old shepherd dog tracking through the woods and brush and sudden canyons in wildlands where maps of some blank and forgotten corners were still mere suggestions of one's place in the world.

Some he found scratched and bruised or limping aimlessly atop a fractured ankle with a tree branch for a crutch, some in the late stages of hypothermia doddering half-naked through drifts in pursuit of ghosts and visions. Hunters, hikers, felons afoot from stolen vehicles at the dead ends of logging roads. All alive. Thirteen months ago he'd found an autistic child, scratched and shivering in the timber in the rain with his lapdog clinched beneath his arm like a shabby carnival prize, limp and strangled. That had been the last. For over a year now there had been only bodies.

The dog was working well, lunging with difficulty through the heavy snow, and Millimaki told him so. "Good Tom. Find the girl." The shepherd stopped to look at him, his tongue already hanging long from his mouth, and he lapped once at the snow and went on.

Millimaki halted briefly to examine new tracks quartering across their path. Prints of deer stove into the virgin snow, overlaid with those of a big cat. The hair along the dog's back rose and his lip turned back quivering to show his gleaming teeth and Millimaki spoke to him again. Other tracks atop the new snow, hieroglyphics of mice and squirrels—frantic senseless diasporas into the perilous open where owls swept down spectral and silent as the night itself. Today, Millimaki thought again. Our luck may change today.

Some ten miles in she lay on her back in a trail under a dusting of new snow with a topographical map spread atop her chest as if in her bed she had fallen asleep reading. Tom sat on his haunches at the side of the trail cocking his ears at Millimaki, who squatted beside the woman, brushing away the snow from her face. He sat looking at her, so white, white as porcelain, her blue lips drawn tight as though in deep concentration, but for all that a peaceful sylvan sleeper, her skis and poles arrayed beside her neatly to be taken up after that brief consultation of the map.

The day was utterly silent and brilliant now, the sun at that hour straight overhead and the sky above the clearing where the woman had stopped was galleried by a coven of ghostly pinetops. Perhaps she'd stood gazing uncomprehendingly at the emerging stars, in their milky light superimposing the enormous order wheeling overhead onto the map that seemed to hold her life in its obtuse loops and lines. Perhaps she would lie down and from that vantage Polaris might appear, or another far sun that could reinstate her in the paradoxical world. For just a moment, a few short minutes. The unknowable stars looking down. A brief nap in the clearing in the starlight.

These are the things Valentine Millimaki imagined. A small bird came to sit on the branch of a tree and took in the scene—dog, man, statue—then flew. He watched it disappear into the sun. The young woman had lost a mitten and her bare hand lay atop the map. Wearing the snowshoes, Millimaki squatted with some difficulty. The dog sat watching him. He removed his own mitten and extended his hand and touched her wrist. As he touched all of them. What remained, he told himself, was not what they had been.

He stood and considered the long trek out and eventual return leg after hours of delay while protocol was satisfied. His day was just begun. His ungloved hand was numb and pale and he stood thwacking it clublike against his leg, the whop whop whop unreasonably loud in the sepulchral stillness. The dog looked at him quizzically. He said, "Let's go, Tom." The dog stood and circled once and looked from him to the woman in the snow. She slept on. "Come on. She's all right now."

Fifteen hours later, at home in his bed, Millimaki thought again of the woman sleeping alone beneath her cold white counterpane in the woods. His wife had stirred when he crawled in beside her, the chill still gripping his bones, phantom pack straps furrowing his back.

"I'm home," he whispered. He shifted closer for the warmth of her, for the life in her. "I found her."

"What?" She spoke from the edge of a dream, her words slurred. "Who?"

"The woman I was after, in the Crazies."

"That's good." From far away, barely audible, she said, "That's nice."

"I didn't get there in time." In the darkness above his head he was seeing the woman again, blanched and rigid. "I didn't make it."

He'd wanted his wife to say she was sorry, that this epidemic of woodenness would soon end. That the next one would be alive and breathing and grateful. To say, "It wasn't your fault, Val. It's not ever your fault."

"Oh, Val," she said, "Please. Go to sleep. I need to sleep."

He put his hand on his wife's warm back and soon he felt through the heave of her ribs the slow rhythm of sleep. After a long while he slept. A wind out of the prairies of Alberta rattled the branches of the box elder trees against the house eaves and the cabin door shuddered in its jamb. It blew and drifted deep all night and the country in the clear blue dawn would be new and immaculate and anything lost in it would be lost until there was little to be found but bones.

He had saved her from that. He had done that at least.

The day following was Monday and after four scant hours of shallow sleep he dressed in the dark to not wake his wife. Lying beside her he was visited that night by the dream that in recent weeks was never far away. In it his mother's mouth was not blue like the woman's he had found earlier nor did it look as it did when as a boy he'd found her but was instead painted the color of cherries or of blood, horrible against the white of her doll's-face.

Palsied and leaden he drove the blank white country through the coming dawn to assume his shift as court security for the old man who had recently taken up residence in the Copper County jail. The hills' incipient green, so faint and tenuous it may have been merely a trick of the eye after months of white on gray, was utterly erased by the storm. Songbirds gathered stunned and mute in the cottonwoods along the creek and on the right-of-way fence wires and the roadway was smeared and littered with gore, deer come to feed on weeds exposed by the county's plows grotesquely disassembled by tractor trailers careening through the dark toward Billings and Cheyenne. Millimaki stopped once to drag a young doe from the centerline of the highway, among the gray and glistening ropes of her umbles a tiny fawn spilling from its caul. Crows and magpies swarmed the humming powerlines overhead, awaiting the tender carrion and greeting with caws and croaks the plenitude of the refulgent day.

The day they'd gone for him, one week earlier, was a day so fine that Millimaki drove with his window rolled down, the ruddy road dust from the patrol car in front of him that seeped into the cab of little consequence because it made him believe in the possibility of spring.

The old man stood up from his chair as if to greet old friends. Millimaki walked down the short length of road behind the other men as instructed, Dobek advancing with his piece drawn and aimed at the man's midsection, Wexler beside him with the shotgun, the barrel wandering dangerously as he quick-stepped through the grass grown up in the center of the lane. It was a mild day but Dobek's shaved head gleamed with sweat. Wexler was pale, his prominent adam's apple jerking in his throat.

Dobek called out as they approached, "Sit in the chair, asshole." Gload showed his hands front and back like a magician and resumed his seat.

"Now on your feet." Dobek and Wexler stopped ten feet short, their guns upraised. They were breathing hard as if they'd run a great distance. The old man put his hands on his thighs and rose with an air of detachment or boredom, unconcerned with the two black boreholes wavering lethally in front of him, his eyes instead searching the pale blue vault above in the direction of the river where he seemed to be expecting something to appear.

"Down on the fucking ground."

"Up, down, up, down," the old man said.

"Down in the fucking dirt, now," Dobek bellowed. "Hands behind. Millimaki, get the bracelets on him." Millimaki knelt and snapped the handcuffs in place. They were barely large enough to fit over the old man's massive wrists, only two teeth of the ratchet end engaging the pawl.

Dobek, his round smooth dome gleaming, stood off several feet with his sidearm leveled at the old man's broad back. One of the older deputies on the force, he wore a tailored uniform that now fit too tightly across his gut, and the short sleeves he favored revealed a faded USMC tattoo on one biceps and on the other some snarling animal—wolf or panther—it, too, indistinct, whether from age or maladroit artistry, but its message of predation was clear. He was an enforcer, a departmental bogeyman to be conjured when all reason failed to mollify prisoners gone mad in their cages. Now he motioned with his chin and the two younger men got Gload to his feet and Wexler began patting him down. In his agitated state he'd leaned the scattergun carelessly against the chair's seat where it teetered, and Millimaki stepped around him and took it up and punched the safety on. Wexler ran his hands up and down the old man's faded shirt and beneath his arms and moved to his feet, slapping and chopping up the bowed legs and finally leering up at the two other men as he squeezed the old man's genitals, saying, "Nothing."

"Who's inside?" Dobek asked.

"No need to holler. I can hear as good as you."

"I said, Who's inside, goddamn it."

"Nobody."

"Nobody's ass. We'll see." Dobek nodded to Wexler, who took up the shotgun, and they moved toward the rear door of the house. "Millimaki, keep your piece on this fuck." He jerked the screen door open savagely and nodded Wexler to the fore and they banged through the main door in combat positions. The screen door, weather-checked and paintless, hung askew, the top hinge screws pulled nearly loose.

Gload had watched them enter his house and when he turned to Millimaki he wore an expression of deep sadness. "Now look what they done to that door."

"That can be fixed easy enough."

"It's got some dry rot. You got to be gentle with it."

Millimaki said, "Is anyone here?"

"Like I said, nobody."

The deputy brushed the dirt and grass from the old man's shirtfront and trousers and brought forward the chair for him to sit. Millimaki turned and looked at the wild orchard where spring was foretold by minute buds and the presence of tiny birds among the brambles. He noted crocuses in bloom along the walk and bright yellow flowers turned toward the sun.

"What are these?" he said. "Daffodils?"

The old man shrugged. He'd begun to watch the young deputy with interest.

Millimaki turned his back to the old man and studied the tangle of trees. "You might have wanted to cut these trees back without any mercy. It's out of control in there."

The old man stared at him with his mouth ajar.

Millimaki said, "What kind of apples are they?"

"Couldn't tell you," Gload said.

Millimaki ducked into the trees and, reaching to a high branch, picked an apple from the previous year that had somehow not fallen, shrunken and hard as ornamental fruit. He rolled it in his palms, sniffed it. Around him the small birds swirled, their tiny black eyes following his every move. John Gload watched him. He looked to the young man in the trees and he glanced at the door of his house where the two deputies had gone and he looked down the narrow lane to the county road beyond.

Millimaki came out of the trees. "Best guess is they're some kind of old McIntosh," he said.

Before the old man could reply, Dobek and Wexler banged out of the house, the older deputy at ease now and smirking and eating a pear he'd found inside. When he saw the two other men conversing, the older man sitting cross-legged in his chair, Millimaki once again examining the apple, the pear exploded out of his mouth. He sputtered, "Christ, Millimaki, I said put your piece on him. Did I not say that?" He'd holstered his sidearm and now he had it out again and pointed at the old man in the chair. "Wexler, did I not say to him, Put your piece on this piece of shit?"

"You did, Voyle. Definitely."

"The fuck's the matter with you?"

"Cuffed and sitting in a chair," Millimaki said. "Where's he gonna go?"

"Fuck." Dobek looked from the young deputy to the old man, who placidly sat in his chair, cocking his long equine head carelessly to the trills and frantic fluttering of the springtime birds in his arbor. The old man's insouciance seemed to enrage the veteran deputy and the flesh of his neck bulged above his uniform collar red as a coxcomb. "Fuck," he said again. Wexler's small blue eyes swung from Dobek to Gload and to Dobek again, reading the veteran's face. He raised the scattergun to his waist, his finger massaging the trigger guard nervously. With his free hand Dobek thumbed a line of sweat from his forehead and slung it to the side.

"There was a time not all that long ago when we'd of just dropped a rope over something or other and been done with this suvabitch. But now." He surveyed with clouded countenance the country around them for all its corruption and inefficacy, the weak imperfect world an insult to him. "Now we got to go through the whole song and dance and the spending of taxpayer money and feeding this suvabitch for ten or fifteen or however too many years to wind up with the same exact thing—a dead fucker hanging."

Wexler smiling, nodding. "Fucking right, Voyle."

John Gload throughout this gazed off wistfully toward the low hills that rose to the north, where juniper and scrub pine grew on stubbornly among the weeds and sage. Great shoals of cumulus scudding on the wind. Dobek stepped up from behind and ran the barrel of his pistol roughly along the old man's bristled cheek, eliciting a sandpaper sound. With the cold nickel barrel he traced the curve of the old man's ear. When Gload snatched his large head to the side Dobek stepped back as if scalded.

Once more he troweled sweat from his forehead. "Okay," he said. "All right. Where's the woman of the house, old man."

"Not here."

"I deduced that all on my very own, asshole. Where'd she go?"

"Just gone," Gload said. "Gone off."

Dobek stood for a moment, tapping his handgun against the stripe of his uniform pants. He exchanged a look with Wexler then turned to Millimaki, his obsidian eyes lingering there longer as if considering his options. Finally he said, "Okay, Wexler, get him in the car. And I want the footwear on him, too."

John Gload's expression never changed as he was jerked

erect and pushed toward the car. He glanced once at the house and once longingly at the wild bosk of trees and he looked briefly to the sky to the south where skeins of thin cirrus mirrored the slow river below. His eyes too swung across Millimaki, who'd stood aside carefully among the radiant spring blooms to let the other two lead the old man away to his fate.

The corridor of cells was belowground and the darkness stayed long there, the sickly purple-blue light from the hissing fluorescents and the light that came in through the two high windows scant at any hour, any season. The snow had begun to melt and water poured from the downspouts of the old building and overran the gutters, cascading down the sandstone block and over the street-level windows in myriad rills. From within, the glass appeared to run and shift like mercury.

The night jailer at the end of his shift walked with Millimaki as if in a trance down the dank corridor and introduced him to the old man and turned and retraced his steps and went out into the light of the new day, which he seemed altogether unsuited for. His eyes were so red and the circles under them so dark, he seemed to be wearing thespian's makeup and the flesh seen above his collar and below his shirt cuffs had the yellow cast of a consumptive.

Because of his age and reputation and the nature of his crimes John Gload was kept out of the bullpen and housed in one of the county jail's hospital cells, different from the six other county jail cages of the general population only in that it was separated from them by a short hallway and a locking door. In the course of his long career the old man had inhabited such lodgings before. As a much younger man he had done ten years in the state penitentiary in Rawlins, Wyoming, much of it in solitary confinement, and on an overhead water pipe in that cell he had done thousands of pull-ups, the only sounds for hours in the near-profound dark his breathing and the mouselike whingeing of the pipe protesting his weight. His arms, even at the age of seventy-seven, were so large that when he extended his hand toward Millimaki he could only get it through the bars just beyond the wrist.

Gload had come forward, his face lit for an instant by the overheads and the aqueous niggardly light the high windows afforded and then receding to shadow.

"We've met," Millimaki said. "Informally, I guess you'd say."

From beyond the lightfall he heard Gload say, "I recanize you from the welcoming committee. The apple expert."

Millimaki drew up a chair from the opposite wall of the narrow hallway and sat. They waited for the call to move across the street to the courthouse. The cells beyond the sally gate were quiet—men asleep, men absent, in court themselves shackled and fearful and sweating in their issue coveralls. Men in their cages atop their bunks biding oppressive time, urgently listening to any voices but those inside their heads.

"It's a nice place you have out there," Millimaki said. "Hope you don't mind I poked around a bit after you went to town."

"Why would I mind? Nothing to hide."

"Good soil. Out of the wind, for the most part. Nice little spot."

Gload nodded. "I appreciate that." Small sounds came from the dark—a striking match, the noise of a tin can sliding. Blue smoke substantiated in the brighter hallway above the deputy's head. The old man studied him, noting the scuffed boots and the khakis loosely hanging on a frame of prominent and elongate bones, the circles beneath his eyes. The lean and hungry look of him.

He said, "Your two compadres have kind of a brisk manner about them." Millimaki sat with his hands clasped, forearms resting on his thighs. He smiled at the floor between his feet but the old man could not see his face and he went on. "You seemed to be the odd man out in that dog and pony show." Again, Millimaki merely sat. He turned one wrist slightly to consult his watch. Finally the old man leaned from his chair, one eye squinted against the unaccustomed light or the smoke from the cigarette in the corner of his mouth to read the nametag on the young deputy's shirtfront. "That's a mouthful. What is it, Finn or something?"

"Yeah, Finn," Millimaki said. "I didn't have any say in the matter. The other half is Bohunk."

Gload smoked. "Hell of a deal." He held a bean can bent to accept a cigarette in its edge and he tipped his ash into it. "I knew a lot of Finlanders and Hunkies down in Butte. A lot of 'em. Micks, too. You take the Harps and Finns and Bohunks out of Butte and you got a couple of Wops and a Welshman standing around a hole in the ground with their dicks in their hands."

Millimaki said, "I'll have to take your word for it."

"Well," the old man said, "that's how it was."

By shift's end the old man was back in his cell, thoughtful and quietly smoking, and Millimaki left him and the jail and drove toward the grassy dune country southwest out of town where above the languid horseshoe bends of the Missouri River a settlement in recent years had sprung up, outsized homes he'd heard the sheriff once call "monuments to power and wealth." On the sandy bluff the surgeon's house where he was to meet his wife appeared fortresslike against the dusk, its roofline a complex topography of hips and gables and Dutch hip dormers and a phallic tower with a dome of hammered copper which at that hour beaconed its russet affluence to the working-class homes on the river below. From the hilltop eminence the prefabs and double-wide trailers looked like shoe boxes or children's blocks set haphazardly beside a papier-mâché stream. The department made calls with equal frequency to the homes of the wealthy for spousal abuse and ODed teens and skeletal anorexic wives on the roadway in their teddies strung out and waving handguns at the passing cars. Millimaki had discovered fairly quickly that the problems of the rich were much the same as those of the unrich, though in the savage glare of the booking-room lights their sportswear and excellent dental work made for more attractive photographs.

What he could see of the yard sloped down to the water's edge, the acreage neatly cordoned from the rampant weeds of the vacant adjacent lots by a welded pole fence of black metal. In the center of the yard a bosk of sculpted junipers in the descending twilight looked like mourners nodding above a grave. A single robin sat atop the fence, a bold brushstroke of color, its breast more sanguine for the backdrop of freakish April snow.

At the sheltered entry, a black iron footman greeted Millimaki and tendered his servitude with an upraised tray and a rictus of gleaming teeth. The woman who answered his knock affected a wide-eyed look of theatrical fear.

"Oh, Gawd," she said. "You finally caught up with me." She threw her hands up, a cocktail the color of emeralds bleeding down her arm, a dozen thin silver bracelets chiming.

Millimaki forced a smile. "My wife is here," he said. The woman went away howling. He found Glenda in an enormous room standing among several men and she managed a quick kiss on his cheek.

Their host called it the great room and from its twelve-foot walls glassine eyes of exotic trophy heads regarded the guests, well-turned-out men and women already aglow and garrulous from drink. Though it was barely spring and there was snow on the ground, a few of the men wore no socks with their tasseled loafers. They were polite. Millimaki sensed as they gripped his hand they were formulating a diagnosis from the dull thrum of his pulse, the red of his eye.

He wandered beneath the gaudy taxidermy and stood finally before a bank of windows watching the evening dim and the great room lights appear as uncertain phosphorescent portals on the black water below. A nurse whom Millimaki had always thought of as an older and heavier version of his wife swept toward him and gave him an uncomfortably long hug.

"Howdy, Sheriff. Come to arrest me?"

"I sort of heard that one already tonight, Jean."

"Oh, shit. I hate being unoriginal."

"That's all right. Yours came with more warmth."

She put her hand on his arm. "Are you okay? Your eyes look like two piss holes in a snowbank."

"Now that's better. That's fresh stuff."

"I mean it."

"I'm fine, Jean."

His wife was across the room, cornered by a man who seemed to be indicating where an incision might be made on her chest. Jean glanced their way and squeezed Millimaki's arm.

"What can I get you to drink, Val?"

"I think Glenda has a head start so I'll have to drive us home."

"She's staying with me tonight, didn't she tell you?"

Above his wife and her companion a leopard was poised to leap from stagecraft cover of savannah grass, its jaundiced eyes bright as candle flames beneath the floodlights.

"Of course. Right," he said.

"I'll just get one more for myself and that's it." Jean moved off somewhat unsteadily toward a table arrayed with bottles and containers of ice. At the same time a Japanese woman who worked with his wife in the ICU approached from the makeshift bar. She had been married to an Air Force major and they'd lived on the base east of the town, a sprawling city-state of tarmac and austere cinder-block buildings where the green of lawns and trees after the brief springtimes faded quickly to the color of the prairie and the window glass in the identical houses shuddered under the bellowing of lumbering cargo jets and where she one day awoke to find the major gone. The surprise of her abandonment never left her face and when she bore down on Millimaki her eyes were wide and her tiny mouth was set in an O. She chattered excitedly about his debt book. Her voice was shrill and her accent thick and he was not sure what she'd said.

"I'm sorry. My what?"

"Debt book, debt book." She pantomimed with frantic fluttering hands the turning of pages. "Book. With all your debt people in it."

"I'm not getting—"

Jean had come with her drink and put her hand on his forearm. "She means 'dead,' Val."

"Yes, debt, of course. With collecting pictures of debt people. How funny."

He began to explain that he took the pictures as part of his work, but she was already reeling off toward a group of men clustered beneath the grizzled head of a Cape buffalo, the great sweep of its horns under the floodlights glowing like burnished ebony. "How funny," he could hear her say. "Debt pictures of debt people." Her voice from across the cavernous room sounded like breaking glass. The men looked at her and as she pointed looked at Millimaki.

Jean said, "I'm sorry, Val. Let's call it a cultural thing."

"Did Glenda tell you guys about those pictures?"

"No, Val. I'm sure she wouldn't have done that."

But she must have said something, he thought. Dead book. Had Glenda called it that? But debt book, that was also true. He did owe something to the dead.

The woman from the front door swept by and spoke without stopping or looking at him. "I'm a goddamn fugitive from justice." She was shoeless, her dress iridescent.

"Somebody's having a good time."

"She's harmless," Jean said. Millimaki saw her across the room. She eyed him malignly from over the rim of her neon tumbler. Her virid tongue flicked like a lizard's.

Like a jackal harmless, he thought. She should be skulking through the veldt among the other predators on the great room's wall.

They drove down the long slope of the hill with the house blazing behind them, and soon were on the river flats. In silence they passed shabby shotgun houses and tire-buttressed trailers where no window lights burned and the river rolled beside the road like oil, in the headlights cannibalized pickups set on blocks, appliances upended and rusting, the acetylene eyes of feral cats.

In the sudden lights of town the traffic was sparse and she directed him wordlessly to the apartment complex. He parked the truck beneath the polar glow of halogens and left the engine idling. The wind shook the lamp poles and the truck shuddered in the gusts. Low gray berms of plowed snow seemed animated under the quaking light.

Millimaki said, "I guess I'd better get going. Tom will be pissing and moaning like I haven't fed him for a month. He'll make me feel like a bad person."

"He'll be fine."

The apartment building was a bleak three-level box, one of several adjacent to the hospital. Everything about was asphalt, everything weirdly pale beneath the wobbling arc lights.

Millimaki said, "At what point were you going to tell me you were staying in town?"

"Well, I thought I did. Didn't I? You can see it makes sense." She extended her wrist toward the dashlight glow to see the watch dial. "I have to be at work in six hours."

"Yeah. It makes sense. I just wish I didn't have to hear it from Jean and look like an ass."

"Jean loves you. You couldn't look like an ass to her. She has a thing for you."

"She's a nice lady. I don't get that kind of take on the rest of the crowd."

She sat rigidly, gloved hands in her lap. "Those are my friends and colleagues."

"Yes, and by the way, did you catch your colleague's slave décor by the front door?"

"Of all the wonderful things in that house, that's all you can comment on?"

"I didn't notice any other racist appointments. He may have had some."

"It's not a slave just because it's black, Val. It's an antique."

"Well, just because it's old doesn't make it not a nigger waiting to hitch up Massa's Beamer after a long day in the OR."

"Oh, for God's sake." She stared into the windshield. The truck's heater fan whirred. After a long while she said dreamily, "It's a beautiful lovely house. I mean everything is so—"

"Everything is so bought."

She didn't turn to look at him. Whatever she saw in the dark glass still held her. "You could have tried, Val," she said at last. "They were trying. They are talented intelligent men."

"Glenda, when I'm expending all of my energy trying not to punch someone in the throat for staring at my wife's ass."

"That's ridiculous."

"I have eyes."

"Yes," she said. "You have cop eyes."

"Cop eyes?" he said. He turned on the seat to look at her. "This is new."

"Just the way you look at things. Eyes that see around corners and under things where nobody else would think to look."

He felt the night's tension begin to veer toward a novel savagery. Unconsciously he dug one hand into the seat as if he might hold them in place against the quickening current. His long exhalation fogged the window glass.

"Okay," he said. "Look, it's just that I don't have a thing in common with those guys."

"You could have talked about hunting. You could have talked about that."

"A goddamn rhino, Glenda. There was not one head shot in this country. Hell, on this continent."

"Well. It's still hunting."

"It is and it isn't. I mean a Chevy's a car and a, whatever, a Lamborghini's a car. The same, in name only."

"But you know what, Val? When I'm with your sheriff's department Neanderthals I try."

"Once. Exactly one party you came to with me."

"That's not true."

"One time. In three and a half years. And 'Neanderthals'?"

"That's not fair, of course. The sheriff seems very nice. One or two others I remember with eyebrows that didn't meet in the middle."

They sat staring out at the desolate lot. Trash cartwheeled past and caught up against cars parked in their numbered spaces. From a gap in a hedge of half-dead arborvitae a lean brindle dog shot past trailing a tether, its hair roached up on its back by the wind and it trotted with its head oddly angled to avoid stepping on the rope. In the harsh odd light its ribs showed clearly. She watched it until it vanished into the gloom between the austere complexes. Overhead powerlines swayed perilously, their shadows writhing on the icy pavement. When she spoke again her voice had softened.

"If the wind would not blow for one day."

"You'll wish a long time for that."

She moved her slender wrist again into the green dashboard light.

"I guess I'd better go in before Jean locks me out."

"Does she have an extra bed?"

"A couch. A foldout."

"That's just torture," he said. "Does she have rocks? Rocks would be more comfortable."

"I'll be fine for one night." She reached over and patted his hand briefly where it lay between them on the seat. "You be careful driving home."

"I will."

They both got out of the truck into the raw nighttime and she ran for the shelter of a stairwell. He stood there for a moment with the wind rifling down his jacket and whipping his pants legs and watched until he saw her on the second-level walkway hurrying beneath weak amber bulbs. She stopped at a door without looking back and disappeared within.

He considered the hour drive to the empty house in the hills where the snow would still be ankle deep. "That's all right," he said. "You can kiss me twice tomorrow night." He got behind the wheel and looked up at the apartment door. "Or a wave. That might have been nice."

During the first week of the trial, the young deputy took John Gload from his cell to the courthouse and escorted him to chambers to meet with his lawyer and he walked with him to the bathroom and during noon recess carried his lunch to him in the holding area. At the dark end of the day he held Gload's elbow like an old companion as they crossed the frozen courthouse yard on the icy sidewalks, the old man in his leg irons shuffling among the stark shadows of still-leafless elms as black as columns of anthracite in the pearl moonlight of early April.

Gload said little during this time to anyone, and Millimaki made no attempt to draw him out. What conversation there was was remote and quotidian, the kind any two strangers might exchange. A word about the food, the weather. For the most part the old man sat before the high bench in the courtroom beside his lawyer with his head erect and unmoving and with his enormous arms atop the table in the pose of a leonine statue. Occasionally he slid a yellow legal pad close and scribbled on it feverishly. At times Millimaki caught the old man looking at him appraisingly where he stood nearby. When Millimaki returned his stare he did not look away and he did not smile.

When the week was out, on a Monday, Weldon Wexler assumed Millimaki's escort duties and would take the old man to and from the courtroom where the nature or duration of his life would be decided. He'd been with the department a year longer than Millimaki and had parlayed this seniority and a troubling knee into a request for light duty, relegating Millimaki to an indefinite period of night shift at the jail. When they passed in the corridor that morning Wexler favored him with a smirk and a short two-fingered salute. He limped away down the bright corridor, favoring first one knee then the other, hair freshly barbered and meticulously combed, his uniform trousers creased smartly, sharp creases beneath the pockets of his shirt. Buckles, buttons, the snaps on his holster, polished to the luster of servingware. The men in their cells who like feral dogs sensed weakness in any form mocked him in hushed tones and would in the deep witnessless hours of the night concoct from his slewing gait and pretty mouth salacious tableaus, hissed from cage to cage to cage like some lascivious burlesque.

Valentine Millimaki would not see John Gload in the light of day for a month and his own wife for nearly as long. He left his small house in the foothills of the Little Belt Mountains as the sun burned to an ember through the timber at the ridgetops even as his wife arrived home and he spent the long nights ambling listlessly about the old building or sitting outside the prisoners' cells, nearly maddened with boredom and claustrophobia.

He found it almost impossible to adapt to this place where in enduring his eight- or ten-hour shift he would differ so little from his charges in their cages.

All but asleep on his feet at the jailer's desk on the third night, he was roused by the appearance through the streetside door of Voyle Dobek and another veteran deputy and they carried between them a slight dark figure seemingly as boneless as a straw man, the toes of his shoes squealing as he was dragged roughly along the polished floor. They turned toward the sally gate, blowing and sweating like draft horses and when Millimaki came forward Dobek said, "Just stick your ass right there, Millimaki, and buzz us in. We'll take care of this blanketass."

When he saw the man next, at three-thirty in the morning, he was shivering violently. The sound of his teeth chattering brought Val to the bars and he saw the man sitting on the bunk with the rough wool issue blanket wrapped around him and cowled monklike over his head. The hand that held the blanket was overlarge for a man his size, abraded and deeply fissured.

Millimaki said, "Are you sick?"

He was a Cree from the Rocky Boy reservation, his face in the beam of Millimaki's flashlight a death's-head of sunken cheeks and eyes in their caves the color of coal.

The man could barely speak. "Them bastards held me down in a g-goddamn puddle and I can't can't can't get warmed up no more."

Millimaki reached through the bars and felt the sleeve of the man's worn western shirt. "You're soaked."

"I'm all s-soakin' wet and I can't get warm."

"I'll get you something."

He had a spare shirt in his truck and he came with that and another blanket and a cup of burned coffee from the office hot plate. He'd expected to smell liquor when he entered the cell but he did not. The small man shook so badly he could not negotiate the shirt's buttons and the deputy was forced to do it for him.

"All's I wanted to do was to talk to her. That was all. I never in my life put a hand on that woman. She's a drunk. I'm worried about my kids."

"Yeah," Millimaki said. "Okay."

"She's taken up with some white dude. I think he might be some kind of meth-head or something. Some junkie. I come down after work and all's I want to do is to talk to her, man. Now I'm fixing to lose my job."

"Where do you work?"

"I bust tires at a place up in Big Sandy. I ain't never missed a day in four and some years."

Millimaki took out his notebook and pen. "Write down the name of the place and your boss." The little man wrote, his knobbly hand working laboriously across the small page, shaking.

"I don't know that you can read that. See if you can."

Millimaki read it back and the man said it was right.

"What's your name?"

"George Gopher. Georgie they call me."

"Drink that coffee."

"I ain't drunk, you know. Them sonsofbitches said I was drunk but I ain't."

"I know you're not. Just to warm you up is what I meant."

"All right." He sipped at the cup, made a face. He held up one arm and the shirtsleeve dangled over his hand. "This shirt's too big for me."

"So sue me. I forgot your size."

"It's all right."

When he left George Gopher's cell half an hour later, the man was asleep on his cot under the two blankets and the hallway was as quiet as a mortuary. One of the tube lights was failing and it strobed weirdly, his footfalls syncopated like an antique movie reel and into this light a plume of cigarette smoke bloomed from John Gload's cell.

The long hallway with its cells had been painted yellow halfway up and it looked as though it had, a half century before, endured a flood of bile. On one of the first nights Millimaki walked down, his boot heels resounded hollowly and above the insect-burr of the tubelights and from the invisible interiors of the cells came the sounds of sleeping men and their smells—sweat and hair cream, aftershave, urine, from some a distinctive metallic smell that Millimaki had decided was the smell of fear.

The thin Cree Georgie Gopher had made bail and was back north earning his difficult living and bearing upon those narrow shoulders the great burden of his endangered children.

Millimaki paused at the end of the hall, cocking his ear at a noise that might have been someone strangling, but it was only snoring or a man in that aphotic place struggling against some malign hands in dream. He was about to turn when a voice said, "Seems you got the shit-end of some stick or other, Deptee."

"You scared the shit out of me, John. I thought everybody was asleep."

"Sleep," the old man said wistfully. "I don't sleep much, kid."

Millimaki approached the cell door and in the slant of light could make out but Gload's disembodied legs and huge hands and wrists. The hands disappeared momentarily and he heard a scritch and then the flare of the match and Gload's visage appeared for an instant from the black like a mask passed before a stage light.

"What's the deal with this Weldon asshole?"

"Deputy Wexler, I think you mean."

"Yeah, Wexler. Sorry-ass little turd. He wants me to call him Weldon I guess so we can be pals." He grunted. "What'd you do to miss out on baby-sitting me, anyways? Seems like pretty fair duty."

"Deputy Wexler has seniority on me. And he's nursing a bum knee."

Gload snorted. A pale cloud formed from out of the dark of his cell. "Right. From chasing bad guys." He seemed incredulous. "That's what he honest to Christ said." He waited for Millimaki to say something but he did not. "Seems to get around on that war wound pretty good unless somebody's watching him." He snorted again. Millimaki would come to understand in the coming weeks that this was what passed for a laugh from the old man.

"I don't know anything about how he got it."

"He tells me you're a farm kid. But he kind of says it like he has a mouthful of shit."

He knew Gload was fishing, whether to combat the boredom of stir or for some other reason, and he chose to ignore it. He had been around enough of these jailbirds to know that it was in their nature to foment trouble and it didn't matter whether it was among the jailed or their keepers. He said, "It's a dryland farm-ranch outfit. I've got a cousin who's running it now. West of town."

"Rich cousin, I'd bet."

"He came down off his folks' place on the Hi-Line. They've done all right."

"I figured as much. Do you wisht you was running it?"

"Not so much. Some of it I liked. Didn't like cows too much but I liked the machinery."

"Farming."

"Yeah. The tedious stuff, dragging a harrow, plowing and seeding. Don't know what that says about me. Probably that I'm boring." What he didn't say was that he welcomed the solitary time within the drone of the engine to think, apart from the room he still shared with his sister or the quiet moments at the supper table where his father's silence broadcast nonetheless a tirade of bone-deep guilt and loneliness and accusation, his eyes from their shadowed hollows radiating a look of grim wonderment at the type of creature sprung from his own loins who could so placidly compose his mother on the floor of a chicken shed and fit slippers on her feet.

There was a long pause from Gload as though from his dark keep he might be reading the young man's thoughts. His hand appeared to tip his ash into the bean can. Then he said, "Well, I must be boring too because I liked the farming. I liked it quite a little." Into the light a blue billow rose and Millimaki watched it twist slowly toward the cracked and peeling ceiling invisible beyond the suspended fluorescents.

"Plowing, mostly. I had to get out of it when I was maybe thirteen or fourteen, but I'd done quite a little up to that time."

A hand appeared, tipped the ash, shifted the can a few inches nearer. "Had a favorite field, too." Millimaki waited for him to go on but he did not. The cigarette glowed and Gload's upshadowed face materialized from the darkness and vanished and smoke rolled out into the lighted corridor. Finally he said, "What about you, Deptee? One you come to like more than another one?"

He had never really thought about it, had merely gone where he'd been told and done what he'd been told and reveled in the earsplitting monotony and the reverie it provided. But now, surprisingly, seated in the dank corridor in the company of a killer, he saw his father's arm extended, pointing like a weathervane east, west, north, as he named each day's work—Schmidt section, McIver place, the Bluff parcel—patchwork rectangles delineated by spliced and respliced antique wire stapled to ancient cedar posts, acres that seemed miraculously to repel rain and to relegate his parents to a life of marginal poverty. He could recall them from the porch watching the gravid clouds veer and tack around them, christening the neighbors' fields with rain while the wind at the storm's fringe scoured the topsoil from their range and sent it aloft where it vanished into the heavens like an apparition.

One slanted parcel ran beneath a butte that had been a buffalo jump and the duckfoot plow each year turned up bones and teeth or an occasional arrowhead or scraping blade three hundred or five hundred or a thousand years old. From the rocky rims above they came thundering, to land broken and bellowing on the rocks below with their eyes rolling white and their tongues red in their red mouths and the women roamed among them with stone clubs and knives laughing in a welter of gore.

It had been a decade or more since he'd felt the big Minneapolis-Moline's diesel rumble through his bones and thought about the buffalo cascading down screaming and he thought about that boy and about his loneliness. He said, "We had some winter wheat put in right under the butte. There was an old buffalo jump there and I used to think about them falling off of there when I was a kid."

Millimaki shifted in his chair, crossed and uncrossed his legs. The old man waited. He had the advantage of seeing Millimaki clearly in the surgical light under which he sat and he observed reflected in the young man's eyes a sudden distance more vast than the blank hallway down which he stared.

"Why, hell, don't worry about it, kid. We're just making talk."

"I'd better do a walk-around," Val said. "I'll come back here in a bit." He went down the aisle and out the sally door. In the office he stood and watched the clock, which seemed hardly to have changed since he'd last checked. He rubbed his eyes with the heels of his hands. Minutes had become hours, hours become days. He watched the second hand creep slowly down the face to assure that the clock had not altogether frozen and the big hand with a savage click at last registered the minute.

He'd not had a chance to read the letter from his sister that had arrived the previous day and now he slipped it from among the meager contents of his lunch, where it had taken on the shape of an apple, and smoothed the pages atop his knee. Above him the jailer sat upon his high chair and seemed altogether lost in the book before him. A moth fluttered down brokenly from the sooty hanging globe light above the man's head and it hovered near his face and alighted briefly on the book he held but he did not move. Millimaki stared at him for a moment then raised a hand and waved it in the air. Still he did not move and Millimaki realized he was asleep, his eyes protuberant and unwavering, gaudy with bruised flesh, eye-whites thatched with veins.

He opened the letter and read of his new niece and about life in Albuquerque, New Mexico, where his little sister's husband was stationed, the letter chatty and loving and without substance. Though she was nineteen years old and a new mother, Millimaki still thought of her as a child. The words were written with large loops and backward slants, I's dotted with hearts. In the end she sent her love and love from the infant he'd never seen and inscribed for him at the bottom of the page the X's and O's of a schoolgirl. So the PS she added hit him like a gut punch: "How old would Mom be now?"

Perhaps being a mother herself now set her thinking of the woman she'd hardly known—who could only be a shadow in her memory, a flicker of a face in profile, a hand in the tangle of her hair, a fragrance vaguely haunting. He both pitied and envied her. Her memories were fleeting and phantasmal, almost a dream of a mother, and so there was little to cherish. But she did not carry, either, the pain of loss.

Millimaki counted the years—their mother would be sixty years old, a middle-aged woman. But he never thought of her as any older than she was the day she died. When he thought of his parents together the picture that appeared was one more of father and daughter—one frozen in time, the other, dead now, too, worn and gray, beaten, his face hard and cracked as trace reins.

And then from this picture, another—his mother on the

porch with one hand to her mouth, another to her throat as the rain blackened the sky to the east or south, watching like someone marooned as a ship beyond signal fire or semaphore plows doggedly on toward a far foreign shoreline, lush and safe.

The jailer in his catatonia stared down unblinkingly. Millimaki imagined the man's eyes drying in their abysmal sockets and clattering out atop the desk. When he consulted his wristwatch he found that ten minutes had passed. Above his head the second hand on the wall clock crept glacially down, its ticks in the silence loud as bell tolls.

As though it were a monologue he had been uttering for hours into the dark without seam or interruption, almost before Millimaki had taken his chair John Gload began to talk again about farming. He told the young deputy that many nights, to combat sleeplessness, as a kind of self-trickery, he revisited a favorite field. He paused to light a cigarette from the smoldering butt of the last, which he dropped into the bean can. He stared after it as if it were of great interest to him. Then he corrected himself, said no, that's not quite exactly right, it wasn't tricking himself but tricking the insomnia, which he imagined as a palpable thing, a kind of shade or haunt that bent over him in his repose, passing rattling hand bones in the air above him to ward off the visitation of sweet slumber. It's common knowledge that every child can sleep, he said. That they hadn't learned how not to. But he had learned to hoodwink the leaning shape, to leave it standing bewildered above whatever bed he'd made or been given, by becoming once again John Gload the child, Gload the farmboy, whistling from the tractor seat in the sunshine of innocence on a brilliant day in a season that never changed in a year that could never be again.

"Not but twelve years old, running a John Deere 3020 and a thirteen-foot duckfoot," he said. "Eight foot of disk and drills." He said it wasn't a particularly good field, in fact being much of it a sidehill it was rocky and dry and for that reason he found it gratifying that it could raise up anything at all. It had been put into barley but it wasn't the satisfaction of any crop that seemed his anodyne but the clear remembrance of the view from the tractor seat as he rounded the field and in a kind of somnolent monotone, an echo perhaps of the monotony of the plowing itself, he described for the younger man, in panorama, what he could see yet—sandstone bluffs bewigged with ancient sage, the stone chimney of a honyocker's cabin standing amid a rubble of rust-colored timbers, the pale green of a river bottom and then, on another turn, much farther, a serrated line which seemed some days mountains within a day's easy walk and on others a mere brushstroke of blue on blue that may well have been a cloudbank or was perhaps nothing at all, a phantasm. Bluffs, chimney, bottomland, mountains—a strange soporific concocted out of days and months and years with duckfoot, disk and drill a half century before.

The field lay in the bed of some primordial sink or pothole, and on the outer passes, the tractor and plow rode perilously on the incline of the bowl and he was forced to put one foot against the fender to maintain balance, riding with a foot braced there and leaning uphill, as though his small weight would be the critical counterbalance against disaster. Beyond the outermost furrows was a den of foxes, the dark aperture facing south, and the young kits in those first warm days of spring would lie atop the mounded dirt and watch Gload unalarmed, when he came close lying low to the ground and then as though attached by invisible wires to the passing machine sit bolt upright when he had gone past, their outsized ears swiveling, small black noses sorting out the scent of a man, the scent of this other creature roaring and chugging and darkening the air with its perse breath.

And he told the deputy that the gulls began to arrive. They appeared first as minute white tufts against the green of the river trees and he turned and made a pass going away and then suddenly they were among the furrows behind the plow, as though like the soldiers of myth they sprang from the ground itself. He wondered how they found him and thought they may have followed the dust cloud or perhaps like wolves or hounds on a blood scent they could smell the new-turned earth. He threw the tractor into neutral and sat watching as the birds gorged themselves on tiny infant mice he had exposed from under small rocks and glistening worms as long as garter snakes, and crickets and partridge nestlings and even above the pothering of the engine he could hear the gulls scream. There seemed to be no communion among them. They fought over every mouthful, the most successful of them gagging down pieces that would have choked a hyena and in the chaos of screeches there were times it seemed they would set upon one another until one gruesome bird remained, engorged and wallowing through the furrows unable even to raise his bloodied wings to fly.

In the end he told Millimaki that that was how he was able to sleep, when he did sleep. He revisited the field as he lay in whatever darkness waiting for the blessing of that oblivion. In the memory he did not know if it was the same day or simply a day each time that was similar but the sun was bright overhead and unobscured and the den of foxes sat erect and regarded him with the same black eyes and like Harpies the seagulls came planing over the rim of the hills. The gulls were the only things that ruined the picture for him, with their rapacious mouths and their screaming, but they were as much a part of the memory as the plow or the field and he could not parse them out. He tried but they would not go and in the end if he could not sleep it was because of them.

"I close my eyes and put my foot on that one step and even that I can see plain as anything under my boot and then I just ride round and round. It don't always work but it works better than anything else," Gload said. His hand came down and he stubbed out another cigarette. His chair squawked as he rose and then all of him was in darkness. "I believe I'll try it right now." Shortly from his own chair beyond the cage bars Millimaki heard the slight musical complaint of the cot's metal latticework and the rustle of clothes or bedding. All along the corridor a chorus of liquid snores, bizarre snatches of dialogue from the fevered drama of mens' nightmares. Often the names of women, slurred and lubricious pleas for that sweet thing. Hushed fervent promises of violent lovely torment. Millimaki listened, the midnight congress between men and their ghosts in this place as conventional as a heartbeat. He held his wrist up toward the light to read his watch and was amazed to see that an hour had passed.

John Gload said, "Good night, Valentine. You might try my little trick next time you can't sleep. In that field under the butte or wherever." He had never told the old man his Christian name. He stood up and stared into Gload's cage and then went slowly down the hallway, his shadow pooled about his boots.

John Gload counted the slow receding footfalls that had for him in that durance become the tickings of a clock, the regular mesh of gear on gear marking the order of time. He closed his eyes. But in a short time he realized that the gulls that night were particularly active, swarming behind his eyelids in a maelstrom of soiled feathers and beaks stained with gore. So he lay in the plot of darkness now allotted him in the world thinking about the woman who waited for him at home.

THREE

The morning following the night on the dam they drove east six hours to Rapid City to exchange for currency what they had earned from their labors: a trunkload of antique glassware. The young gay man they had kidnapped and murdered had inherited much of the collection and had added to it over a decade, never dreaming the seashell plates and fluted glasses so lovingly arrayed about his dead mother's house where he lived yet would be the vehicles of his own death.

They drove the bright spring day in near total silence, the kid sleepy and still pouting from Gload having stuck a gun in his ear and the cold and quiet atmosphere suited the old man.

In Roundup they stopped to eat and the kid, revitalized at the prospect of food, flirted with the waitress. She was a girl of nineteen or twenty and White stared after her stout bare legs as she walked away.

He said, "How'd you like to have those clamped around yer ass?" Gload looked up from his paper briefly and looked back. "She'd about buck you off and that's no shit," the kid said.

When the girl came back with their platters, Sid looked up at her. Above her left breast was a tag with the name Jessy laboriously printed in childish block letters.

"Jessy," Sid said. "Hey, now, what's the name of the other one?" The girl set the plates down and looked over her shoulder.

"I'm the only one on today," she said. She smiled down at him, a pretty girl twenty pounds overweight with gaps in her teeth and sorrel hair in a knot atop her head, the seams and buttons on her uniform restraining burgeoning excesses of soft flesh at hip and bosom.

Sid shook his head. "No, the other one." He pointed at her tag, at her breast. She shook her head in confusion. "Hell, your other tittie," he said. "This here one's named Jessy, I can see that, but you ain't named the other one."

Gload looked up at the girl briefly and then at White. "Shut your mouth," he said. He spun his plate of eggs and ham around in front of him on the newspaper and began eating and those were the last words spoken between them until they reached Rapid City three and a half hours later.

The building was weathered board and bat, proclaiming in great red letters on its façade: "Old West Trading Post." The duckboards leading to saloon doors lay in a piebald shade beneath an archway of woven antlers. A marquee atop an iron pole of rudely welded four-inch pipe rose from within a ring of whitewashed stones, bearing skyward its message: "Coldest Beer in the west, postcards, IndiaN beAdwork, friendly. Clean rooms afFordable. Genuine antiquEs of the OLd West."

Gload pointed wordlessly and Sid nosed the big car up to a

hitching rail. He swung the door open and said, "Stay in the car."

"We're partners on this deal," Sid said.

Gload, standing outside the car, leaned his head down to speak into the open door.

"Stay in the fucking car."

In ten minutes he came back. White sat brooding with his boots propped on the car's dash, his arms crossed at his chest.

Gload said, "Get your feet off of there. We'll meet the man tonight, eight o'clock. Drive around to the side over here." He fumbled with the plastic key fob. "One oh one." He glared at the swinging doors and at the name in foot-high gold letters above them. "Colonel," he said. He spat onto the gravel between his feet. "What's he a fucking colonel of?"

"I don't know."

"Colonel of bullshit, maybe."

"What'd he say?"

Gload went to the passenger side door and got in. "One oh one," he said. He pointed with the key. "Over there."

"Don't I even get my own room?"

"Once we take care of business you can get you a room and stay a month for all I give a shit," Gload said. "Until then we stay together." He looked over at him. "Partner."

Full dark at that early hour afforded them cover to unload from the car's trunk the boxes of plates and cups and saucers, glasses, glazed and painted bowls and all manner of dishware, the uses for which Gload could only guess. He had no more interest in them than in stones or books or the workings of a car's engine. He was in many ways as simple as a child, though without a child's curiosity. In the efficiency of his work he took pride though not necessarily pleasure, any more than would a man running sawlogs through a mill or for his prescribed hours soldering senseless components onto a board. He was handy at his work and it afforded him a living. His pleasures were few and modest—sitting in the sun at the door of his house in the orchard above the Breaks; a slow drive along the vacant county gravel roads with Francie to park finally above the river to watch the sun fall down toward the crimson close of the day. Once a year he loaded a stout pole and reel and drug the muddy Missouri bottom for paddlefish.

The Colonel, a small wizened figure seeming smaller yet within his huge swivel chair, instructed Sid the Kid to display the goods on a long folding table, making benevolent sweeping motions as he spoke and when this was done he got up with pipe in hand and walked up and down before them as if inspecting troops, picking up an occasional saucer or bowl to squint at runes on its underside. Gload had taken a chair opposite the Colonel and the exhibited wares, that he might see the man's eyes. He smoked and appeared to pay little attention to the production. Like a tradesman, his talents were primarily manual—the use of a knife, manipulation of flesh—but they ran also to cards and the reading of men's faces. So when the Colonel sat back and packed his pipe and said a number, Gload stubbed out his cigarette, stood and walked through the door into the night without a word, as though he were taken with a mild whim or notion, or had remembered suddenly some domestic errand. The Colonel and Sid White sat quietly dandling their feet in their chairs. They did so for fifteen minutes. The Colonel began to swivel and fidget in his chair and Sid began to sweat.

As if to answer a question that had not been asked, Sid said, "Well, hell, I don't know. He might of had, you know, one of them deals." He made a rotating motion near his ear. "A stroke." He rose. "I'd best go and check on him."

As he left the room the little man said, "It's a generous offer, tell him. A handsome offer."

Gload sat in the room, smoking. He had turned on the TV but did not seem engaged by it. He sat with his head leaned back on the chair watching the smoke curl up to the ceiling. He had put his slippers on.

Sid looked at him incredulously. "What're you doing? He's waiting back there."

Gload smoked. Presently he spoke, very slowly, as if instructing a child. "How much did the kid who previously owned all that shit say it was worth?" He continued to study the smoke, White presented with a view of the bristled hollows of the older man's throat.

"What he said might not of been right," White said. "He might of just been a fag trying to be Mister Big Shot."

Gload only sat, waiting, his head back. One slippered foot jounced up and down to some slow rhythm sounding in his head.

"Okay," Sid said, "he said seventeen-five."

"Seventeen-five," Gload repeated. "And your new buddy over there, the Colonel, offered what was it again?"

"It's a handsome offer."

Gload's eyes were small and black like a pig's and when he dropped his head and turned them on the kid, in the fluxing television glow they flashed a brief radioactive spark.

"Okay, okay," the kid said. "Eight thousand dollars. That's a shitload of money for dishes."

"Eight thousand dollars. A difference of what?"

Sid sat figuring for some time. He began to cast about for pencil and paper.

Gload said, "Nine thousand five hundred dollars."

"Right. Nine-five."

Gload held a single finger aloft as if to admonish White to listen to something outside the room. White looked about, his head canted.

"What?" he said.

"That," said Gload. "The sound of the Colonel making money off other people's sweat and travail."

White stood helplessly, his hands outstretched in an attitude of supplication.

"Travail?"

"My sweat and travail."

The kid said, "Well, what do I tell him?" A vision he'd begun to concoct of himself attired in a western-cut Porter Waggoner–style suit, its trouser pockets ballasted with folded bills in a begemmed clip, began to wobble and fade. Even half of the money the Colonel had offered was money beyond reckoning. He had worked washing dishes in an Italian restaurant in Black Eagle and he had sold batteries stolen from cars and he had once worked briefly as a hay hand in the Judith Basin, feigning heat sickness after one long hot morning atop a haystack, riding to town on the bus and licking his blistered palms like a dog. From that foray into ranch work Sid White considered himself a cowboy. Four thousand dollars was the stuff of hallucination. "He ain't going to sit there and wait on us forever."

"With an offer of what he said he can sit and wait till doomsday comes," Gload said. "If you come back here without a number in your mouth that is twelve thousand then I am gone home. And I'll not send you back with a different number. I'll not dicker like a Mexican over a clay pot. There is one number that will work and I just told you it."

Sid White stood openmouthed in front of Gload, who had by then turned to the television and begun roaming the stations, his face no more than a foot from the screen as he turned the dial, its crags awash in a kaleidoscope of lurid colors. This old man, White thought, is going to get me fucked over. He considered his options and decided that should the numbers not work he could come back with something in his pocket to take care of John Gload. Gload was an old man and the kid didn't care about all the things he had supposedly done a hundred years ago. He wastes one queer, so what? He would still go down with a blade in his spine, same as any man would. He could make a deal with the Colonel, he was sure, and who would miss this sonofabitch with anyway one foot already in the grave?

"We could go ten," the kid said. "Show our good whatchacall. Intentions."

"I am leaving in the morning with what I said or nothing," Gload said to the television screen. "And the shit goes back in the trunk."

In ten minutes the kid came into the room and sat on the edge of one of the beds. Gload did not look up. White sat with his hands on his knees, his mouth slightly ajar. He sat so for some time, his tongue darting out with the regularity of a heartbeat. Finally he said, "Well, I will be goddamned all to hell." He looked at Gload then. "He said come in in the morning and he'll have the money." The kid was looking at Gload's great sloping back beneath a T-shirt worn to near transparency. A gray fringe of hair bristled at the neck. "Hey, old man, I said he'll have the money. What you wanted, twelve grand, all of it." He shook his head. "He didn't piss and moan or nothing. Just sat there for a half minute and said it: come by in the morning. Unfuckingbelievable." He was about to clap the old man on the back, but thought better of it.

"You are something else, you know that?"

Gload looked up then. He said, "You left the door open."

Morning, heralded by a raw wind that pawed and moaned at the door and by a bar of wan light beneath the draperies, saw John Gload paring his nails in the coned light of a bed lamp and on the twin bed opposite Sidney White was an inappreciable bundle, as though beneath the horse blanket bedspread stickwood and stones were arranged to approximate the shape of a man. A faint whistle issued from under the covers and on the pillow Gload could see but the top of the boy's head, a medusa of lank blue-black stringlets against the linen. He sat with the knife in his hand for a long time.

An hour later White sat in the passenger seat of the car, bleary-eyed and shivering in his thin denim jacket, and watched as Gload came from the Colonel's office, slewing bearlike down the ludicrous duckboard walkway. The car was loaded and running and John Gload settled behind the wheel. From an envelope he counted out ten five hundred dollar notes and handed them across to the kid.

"This ain't half," White said. "I can figure that much."

Gload levered the car in gear and pulled onto the highway west, the asphalt a ribbon of brass unspooling in the rearview mirror, wherein small birds feeding at the road edge rose like sea spume and tumbled shimmering in their slipstream.

"You were ready to settle for four and you get five," Gload said. "What you might call a 'handsome offer.'"

The kid regarded Gload's profile, adamantine as those granite visages chiseled from the mountain a few miles' drive south.

He fanned the money in his hands—new stiff bills, undreamed-of fortune—and knew it was pointless to argue. As they sped past the array of strip malls and truck stops, he sat with his forehead against the side window. He said, "What a fucked-up town."

By the time they got to Miles City the kid's mood had brightened considerably. His head swiveled as they drove through town and he took note of the number of bars and of the garish rodeo posters in shop fronts of bucking and rearing horses and he goggled at teenage girls with books clamped to their chests and their long hair swaying down their backs. Suddenly he turned to Gload and said, "What's the best hotel in this shit-hole?"

"Pioneer, I suppose. Used to be anyway."

"Drop me off there."

"It was on the other end of town. We passed it."

The kid seemed not to hear. He sat with his face pressed to the window glass, patting his left breast pocket wherein the folded bills lay, and Gload shook his head. It would not be long, he knew, before the kid and money parted company. He slowed and glanced at his mirrors and U-turned the car in the wide avenue, cranking the wheel around with one finger.

"If I can't get laid here," the kid said, "I don't have a hair on my ass."

Having retrieved his small gym bag from the trunk, the kid swung open the passenger side door and leaning in made a gun of his thumb and forefinger, aimed it at the old man behind the wheel. He said, "Okay. I'll catch you back on the home turf, pardner." Gload bent down to watch him mount the hotel steps, swaggering atop three-inch riding heels with his jeans stuffed bronc rider style into his boot tops. He paused at the door to rake back his snarled hair and turn up his collar and he swept into the lobby like some kind of outland prince come to take the little town by storm. For all that, Gload thought, he was no more than a boy.

Some time later he stopped the car at a small creek which like an oasis in the bald prairieland along its course supported a stand of old cottonwoods. He walked through the tangled ditch weeds into the trees, the trunks gray and immense as menhirs. An incongruous crane labored up from the bracken along the muddy stream, towing its lean shadow through the heeling bluestem toward water rumored in the distance by a slash of green. Gload stood and relieved his swollen bladder against a tree and stared up into branches so high the ragged April scud seemed caught there like wisps of tapestry, a high circling bird caged in a wickerwork of pale spring bud. He stood for a long while, until the earth under his feet became as capricious as the deck of a ship. The line of song in his head was this, from when or where he could not remember: "Above Earth's Lamentation."

FOUR

They'd come for Gload in the late afternoon. He'd had time to put things in careful order and he sat for perhaps the last time on his chair, listening to the calls and flutterings of birds just arrived north and looking at the desolate faces of last year's sunflowers at the orchard's verge. He felt strangely at peace. He got up once and walked down the little orchard lane, bordered already by senseless weeds woven like basketry and he stared long across the sage where the river was. He kept his eyes there as he walked and soon they appeared, like wind-borne trash, rising and falling from view and appearing again, kiting effortlessly on set wings. The old man felt their terrible eyes on him.

The wind shook the trees and their branches gnashed and shuddered and the wheat-pale needlegrass down every row lay on the ground. He stood at the prescribed spot looking through the gnarled trunks beyond which the sun burned slowly down. He moved forward a few paces and looked and he moved back, trying to see it as a stranger might. He squinted his eyes and through the ruddled apertures the cured orchard grass and the dark slender tree boles quaking against the sky were an impressionist's blur of blue, ocher, dun. The grass bowed and hissed in the wind and waiting he heard the dull pong of the harrow tines, hung in a tree like a rude mobile or wind chime, and then he went back.

Long before they arrived he could see the dust trail, patrol cars dragging a dirty cumulus across the evening sky, and he could see within it lights throbbing like a foundry fire and finally the cars themselves appeared, bumping and slewing up the narrow road, their windshields aflame.

They found a house in neat order, dishes washed, bed made, plants in pots set up to the south-facing windows newly watered. They found Francie's clothes and perfumes and creams, her shoes paired and aligned in a closet. They asked about her and John Gload told them she was gone and he did not lie.

Five weeks later, astride the chair in his cell, John Gload recalled the moment under the cottonwood trees, not as one of the greatest miscalculations of his career but the instant of its realization. Standing pissing on a tree and embarked upon one course of action, the other concocting itself like a visitation out of the leaves of the trees.

That morning Sid White had been led shuffling into the courtroom and he wasn't in such spirits as Gload had seen him last. He sat hunched and childlike in a strange purple suit piped in gold and around his gaping shirt collar a bolo tie cinched with an outlandish shard of turquoise. Entering he did not raise a hand in greeting or so much as meet the old man's eyes, as he seemed altogether transfixed by the troubling new jewelry adorning his wrists and ankles.

Out of the cell's tangible dark Gload alchemized an early morning in Rapid City. He sat beneath yellow lamplight with the knife in his hand as the kid slept and it would have been such an easy thing, a simple matter of drawing back the coverlet, getting a grip of hair and pulling the blade across Sid White's throat. For that matter, he could have gotten in the car, driven back from the grove of cottonwoods a scant hundred miles and waited in the room in Miles City for the kid to come back drunk. In a way, he thought, it was like two mistakes, one stacked on top of the other. "I could of had him rolled in a bed quilt, into the trunk and underground and it wouldn't of cost me no more than two hours tops," he said.

As he spoke, the young deputy who had befriended him came to sit in his accustomed chair. Millimaki thought with the appearance of Sid White today that the old man would be inclined to talk. He seemed, though, to regard Millimaki as no more animate than the chair he occupied. Gload sat back and disappeared into the darkness and a match flame revealed a ghostly theatrical mask of profound abstraction.

Millimaki said, "Did you say something, John?"

The old killer said, "For example, there's one thing that if I would of done it and if I would of followed my goddamn instinks I'd be sitting in my little trees right now with a blanket on my lap. Instead." He raised his hands palm up, turning his head left and right, inviting the attendant darkness to regard the conditions of his current life.

Val turned in his chair to see if perhaps someone had come silently to stand behind him.

Gload sat astraddle his chair, his hands atop his knees and his chin nearly on his chest. He looked very old then, his thin gray hair awry and hanging before his eyes and Val could see deep vertical creases in his neck like watercourses.

"What one thing, John?"

Gload shook his head ruefully.

"The trouble with being old in my business is that all your old partners are dead or laying up dying slow in the joint somewheres. I was plumb out of good help, is how I come to get White. The young blood," he said wearily. "Good Lord." A hand rose from his knee as if of its own accord and he sat looking at the burning cigarette there and then put it to his lips. He spoke squinting through the smoke. "I tried to show him some things, but the way it is with these young guys is they already know everything and they want to be the boss. If they don't know shit from apple butter." A pause, a long liquid exhale from the shadows. "Golf clubs," he said. "Sweet Jesus."

"What? Golf clubs? Are you talking about Sid White?"

Gload continued. Millimaki felt invisible. "There's times when you do that—look back and think, I should of done this or that or some other thing. Like with that kid. I don't have a lot of those times, a handful, but what I do know is that you can't never ever let them get under your skin. You did what you did at the time and at the time it was right. I regret almost nothing. This thing here lately. Some others. But I ain't been eat up by them, either."

Val consulted his watch and waited. The night was well advanced. The old man sighed and Millimaki thought he might continue but he withdrew without a word and from the darkness came the creak of bunk chains.

Val sat for a moment longer and stood to leave. From the dark came Gload's voice. "Television. That's the problem," he said. "They seen it all on the television."

FIVE

When Millimaki pulled into the yard the rancher who had phoned in the plate numbers stood leaning against a porch post, at four in the afternoon red-eyed and holding a tumbler a third full of something that looked like tea but was not. He did little more than point with his glass hand toward the low ridge where the car was and seemed otherwise indisposed to talk. Two scabrous heelers came on a dead run from a hay barn that leaned from its footings six inches from plumb and they made immediately for the flanks of the tracking dog and Val was forced to kick at them. When he turned the man had gone in, and when he came down off the mountain four hours later in the semidark there was no light burning anywhere on the place.

It was a seldom-used ranch road the missing old man had taken, an apparently random turn from a random highway at the end of a fuddled and reckless drive. He had laid down the right-of-way gate and driven over the gate wires and posts and in the old Buick had bucked and churned upslope until the tires sank axle deep in the mud of a seep-spring.

On the floorboards of the LeSabre were newspapers and balled filthy clothing and the dog snuffled at them, looking at Millimaki with his sad wet eyes and then set out lunging at his lead with the scent in his nose. The road wound steeply upward through sparse dwarf pine lopsided and scoured by the vicious winds that inhabited that place and then along a ridgetop where rocky spines like the backs of antediluvian plated beasts protruded from the soil. The wind did blow and it moaned among the trees and the dirt from the bare ridge seethed in the grass as the dog surged ahead, whining. Below and ahead of them an ancient tree rose from the center of a great rock, its limbs accoutered with crows. As man and dog approached, the birds rose by twos and threes croaking, their black beaks agape like panting dogs', and their ragged wings beat furiously to hold against the wind.

He had apparently tripped or had suffered a seizure or heart attack on the ridge and then had fallen head over heels like a circus tumbler, becoming lodged head downhill in the split trunk of the tree the birds had occupied. Old sawyers called these trees schoolmarms and the man's head was wedged in the V of the trunk and was enlarged and black as a chunk of coal. His footfalls soundless through the pine duff, Millimaki circled the tree slowly, the film in the 35mm advancing with a whirr. He photographed close-up the terrible thing and then with some effort pried it from its horrible cunnilingual embrace and laid it back, where it sat rigored on the sidehill like a charred gargoyle. The dog sat whimpering. Millimaki snapped more pictures of the troll-like thing balanced on the slope and finally for his own purposes photographed the tree itself, groping freakishly into the daylight and wind as if from a stone egg, with its complement of funereal birds returned raucously to claim their rightful place.

The mountains there were beyond the truck radio's range and by the time he roused the rancher to call the coroner for permission to remove the body it was near dark. The rancher sat nearby at his kitchen table listening, dressed in the coveralls he had slept in. Millimaki negotiated the use of an ATV and a small cart. The exchange took perhaps ten words. The vehicle's headlight when he arrived once again on the mountain pulsed bright and dim apace with its ragged idling and in this weird light he bagged the awkward corpse and rolled it onto the haycart among fencing pliers and staples and metal posts and at his truck loaded it with difficulty into the bed like a bale of wet hay.

By the time he exchanged vehicles and made the drive to town through the dark on the empty highway and delivered his package to the morgue it was nearly six o'clock, and when he at last got home his wife was gone to work and his bed without her in it seemed as cold and bleak as the coroner's trestle. An owl's insistent call from the pines behind the cabin was a din within which he could not sleep.

The sheriff sat rifling through a drawer in his desk and Millimaki could hear pens and loose change and perhaps pill bottles and cartridges clattering and then the man said, "Well, shit." He looked up, surprised to see the young man standing there. He sat back and regarded him. "You look about half like a raccoon, Val, with those eyes. You been cattin' around when you get off shift?"

"No, sir. I just haven't figured out how to sleep yet."

"Well, hell. It's not your first graveyard."

Millimaki thought of the bright empty cabin without his wife moving about in her stocking feet, the muffled companionability at the verge of his sleep.

"I slept better when my wife was home. Since she started working, I don't know, it's too quiet."

The sheriff nodded absently. "You'll get it figured out. It takes a while. And about the time you do, it's time to go back to the real world." He looked down at the open drawer once more and then slid it shut. "I've got the finest system in the world for losing shit I need."

Millimaki stood. Out of boredom he'd eaten his lunch too early in his shift and now he felt the bad office coffee eroding the walls of his empty stomach. It churned and creaked and he hoped the sheriff would not hear it.

"Goddamn it, I'm sorry. Your wife's name is . . ."

"Glenda, sir."

"I've got a pretty good system for forgetting shit, too. For Christ sake. Glenda. That's right. She's a nice girl. A nurse, isn't she?"

"Yes, sir. An ICU nurse."

"She been chasing you around when you get home?"

"If she was home she might. Or me her. But she's gone to work by the time I get home."

"Right, right. You just said that."

As if some order in the tumult of papers arrayed across his desktop might be disturbed, he delicately lifted one then another and peered under them. "What is that drive for you, an hour or better?"

"This time of year little over an hour."

"Uh-huh." He patted down his shirt, felt in his pants pockets. He called, "Raylene!" There was no answer from the outer office. "Goddamn it." He picked up a page of paper and held it away from himself and stared at it, scowling.

"You know about Gload, then," he said. "I mean you read his sheet and all that."

"I did some, since we brought him in. I didn't spend a lot of time on it."

"You know there are cops in this town, hell, all over this state, that if they were to pull over John Gload by accident would just about piss their pants? I mean old-time bulls, old-time tough beat cops and sheriffs, sonsofbitches who have seen it all."

Millimaki said, "Officer Dobek did seem a little on edge."

The sheriff smiled grimly. "Not having been there, I can only guess that's a decided understatement."

"But I did hear that about Gload from somewhere, yes, sir." He thought about the old man stiffly astride his chair in the cell and his slow careful trudging along the icy walks, as though afraid in falling he would shatter like crockery. "It's hard to believe now."

"Don't be fooled by that smile, Val, or him being an old man. You've seen those hands. He could squeeze juice out of a stove log."

"Yes, sir. That's true."

"Take his sheet home and look over it. Study it. Hell, it might help you get to sleep, though it's more likely to make you lock all the doors and sit up with your gun in your lap. I think we might finally have him on this thing, but there are a lot of unanswered questions floating around with Gload's name hanging off of them."

He shuffled more papers, patted his pockets again front and rear. "Anyway, the shitty thing is this, Val. I'm keeping you on nights. For one thing that old man has a hard-on about Wexler but also he seems to like you. I don't know what it says about you and maybe I don't want to know. He hates cops. Just hates cops like all get-out. But he talks to you. If you could just keep your ears open or maybe even steer him around to talking about some of the shit you'll read on his sheet." As he spoke the sheriff was variously leaning back and hunching forward in an effort to read the print on the files and forms fanned across his desk. He said finally, "Well. It's a long shot. We might be able to clear up some of these things that have been left unfinished since he showed up in this country. And that was a hell of a long time ago."

"All right."

The sheriff eyed Millimaki. "What the hell is it about you, anyway, and that old killer?"

Millimaki thought for a minute. His head felt fat and his stomach rolled dangerously and his eyes burned. "We talk about farming."

The sheriff stared at him. "Farming."

"Other stuff. But farming, yes, sir."

"Well, I'll be damned." He waved Millimaki away and began running his hands beneath the papers on his desktop, feeling his pockets. "Would you please for the love of Christ ask Raylene when you go out if she's seen my glasses anywhere?"

"Do they look anything at all like the ones you have on your head, sir?"

"Oh, for Christ sake." He reached and took them down and glared at them maliciously and then as if addressing them he said, "Lest you think me a fool or a liar, Deputy, I'm one of them who wouldn't ever want to run into John Gload with no bars in front of him."

"I wasn't thinking anything."

They were half-glasses and seemed indeed to not fit the sheriff's handsome face and he set them with distaste on his nose. Over these he looked at Millimaki for a long second. "I don't believe for one minute that you're ever not thinking, Deputy." He opened his drawer again and began to set things in order. "Come and see me next week if I forget to send for you. And disregard that it's eight-thirty in the morning and try a glass of beer when you get home. Used to work for me and near as I can tell I never turned out to be a juicer."

When he came out into the outer room a large woman with voluminous red hair set atop her head with two sticks looked up from her desk. She wore an elaborate betasseled shawl held in place over her capacious bust with a pin of pewter or silver in the shape of the state of Montana and she held the telephone receiver pressed against her shoulder with her chin. When she saw Millimaki she said, "What's he caterwauling about in there?"

"It's nothing. He couldn't find something but then he did."

The woman squinted at him, her head cocked oddly, still clenching the phone to her shoulder. "Them goddamn glasses, am I right?" she said. "If he wasn't so vain and would just get a chain for those things." Her manner was proprietary and kind for all she meant to appear the picture of stern subaltern righteousness. She spoke curtly to someone on the phone. When Millimaki looked back from the door he saw she was smiling.

He had spent one normal evening with his wife, though he found himself dozing off during supper and during conversation, and then in their bed later, even as his wife breathed beside him, he could not sleep. Nor the next day. Knowing the dark confinement awaited him he pottered around the empty cabin in his slippers like a shut-in, the early spring sunlight an admonition or taunt. By the time he resumed his shift at the jail, except for those brief snatches in chairs he had barely slept for thirty-six hours. His wife when she left had not bothered to kiss him good-bye.

Gload said, "Good to see you, Deptee. Where you been hiding?"

"I got called out on a lost hiker."

"Have any luck?"

"I found him, if that's what you mean."

"Found him cold."

"Yes."

"Found another one cold and now you're back on shit duty nursemaiding the old man."

It had become their routine. Gload pulled his chair to the bars and arranged his smoking gear beside him on the floor and on his knee balanced the tin bean can, and the young deputy sat his chair under the bank of lights, their faces long waxen caricatures under the purpled sheen.

Gload said, "All manner of excitement while you were out. Brother Wexler hauled in some dangerous criminals, three kids he caught with a twelve-pack of beer. He put 'em in a cell next to that short-eyes asshole and left 'em. Forgot to call their parents for three hours."

"They were minors in possession," Millimaki said.

Gload smoked within his shadows and continued as if he hadn't heard. "Come and sat here and bragged about it to me." Val could hear the old man's breath quicken. "I could hear that fucking pervert Shoals whispering and one of them boys for a long time crying down there."

"He's a letter-of-the-law man. Those boys were in violation of the MIP laws."

"You'd of cut them loose, wouldn't you of?"

"They had violated the law."

Gload hissed suddenly, "Fuck that. You wouldn't of done it. You'd of taken their beer and followed them home and cut them loose, goddamn it."

Millimaki sat. John Gload was breathing heavily.

"Wexler's the worst kind of asshole. I would bet any money you care to name he was a little picked-on turd his whole life and now he's got just a little bit of whack and he's making everybody pay for it. I seen that kind pretty near my whole life. Thousand bucks says he was a turd all his growing up and now he's getting his paybacks." The killer's hand appeared in the light, ghost-white, pointing down toward the now empty cell where a third-offense child molester had recently slept. "Doing shit like that."

Millimaki knew Wexler was capable of such things and he despised him for it and suddenly he hated all of it, the incremental passing of the hours, the eternal darkness he seemed to reside in, the smell, the pettiness and small cruelties that populated his life. The unnamable tension that was present on the rare occasions these days when he saw his wife, who seemed to feel he had chosen this imprisonment as a way of not seeing her and not dealing with the issues of married life.

"I'm right, ain't I?" Gload said.

"I wouldn't know."

"You wouldn't know," Gload repeated. "Don't fucking bullshit me, Deputy. I thought we were friends."

"We're friends, John, inasmuch as you're in there for possibly killing somebody and I'm out here making sure you stay alive to be punished for it."

There was only their breathing, the sound of the lights. Past the high small windows that fronted the sidewalk and street a brief shadow went. Finally Gload said, "I don't want no more company tonight." He stood up and receded suddenly into the gloom of his concrete cage. "You go on and eat your lunch."

Valentine Millimaki sat for a long moment and then stood and turned. But he heard Gload behind him hiss, "I would put him in a hole in the ground, Val. I would put him under and you nor your dog nor anyone would find his ass until his bones were as white as Custer's."

The voice was one he had not heard from Gload before, had not heard in his life, and he stared into the cell as if he might see this other animal that had taken possession of that place, come from some other more calamitous dark. As suddenly it was gone.

"Go on and have your sandwich now," Gload said. "I'll see you tomorrow."

Gload had been in court all day following and seemed worn out by the day's endeavors. When Val came on shift the old man was asleep on his thin cot.

He ate his lunch in the jail's foyer, leafing through the battered magazines, and afterward filled out some paperwork at the request of the jailer. When he walked back through the corridor of cells he could see from a long way off the smoke materializing from the black of Gload's cell.

He took his accustomed chair. Gload spoke a short while of

the day's events in the courtroom, what the prosecutors had said, what his defender had offered by way of rebuttal.

"You know one of them sonsofbitches used a word I never heard before. Maybe you know it. I wrote it down here on my pad." He turned and reached just beyond lightfall to the tiny desk cantilevered by chain from the wall and took up a yellow legal pad. Oddly elegant writing on the lines and baroque fretwork penciled in the margins of imagined creatures and strange faces that may have been caricatures of courtroom players—lawyers or judge or baliff—elongate and leering like those in a funhouse mirror. Gload ran a finger down among his sentences and stopped, tapping the page, and he cast his eyes toward the hall ceiling lights. "Turpitude." He sat staring at the word, twice underlined, his long sloping horse's brow furrowed in concentration, as if the meaning may have been revealed in his recent dreams if he could only conjure it. Finally he said, "No, I haven't never heard that word."

"I never heard of it either," Valentine said.

Gload smiled at him. "Thought you were some kind of college boy."

"That's one I missed."

"He said, 'This man's life of turpitude' and one other time. Seemed pretty proud of it."

"I've got to go on up for a while," Val said. "Want me to look it up?"

"I'd appreciate it."

The old man listened to the clop and rasp of Millimaki's steps diminishing down the darkened hallway. He tried to remember the dream he had had while he slept earlier and could recall only a chaos of amorphous people aswim in that murky realm wearing each other's heads and loosed in the court were the cobbled beasts of sleep—minotaurs and griffins and creatures seen only in the mythology of men's sleep.

He sat smoking in the dark, reading by its sounds the hour of the night and he was smoking still when the deputy came back. The younger man sat down as before on the ladderback chair and said, "Baseness, vileness, depravity." He had written the words on his palm and he turned it to Gload as proof and turned it so the light would fall on the words, large block letters on the farmboy's hand like jailhouse tattoos. Gload smiled above the cat-eye ember of his cigarette, imagining Val's hand with its message easing up the flannel of his young wife's nightdress.

"Well, thank you. I didn't figure it to be anything that might be complimentary."

"Nope. I guess you could have figured that much."

Gload told the young deputy that he sensed something in the demeanor of the state's attorneys. Above their opened files with their heads inclined together like children at a game, they seemed to have an unusual sense of confidence. His own attorney he thought of as little more than stage dressing. He had done work in the past for Gload and some of his contemporaries, but a proclivity toward fortified wine had much diminished him in the ensuing years, and the papers he compulsively shuffled above the table trembled alarmingly, his handwriting a faltering scrawl that for all its illegibility may have been another language entirely. He sat dwarfed beside John Gload with a fond look on his face, a strange small man of indeterminate age around whose balding head ran a lank fringe of hair like inexpertly dyed tree moss. At the end of the day he laid a hand on Gload's shoulder and went out, to be seen no more until morning.

"I don't think my little friend Calvert C. Benjamin, attorney at law, knows shit from Shinola, Val," Gload said. "Them other guys are holding some kind of hole card, I can tell you that, and he's a man wandering in the dark." He gave Millimaki a hard inquiring look.

"I don't hear a thing, John, swear to God. By the time I come on shift there's just me and the jailer and the janitor, and he's deaf as a rock."

"Yeah. Well."

"Anything the state's guys have, your guy'd have too, John."

"True enough. The sonofabitch might just not know what to do with it. But something's up. I can feel it and I smell White."

Gload looked beyond Millimaki to the small arched windows opposite, high up on the wall, and watched as phantom legs scissored across the rectangle of dull yellow streetlamp. The old barred windows let in the wind with a faint moan and it swayed the tube lights overhead on their chains in a barely audible metallic creaking like the turning of a distant windmill. From somewhere down the line of shadowed cages a man coughed deeply and swore.

Gload said, "The good deputy Dobek stopped by earlier to tell me how I'm going to piss my pants when they drop the trap and that my eyes are going to pooch out of my head and shit like that." He snorted. "Hell, they ain't hung nobody in this state for twenty-four years, he ought to know that. But it was sort of sweet of him to stop off and share all that with me just the same."

"I'm sorry about that, John, I really am."

"I believe friend Wexler was there, too, down the way where I couldn't see him."

Gload beyond the latticework of shadows drew on his cigarette and leaned back, and the shadow line clove his face. His eyes were gone. Smoke in twinned plumes hissed from his nostrils. Down the corridor a lodger coughed again and another in his troubled slumber whimpered like a child and John Gload snorted his facsimile laugh. "The wicked flee where none pursueth," he said. "Even in their sleep."

"Bad dreams," Val said.

"Bad dreams. Right." He paused, nodded his head slowly up and down as if agreeing with some muttered point put forth from the obscured region behind him. He inclined into the light, pointed two fingers at Val with the cigarette clenched between them. "You earn those, Val. They don't just show up on their own."

He blew smoke at the floor, leaned and tipped his ash into the bean can. "When I don't sleep it ain't because of bad dreams. It ain't because of ghosts or nothing like that. So what does that tell you?"

"Don't know."

"I don't know either." He studied the polished concrete between his feet. He looked up. "Yes I do. I know what I am, Val."

He was quiet for a long time. He was about to speak when the man cried out from the grip of his troubled sleep and seemed to wake himself and he was cursed by men in adjacent cells and curses and threats went from cage to cage like an echo. Millimaki stood and went down the corridor a short way and stood listening until the noise slowly subsided and there was nothing to be heard but snoring and soft and regular breathing and over all like a swarm of electric bees the maddening hum of the fluorescents.

When Millimaki returned and resumed his seat, Gload said, "Dying is something I ain't afraid of, Val. Don't worry about that shithead Dobek. For one thing, they won't hang me or shoot me the juice or whatever. I'm too old. That'd be bad press for 'em. Hanging is a young man's deal. Nobody gets any satisfaction from jerking an old man's neck."

He paused to shake out a smoke from his pack and kindle it from the previous one and he did so in the dark as a blind man would, by touch and sound, movements done a thousand times in a thousand darks.

"But I will say this—I don't much care for the idea of dying in lock-up. That's just pitiful. You're dead in a field of other loser cons like you were throwed in a landfill."

"That's only if the family doesn't claim the remains."

"First you got to have family."

"But you have someone, John, right? Your wife, is it? The woman out at your place?"

"Nope," he said. "No one."

"Well, I saw her stuff there. We saw a woman's stuff."

"I ain't saying she wasn't there. But like I told you before—gone."

"She'd come back for that, would she not?"

From the shadows Millimaki heard the faint creaking of the chair as Gload shifted his weight. "No," he said, "she will not come back."

Millimaki said, "You never said. Is it your wife?"

In the ensuing pause it may have been a sigh he heard or it may have been a mere exhale of smoke and then from Gload's private darkness could be heard nothing but the faint crackle of paper and tobacco as the old man drew deeply on his cigarette. Millimaki waited, staring into the shadows, but the conversation seemed to be at an end. For these long weeks since he'd been to Gload's house he imagined the woman back, pottering from lonely room to room and tending her frail blooms in their narrow beds, leaning at a window jamb a hundred times a day to witness her man's return when such a returning was as improbable as resurrection.

"My wife won't come here," Val said. "One time when I first come on the department and that was it. Something about this old building gave her the willies."

"Well, I'm on her side about that."

He'd thought introducing his own wife into the conversation might pry loose from the old man's mouth words of wife and marriage but it would not. Finally he said, "Don't you have some other family somewhere, John?"

Blue smoke rolled into the light as the old man spoke, and his voice was newly animated. "Only one there ever was was my dad and when he died it was really the end of anything you might call a normal life for me."

"When did he die?"

"Oh, well. That had to of been sixty-some years ago now."

"You must have been just a kid."

Gload in a muttering undertone toted the years and decades on his thick fingers and then said, "Sixty-four years ago to be exact. And yeah, I was just a kid, Val. But I remember it clear as yesterday." And he began to talk and the details were, even for Millimaki, vivid as any recent memory and the old man talked without pause for a very long time.

SIX

They lived in east Fergus County on the Judith divide and his father ran a few black cows there in the foothills of the Little Snowies and it was there that Gload did the farming that inspired his dreams, a boy all but running the place while the elder Gload, in lieu of more conventional cash crops, kept the operation afloat primarily through poaching and poker.

At their backs as they drove toward the neighbor's hunting shack, late January of John Gload's thirteenth year, was a tide of charcoal Alberta clouds, vanguard of the storm that would orphan him.

The shack sat in a round hollow among the stunted bull pines of that country, situated to be out of the wind and with an eye toward invisibility. While his father and two other men went about butchering a pair of mule deer does and a calf elk jacklighted some days earlier in the Missouri bottoms, young John Gload sat on an upturned crate, sharpening as needed an eclectic collection of knives, his hands even at that age quick and dexterous and the blades as he passed them over the oiled stone appeared liquid as quicksilver. The men sawed and cut, drinking as they did so from a bottle stood among the chunks of meat on a table cobbled up of lengths of stove wood and a sheet of warped plywood. There were two rank-smelling cots in the shack, pushed to the outer walls to make room for the bloody work and in a dark corner a box of rags where a mongrel bitch lay watching the men through hooded eyes. At intervals she would venture out and lap at the thick black pool growing beneath the table until one or other of the men kicked her away. She looked to be part coyote, her lip curled in a perpetual leer to show wretched teeth the color of clay. Her piebald pups in the box mewled piteously at the sudden cold and young Gload stood over them counting, assessing which would thrive, which would perish.

The storm had reached them even in that sheltered place and it sucked and moaned at the door and sent slender serpents of drift into the room. Each man's shadow loomed and shrank beneath the penduluming lantern. Two propane heaters were set to burn but still the butchers' breath blossomed whitely and when they could no longer feel their hands the work was halted. The boy had hoped to take home one of the pups but instead they carried out only packages of meat haphazardly wrapped in butcher paper and bound with electrical tape, the box weeping a thin vermillion trail atop the snow.

The truck was a 1924 four-cylinder Chevrolet and it veered and slewed like a carnival ride along frozen ruts as they climbed through the slanting snow, the blunted trees on either side stuttering and nodding and when they came up into the open parklands the wind hit them full force. Ice crystals blown through the shrunken doorseals shimmered like mica in the green dashboard glow. Four miles out they became high-centered on a wind-scoured drift. The crust was hard as pavement and the truck with its narrow tires had rolled atop it and then simply dropped. The wind howled and the snow swooped down from the yawing treetops into the clearing and broke against the truck like an ocean surge. His father dug around the tires and the wooden spokes with a spade and he would jump in and gun the engine and move ahead a foot or two and then the truck would sink. John Gload could see his father's face red and glistening in the headlights as he drove the spade handle down into the drift. It sank to the blade. He stood up into the light and held the shovel up to indicate the depth and shook his head. Gload remembered that his father's hat had fallen off and his hair stood up crazily above his bone-white forehead. After an hour of digging and rocking the truck and more digging, they had progressed no more than ten feet. Neither could they go back, as the snow filled in what tracks they had made until it appeared as if the Chevy had simply been set down like a toy in the center of the drift. The storm raged out of the north and there was little to the world beyond the twinned cones of light the headlights threw and black pines at the limit of their vision stood cowled and sinister as executioners. His father stood the spade in the drift and clambered into the cab.

"Whew, boy. I think we fell into some kind of a glacier or something. We must of drove around it coming in." He sat in the driver's seat panting and sweating. "I don't think there's no bottom to the sonofabitch."

He started the engine to warm them, the laboring cylinders barely audible above the wind yowling at the doors, the grainy snow like locusts seething across the metal of the hood. From beneath the seat his father retrieved a pint bottle of J&B and drank from it.

He told his son he was going to make for a ranch house he knew to be just off to the west. "Just down through this little bit of timber," he said. "It's closer than the shack is." He looked at the boy and smiled. "It's not no more than a little hike." He told his son to stay in the truck and for no reason to get out. If he had to pee use the empty beer bottle that had rolled from under the seat. But wait there for him. Run the engine every little while and keep the window down a crack. In the dash glow he examined the level of the bottle, dropped it into the pocket of his coat and stepped out. With his hand on the door handle he seemed to hesitate, looking once back the way they'd come, once up to the white and swirling heavens and then he'd turned and set off into the storm. Young Gload could see him clearly for a while and then as a dark shape wavering against the black pines and then with his face pressed to the clouded window glass young Gload's father became a part of the dark itself.

"He didn't get too far, Val. I guess he was a little turned around because he wasn't headed for nowhere. Nearest house in that direction, I heard some of them sonsofbitches say, was ten miles, prit-near to Grass Range. By the time they found me I was almost done in myself. I wound up losing toes on this one foot."

Millimaki sat staring down into the cell, hypnotized by the disembodied voice. Gload may have thought the deputy was staring at his foot or merely meant to prove the validity of his story, but he shucked off a worn brown brogan and brown sock and thrust into the slant of light a strange foot, very white, two-toed, looking more like the foot of a large, strange bird than a man's.

"They brought me to a ranch house and put me in somebody's bedroom. Guy who owned that little cabin, my dad's partner, he found me there, come in and called me a little sonofabitch for telling them sheriffs where the meat was. But I hadn't told them nothing. That cold bastard, kid who just lost his old man." He sat shaking his head there in the dark. "Wasn't long after that that I seen them carrying him."

Gload leaned forward into the purple lightfall and Val could see him studying the floor, his bare, strange, dead-white foot. Finally he said, "Just a little hike, is what he said. And I always remembered him sort of hesitating there by the truck and him knowing I was watching and I think he set off like he was sure just so I wouldn't be scared. I do believe that to be true. Standing there," Gload said, quietly. "Didn't know north from east."

He had last seen his father carried between two sheriff's deputies across the drifted ranchyard, just a shutter-blink as they passed what view he had out the window, left to right between folds of drapery behind which he sat with his black and swollen feet in a pan of water. It was a misshapen thing they carried, as brusquely as you might a hay bale or furniture piece, and it left in the unblemished snow, when they'd passed from view, a strange drag trail, as though the two men between them conveyed a fairy-book dragon, its tail and wingtips unsteady above the alien snow.

From some distant duct-grate or from the imperfect street-level windows, a breath of air set Gload's bare lightbulb swaying, the pull chain tinkling softly and he turned his gaze upward. At the corners of his eyes were long deep crevasses disappearing into his sparse hairline, and from his chronic sleeplessness, as if drawn with a pen, his inflamed eyes were rimmed with red.

From the endeavor of the long narration and the reliving of the winter night that would re-create him in the world, he seemed depleted. His voice when he at last spoke again was faint and hoarse.

He said, "I went from there to a hospital to an orphanage run by these strange ladies dressed up in black, all in the matter of a few weeks. I gotta say, it was a tough old time for a kid."

"I imagine it was," Millimaki said. "My old man went down for a nap and just kept sleeping and that was bad enough."

Gload stared out through the bars. He sat erect in his chair and raked back the thin strands from his forehead and cleared his throat. "When did this happen?"

"Oh, that's been a year now. Year and a half."

"You lost your old man?"

"Sixty-two years old. Died in his chair."

"That's tough."

"He was a decent man. Had this kind of crazy temper but he only hit me once and I had it coming."

"Died in his chair," Gload said. "And you felt like you should of been there."

"Oh, I don't know. Not so much. My cousin was there to check on him every day."

"Felt like you could of done something to prevent it, I imagine."

Val stared in at the old man. "It just happened. His life was hard."

"Sixty-two years of age. Lost your old man at a young age,

same as me." He paused conspicuously to allow the gravity of kindredship to fill the moment.

"Not all that young," Millimaki said.

Gload went on as if he hadn't heard. "And your mother?" he said. "Where is she?"

"Gone a long time now."

"And I bet she run off on you all, didn't she, same as mine? I bet she skipped out."

Millimaki stood up. "Like I said, it was a long time ago."

Gload's hands appeared. He grasped the bars of his cage and leaned his face into the fluorescent light. "We're just a couple of hard-luck orphans, ain't we, Valentine?"

The old man's face was a smiling deathmask in the hard chemical light. Millimaki excused himself and picked up a small brown sack he'd had beside his chair and down the way Gload could hear him talking to one of the men. He came back shortly and set down his bag and settled into the chair. Gload raised an inquisitive eyebrow.

"This Grogan's got some kind of croup. I been giving him some cough dope from home. The store-bought stuff doesn't seem to be doing much."

"Like a goddamn TB ward in here," Gload said. "Been listening to him cough up his lungs all day." He sat slowly pulling on his sock, lacing his shoe, and with a cigarette stuck in the corner of his mouth he studied the young deputy. "Goddamn bleeding-heart cop. Christ on a crutch." He snorted, shook his head in amused disbelief. Smoke plumed from his nostrils. He wiped the toe of each shoe on the back of his dungarees and examined them in the light.

He said, "What time you got, Val?"

"It's a little after one. Ten after." Millimaki consulted his watch and as he did the clock in the Catholic church three blocks away tolled once. "There you go. I might be a little fast."

"Did you eat yet?"

"I did. Just before I came in."

Gload considered this. He stood and moved his chair next to the bars and arranged his smoking gear on the floor and rested the bean can on his knee.

"Why don't you move over just a bit closer, Val, so we don't keep these assholes awake. Unless you got things to do."

Val checked his watch again out of habit and sat with his head cocked, listening for a moment to the sleeping corridor. Grogan slept on, the others slept or silently listened. "Not really," he said. He picked up his chair and carried it nearer the bars, just beyond arm's reach. He settled it there, sat and crossed his legs, and in the shadows Gload, still watching, smiled.

"Still don't trust the old man, Val."

"Policy, John. You ought to know that."

Gload leaned forward just enough to meet the deputy's eyes. His look was fond. "Val, I'm going to tell you some things and you can tell the Old Bull but I suspect it won't make no difference to me at this point."

"You know I'd be obligated to report anything concerning illegal activities, so you maybe want to just stick to safe subjects."

"Policy."

"However you want to call it."

"Well, you let me worry about it, Val."

"I just want to be clear on that."

"You are perfectly clear, Deputy."

"Okay."

Having shifted forward, Gload now sat half in light, half in dark, and he looked to have been sheared in two and set for display, head and shoulders of a taxidermied felon, a trophy displayed for tourists or schoolchildren in a diorama of prison life: table, chair, cot. Killer.

He lasted no more than six months at the Catholic orphanage where he was remanded as a ward of the neighboring state where the bones of his mother were buried. The first months there were marked by long gloomy silences and merciless teasing as the boy sought for his solitude the comforting dark of closets and gardening sheds and kitchen pantries. Then he began to fight. For young John Gload there was nothing of sport in these contests, and almost from the first, blood was the common consequence, as if like some pagan sacrament they could not be otherwise consummated. Boys three and four years older and twenty pounds heavier went about with torn ears and gouged eyes, the corners of their mouths split where Gload had jammed in his fingers and simply pulled, as though trying to tear a gunnysack. The screams of his dorm mates or threats from nuns or priests went unheard and Gload was more than once blindsided with a sap by one of the tough old Jesuits as he worked blood-speckled and stoical atop a boy who may have simply laughed at the wrong time.

Few of the residents or staff was saddened by his departure and when he set out under a shard of moon wending westward on his barely healed feet he was neither sought nor reported missing. He progressed across that state afoot and by car. He shared the back of a pickup with a six-year-old girl alone with her 4-H hog which was so huge it might have crushed and eaten her. He rode in an Oldsmobile with a candy salesman from

Duluth, Minnesota, who offered him twenty dollars to show his underwear. There were two phlegmatic wheat farmers, brothers and perhaps twins, so preoccupied with the clouds marshaled in the skies over Canada just to the north that they abandoned the road altogether and drove cross-country through fallow and farm toward a strange metal structure bristling with antennae which they called the Weather Temple of Christ Jesus and offered to let him stay and pray if he could prove the purity of his heart and he rode with a half-mad rancher's wife abroad at midday drinking, who would have killed them both on a bridge abutment had not Gload taken the wheel as she nodded into unconsciousness. By these and other such means he crossed the border back into the state of Montana in the summer of 1947.

In the little town he arrived at that afternoon, boys his age on bicycles stared after him and there were boys walking toward the river with fishing poles on their shoulders and except for the filthiness of his clothes and the look of the wolf in his eye he may have been just another of them.

He was hot and tired, having walked several miles that morning from the highway where a car had dropped him off. The air was syrupy with the smell of roadside sweet clover and his pants cuffs were yellow from it as though he'd walked through a field of chalk.

He had seen her as he passed down a neighborhood, an older woman in her bathrobe kneeling on a gardening pad behind a wire fence and turning the soil in her flowerbeds with a hand trowel. A tiny ivory Pomeranian attended her and sat panting in the shade of a lilac. Gload went down the street and returned and as he did he saw her get up and put her hands to the small of her back and look up at the sun. She bent to speak to the dog and it rose and began yammering and running in circles like a wind-up toy.

He went in through a back gate, pausing under a hanging feeder where small yellow birds fluttered, raining tiny seeds down on him. A bird flew up onto an overhead branch gaudy with purple plum blossom and began a long sweet canzonet as if in greeting.

He went silently in the door and among the rooms looking for he knew not what. He pocketed a hairbrush, a watch, change from a china bowl on a nightstand. He felt comfortable there, as though these smells and plaster saints and faintly ticking and chiming clocks were the things of his own childhood, the ghosts of forgotten longings. When the old woman came into the room, young John Gload stood before a mantelpiece studying the faces in framed photographs as though among those grainy images he might find his own staring back. She did not speak but only gazed openmouthed to find this ragged boy in her house. The Pomeranian began to yelp and it lunged and sank its needle teeth into John Gload's bare ankle and without thinking he snatched it up and threw it against the wall. It was only then she began to scream. Young Gload in one motion picked up a table lamp, swung, and hit her above her left ear with its heavy leaded base. He was surprised that she went down as hard and as fast as she did and she lay on the carpet in the summer sunlight perfectly still.

He set down the lamp on the table, aligning it in the dustless circle where it had stood and he looked at his hands. He studied the small crimson mark on the wall where the dog had struck, a small runic daub like a cave marking, and he stood above the clutch of animated rag where it lay working its obscene little mouth soundlessly.

Finally he stood over the woman. She was very pale and lay with her arms outthrown and one leg crossed beneath her as though she had only misstepped while dancing. Kneeling, he opened her robe and carefully straightened her long limbs, so light, he thought, as if the bones of her had already begun to go to dust. He raised her pale shift and examined the parts of her that boys at the orphanage had whispered about and he'd seen in nudist magazines some of them kept hidden from the nuns. He lay atop her fully clothed and after a while he put his arms around her and he spoke to her, said the name of one of the girls from the sister orphanage he'd once danced with and he said some of the things the other boys said in the locker room after gym class. The woman's eyes were half-closed and from one nostril a single drop like a viscous red tear appeared.

He stood up. The little Pom dog lay as before and made a snoring sound and then was still, one eye agape, slightly bulged and aglow from the long afternoon sunrays breaching the gauzy curtains. He looked at the woman again and presently went to her and arranged the folds of her robe over her breasts and withered limbs. There was a small pillow on the sofa, a purfling of white lace for a border and incomprehensible words lovingly needlepointed across its face. He placed it under her head and but for the blood at her nose and the crease above her ear that had by then begun to leak a crimson pool beside her, she may well have been asleep.

In the kitchen he stopped and chose an apple from a turned wooden bowl and he stood in that bright clean room looking at the apple in his hand. He set it on the counter, returned to the outer room. Rummaging in a drawer he found a pair of men's socks and he dabbed at the blood on his ankle with them and put them on. Passing the woman again he paused, looking down.

He took the pillow from under her head and placed it over her face, reading again the words stitched there—foreign, hopelessly untranslatable, and for all that unforgettable, as he felt they were meant to convey a message, tidings as obscure and cataclysmic as the goldfinch's song.

Leaving, he took the apple from the counter, closed and locked the door, and walked west progressing unhurriedly in his strangely nautical gait under an arcature of ponderous elms, more birdsong in his ears.

When he had finished his long narrative, the old man sat back stiffly with a barely audible groan, whether the protest of chair slats or of old bones Millimaki could not tell. He straightened in his own seat and was himself stiff and when he checked his watch from long habit he realized his shift was nearly up. His stomach creaked and turned. The corridor was brighter now with the marginal light from the high windows, and the new day was announced with the sound of men urinating and the striking of matches. Grogan had begun to cough.

Gload seemed to have gone far away in conjuring such memories and from his private darkness he was a long time speaking. Finally he leaned his long face out into the purple light and raised his eyes to look at the deputy as if he might read something in the younger man's face.

"Funny, ain't it, Val, I started out the way I did on account of a little Pom dog?"

"Wait," Val said. "An apple? You ate an apple?"

"An apple, why not? Yeah. That's not important, Val, but here's the deal." He sat with his forearms upon his knees, gazing into the palms of his enormous hands as if recorded there among the ridges and cracks was the transcript of his life and he was merely reading it aloud. "Along about two miles later I sat down on a railroad berm to catch my breath. It was an interesting moment. By the time I ate that apple, I didn't feel a thing about that woman." He rolled his eyes up to regard Millimaki, his hands still open on his knees in a sort of offertory pose. "Val, I knew right then I'd never in my life have to do a regular day of work again."

SEVEN

He stood at the top of the steps taking in the morning. The birds in the elms across the street in the courthouse park sang and the sun through the branches mottled the damp walkway paving stones, in the periodic light the newly cut grass gleaming as if sown with diamond parings. Having emerged from the chill and artificial light of the jail into a golden April day of birdsong, Millimaki felt more than ever like a prisoner himself. A place of perpetual dark, where even on a glorious spring day the gloom did not abate entirely but merely withdrew, receding like a fog to linger near the ceiling where the light chains were hung. When he shaved in the late afternoon the outlier's eyes that stared back were braided in red, the skin pasty, even yellow. He examined the backs of his hands in the daylight and they seemed to him soft and pale as a child's. He worried that some jailhouse pathogen had invaded his body, contracted from a handshake, a cough, a sneeze. Or that he was simply becoming

Gload. He wondered, too, if he had caught insomnia like a virus from the old man and could blame him for the sleeplessness that seemed without remedy.

Uniforms were arriving for their shifts and he watched as Weldon Wexler parked his car in the lot across the street. He watched as he righted his nightstick and holstered sidearm and stooped to adjust his hair using the car window as a mirror. Then he stood and turned. He set off across the street and then he began to affect a slight limp.

Val met him at the bottom of the stairs.

"You can go home to your wife now, Millimaki," Wexler said. "She's a little wore out but otherwise just fine."

"You know, Wexler, even if I liked you that wouldn't be funny."

"I think we might of woke the neighbors with all the moaning and screaming and carrying on. But I just went out and told them, 'Go back to sleep, I'm an officer of the law.'"

"Technically I guess it could be said that you are. You have the uniform."

"You might try a little spit and polish yourself, pardner. You look like you just come from milking the cows."

"What do you know about Dobek paying a call to Gload?"

"So that's your problem? What, did we upset your pet killer?"

"There's no need for that."

"Listen, pardner." Wexler ascended two steps that he might look down on Millimaki and when he spoke it was to the air above his head. "Let me put it thisaway. I intend to get information out of this Gload that could clear up God knows how many open cases. If by scaring this suspect we can get him to talk about some of these things then I will do that."

"For Christ sake. Scare him? This guy has been letting blood out of people for a half a century. He's seen and done about every shitty nasty terrible thing there is to do. Do you really think you can scare anything out of a man like that?"

Wexler's smile was thin and insincere. He put one hand atop his holstered pistol and the other on the knob of his nightstick and stood erect and spraddle-legged, a pose perhaps seen on television and practiced in front of a mirror. He said the name Valentine in a way Millimaki had not heard since his days on a playground. A sneer, a taunt. "Valentine," he said, "if I can't scare him, I'll be his buddy. Just like you." He leaned down and held two crossed fingers in front of Millimaki's face. "This tight. Asshole buddies."

The river was two miles from the jailhouse and he drove there, parking beside the riprapped bank where, beyond, the water lay flat and calm as a lake. Everywhere movement filled the morning sky, rafts of ducks rising up and ducks moving back from stubble fields on the benchland and their cries came to him sounding all the world like the cries of young children, as if playing pirates they stood off there on a raft on the smooth water. The river's organic smell rose to his nostrils like the breath of a living thing. On the far shore the rusted stacks of a refinery stood ranked and steaming against the sky like artillery and with the coming of blue twilight the compound there, with its pulsing lights and tongues of ultramarine flame, would look like a city besieged by war.

It was nine o'clock in the morning and he drank a beer, watching the ducks move off the river and circle and gather and in hundreds and thousands, in a cacophony of chatter, drift north toward the marshes and potholes of Canada. He lapsed briefly into addled sleep and the choir of waterfowl became in his dream the voices of people calling his name from a senseless other-world of dark trees as animated as snakes from whose coils the pallid victims of his searches reached out, weeping.

He awoke with a jolt to find a city patrolman standing beside his half-opened window.

"What's up there, Millimeter?"

"Officer Moon. Jesus." Millimaki pawed at his hair and wiped at the sheen of clammy sweat that had formed on his forehead during his brief sleep. "You're like a goddamn thief in the night."

The officer smiled, revealing movie-star teeth. He was a farm kid from the Hi-Line. They'd spoken a few times at cop functions and found they had in common a desire to see nothing more of lean cattle or machinery stitched together with baling wire and prayer or to wake to the sound of flies snarling at the window glass. Despite his gym-rat physique, Millimaki knew him to be a gentle man and a good cop. He wore mirrored sunglasses and Millimaki could see his own bleary face in them, a newspaper crumpled on the seat, the beer can between his thighs.

"You were twitching there like you had jumper cables hooked to your ass."

"No shit?"

"Yes you were. You doing okay?"

Millimaki attempted to smooth his uniform shirt. The cruel light pierced his eyes and he pressed his thumbs to them to damp the pain.

"Except that I can't sleep anymore," he said. "I get off, my wife's gone to work, I go home and I can't sleep. I just got off shift." He looked at his watch. "Well, two hours ago. I get home and I'm dead-ass tired but I'm wound up tight as a two-dollar watch."

Moon stood up and surveyed the brilliant day and the silken river with its myriad birds and he looked back to his idling patrol car. His uniform shirt was tailored, the sleeves cuffed up to show his biceps. He removed a small notebook from his breast pocket and began to write in it. "Used to take me about six of them sonsofbitches to fall asleep," he said. "It was terrible." He turned the tablet for Millimaki to read, running his finger beneath the printed letters as if instructing a child. "So this here's the answer. It's herbal, all natural, no side effects, nothing. It's goddamn magic."

He tore loose the sheet and held it through the window with two fingers like a traffic citation. "Yeah," he said, "I was starting to get a belly on me." He rubbed his hands over his flat shirtfront. "Knocking out eight hundred sit-ups a day and still getting fat. All that beer." He had been bending down to talk to Millimaki through the side window. He stood again and put his hands on the roof of Millimaki's truck. "Course, I was drinking in the bosom of my own home, not down by the river like a high school punk."

"Well, Patrolman Moon, maybe I will just pick me up some of these hippie pills. Then I can catch up on my sleep in the Daylite Donuts parking lot during duty hours like you."

Moon backed away from the car. "Please step out of the vehicle, sir. I'm afraid I'm going to have to crush your head."

"Moon, man, listen to yourself." Millimaki ran a hand over his eyes and suddenly felt he could sleep there or anywhere for a day and a night and intersect the right world of diurnal creatures the bright morning that followed. "If you're this way with a fellow officer, I can't imagine you're too cool with the citizenry."

Moon smiled. "Seriously, Val, get you some of those things

and go home and get some sleep." He reached in suddenly and took the beer from between Millimaki's legs and pitched it into the willows. "You fucking rummy."

He made the hour's drive home in a haze. All along the creek the cottonwoods and alder were in a frenzy of new leaf and calves ran and leapt along the banks where their mothers stood feeding, drowsy and hock deep in the vivid turf. He drove with the window down. Meadowlarks and red-winged blackbirds sang on the fence posts at the road edge and from the willows along the stream. Through the window the bright notes he had heard all his life fell garbled and indistinct on Millimaki's ears like the song of some alien species.

At home there was not the usual note from his wife and there was no dinner made and there was little to indicate she had even been there recently. He sat in his chair in front of the fireplace. There were bone-white ashes stirring on the cold grate. He sat for a long time looking into the white jailhouse hands in his lap.

"He's not a carpenter, Mother, and he's not a mechanic and not a whatever they are, road worker to fix the road."

He shuffled from the bedroom in his bare feet. His hair stood up on his head in a ragged coiffure and his eyeballs felt as if they'd been rolled in sand. Her back was to him and she leaned over the supper table, supporting herself on one arm, the phone pressed to her shoulder. He could see the boyish outline of her narrow back through the tight yellow T-shirt, the bones of her spine, the effect vaguely serpentine, and he fought the urge to run his hands down the length of it.

"I don't know," she said. "It is the way it is." She stood listening. "I'll have to live with it. Yes, Mother, thank you, that's very sound advice."

She held the receiver six inches away from her ear as though it had suddenly become hot.

"No, I'm sorry." She said it again, weakly, resignedly. "Yes. It's the way it is." She listened. "Yes. Love to Daddy, too."

She set the phone deliberately in its cradle and stood leaning with her fists balled atop the table, her head bowed.

To her back Millimaki said, "Who says I'm not a carpenter?"

She spun quickly. A gold strand of her hair caught up on her angry mouth and she swept it away. "Jesus, Val, don't do that." She glanced down at the phone on the table as if it had betrayed her and looked back at him. "I thought you were asleep. You should be."

"If you need a carpenter I can give you plumb and level till hell won't have it." Like a supplicant he stood before her in his ragged pajama pants, his hands upturned, his eyes from the luminous April daytime asquint after the shuttered gloom of their bedroom. He studied her face. Too often lately it had been a geometry of sharp lines and hard shapes and in the brief and infrequent intersecting of their lives she had been immune to his teasing, which in their marriage had been the ice breaker, the mender of rifts, the poultice on the inflamed wound of an argument.

"Is it too much to ask, Val, that a door actually works?"

"No," he said. "It is not. Most definitely not asking too much."

"I've fought that door since day one. I practically broke my thumb trying to open it today." She held up her left thumb as she spoke. "And it lets in the dirt and the snow and God knows what else. Bugs. Snakes. Absolutely from day one. I hate it."

"Okay, Glenda. But not snakes."

"I detest it."

He was smiling at her. "It's an awful thing to hate something as lovely and practical as a door."

"I'm just not in that kind of mood. I'm just not." She glared down at his bare feet. "And, God, where are your slippers?"

"I'm all over that door," he said. "Like white on rice."

"Just don't. I'm not kidding, really."

He spent two hours planing the door edge with his grandfather's old jack plane until the door swung freely on its medieval hinges. The bright excelsior from the plane lay in ribbons about his feet. His palms were raw. The cabin atop its unmortared foundation stones heaved and shifted like a trawler with each frost and thaw. In a few months the door would come untrued. He had learned to wait it out. October would see it stuck again in its skewed and unplumb jamb.

They ate dinner in near silence, the sound of fork on porcelain overloud in the still room, and then, as was their habit, left the table with its unwashed plates and empty wineglasses to take a drive. In Glenda's pale yellow Datsun they wove slowly down the hill, negotiating ruts and rocks exposed by the rains of spring, and onto the highway blacktop. Twelve miles on they turned onto gravel that wound south and east toward the old mining town of Hughesville. The sun burned in the mirrors and dust rose roiling bloodred behind them. From the limestone canyon walls, grave ill-formed statues and faces took shape among the shadowed clefts and spires. Glenda stared out the side window. Cow elk with their speckled calves stood off in the sparse lodgepole and reddening willow and sumac along the stream, eyeing them warily, and when Val pointed them out her head did not move and she did not speak.

They parked in the barrow ditch and wove through the

trelliswork of brush to the small creek. She took his hand mutely. At the bank they stretched out in the grass, the burbling lullaby of the water in their ears. In a very short time he fell asleep. He awoke from a sumptuous dreamless nap and Glenda was gone. He found her in the car, curled on the backseat like a child. He got in and eased shut the door. She did not wake, or pretended not to, as he drove home through a cool blue light descended upon the canyon. Above, the day diminished in a brilliant unfurling of color, the tottering pines atop the ridges as vivid as candle flames.

The little car rattled and bumped slowly once again up the hill to the unlit cabin. Millimaki stood leaning on the hood of the car for its warmth and his wife lay as before on the rear seat. The dog had come to the wire of his kennel and he whimpered softly.

As Val stood, dusk went to dark. From among the crevasses in the coulee rimrock to the south bats emerged by the hundreds and they swarmed among the constellations burning coldly through the black palisade of the pines. The single yard light had flickered on. He went to the rear door to wake her. She lay with one hand beneath her head and he stood looking at her through the dusty window glass. In the queer light she looked made of wax.

EIGHT

As he'd been instructed, Val after his shift the following week reported to the sheriff's office where he was ushered into the inner sanctum by the secretary with a brief backhand wave, the woman's eyes, inches from her monitor's screen, blank and iridescent as an insect's. Within, Millimaki stood before the man's desk with its bedlam of paper and plastic bags with esoteric articles enclosed and he felt a sudden pang of guilt, as though he were about to violate some priestly pact.

The sheriff regarded him over the top of his half-glasses. He said, "Did I send for you?"

"Sort of, sir. You told me last week to come and talk to you. About Gload. You said if I heard anything."

The man stared at Val critically. "It would seem the remedy I recommended for your malady has failed to work."

"I've been trying it. For some reason drinking beer that early in the day gives me a headache."

"It's not early, exactly, when you're on graveyards. For Christ sake, it's Miller Time."

"I can't get my head to figure that out."

The sheriff wagged his head sadly and the glasses that seemed so out of place on his face slid to the end of his nose. He pushed them up and leaned his head back to study the younger man through the magnifying lenses, as if that scumbled focus might present a more lucid picture.

"You still partnered up with that old man?" he said.

"I guess so."

"You must be his long-lost spawn, for Christ sake. I never knew of him to say much more than two words to any uniform and those two were 'Fuck you.'"

"I can't explain it."

"On top of that he's been talking to Wexler and that really puzzles me. Maybe the old sonofabitch is getting soft. Or soft in the head."

"I didn't know that."

"That he was talking to Wexler or soft in the head?"

"Wexler."

"He never mentioned it?"

"Well, just that Wexler had been to see him. Not so much that he was really talking to him."

"Maybe he doesn't want to hurt your feelings."

Val didn't say anything. The sheriff busied himself with the mess atop his desk.

"So what do you have?"

"He told me about an old woman he killed."

"The hell he did." The older man took down the glasses and set them among the papers strewn on his desk. He was suddenly interested. He rifled through the top desk drawer and came up with a small brown pipe, looked into its bowl and put the stem in the corner of his mouth.

"Yes he did."

"Terrific. Did you see anything on his sheet about it?"

Millimaki held his wrists crossed before him and he held his cap by the brim and stood staring at the county logo on the face of it. "I don't know if this is what you had in mind when you said to come in, sir."

"Well, you let me decide that, Deputy."

"It was over east, in Wibaux, I think."

"And? That doesn't make any difference."

Val looked out the window. "He was fourteen."

"Fourteen years old."

"Yes, sir."

"Christ, that had to have been, what, sixty-some years ago?"

"Sixty-five."

"Well, that doesn't do us a lot of good, does it?"

Millimaki stood fingering the bill of his cap. "He said it didn't bother him. Not for long, anyway."

"Well, that's our boy."

"That he saw after that he wouldn't have to do real work ever again."

The sheriff sat back in his chair. "The beginning of a long and colorful career." He placed his hands together beneath his chin as if in prayer, steepled his index fingers as in the child's game. He ran his eyes over the thin sallow figure of the young deputy.

"And how is Gail?" he said.

"She's okay. It's actually Glenda."

"For Christ sake, of course it is."

"Fine. She's fine."

The sheriff stared at him. Val looked toward the single window, high and arched and brilliant in the early morning despite the calligraphy of water streaks and splashes of bird shit from the vile and mumbling pigeons roosted in the rain gutters at the roof edge. Because it had once been part of the jail itself, there were bars on the window, and their shadows lay across the floor and laddered the far wall.

"Your mouth says fine but your face says otherwise."

"She's having a hard time with me being on nights."

"Harder than you."

"Harder than me, yessir. I think so."

"It's tough. I know. I did it. We all did it."

"I know. I'm not asking for anything."

"I know you're not. I couldn't hardly change things, anyway, Val. It's all low-man-on-the-totem-pole stuff. You know that, don't you?"

"I do."

"This might not be the best analogy, but it's kind of like breaking a horse. It's tough on everybody at first and then pretty quick all parties involved don't think anything of it. It's just how it is."

"I might choose to not tell her that comparison if it's all the same to you."

"My wife if she heard it would leave me singing like Liberace for a week. For some reason women don't like being compared to livestock." He removed the cold pipe from his mouth and sat looking at it. "And that might be the extent of my wisdom on the matter."

"That's more than some."

The sheriff smiled. "More than some, yes it is." He put the pipe in his mouth again and began to pass his hands over the mess of files and paper on his desk as if waiting for one or the other to insinuate its urgency. He said, "Do you feel the need to take some time off? I could arrange that."

"No, sir. It'll be all right. Plus, I don't think it's a good time to lay off as far as Gload's concerned."

"Well, as far as that goes, I don't think it matters. It looks pretty good we've got him on this guy up north of town."

"I didn't know that."

"You read his M.O. on making his guys anonymous, did you not?"

"Where he takes the teeth and hands? Did he not do it this time?"

"Oh, no. Our boy is thorough. It isn't that. But it seems this poor kid had had open-heart surgery here a while back. Two years and some. What they're saying is that they can identify him by the way he was put back together. The chest-crackers have a kind of signature way of wiring them back up."

"I didn't know that."

"Hell, I didn't either. And safe to say John Gload didn't or he'd have carved the chest right out of him and thrown that in the drink, too."

"Is that what he did with the head and stuff?"

"What the kid White said. Threw them over the dam. Hell, that head's probably rolling along outside of St. Louis by now." The sheriff pointed his pipestem vaguely out the window to indicate where that city lay. "Anyway, your old boy's going away until he dies. It would be nice to know where all the bodies are buried—metaphorical and otherwise—but you don't have to milk him anymore if you don't want. He's had it." He looked down, selected an envelope seemingly at random and studied it through the half-lenses of his small glasses. He said, "The *end* of a long and colorful career."

"I guess so."

The sheriff laid the envelope down and became preoccupied with some other and he turned his head oddly to read it as though it were fixed to the desktop and could not be turned. He rested his elbows atop the clutter and held the pipe by its bowl in one hand and sat reading. Millimaki stood quietly. Then he put his cap on.

The sheriff did not look up. "Remember what he is, Val. Think of what he did to that young man out there and how he did it and how many others he did the same way. He doesn't deserve your pity."

"Yes, sir."

He was almost out the door when the sheriff said, "And, Val. That was good work on the old boy with the Buick or Pontiac or whatever it was. His family was very grateful."

"Buick, sir. And it wasn't anything, really. He didn't get too far and Tom went right to him."

"Well." The sheriff laid his pipe carefully on the jumble atop his desk, as if it might shatter or disturb some order there known only to him. "How long has it been?"

"Fifteen months and a couple weeks. Or thereabouts. Not that I'm counting."

"You'll get past this streak, Val. It all equals out."

"How so?"

"Hell, I don't know. Just that some you find alive who should be dead. Some you find dead after a warm night in the trees with nothing more than a bruise on their shin."

"With all due respect, sir, that doesn't even make sense."

"It doesn't have to make sense, son. You should know that much by now. But it's the way it is."

"I'll just have to trust you on that point, sir."

"You do that." He took up the unlit pipe and stuck it in his mouth and waved Millimaki away. "Now go home and be nice to your wife."

That day he forsook his routine beside the river and drove north of town to view the scene of the disinterment. The yellow crime scene tape had been left or forgotten and it writhed among the weed bines like some exotic jungle viper and flapped and snapped in the wind. He sat on the ground near the very place John Gload had stood conducting the young man's burial with the barrel of his pistol. Millimaki could see where the hole had been, the earth dished and dark from having been so recently turned and much of it had been sifted for evidence. It lay at the edges of the hole as fine as talc. He imagined the thing they'd dug up would have been, after two months, no more than a rawhide headless mannequin, the incriminating Frankenstein scar at its breastbone hidden beneath dirty rags. For John Gload there would have been much sawing and twisting, stubborn elastic tendons to be cut or bent over a knee and snapped. Vertebrae would have to be unlocked, the head twisted. He tried to imagine the sound. Little blood had been found at the scene, so Gload must have bled the victim somewhere else. There had been a time, he thought, not long ago, when coyotes had come tacking out of the night with the alien scent in their nostrils to roll in the gore and muddy their teeth.

He took up a handful of dirt and let it sift through his fingers. The wind came down from the northern benchlands and rattled the strange larval pods on the yuccas and brought the faint thin cries of gulls he could see afloat and stationary as kites against the morning sky. He tried to reconcile the avuncular old man tendering comfort and counsel from his dark cage with the creature who could placidly dismember a fellow human being. A lifetime ago while eating an apple (an apple, Val thought, like me that day, eating that apple) beside railroad tracks on a golden spring day, John Gload had observed in himself with a curious detachment the absence of passion. Perhaps he was somehow exempt from responsibility at all, could no more be blamed than a child born without feet could be blamed for his inability to run.

Millimaki sat in the dirt staring blankly at the grave, benumbed by his sleeplessness. Gload seemed capable of kindness, but it may have been just a kind of vestigial feature, like the webbed and blunted limbs of thalidomide children—a half-developed grotesquery that made him more pitiable for the reminder of what it might have been like to be whole.

For the rest of us though, thought Millimaki, the distance from reason to rage is short, a frontier as thin as parchment and as frail, restraining the monster. It was there in everyone, he thought. It was there in himself. A half second of simple blind fury and the hatchet falls down. He stared at the patch of turned earth where so recently a body had been. At some point, he thought wearily, it was only meat.

He sat for some time, the wind coursing through the sparse bluestem and whipping the yellow tape. His pallid hands were in his lap and he stared into them. The sun felt good on his face and he closed his eyes. Fifteen minutes later he woke with a start. He'd fallen asleep sprawled in the grass above the grave and when he raised up there was dirt stuck to the side of his face and one arm was numb and dead. He sat up looking around wildly, as if someone might have crept up on him in that lonesome place. "For Christ sake," he said aloud. "Look at your ass, sleeping in the dirt like a bindlestiff."

The weeds had grown up in the road between the wheel ruts and they hissed along the undercarriage as he climbed toward the cabin. On the opposite coulee side among the rimrocks, marmots scuttled and froze and it appeared at that distance that the rocks themselves moved. The church-steeple tops of the lodgepole behind the little house quaked in the wind. His wife's car was still in its place and he could see Tom pacing in his kennel. He parked and walked across to the dog run. The shepherd sat and whined. "Hey kid, how you doing?" He stroked the dog's nose with two fingers through the chain link. He looked toward the house, and the windows in the early sunlight dazzled his tired eyes.

He went in and hung his hat on a 16-penny nail driven into a wall log and when he turned he saw her standing at the sink in her street clothes and she didn't look at him.

"Hey," he said, "how come you're not at work?"

"It's my day off. You should know that."

"Is it Tuesday? Man, my head-clock is all screwed up."

"Your everything is screwed up, Val."

He expected her to turn and laugh but she did not.

"What's Tom doing locked up?"

She didn't answer.

"Glenda," he said, "why's the dog penned?"

She spoke to the window. "Because he kept following me around." There were no dishes in the sink and no water running. She stood gripping the counter edge. "Every time I made a trip to the car he followed me and he followed me back and I just got tired of it."

He stood for a while looking at her and then walked onto the porch. He could see boxes jumbled in the backseat of the Datsun and clothes hanging from the hooks above each side window. He went back in and stood behind her. The window was a bright rectangle framed with box elder trees and the coulee rim beyond was green with spring and the sky the kind of blue, with its Van Gogh brushstrokes of cloud, that had made them, in the early years, jump in the truck and drive the country with no purpose whatever. It was enough to be together under the spring sun in the greening and open country. He stood looking out at it, over her shoulder. Her yellow hair glowed with the sun in it and he suddenly wanted to take it in his hands, press it to his face.

"It's a driving-and-drinking sky we got today."

She studied her hands before her, glanced up briefly to the perfect day. She said, "Where have you been? You should have been home two hours ago."

He made a wiping motion across his face. There was still a trace of dirt on his cheek and in his hair. "I had to go up north of town and look at a site. Really, I forgot it was your day off."

"A site," she said.

"We found a body up there."

She turned then and he could see she had been crying. "Oh. Well. A body. That's okay. At least someone you can relate to."

"What's going on, Glenda?"

She looked at him. "What's on your face? Jesus, Val, you look like a homeless man."

He said, "I want you to tell me what's going on."

"I'm going to stay in town."

"Tonight?"

"Tonight. For a while."

"How long a while?" Millimaki said.

"I don't know. Indefinitely." She put the back of one wrist to each eye in turn and swept back her hair as though to put herself right. "I would have to say indefinitely."

"You seem to have it all mapped out," he said. "Isn't this something that we ought to have at least talked about beforehand? For Christ sake, Glenda."

"I tried to talk about it but every time I looked up you were asleep or on some other planet."

"That might be a little bit true, but goddamn it, I can't sleep anymore."

"But it's more than that."

"More than what?"

"More than your emotional absence."

He looked at her. She had composed herself in earnest and stonily studied a point above his head. "That sounds like something out of a book," he said.

"It describes our situation."

"When did this turn into a situation? For Christ sake, I come home and take off my hat and I'm in a situation."

"All I know is I can't think here and I have to have time to think."

"You've got all the time in the world for that."

"You're not listening, goddamn it. I said I can't think *here*."

"Why not? I thought you loved it here. You've said that any number of times. This is your house, goddamn it."

"I can't think." She enunciated each word slowly, as if she spoke to a foreigner or a lip reader. "And I feel small."

"All this goddamn thinking," Val said. He rubbed his hand over his face. He felt dull, his arms heavy as stones. He stared at her. Everything she said—her posture, the set of her jaw as she spoke to somewhere beyond him—seemed rehearsed. Millimaki in his fatigue fought the feeling that two other people were playing this scene, their doppelgängers, while he and his wife stood to the side merely watching.

"What's all this goddamn thinking about?"

"Well, there it is. You don't even know."

"Okay," he said. He ran his hand in a washing motion over his face again. "Okay, what do you mean 'small'? Let's start with that. That doesn't even make any sense to me."

"It means I feel unimportant. In your life and just in general. And it's exacerbated by this place. I feel like it's swallowing me up."

He reached out to touch her crossed arms, to make some contact while reason and his own center were flying about the room. She took a half step away.

"That's not one of your words," he said. "It doesn't even sound right coming out of your mouth."

"It means it makes it worse here."

"I know what the fuck it means. But you're not the one saying it."

Her words came in an exaggerated calm, as though to counteract his urgency. The room darkened suddenly, whether from a passing cloud or from some dimming behind his tortured eyes he could not tell. The exertion of mustering reason sufficient to the moment was enormous and his head swam.

"I need to have time to think and I can't do that here, now. That's what I'm saying."

"You said it's swallowing you up."

"It is. Without you here I'm more alone than alone." This thought seemed to suddenly attenuate her resolve and she began to cry again. "You don't know. You couldn't, because it's so much a part of who you are. But not me, not by myself." She repeated, "You don't know."

"What? What don't I know?"

"At night. At night. It's awful."

"Why?"

She'd evidently not planned to let the conversation go this way and she paused to consider her words. "At night, outside the house is inside with me. It comes in with me and it's like I can look down at myself and all I see is me in the bed and there's nothing between me and everything out there." She swept her hand toward the bright day. "Val, you don't know. You couldn't know. I've been sleeping with all the lights on. And don't you dare say anything. One night an owl was in the house."

"That's just crazy."

"I told you, don't say it."

"There isn't a way for it to come in here, Glenda."

"It was above the bed and it was just up there and beating the air with its wings. Fanning the air."

"For Christ sake."

She covered her face. "I could feel the air moving."

"No. It couldn't have come in the house."

"And then last night, on the porch, there were coyotes."

"It's just nightmares, Glenda."

"Don't."

"For Christ sake, Tom would have gone ape-shit if coyotes were on the porch."

She pointed toward the front door as if to present concrete proof and he could see her hand trembling. "I heard their toenails on that porch, Val. I heard them breathing."

"No. They wouldn't come up there."

"Clicking. A clicking sound." Her hand went to her mouth. "And that fucking door. They could have just pushed on it and come in."

"Okay, listen. It's nothing. It's the branches on that box elder rubbing against the house. That's all it was, Glenda. I'll cut them back. Right now, today. Just branches in the wind. I'll cut them all the way back."

"Not branches," she said. "Or the wind or anything. You will not talk me out of this because I know what I know."

Millimaki closed his eyes. He felt behind him for the arm of the couch and sat down heavily on it. He said, "Glenda, I'm absolutely all in. I can't find my own ass with both hands. Can't we just talk about this tomorrow? I just need to sleep. This isn't fair right now. I can't figure out what it's all about."

"It's about what I said it's about. That's easy enough, isn't it? I can't stay here. When we had it together, I felt above it or at least a part of it. But alone here I'm no more important than a bird or a tree. Whether it's a nightmare or whether it's real, what it means is that this place is swallowing me up. It's a part of you, Val, but it's swallowing me up. The more you fade the more it swallows me up."

Val looked at her bleakly. "You act like I'm a ghost. I'm your husband. I'm sitting right here."

"No. You're right, that's perfect. That's exactly what you are. A ghost." She took a long deep breath, seeking oxygen where it seemed in insufficient supply, and released it slowly. "And I don't know where you are, Val. I think probably out with all the dead people you find out there. They're easier. You don't have to talk to them. You bring home their goddamn pictures like they were family or some secret girlfriend. Jesus Christ, Val, that's what you are, no more than a ghost yourself, walking around with all those dead people in your head. I won't stay with a ghost, Val. I won't do that. And I won't become one myself."

When she had gone, Val stood with his coffee out on the porch in the dizzying light of late morning. He had moved about the kitchen woodenly as if in a dream and his hands seemed to him pale creatures crabbing among the cups and plates of their own accord. He realized as he stood at the sink that she must have watched him drive up and move around the yard and to the kennel and mount the stairs with his slow geriatric tread. He tried to make out in the window glass the face of the stranger she'd said inhabited her husband's skin and saw in the silvery pane a parody of himself, got up in fard and eye black and wrinkled khaki, who in wearily ascending the steps entered the middle act of a pedestrian tragedy. Or worse, he thought, she'd seen the ghost of the man she had married, no more than a bleared outline of opaque glass in her husband's shape through which she could see the grass, the dirt, the trees beyond.

Far below through the greening trees he could almost see the place along the creek where they'd swum one afternoon in their courting days. To get there they pushed through undergrowth and came out near the creek and from the tall grass and thin willow stems at their elbows rose a cloud of small orange butterflies and they went before them on the warm air like a blizzard of flower petals strewn before heroes. The stream swung fast and clear out of impenetrable brush as if emerging from a cave, curved languidly and pushed murmuring against a steep cutbank where the roots of a toppled cottonwood splayed above the current. They spread a blanket on the warm sandy shingle and while Val was making a fire he heard a splash and saw her golden head bobbing with the current and then as he watched she rose glistening from the stream below the bend like some fabled huntress, dripping and naked and all but aglow from the sun and the cold water. He stood with a stick in his hand staring foolishly. From habit, as he'd done as a boy when there was something he desperately wanted, he said a prayer: dear God let this woman stay with me, let me not ruin this, let her marry me and I will be good and pure forever and then as she came on, placing her tender feet carefully on the gravel, milk-white skin bejeweled in the sun, all prayers evaporated and in the center of all the universe was only her. And he would at that moment have done anything to have her.

Now as he stood on the porch he realized he would do it yet, if he could only discover the correct god, tender the proper coin. He gazed at the creek far below, chromium glintings through the cottonwood and willow. He slung the coffee out onto the dirt. The dog Tom from the fenced run sat watching him and when Millimaki went inside he turned to stare down the narrow lane where the car had passed and where a veil of dust hovered yet above the tracks like mist. In the creek bottom the crowns of the cottonwood trees were gilded by the sun's rising above the coulee rim, so bright and substantial they looked to have been held by the roots and dipped in a vat of molten gold. Sparrows had come to peck like yardfowl in the spare expanse of lawn and their shadows lay long across the grass in the shape of exotic giants—egrets, flamingos.

In the coming days and nights he went about his duties mechanically and at home he could not bring himself to sleep in the empty bed. He awoke late afternoons dull and sore from the recliner or the couch and found the only thing good about his life then was that he did not have to speak to a living soul. Even

Gload left him to his thoughts during his interminable shift and required from him only his presence, as if like a hearth fire the young man's bleak thoughts and brooding were a comfort to him. He sat for many hours beyond the bars transfixed by the disembodied brutal hands hanging in the light and before long they began to articulate some feeling within him. Sitting around the cabin in the mercurial spring days among his wife's things, the scent of her still lingering in the bedding and closets, he found to his horror that he missed the old man's company.

He watched the storms roll in from the west, erasing the sun as fully as an eclipse, and then the rain slashed down, ripping at the new leaves on the box elder and lilacs and gouging troughs in the road. Then as suddenly the day was brilliant again, even as the rain sluiced from the porch roof in an effulgent cataract. Looking out it was as though the two hemispheres of his brain were at war, each eye viewing different worlds—one brilliant, the other black and violent. What peace he had came upon him in the mausolean dark in the company of caged men where speech was not required of him—there among sociopaths he was disburdened of the weight of sociability.

Once during this time he called his wife. While he waited for her to take the phone he could hear through the vacant earpiece garbled voices speaking the idiolect of the ICU. Another language entirely to speak of the ill and dying. When she came on the line he realized that he had nothing to say. He asked how she was. She was fine. He asked when she could be coming home. She didn't know. Silence. He pictured her standing impatiently at the nurses' station, beyond her the enshadowed ranks of beds and their still tenants in thin cotton habiliment festooned with luminous tubes. For reasons he wasn't sure of, he told her he and the dog had found a young girl in the river who had been raped and strangled. It wasn't true. After a pause she said, "How awful." Someone spoke to her and he heard her say, "Bed Seven," and she said to him, "Val, I've got to go now."

"She was eight, this girl. Did I say that?"

"Yes. I'm sorry. I have to go, Val."

"All right."

"I'll see you."

"You'll see me when?"

"I can't say a time. I'll just see you."

"I could come by there."

"No," she said. "That's not a good idea, Val."

"Then come by the jail. I've got nothing but time there."

"Val, you know I hate that place. I won't come there."

"I know."

"Val. I have to go."

"Fine."

He waited for her to say something more. In the long pause before she ended the connection he could hear in the background the chirps and bleeps of the machines that became for the people lying there as much a part of them as their skin or veins. He waited. He heard a man's voice say her name and then she was gone.

From the couch among his twisted bedclothes he heard the tree limbs rubbing along the house eaves, a sound that to her had been the vile nails of predators seeking her innermost part was for him a balm and a caress on his troubled ear. Nothing, though, seemed to touch his sleeplessness. It was as durable as stone and had become as chronic as Gload's but without even the soporific of the plowed fields of his youth to remedy it. He considered her accusation that he consorted with ghosts and it was certainly true. But the dead were a part of her work, too.

She seemed to be able to leave them, though, and at the moment of their passing they became as inanimate finally as the burbling machines whose tubes and wires were meant to keep them alive. She'd told him that they were gone for her then and that was the end of it. And in telling him he sensed even an animosity toward them as if, as the unreliable cog in the mechanism, they had betrayed her. She was not to be blamed for wanting to forget her failures. Certainly, he thought, some of it was professional bluster, but still she seemed as dispassionate in her way as Gload. He envied them both.

But he was at home with the dead, she was right. And whether they sought the open country for their death, or death sought them there, it little mattered. In either case kindred souls, Millimaki and the dead, met under a companionable sky and the encounter was good for all. In the reticence of their company Millimaki found peace and for their part the dead would be brought home to rest among their kin beneath the verdancy and perdurable headstones of cemeteries. Their bones would not be gnawed and broadcast like fallen branches down anonymous canyons. And that, too, was a comfort to him.

Without the woman around and in the absence of work in the woods, the dog Tom became possessive and if Val stood anywhere for any length of time came to nuzzle his hand. He took the dog walking in the trees behind the house and Tom loped ahead, leaping and running his nose under the leaves and pine duff and then came back and went to heel when he saw Val unaccountably standing still as stone, as if he required guidance through foreign terrain.

NINE

Seen from the street they may have been a young man and his grandfather, taking the spring air among the elms in pale leaf. Millimaki in escorting the old man back to his cell at day's end allowed him to sit on one of the benches in the courthouse park and smoke. They sat side by side, Gload in his orange county jumpsuit emblazoned with PRISONER on its back and the deputy with his arms over the bench back listening. The great gray trees and the wind in them moving the leaves seemed to evoke memories in the old man and he sat with his cuffed wrists upon his knees and he would occasionally lift his head and draw in a great breath and expel it, savoring the air of freedom as though from a mine shaft he had risen to safety from the corrosive dark.

Val took the old man's Camels from the breast pocket of the garish suit and shook one out and when Gload selected one he lit it for him. They sat watching the cars pass on the street and the birds flare overhead. Finally Millimaki said, "John, you know Sid White took them to a body up north of town."

Gload sat with his head back following the birds with his eyes. He raised his paired hands to his lips and drew on the cigarette, expelling a long slow plume.

"Yeah, I heard that."

"They're saying they can tie you to this guy."

The old man lowered his head and sat erect and strangely formal, staring into the middle distance. "Don't think so, Val," he said. "They can't bank their whole case on White. For one, he's got a record. Not what you might call a credible witness." He snorted, shook his head in disgust, or amusement. "And look at him, sitting there in his Grand Ole Opry suit."

"No. Beyond just White's say-so."

Gload said casually, "It's just bones, Val. Could be anybody."

"There's some identifying feature."

"Don't think so."

"The thing is, he had open-heart surgery. They tell me that every surgeon has a kind of signature way of putting the guy back together. They string wire across his breastbone in a particular way. They're saying they can tell who it is from that."

Gload rocked forward and turned to Millimaki with a bemused smile. "The hell," he said.

"They'll be talking about it this week. Charts, photographs, the whole deal."

"Well, by God, I got to say that's a new one on me."

"Did your lawyer not say anything about it to you?"

"Oh, Jesus Christ, Val. You seen him. That man is three sheets to the wind right this second I guarantee you and we've been out of court for, what is it?"

"An hour. Little more."

"There you go. Right now, drunker than ten Indians. Guaranteed."

"You could petition for different counsel."

"What, a P.D.?" He snorted, smoke erupting from his nostrils. "No, it don't make any difference, Deputy." He cast a sidelong glance at Millimaki. "Ain't you on some kind of ethical thin ice, here, Valentine? Offering legal advice to a felon?"

"Like you said once, we're just talking."

The old killer sat staring at Millimaki's profile. He looked down at the handgun and baton on the deputy's belt and he looked over at the old sandstone jailhouse across the street. He looked for a long time at Millimaki again.

"You look like a goddamn scarecrow, Val, you know that?"

"I've been hearing that a lot lately."

"Your missus not taking care of you? Is that the deal?"

Millimaki turned to stare after a car passing on the street and the old man watched him closely. "Something like that."

"Smoke me, will you please, Deputy?"

When he had smoked for a time Gload said, "Your friend Weldon come a-courting me."

"How do you mean?"

"Wants to be my boyfriend. And he seems pretty intent on stealing your thunder."

Millimaki laughed tiredly. "I don't have any thunder to steal, John."

Gload swung one knee up and clasped it with his manacled hands. He gazed into the rustling dome of greenery overhead. "You got to see all this through that shitbird's eyes. He knows you have the Old Bull's ear and any fool can see he's got some kind of soft spot for you. This turd Wexler, he figures it ought to be him who's the number one son, being as he's been around longer. And him being such a spit-and-polish troop."

Val turned to him. "And how would you come to know all this?"

Gload thrust his chin in the direction of the jail, some hundred feet from where they sat. At that moment the topmost course of stones was awash in rose light. "It's a small town in there, Val."

"Well, in any case, he has been on the force longer than me," Val said. "That doesn't change."

Gload looked once more into the treetops. He was smiling. He said, "It was Weldon's day off today."

"I know. That's why I'm here in the wonderful light of day."

"I got a feeling he spent the day getting his ass full of prickly pear."

Millimaki turned to look at him then. "Why would you have a feeling like that, John?"

"Here's the deal, Valentine. He's got it in his head there's bodies buried all over the place out there, other side of the river. A regular goddamn battlefield. Figures if he can find them he'll be the man of the hour. Detective First Grade. And especially," he said, "if he's the one finds them instead of you."

"How'd he get an idea like that?"

The old man leered and began to shudder imperceptibly. "Ambition is a dangerous thing, Val."

"You shouldn't do that, John, no shit. He could make it bad for you."

The old convict shook his head and his black eyes sparkled. The shuddering became more pronounced and Val thought he might be cold in the orange suit, thin and loose at the seams from a thousand launderings. "Oh, Christ," Gload said. "Oh,

Christ almighty, it would be worth it." He wheezed and water sprang up in his eyes. "I got this picture in my head of him running up and down them hills with his notebook and a spade. Running and writing and digging and running some more. Oh sweet Christ on a crutch." From his pursed lips came a series of snorts and sharp breaths. Val for a moment thought he may be beset by a fit. Small tears began to leak from the corners of Gload's eyes. He leaned forward over his knee, shaking and swinging his great head like a drunken bear. Finally he wheezed, "Good Lord." He ran the backs of his chained hands across his eyes and passed his hands over the huge dome of his head to lay back his hair. It was as close to happy as Val had ever seen Gload and the old man finally sat gasping and smiling his strange equine smile. The sun had fallen behind the courthouse and as they sat on their bench in the long blue shadow, small birds came and went to nests hidden among the leafed branches of the elms. Gload turned his attention there and seemed to address with great seriousness the trees, the sky beyond circumfused at that hour with sorrel light.

"He'll take your legs out from under you, Val, make no mistake about that."

"I'm not worried about it."

"You oughta be. I'm dead serious about this."

"John, I imagine you've heard the old thing about honor among thieves. Well, there damn sure is honor among law enforcement people, too."

"Total bullshit, Valentine. What there is among thieves is turpitude." He smiled. "Now that right there is a hell of a useful word."

The old man stared after the sparrows long after they disappeared into the dusk of the leafy canopy. The church bell began to toll and he looked to Val's watch, which he held up for Gload to read.

"We ought to get on over, John. You'll miss your supper."

Gload dropped his head and seemed to study the tops of his shoes, the thin, dechromed chains around his socks. Presently he said, "In any profession you care to name there are the good and the not so good. Not necessarily good and bad, just good and something short of that. Think about it. For every doctor graduated first in his class there's the one who come out last. Still gets to call himself a doctor, though. Teachers the same. And cops. They ain't all going to be good. There's degrees. It's a simple matter of fact. Fact of life."

"I won't argue that. But it's just that some guys have a different approach than others. Doesn't necessarily make them bad cops."

Gload only smiled. "I'm going to tell you a little story here, Val."

Though he had only just looked at it, Millimaki consulted his watch again. "You're going to miss the meatloaf, John, if we don't go over."

"Couple more minutes."

"About the only thing worth a damn."

The old man looked over at him. "It is a loaf, true enough, but meat? The jury's still out."

"In any case."

The old man sat forward again, his chained hands balanced on his thighs like a man at prayer. Then he sat back against the bench and patted his breast pocket. "Oh, hell," he said. "Would you do me the favor, Val?"

The deputy reached into the breast pocket of Gload's coveralls and removed his smokes and matches. He shook out a cigarette and the old man took it and put it to his lips, his hands in their cuffs paired holding it there as if it were imbued with a great weight. Val struck the match and held it out and the old man moved his head to the flame in a benedictory nod. He drew on it and took it from his mouth with his paired hands. A car went by on the one-way street, teenaged boys already drunk on a beautiful spring evening and they hooted and jeered at the two men, the words tumbling away down the avenue in the rattle of muffler and the blue contrail of exhaust. Faggots. Jailbirds.

"Tough guys," Val said.

"Just rudeness is what it is."

As they watched the car recede, the streetlights began to flutter and shortly the light above the jailhouse door came on. Val said, "I need to get you back."

"A minute, Val," he said. "Humor an old man. Then we can go in." He smoked. "This is something that happened here, oh I guess thirty years ago now." He stopped and smiled, looking as he did again into the green vault overhead. "Thirty years. Jesus Christ. The years do go." And still gazing fondly upward he began to recount a night from his young manhood. It was a time, he said, when he was at the height of his powers. "Not bragging or anything. But I was."

He asked Millimaki if he'd ever told him about his days playing cards in Butte and the deputy said he had. He said there had been a card game with a Chinaman and that he was a real China Chinaman and that he could be barely understood. But poker was a language unto itself and besides it was a game that required little in the way of speech so it didn't matter. The game went long into the night and Gload was well ahead and going along nicely but what caught his eye was the rings on the foreigner's fingers, outsized and electric beneath the low lamp. He recalled that the man was a bit of a dandy, his hair upswept with reeking pomade and gleaming blue-black like a plasticine hat. The Chinaman twisted the rings on his fingers in sequence, a kind of nervous tic, changing the fanned cards from hand to hand, and though Gload could not read the tic as card-tell he read in it the value of the rings.

Gload paused, smiled. "Let me tell you something, Val. It's just like a guy with a full wallet and maybe you didn't know this, but a guy with a full wallet will keep reaching back and putting his hand on it, patting it, like. That's a giveaway. That's just a little tip for you or cheap advice, if you happen to be the guy with the big wallet. So I knew this Chinaman's rings were worth something, by the way he was fooling with them." Val waited, thinking more advice was forthcoming but Gload only sat, erect and staring into the trees and then he continued.

The man was a big bettor and a fair enough cardplayer and he turned the rings constantly, good hand or bad and Gload quickly gave up on that as a way of reading him. His plans began to shape themselves out of the smoke and gloom and they went beyond a game of chance. Chance was not at issue. The night wore on and John Gload from behind his cards studied the man for size and weight, for the fight in him.

Finally he said only that it was a good score. When the game broke up he merely rose and followed the man casually into the alley and killed him. He'd not seen him upright for the entire night and was surprised at how small the man was and how insubstantial, almost like a child in his embrace.

Gload paused and requested another smoke, lit it from the short butt of the previous one and then methodically ground out the stub on the edge of the bench and put it in the breast pocket of his jumpsuit. Millimaki sat mesmerized, found he'd been holding his breath. The old man said, "The hell of it was, I couldn't get them rings off. Sonofabitch Chinaman must have been eating salt by the fistful." He paused, flexed his own thick fingers. "There's some more cheap advice for you, Val—go light on the salt. Salt killed more people than Hitler. Or that other one. The Russian."

With his head down and occasionally turning to regard Millimaki's face, the old man talked on for some time. Val looked over at the jail across the street where already the windows with their latticework of dark bars were burning yellow in the failing light. The small plain birds rose chittering into the harbor of trees.

The old man saw Millimaki look toward the jail and said, "Bear with me just a second. This is going somewheres, I promise."

One of the other players found the luckless Chinaman, sitting spraddle-legged on the alley bricks, the pool of his blood throbbing in the light of a single neon beaconing its lurid color in that dim place. John Gload had held the oriental's throat with one hand against his calling out and when found the little man with his scent of sweet flowers sat with his windpipe crushed and mouth agape as though poised to burst into song. His eyes were wide and they pulsed in the light too with blood pooled at his hands and the great puddle of it between his legs, seeping slowly then from the hole just below his sternum.

The cardplayer had gone into the alleyway to relieve himself but instead stood gaping and vomited down the front of his shirt and ran wordlessly back into the room where the players save two still sat about the table smoking and finishing their whiskey ditches before going home. They stared at the mute ashen statue pointing toward the dark and they rose and followed him and when the police arrived they found them circling the Chinaman and the Chinaman held his place in the circle much as he had earlier.

The players spoke with the police in their turn and dispersed, some to their sleeping wives, some to spare and musty bachelor rooms two floors above the card room that would seem that night emptier still.

Among the bills and change in his pocket the Chinese man had an assortment of pills in a plastic bag and John Gload folded the bills into his own pockets and emptied the pills with a grunt of disgust and put the man's fingers with their contrary prizes in the bag. He went unhurriedly down the cobbles of the dark alley and kept to the shadows of the awnings and coigns of the old union halls and by the time he got to his car, no more than ten minutes had passed since he'd thrown in his last hand.

Through the starless night he drove north with the window down despite the cold. He stopped at a roadside pull-out at Elk Park Pass where icy spring water came sluicing from a pipe into a stone trough and he washed his hands and the knife and stripped off his trousers and shirt, which were damp yet and stained with the dead Chinaman's dark arterial blood. He transferred his prizes to the pockets of his fresh pants and then went lurching like a blind man among pines and brush in the pitch-dark and buried his clothes under duff and deadfall. At the car he pared his nails beneath the dome light. He looked into his red eyes in the rearview mirror for a long moment and palmed back his hair and pulled once again onto the blacktop. Twice as he drove he was forced to swerve the Oldsmobile into the ditch weeds to avoid mule deer standing in the road like lawn statuary with phosphorescent eyes. Gravel rang in the wheelwells.

The radio in that remote country was alive with static but he hummed to the sporadic music nonetheless and the pavement rolled along under his headlights like an endlessly spinning stage prop.

The sun rose red and irresolute in an August sky hazy from distant fires and found John Gload that morning passing through high plains and the buttes of famous western paintings in the near distance began to take shape in roseate geometry, their tabletops afire and from the shadowed slopes birds of prey drifted out over the ripening wheat fields. The highway patrol car passed him going south and he could see its occupant's head swivel and in that instant the light on the cartop began to pulse and the car swung about on the steaming asphalt, through the median in a maelstrom of dust and trash and was behind him, wailing.

He erupted out the passenger side door and through the ditch weeds and took the barbed wire right-of-way fence with one step. The wheat stalks rasped against his legs as he ran but because of the slope of the ground and the difficult purchase of his feet in the soft furrows he seemed to proceed as if in some recurrent nightmare of running and the near-ripe grain flew about him like bees driven from a hive and then he heard the hiss of the first bullet and felt it go by and splat into a rock twenty feet beyond him at the level of his head and so he stopped. He fell to the ground as though in exhaustion and with his head below swaying grain he pulled the Chinaman's fingers from his bloodied pockets, took them from the plastic bag, dug a hole in the soft earth and put them in. He continued forward on his hands and knees, dug another hole for the knife and then he stopped.

"All right, all right," he called. "You got me."

He did not turn but could hear the thud of the patrolman's boots coming across the field and then he could hear the whish-hiss of the wheat stalks on his trousers and then at last the labored breathing.

"Don't move a fucking muscle," the man said. He was breathing very hard. "You sonofabitch."

"You got me," Gload said. "I know I must of been speeding. Didn't know that crate could even go that fast."

"Shit, speeding," the officer wheezed. "My ass speeding."

"Well, I ain't drunk, if that's what it is," Gload said. "I'll walk the line for you. I'm cold sober."

"Shut the fuck up." Gload had taken a kneeling position, still facing the way he had run and he could see ahead of him a small plane in the distance lift off into the perfect blank sky without a sound. It seemed to arise from among the strips of wheat. He felt the barrel-tip press into the base of his skull.

"This is definitely cocked and I'm nervous and I'm breathing real hard," the patrolman said. "And there ain't anybody around for a long long ways to tell how it was you come to have your face splattered on the ground. So don't twitch a eyelash while I put these on you. Put your hands back."

"No, sir," Gload said. "I ain't going to die on account of a speeding ticket."

"Stand up now."

He stood. He turned to face the man then and the sound of the Beechcraft suddenly came to him and above his breathing and the hard breathing of the patrolman he began to hear the whirr of grasshoppers among the amber stems and from the right-of-way fence posts the warble of meadowlarks proclaiming the glory of that day.

"Okay, goddamn it, where's them fingers at?"

"I'd show you but they're cuffed up."

"The Chinaman fingers, asshole."

"Chinaman fingers?"

The plastic bag he'd thrown aside hung atop a clump of wheat stalks and wavered there. The patrolman glanced at it briefly and Gload thought, Blow, wind. He jangled his wrist cuffs and the man looked back to him and the bag filled with air and went skeltering over the grain field like a child's balloon and disappeared.

"Here. Stand out of the way." Gload took two sideways steps in the wheat. "Stand there." The patrolman, a man of perhaps forty-five, began to search about in the wheat, one hand with his service revolver held straight out and his eyes sweeping the ground under their feet. From a distance he might have seemed to be performing some strange ritual dance with the stoic and smiling John Gload for a partner.

"Are they in the car?" he said. "You wouldn't have left them in the car, would you?"

"Officer, you're making my head hurt."

"Shit."

They made their way back through the grain field and at the car the lawman spread Gload on the hot car hood. He sifted through glove compartment papers and with the barrel of his pistol pushed aside crumpled receipts and week-old newspapers lying on the floorboards and atop the Oldsmobile's commodious seats. He took the keys from the ignition and opened the trunk, rummaging for a long while among suitcases and tire chains and an enormous tackle box full of rusted treble snagging hooks and comical oversized lures on wire leaders, raising his head occasionally to scowl at the implacable John Gload. Fifteen minutes later, red-faced and profusely sweating, he leaned against the car's rear quarter panel.

"Goddamn you, Gload," he said, "you didn't eat the sonsofbitches, did you?"

The old man paused in his telling, smiling, and held up his forgotten cigarette to display its long ash and he sat for a moment with his head to one side listening to the twilight birdnotes from above among the tender leaves.

"Sheriff was so pissed off he sent ten men out there to search that field, up and back, on their goddamn hands and knees and one with a metal detector, I heard. There was a track in the wheat there looked like somebody had drove a truck through by the time me and that highway patrolman got through, so no mistake where we'd been at. Never found nothing." He smiled at Val and shook his head. "That just about damn near killed them. They had to cut me loose."

He sat back then and waited, counting to himself one two three four.

"So what happened to the fingers?" Val said.

Gload smiled. "What do you think?"

"Coyotes? Hell, I don't know. Birds?"

"Val, Val, Val." The old man sighed, as if the task of imparting his knowledge were too cumbrous a burden. "It's just like I said. Any line of work you care to name you got what you call degrees of good. Might be the doctor who's the best doctor in the world at what he does but he cheats on his missus. Or say a priest who will sit all night holding the hand of some poor sonofabitch rotten with the cancer and crying for Jesus and this same man of the cloth pounds down a fifth of Seagram's before lunch. And there are cops who steal, Val. Make no mistake about that."

"The highway patrolman?"

"Give the man a cigar."

"I would doubt that," Val said. "I think that's real unlikely."

Gload went on as if he hadn't heard, his voice distant and quiet with wonderment. "Fucker came within two inches of shooting the top of my head off, then saves my ass out of greed. But can you blame him? Makes probably a thousand a month chasing drunks and scraping people out of burnt cars. He gets a chance to give his girlfriend something nice for once and have a little walking-around money." Gload laughed his croaking laugh. "And nobody out nothing except me and that Chinaman's cat. Bet he puked his guts up, though, getting them rings off. Hell, Val, he earned it right there."

Millimaki shook his head in disbelief.

"Here's my point. Is that if that poor sonofabitch did that for just a little bit of pocket money, don't think for a minute that your pal Wexler wouldn't blindside you for the sake of his so-called career. You know him. He's more than capable of doing that. I just want you to know how things work, Val. I just want you to realize how the world works."

TEN

"A story about a Butte Chinaman and some rings," Millimaki said.

"Oh, Christ, yes."

"Something about fingers and an HP officer."

"Ancient history, Val." The sheriff waved a dismissive hand. "An old story before my time and most likely without merit."

Millimaki experienced a moment of great relief. The prospect of recalling details of Gload's tale of dismemberment and implied departmental failings left him exhausted. Beyond that, he realized with some surprise, he would have felt a sense of betrayal.

"In any event, Deputy, I mostly called you in by way of a follow-up. The last time we spoke there was an issue or issues with your wife. Has that situation improved?"

Millimaki had taken the hard chair opposite the sheriff's desk and he glanced toward the door, beyond which Raylene sat at her vast desk, more formidable at her station there than the ghoulish nightshift bailiff.

"Don't worry about her, Val. Until she finishes her morning crossword she doesn't pay a lick of attention to me. I could be cold as a dead cod in here. When I have my inevitable myocardial infarction I hope it's in the PM."

Together they regarded her back, a broad expanse of garish tropical blooms. Her head beneath its plumed vortex of hair nodded above the page.

"You can close the door if you want, but that usually just sets off her radar."

Millimaki had finished his shift twenty-six hours earlier and had forced himself to stay awake until dark and still he'd hardly slept. The cabin door from its planing now shuddered under the wind and when he'd gotten up and shimmed it tight with two table knives it instead produced a muttering as though words were forming in the outer dark and came encrypted through the moaning gaps. At some point in the very early morning he dreamt again of his mother, her stained lips forming these night sounds into words he could not decipher, though he woke and lay among tangled sheets for an hour trying. He knew he should sleep but the image would not abate. He relented and sat on the edge of his bed watching the new long day paint the windowpanes. Now he sat in front of the cluttered desk blearily regarding his unpolished boots.

"She's staying in town with a friend," he said.

"Ah."

"She's going to stay in town for a while," he said. He looked up, his gaze reaching no higher than the sheriff's chest. "We needed some space. Well, she did anyway."

"Yes. Space. Space is a common theme."

"That's my word. The conversation was a bit more involved than just that."

The sheriff leaned back in his chair. He rested the tips of his index fingers in the slack underside of his jaw. The chair as he imperceptibly rocked emitted a faint feline noise.

"The department is a testing ground for marital Darwinism, Val. This is what we do, one might say what we love to do, but it is frequently opposed to or at least makes difficult the husbanding of marriage. I mean that in the agricultural sense, husbanding. There are additional factors, such as a spouse's profession if there is one outside the home, children from the union. The strongest—" he said.

The younger man had turned his gaze to the streaked single window with its latticework of bars and seemed altogether lost there. The sheriff was unsure if he'd even heard. In any case he was embarrassed to have spoken aloud the philosophy he'd formulated through years of such counseling, years of his own uncounselable grief. He noted in the cruel light the deep furrow that had appeared between Millimaki's brows since he had last seen him and that his pale eyes within their dark grottos were set in a perpetual squint, as if in seeking sense in his world, or succor, he had taken to examining life at the level of mites or atoms.

"You know, Val, my old mother always said that if you make a face long enough it'll be stuck that way."

Millimaki stared into the bright spring day, a long horizontal shadow across his eyes like a man masked before a firing squad. "Does it mean we make a choice?" he said. "Because it seems like it means that if you choose to do your job, I mean to do it right, then your marriage isn't anything more than two people sharing a room for convenience. One gets in bed when the other one goes off to work."

"I'd have to say that that's kind of a harsh view of things," the sheriff said. He slid open a drawer and rummaged about. He came up with his pipe and stuck it cold in the corner of his mouth. "Okay, maybe my theory is just so much happy horseshit, Valentine. Maybe it's just luck. Or chance, whatever you choose to call it. I've seen it a hundred times. Who you marry just goddamn turns out to be some other person after a while. Grows up into somebody else. Not better or worse. Just different."

"You put barley in the drills and six months later it comes up rye."

The sheriff smiled faintly around his pipestem. "Okay, something like that, if we want to keep the agricultural analogies going here." He waited. He dug in the bowl of the pipe with a bent paper clip. Millimaki could see yellow birds, tiny and electric, pinballing from limb to limb in the elms across the street. He thought they might be finches. He watched them through the stained window glass, feeling momentarily as if he were in a cage looking out and the brilliant birds mocked him, flitted about imponderous and free in the wide world. He said, "I guess you get used to the bars after a while."

The sheriff turned to the window, observing as if for the first time the rusty bars there, then looked again at Millimaki. "You could talk to one of our counselors, Val. There's no shame in that."

"I thought if I discharged my weapon. Something like that."

"That's not the only reason we have them."

"I just need some solid sleep."

"We could get something for that. Whatever you need. One phone call."

"Thank you, sir."

"I'm not all that good at pats on the back, Val. I hear it's one of my many failures. But you're a good officer. And I've not seen anyone better with a dog. Not since I've been here." He took the pipe from his mouth and examined the bowl thoughtfully then set it on the desk. "In many ways you remind me of me."

"And you're still married."

"Yes. Well. Again and still."

Millimaki turned from the window and looked at him. "I didn't know that."

"It was a long time ago, Val. Don't extrapolate anything from that."

A car passed on the street below. In the ensuing quiet only the rhythmical mewing of the sheriff's chair. Finally he said, "Was Teagarden here when you started? I can't recall."

"No, sir. I remember hearing the name."

"Ed Teagarden—married thirty-two years, the whole time he was on the force. Nice woman. Good woman. And smart." He stopped abruptly then, remembering, and began to busy himself with the seeming unfathomable jumble atop his desk. His glasses were revealed and he put them on and looked down. He took them off and examined them as if they might be glasses left behind by someone else and then set them on the desk again.

"Yes, sir. That's it? He was the only one?"

"No, hell." The sheriff scanned the desk as if an answer might appear there, among the envelopes of overnight mail and yellow and red carbons and triplicate forms requiring his signature a thick dossier on the long and happily married men who had served under him. "Well, the only one comes to mind. There must have been more. I'm sure of it."

"Dobek?"

"Voyle Dobek. Wedded four times that I'm aware of. But he's Dobek. He is not representative."

Millimaki went out of the office, his feet heavy and his head dull. As he passed Raylene's desk he paused and seemed to study with great concern the floor beneath his feet. The secretary glanced up at him from her folded paper and after a moment looked up at him again and laid aside her pencil. "Can I help you, Deputy?"

Millimaki said, "Is it too early for a goldfinch?"

ELEVEN

They tracked him along a dry watercourse in country that had been mapped for a hundred years but, like the charts of ancient seas with their dragons and monstrous waves, its details were little more than conjectural. There was in some years grass enough for cattle but the getting them in and bringing them out of such broken and waterless territory proved an enterprise of insufficient profit. Cattle wild as elk were said to live there, their numbers checked now by big cats and spectral wolves, drought and blizzard.

The ground underfoot was hot and the very air seemed to shudder in the heat and everywhere was the hiss and crackle of grasshoppers. "You got a lot of heart for the old crazy man they say you are," Millimaki said. The dog stopped to look back at him, his tongue lolling. They had already walked five miles and he could see ahead for nearly another mile into the empty country. A hawk far to the north circled above the invisible lake. A sparrow on a sage limb dazed by heat. The dog sniffed briefly at a cow dead some two or three years, disarticulated by flash flood or scavengers and it looked to have fallen from the sky and burst apart. A tatter of red hide lay across the cage of ribs like parchment.

In pursuit of God knows what the old man had walked into that bleak quarter in the third week in July from a scorched and dust-blown campsite on the shore of Fort Peck Reservoir. His family searched for hours, until they feared becoming lost themselves in the utter dark, and the following late morning Valentine Millimaki arrived, having driven straight into the sunrise for three and a half hours after his interminable graveyard shift. He stood beside the exploded Hereford at seven-thirty in the evening and was himself beginning to suffer from lack of water and sleep.

"I set him up with a pole and a chair and a gob of worms and then we took the boat out," the man said. "We weren't gone but half an hour and he's nowheres. Must of started walking soon as we started the goddamn motor."

"So you were gone about a half an hour."

"Something like that."

Val looked to the man's wife for confirmation.

"I wish you wouldn't swear right at this time," she said to her husband. She turned to Millimaki. "It could of been an hour," she said. "Up to an hour."

"Might of been," the man said. "It was like somebody just called him away to supper. Pole laying right there next to the chair with the line still out. It was all snagged up by the time we got back. I had to bust it off."

The missing man's daughter stood with her husband near the

lakeshore, very slender and pale, holding herself quite still as if, like gossamer or a clutch of down, she might come apart in the merest movement of summer air. Both of them from their frantic pursuit of hunch and shadows among the hills and along the beach were sunburned a terrifying red. She said, "It's like a switch you throw." The irises of her eyes were the color of sapphires and seemed to Millimaki about to liquefy, integuments too frail to restrain such pain. She studied the infinity of sky beyond his head. "He'd be so good and normal, calling me by my right, real name and even the kids' names and then it's like a switch. He'd get this terrible look on his face like who was this stranger in his house trying to make him eat poison food. That's how it was."

"We fed him good," the man offered.

"That's not what I'm telling him," she said.

"I know it isn't."

"Then just don't say anything."

She wept openly then, hugging herself like someone standing in a cold place. "Oh, Daddy." Her husband seemed not to know how to comfort her, his hand wavering in the air above her head in a gesture of blessing and finally he merely rested it on the back of her sunburned neck.

Shortly and with a visible effort she composed herself. "He'd say he heard her calling, say, 'There's Clara,' and up he'd get, didn't matter from where. From the dinner table, wherever. In church. Up he'd get and go off."

She stood with her red arms at her waist, the man's hand on her neck. Beyond them the two children sat in the dirt in their bathing suits disconsolately batting an inflatable ball between them. The boy wore thick glasses and he looked up at Millimaki with enormous magnified eyes.

"So I know where he went," the woman said. Millimaki looked at her and her husband looked away. "He's gone out there looking for Mother," she said. "She's been gone three years and he's out there looking for her in the hills."

Tom sat at heel watching the ball and when the woman began to wail he turned to her, cocking his head side to side.

"I'm sorry," Val said. The couple stood before him, the water beyond their backs as flat and reflective as plate glass. "Can you tell me what he was wearing?"

"Ain't like there's anybody else out there to confuse him with," the man said.

Val looked up at him. Far out in the dazzling lake a floating island of ethereal blue pines and sage frissoned in the heat haze—a realm of myth as axiomatic as the ground under him and then that quickly it was gone.

"Colors," he said. "I like to know what colors to look for."

"T-shirt and these brown pants he always wore," the man said. "Them khaki pants, same as he wore to work for thirty years, sweeping at the school." He shook his head. "Some whatchamacall pull-on type shoes 'cause he couldn't work the laces no more. Is that sound about right, Honey?"

The woman wiped at her eye with the back of her wrist. "A white T-shirt," she said. "And a cap. I put a cap on his head when we left, for the sun. Just a ball cap of Jamie's. I don't know what was on it. It was black, I guess."

The boy looked over, pouting. "It was NASCAR and it was my favorite and now it's gone."

The man turned to him. "Don't you start that again."

"'S true, though."

"What color, son?" Val said.

"Purple and yellow and red with 26 on it." He stared at the dog. "Can he find it? Can Whatever-His-Name-Is find it for me?"

"He's Tom. He'll give it a heck of a try."

"Just a white T-shirt," the woman said. "And the cap and the pants."

"All right."

Heat waves shimmered up from the camp trailer, the blue tarp canopied over the doorway casting a rhombus of meager shade. Two cinder blocks secured it atop the trailer and through the grommet holes two poles held it bellied over the dirt where spavined lawn chairs had been placed.

"I'd like some more water for the dog, and could you get a piece of your father's clothes for me? A shirt or pants, something like that. It'll help the dog getting started."

Val went to the truck and began provisioning himself for the long day. The man came over, holding a pale blue windbreaker that had been his father-in-law's.

"Sorry for what I said. It's been pretty tough around here. She's blaming me for it. I know she don't mean it but she is."

"Don't worry about it," Val said.

"I looked everywhere." He gazed out over the flat surface of the lake. "Could he be out there? He might of just waded out in the lake and that was it."

"Could have," Millimaki said. "But Tom didn't show any interest there. Sounds like he went walking. Pretty common with Alzheimer's. They just walk and walk."

"Don't I know it." The man stood awkwardly with his huge laborer's hands buried in the pockets of jeans that had apparently been sheared off rudely at the knee with a knife or an ax. The tops of his gnarled feet were crimson and peeling. "Sometimes he just pissed in his pants," he said. His voice cracked. "Sitting there. My wife changes him like a baby."

"You did good," the deputy said. "You did all you could."

"I might go along with you."

"No. Stay with your family. Tom anyway gets all flummoxed if he's got to keep an eye on more than one."

"All right. But ain't there anything you want me to do?"

"If I don't come back call out a sheriff and his dog."

"Oh, hell." The man took off his hat and ran his rough fingers through his hair and regarded the vast country sprawled behind them.

"I'm kidding," Val said. "But you might get a good fire going once it gets dark and keep it going. Should be able to see it from a long ways off. Maybe get your missus to sit out there with you. Give her something else to think about."

He adjusted the canteens on his belt and called the dog to heel and began to walk away when the man called after him. "Listen, I know you're thinking what could he catch out of there." He waved behind him at the murky lake just then the color of calcimine under the featureless sky. The water hissed softly on the graveled shingle. "I just wanted him to have something to do. Anyways, he might of tied into a carp or a goldeneye, something to tug on the line at least."

After they set out the shepherd was immediately drawn to a streambed entering from the south and the going in that direction was slow: deep troughs and cutbanks and a twisted wrack of weathered plank and post and deadfall from some headland flood of the previous spring. Queer rocks lay atop the dirt as smooth and round as Jurassic eggs, and pinecones tumbled and abraded by the torrent lay all about like spined sea creatures of a past age. Grasshoppers wheeled up before them and rattled off into the weeds and sage.

They walked on for some time, the dog working back and forth across the wash. Juniper and pine appeared atop the banks, the larger trees displaying weeping blazes where porcupine teeth had been at work. Roots snaked exposed over the parched ground, encircling stones as though to squeeze sustenance from them. Sandstone scarps filigreed with fossil fish and shells projected atop the cutbanks like the pulpits of sailing ships and everywhere startling columns of the ancient stone wind-carved and pocked like sculpture from a fever dream.

Atop a small rise an hour later they came upon a low homestead cabin of notched and squared-off logs and the dog raised his nose and angled toward it. A flicker of hope invigorated Millimaki and he jogged up the bank on which the cabin stood, the black rectangle of its doorway promising the only substantial shade for miles in any direction. They had not seen where the man had spent the night and Millimaki prayed he might be resting his old bones in the cabin's cool interior.

But he was not. Tom whined and circled in the dusty dark and Millimaki could see in the pale dirt, among tracks of pack rats and skunk and badger, the man's shoe prints trod in a circle no larger than a barrel lid. He had stood there turning and turning about for some time and had at last gone out into the bright alien world again.

It was very quiet there. Tom lay in the dirt panting. The cabin door was stove in, hanging atilt from a hinge fashioned from a boot sole and Millimaki, dizzy and half-blind in the sudden twilight, stood looking back the way they'd come. It was a strangely resolute course for a man who'd had difficulty navigating the hallways of his daughter's home, a track not at all like the zags and insensate back-loops of so many of the poor souls he'd pursued over the years who'd wandered crazed or hypothermic through deadfall or thigh-deep in freezing creeks or like maddened fugitives scaled sheer cliffs, leaving bloody fingernails wedged among the fissures. The frightened woman at the campsite had said her father had gone off in search of his dead wife and perhaps she was right. He seemed to be drawn by something, and as Millimaki stood atop prints of the old man's cheap shoes, the word "quest" came into his bleary head. Quest, he thought. What the hell, I'm losing it.

He had not slept in more than twenty hours, and fatigue crept down his bones in a slow paralysis. He imagined the old janitor himself standing there earlier, the adze scars on the logs transubstantiating into some long-ago wallpaper pattern his wife had chosen for their home. Where swallows flitted now among the bellied pine poles of the ceiling he heard the twitter of his children from their bedrooms. And then her voice again. It had brought him here but now moved on, a faint and musical rendering of his name on the wind and in the branches of the trees.

Shadows like viscous ink slid down the coulee sides and gave sinister shape to the sandstone totems and crags accoutered with high-water jetsam and there were shapes enough among them to populate any dream or nightmare, even in a sound mind. Box elder trees with their eveningtime shadows came to resemble groping mandrake creatures, and raptors planing high overhead gave voice to them, and the roots of the dark pines lay atop the rutted ground like vipers.

The day was far advanced when Millimaki and the dog stood among the bones of the ill-starred Hereford. He stared at the bleached jumble about his feet as if it might be an augury he was meant to decipher but in his diminished state he could hardly unriddle the mystery of his own compass. He was astounded the man, eighty-six years old, could have come so far in such country, driven it seemed by a love that had endured fifty years to pursue glimpse and figment, the specter of his wife beckoning at each bend of the baking streambed. Or was it that, like Tom, he merely followed the scent on the breeze of lilac or rosewater or the redolence of the soap that for two thousand nights she'd used before she came to lie beside him in their bed. Such feelings for Millimaki were as cold and remote as an expired star and he was better able to conjure images of the old man's wife than of his own, grown faceless and undefined in the mere weeks since she'd abandoned him.

Millimaki rubbed at his afflicted eyes and consulted his watch. When he stared up and addressed the sky, gone lavender at the late hour, his tongue felt thick. "Where in the Christ are you, old man?"

The dog Tom at that moment began to whine, circling near a ravelment of roots and deadfall piled up by a long-ago flood; it looked like the den of some Pleistocene rodent. The grandson's cap lay in the dirt and the ground was scuffed and gouged by the man's shoes as though he had struggled there with a phantom.

The dog's tail began to wag furiously and he bolted away, pink tongue hanging long from his mouth. He ran ahead and waited for Millimaki and ran again. After nearly a mile of this, the deputy saw a snatch of white far ahead—a color, save for bones, absent in all the dun and darkening landscape. He did not trust his eyes. He shambled the last short way on feet heavy as bricks.

A magpie stood on the man's very back, pulling at the fabric of his shirt almost as if it merely wanted to wake him from his sleep. It flew on their approach and from a juniper branch assailed the dog with splenetic speech so nearly human the dog stood and stared. The man lay on his face and seemed to have fallen headlong as though pushed from behind. Every inch of his exposed pale skin was terribly burned and shot with blisters and he lay in the dirt slowly baking.

He had been bitten by a snake high in the groin, his left leg swollen horrifically so that the fabric of his trousers was stretched tight and discolored by the thin fluid seeping from the wound. The snake was a prairie rattler probably five feet long and thick as bridge cable and wound around the old man's arm like strange Egyptian bijouterie. It seemed in his confusion and rage he had grabbed the snake behind the head and just hung on. The dog sniffed at him and warily sniffed the snake and finally merely sat. Val took out his small camera from the fanny pack he wore and circled, taking his pictures of the ground and the man in his repose and close pictures of the wound in the bloated leg. He snapped a frame of the snake locked in the man's grip, an image he'd later think seemed strangely mild and as unthreatening as a sock puppet, with its extended tongue a thin filament dry as a strip of felt. At last he sat beside the dog, in the cup of his hand giving him long drinks of water from one of the canteens. He'd saved it for the old man but now he and the dog drank deeply. As the poison moved in his veins, the man with the snake in his grip plodded up the narrow watercourse for nearly a mile toward the timbered headland above, which now, as Millimaki sat regarding his rigid shape, sent down from its slopes on the breeze a perfumery of sage and juniper and pine. Millimaki was very tired and sat looking up at the bluff and at the trees silhouetted on a sudden pearl light. Presently he rose and moved to the corpse and turned it over. It was a wooden thing, a carving attired with a workman's costume and a thespian's mask of awe, of wonderment, eyes agape and painted the same heart-rending blue as his daughter's.

Shadows lay long across the ground and stars began to materialize and from the uplands stretching off toward the Judith River Millimaki heard the first tentative yawps of coyotes. He closed his eyes and rested his forehead on his knees. The dog slept. The old man slumbered rigidly near his feet.

And then he saw her, standing young and fresh and a little impatiently on the bluff, the wind moving her hair. She waited and soon her knight, this haggard warrior—burner of trash, sweeper of floors—went to her. And there was nothing else but her, not the crushing sorrow, not the sun that baked his skin or the pain in his leg or the vile writhing thing around his arm. His steps were light and he gained the top of the hill with scarcely a breath and they stood together on that palisade gazing out over the green and perfect flowering prairielands of their life. In his dream Millimaki watched as Tom scrabbled up the rocky slope and circled whimpering and at last lost the scent he'd followed as it spiraled into the troposphere like a wisp of smoke.

Millimaki woke and sat looking fondly at the dark terrible shape and then put his head on his knees once more as the blue dusk settled over him with the whisper of bees. Tom came to nuzzle him, staring into his face with sad moist eyes and finally lay down beside his feet. A three-quarter moon ascended above the hills and all was silvery light. Millimaki was reluctant to leave the old gentleman's company.

He held the dog by the collar and stood for a long time in the dark. Driftwood in the fire snapped with the sound of breaking bones. When he approached, the man and his wife sat stupefied before the flames and they stared at Millimaki wide eyed and amazed as though he were the conjurement of their bleak thoughts, a figure portioned out from the darkness itself. Beyond them the lake was a sheet of quicksilver, so flat and calm Millimaki could make out gulls or ducks arrayed on its surface hundreds of yards out and could as well have been a fleet of ships at anchor.

"God almighty, you scared us, Deputy."

Millimaki stood in the circle of light. "Could I get a drink of water for Tom?"

The family had drug up a cottonwood log from the lake that had been worn white and smooth as a great tusk and he stepped over it and sat. The dog disappeared into the dark and could be heard lapping endlessly at the lake edge. The man set the bowl down next to Millimaki.

"Anyways, in case he wants it," he said. He handed Millimaki a long-necked beer, its sides pearled with dew. Millimaki felt something in his pocket and he fished out the boy's cap and set it on the log beside him.

The woman had not taken her eyes from him as he came up and sat and she said at last, "He's dead out there, isn't he?"

Millimaki regarded the shifting coals. "Yes, he is," he said. "I'm sorry."

"I knew it, anyways," she said. "It's all right. It's what he wanted."

"He was a strong man. You didn't tell me that," Millimaki said blearily. "He went a long ways." The heat and lack of sleep and general unnamed sadness lay atop him like a succubus. He sat with his forearms on his knees and was surprised to find a bottle in his hand. He couldn't bring himself to tell them about the snake and it seemed sufficient tonight that they picture their father intact and comfortably asleep under the cosseting sky. Almost to himself he said, "I can't believe how far he went. In that heat." He shook his head. "Might have been seven miles. More maybe. Eight or nine."

"He's done that a couple of times back at home," the husband said. "One time they found him out by the airport, better than twelve miles from the house."

"Anyways, it's what he wanted." The old man's daughter wore a thin sweater thrown over her shoulders and she pulled it tighter around her. "He's with Mother now."

The man sat sunk in a canvas camp chair, a beer bottle dangling from his hand while he stared back at the sputtering coals. "Why couldn't he of just died in his chair at home," he said. He shook his head. "To go out there in that." He tipped his bottle vaguely toward the Breaks, the headlands and blunt pines rumored against a backdrop of outrageous starfields. "It's awful. It's undignified is what it is."

"I won't hear that," his wife said. "Lawrence, I won't hear it."

"Well."

"It's not true." She was quiet for a long while. The fire welled brightly as a breeze rose up, collapsing wood sending up a rosary of brilliant embers. A luminous cloud lay across the moon.

"He was on a search is what I believe." The woman paused,

her face in the firelight ruddled and exaggerated as a native mask. "A kind of search. I can't think of the word."

Millimaki did not look up. He spoke almost as if from a dream. "A quest," he said.

"Well, yes." She looked at him in surprise. "That's exactly the word. A quest. He was. He's been on a quest for Mother since she died. Far as he was concerned, she was somewheres just out of sight, just around the next corner. And don't look at me like that. Do you have to look at me that way?"

Her husband said, "I wasn't looking any way."

"I know that look." Her voice quavered. "I know that look, Lawrence."

The man stared at her for a long moment. The wind passed over them and Millimaki imagined it bringing the old man's scent out across all the broken implacable country, to all the hunger that resided there and the wind blew the woman's pale hair across her mouth and sent a chill down her frame. She was still, in middle age, as slender as a girl.

The man cast his eyes sidelong to look at Millimaki. "Deputy," he said, "don't you have someone waiting on you? You must want to bust out of here and get home."

Enthralled by the pulsing coals and numb with fatigue, Millimaki registered the words slowly. Both of them watched him. The wind blew. Their shadows loomed and collapsed and loomed again on the ground beyond them.

"My wife," he said stupidly, "she—"

"That's right," the man said. "Go on. You don't need to wait on us. You go on and be with her."

With that he set his bottle down carefully next to his feet and stood up. Millimaki watched him. He circled out into the dark and reappeared behind his wife, his face red and demonic in the upflare of the fire and his hard hands aglow and he wrapped his arms around his wife's shoulders as tenderly as if he were trying to contain a cloud. She reached up and held his forearms in her small hands and began to softly cry. "Oh, he was, Lawrence. He was."

The wind swept down and the old man's daughter wept, repeating, like an affirmation of her father's simple life, "Oh, he was, he was, he was."

TWELVE

"I suppose I ought to mention this one other thing, though it don't amount to any mystery or anything. When I was a young buck in Deer Lodge I had to get a guy who was after me. They never could prove who it was, though I had to do a two-week haul in Siberia East because they knew more or less what was going on and they figured it was me. There was a corner by the cellhouse, the only place the towers couldn't see and I got this guy over there. There was a kind of outdoor urinal there that you maybe've seen if you've been there. A piss trough. Lot of shit went down there, guys trading dope and getting it on with one another and shit like that and I figured he'd come over when I was taking a piss just to have a look and of course he did, hissing terrible awful things to a boy. Yeah, that was the deal. You could find out easy enough I guess, if you cared. I don't remember his name but he was a fat dago fairy from Butte, Montana, and he deserved what he got. It was that I didn't have no choice is why I don't mention it much and he come over and I put a shiv up under his fat gut and just pulled it upwards hard as I could and he fell down hard with his blue guts spilt out on the stones like a steer you'd butcher. And then I went and pissed the blood off my hands and walked away and that was that.

"I'm tired now, Val. There wasn't anything more to it than that. Good night."

THIRTEEN

He held the crude map in his hands and surveyed the country below him. He looked at the page then turned it half around and looked again. It was like a child's drawing. The old criminal had drawn horseshoes to approximate the upper and lower dams and inverted Us with strange diacritical marks to indicate hills with their sparse native vegetation. He had incised thick black lines apparently with the paper poised on his knee because in places the paper was torn through, these meant to represent coulees, which converged like veins into a river replete with tiny waves and gulls. To Wexler finally it looked like an idiot's rendering of a storybook land. The old man had drawn in trees and a series of inverted Vs that might have been distant mountains by which to orient oneself, and finally in various places he had marked a number of bold Xs. Wexler stared all around. He turned the pages once more.

By the time he returned to his car the sun was nearly down.

He sat on the bumper, with a stick chiseling mud from the soles of his boots. When he was done he took the old man's map and oriented it and sat looking up into the coulees he'd walked, which at that late hour lay in cool blue shadow. Beyond the bluff tops he could see the peaks of the Highwoods purple and insubstantial in the distance as a reef of summer storm cloud.

With the folding entrenching tool he'd dug three holes that day that had yielded nothing but rocks and the ironlike roots of sagebrush and one ancient bone that may have been the pin-bone of a cow or buffalo. Wexler had examined it for some time and had laid it alongside his own thighbone and finally had thrown it away in disgust. Now, sitting at his car, he studied the maps once more in the failing light and looked to the north again and finally balled up the pages and threw them into the ditch weeds.

"Goddamn you, old man," he said. He seemed to address the papers now fluttering like wounded birds in a snarl of mullein and hemlock. "If you're screwing me around I swear to God I'll make your hayseed boyfriend wish he'd never left the farm."

Walking in a daze, Millimaki followed the old man as he trundled slowly down the corridor, his shadow on the waxed concrete, giant and dwarf, as he passed beneath the buzzing overheads. From the cells some of the men called to him. Gload went along as if he were walking alone in his orchard and the voices of the inmates were to him less consequential than the trill of birds in the apple trees. They'd just returned from the infirmary after Gload had complained of chest pains and dizziness and the caged men behind the safety of their bars called him piker and scammer and goldbrick. Millimaki turned to one man whose narrow head nearly fit between the bars where he stood hissing a disjointed litany of obscenities.

"One more word and it's lights out, right now," Millimaki said. "Get back to your cot or I'll call for Dobek."

The man hissed a long "muthafucka." Millimaki swung his baton viciously and hit the bars above the man's head. "Get back to your goddamn cot, Murphy, or I swear to Christ I'll come in there and crush your head myself." He had raised the club again, his hand tingling and aflame and felt in that incandescent moment if the face appeared at the bars he could turn bone to gruel. But the man whined and slunk soundlessly into the shadows and could be heard for many minutes in conversation with himself there.

Gload stood before his cell door and waited for Val to turn the key in the lock and he went in without a word, though in passing he eyed the younger man with a bemused expression that furrowed his immense forehead. Millimaki heard him sit in his chair, saw the match flame erupt in the gloom.

"Would you like to talk about it, Val?" he said.

Millimaki with the keys in his hand stood outside the door. The men had settled down in their cells, but for Murphy, who addressed the dark recesses intimately in two separate voices, two separate selves. His moist and horrible lips made the sound of dripping water.

"Did you say something, John?"

"I said you might want to get it off your chest, whatever it is that's eating on you."

"It's late, John. What don't you get some sleep? That's probably all that's wrong with you."

"That ain't going to happen. I can feel it. Not tonight it ain't." He lit another cigarette and his mask appeared briefly hovering in the dark. "Take your walk, Valentine. I'll be here should you feel the need to talk."

Millimaki made his rounds. The jailer, who with every long week seemed to become more like the statue of some Old Testament god, gazed down from atop his platform with hollow eyes, his face carved from yellow stone by indifferent hands and deeply shadowed from the sallow overhead globelight. No longer sure when he was awake or when he slept, Millimaki had quit trying to speak to him and so sat silently filling in the night's required forms and eating an apple from his simple lunch. A soft rain fell and muted the church bells tolling the three o'clock hour, and the lacquered street beyond the jailhouse door reflected the streetlight's purple albedo and the lights of the infrequent passing cars. The phone rang and he turned to watch the jailer, willing him to nod and hold up the receiver toward him. The rain did not matter nor the hour. He would go to her then or anytime and pack her things into the truck to bring her home. The jailer from his imperious elevated seat would say to him, "It's your wife, Millimaki," and he'd go out under the weeping eaves and pass under the streetlamp. He could see himself doing it, getting up from his desk and opening the door to the slow gong, gong, gong, and feeling the cool kiss of mist on his face.

But the jailer only leered from his seat and half turned away from Millimaki for privacy and so he went through the sally gate and down the corridor of cells.

As if because he was cursed to sleeplessness, John Gload had become expert in the nuances of sleep. Sporadically, in stretches of months, sometimes years, he'd had time to decipher the night's minute tickings, the folds and creases of it while caged men near him slept, twitching or writhing in unconsciousness while their breath rifled in and out through constricted throats and nostrils that had been malformed in fights and those still capable expiating their sins in the confessionals of dreamland. For some the commodious limits of the cell became in nightmare the close configuration of their own coffins and they battled their rough blankets as though they were the winding clothes they'd worn to the grave and there were others who relived in prurient languor trysts with women gagged with their own hosiery or mute children or other weaker men waylaid in the showers of a recurring incarceration and John Gload read in these moans and sighs, in the wet and strangled sounds in their mouths, the sins of flesh duplicated in their slumbering. Dead people paraded through Gload's dreams, too, but he was untroubled by them and though they were his victims and wore rubious scars, they seemed no more strange to him than the random beings populating any man's dreams.

"They're all asleep, Val," the old man said.

Millimaki paused, his shadow leaning to merge with the dark of Gload's cell.

"Why not pull up your chair, Deptee?"

Gload had come to the bars from his chair and his hands dangled atop the door's horizontal cross member, the cigarette smoldering at his stained knuckle. He stood with his sloping equine forehead pressed to the bars. Rarely in their talks had he come forward from the gloom and Millimaki had long since grown accustomed to speaking to a voice in the dark and hearing one issue from the dark and their relationship because of that had taken on the aspect of priest and confessor, the roles unfixed and seeming to change by the minute. The old man stood staring at the ember of his cigarette, waiting.

"Why not sit for a bit?"

Millimaki stood. He listened. Lights flared in the street-level window, and tires on the wet pavement beyond made a brief adder's hiss. He turned and found his chair against the corridor wall where for the first time he noted the paint peeling in long yellow skeins and it lay on the floor like molted skins and the walls wept a drapery of griseous stains under every window where water had breached the rotting jambs. He brought the chair forward and sat heavily.

"This new Murphy guy seems to of pushed some kind of button on you," Gload said.

Millimaki ran his hand through his hair and massaged a spot at the base of his skull. "He just happened to be within reach. I lost my cool."

"I wouldn't give it a second thought, Val. He's a bad one."

"Not many wind up here for their good Christian deeds."

The old man smiled. "You're right, Valentine. But there's bad and then there's crazy. With your crazies like this Murphy you lose the whole benefit of knowing what they might do next. I've walked a wide circle around his type my whole life."

"And it's served you well."

Gload sat frozen with the cigarette halfway to his lips. "Your point being that I'm in this place and so is he and so what have I gained."

With the heels of his hands Millimaki ground at his eye sockets and he sighed. "I'm sorry, John. I'm not much in the way of company tonight."

"I hear you had a walk in the toolies with your dog. Is that the problem?"

"Like you said, it's a small town in here."

"Nobody has nothing to do but talk, Val. Myself I mostly listen."

"Not much of what these guys say would seem too interesting."

"So you found another one cold and stiff. You're on a bum run of luck, Valentine. But that will change."

"I keep hearing that."

Gload stood with his arms through the bars. When he pulled his head back to bring the burning cigarette to his lips, two faint outlines of the bars were pressed onto his forehead.

"You haven't had a lot to say these days, Deputy. What's on your mind?"

"Very little, John. Sleep. Sleep is on my mind."

"You could try my little trick."

"It's three in the morning and you're standing here talking to me. Not a particularly good advertisement for it."

"Sometimes," Gload said. "Sometimes." With his Camel clinched between knuckles he sat hingeing his wrist up and back, watching in the gloom the tiny bolide of its burning tip. "Tonight I thought you might want to talk."

"So you stayed up to talk to me."

"I'm sorry that after what we been through you'd be so surprised by that." He blew his smoke toward the overhead lights and watched it vanish. "Yes, Deputy, I stayed up to talk to you."

It was out of his mouth before he'd time to consider it and in the intervening short moment of silence afterward he felt ridiculous. "It's my wife."

Gload received the news with gravity. He ground out his cigarette in the tin can and the chair's legs chirped as he inched it closer to the bars and he composed his hands in his lap like a man at prayer. "You sorta had that look," he said.

"She's gone to stay in town with a girlfriend. I hardly saw her before. Now I never do."

"That's no way to carry on a relationship. If I was to add up the days I was gone while I was with Francie I'd say it was damn near two of the five years. I don't recommend it."

"Francie. That's your wife?"

"Not wife, exactly."

"What then?"

There came a long pause during which the sounds of the old building seemed to insinuate themselves overloud like crickets on an August evening. Fans whirred somewhere far away in its mechanical heart and its breath came fusty and dry from the ductwork. Gload's voice when he finally spoke was scarcely louder than the indifferent mutterings of the air conditioner.

"You asked me once before if she was my wife and I never answered you which was rude and I apologize. But I hadn't ever the need to describe her to anybody which you'll think is kind of peculiar but I guess that tells you something about how we lived. Not exactly out in the public eye much, so to speak."

"So would you say 'girlfriend' then? Or your 'Old Lady'?"

"Old Lady," he snorted. "Gah. I hate that. Sounds like some of that bullshit biker talk." He paused to draw on his smoke and exhale into the light. "No, and I'm too goddamn old for 'girlfriend.' So I guess 'wife' is the best one. It's how I feel about her anyways."

"And she left you."

"What I said was—" What he'd said was she was gone and that was a different thing entirely. But from his innominate shadows he could read in the young man's eyes—insomniacal and familiar, so much like those that regarded him in the scarred and untrue polished metal of his cell's mirror—a need for the comfort bestowed by mutual anguish.

"Yes she did," Gload said and thought, My little Francie. "She left me for something better."

Millimaki nodded. Like two men at a campfire they sat listening to the night sounds in the dark beyond their strange violet circle of light. Millimaki had closed his eyes and soon his head began to bob as if the bones in his neck had turned to jelly. He lurched upright, his eyes wild. The old man had been watching him solemnly.

"Shit," Millimaki said. "I need to get up and get moving before I crap out right here."

In his weariness Millimaki in rising placed a hand on the flat horizontal bar of John Gload's cell and the old man reached and laid his enormous paw over it. Val stared at the great hairy thing, white and thick and heavy, and made no move to pull away. The old man left it there for a moment and then it was gone into shadow. It was the first human contact Millimaki had experienced in weeks. The last person he'd touched—the old janitor wandering in the badlands in search of his young bride—had been made of oak.

Gload sat back. "I feel like I want to tell you this one thing, Valentine. Sit down. Sit for just a minute."

Millimaki hesitated briefly. He cast his gaze to the right where the nicked and rusty bars on the cells seemed to diminish infinitely like notches numerating the dead. The caged men behind them slept on.

When the deputy had taken his chair, Gload said, "One thing I always did, Val, was to live my life. It wasn't a particularly interesting life but it was on my terms. Now in here I'm just living it out."

"I'm not sure what you mean."

"Now it's just waiting. It's only a life technically because you're breathing in and out. Putting in the time until you clock out." He brought forward his chair with a squawk yet again and slid his bean can beside his foot.

"I was in this little town once some years ago over east of here and every day I'd walk past this place for old people. Hospital for old people. A whatyacallit—old folks' home?"

"Nursing home?"

"I don't know. Whatever they call it these days. But with this line of people sitting in their chairs or wheelchairs just looking out. Me walking by was the best part of their day. A week I went by there every morning on the way for a paper up the street and back and I seen them there, heads moved all of a piece to follow me just like cattle. They were just living it out, you see what I mean, Val? Waiting it out. And one day I just turned and went in. They were sitting there, didn't look at me at all because it was out the window where the world was. Didn't even turn their heads. They were nothing but sticks in clothes. Blankets on their laps, hair standing up all which-way. I just stood there. Pretty soon I folded the paper and put it in my back pocket. I thought that in about half a minute I could snap their necks one two three down the line and then this pogue comes in eating a chicken leg in his dirty white jacket and says can I help you and then that was that."

Millimaki studied the old man or rather studied the space he knew him to occupy in the dark and then from that space smoke rolled into the artificial light.

"You're serious."

"Serious as God." Through the bars a hand appeared, corpse-white in the light and brutal, two fingers held a fraction of an inch apart. It was not at all the same warm thing that had rested on his own hand a few short minutes before. "That fucking close," he said. "I was fixing to do it and I could of. Don't think I couldn't."

"An act of kindness, then?" Millimaki said.

"In that case I believe it was mostly just impatience on my part."

"Those people had memories at least. To go back to."

"They had shit, Valentine." Gload tapped a finger twice above his pendulous ear. "There was nothing upstairs but oatmeal." He sat back into shadow and was quiet a long while. The tube lights throbbed and hissed. Millimaki waited. "But it would of been a kindness, Val, yes indeed. Or a blessing, some might call it, who believe in such things. Like you. Didn't you not tell me once you were a mackerel snapper?"

"I was raised that way. Pretty sure I never mentioned it though."

Gload waved away the remark, his hand winking into the light and gone again. "Anyways, you have to see what I'm getting at."

"I'm tired, John. Maybe you could help me see your point."

"Like people at the end of the line. Like some of the folks you find, Valentine. They would of been better off dead, is my point."

On the thin mattress Gload lay atop was a cartography of a thousand stains and there were more stains and thin fissures like the veins in a leaf on the ceiling above his head in the muddled dark. Across his counterfeit heaven, visions of Francie came and went like the random flares of headlights through the high corridor windows. As if he looked at her again through the old imperfect panes of their house or one washed with rain, her face was blurred. But her singing was in his ears, her voice calling his name as if it were a chant to ward off harm and finally on that vile cot he could nearly feel her, her leg seeking him out from her own nether bed.

My wife, he thought. Then to test the sound of it he said it aloud, but because he didn't want to share it with the animals nearby in their cubicles he said it softly. "My wife, Francie." He swung his legs and sat on the cot's edge, smiling, and he spoke to her then softly. "I marry you now. Before whatever god you'd pick, it don't matter. You're my wife and I'm your husband."

And when they talked of her from then on he called her his wife and it was not lost on Millimaki and when he asked about where she was or where he thought she might be Gload smiled wistfully and Millimaki felt a terrible fear for her because he had seen that smile before and he knew what it meant to be so spoken of by John Gload. He'd smiled telling him about a Chinaman and about an old woman and her Pom dog sixty years dead.

Hours later while sitting in the Blazer in the shade a towering prairie cottonwood in full leaf cast onto the shoulder of the two-lane highway, not far from where his wife those few years ago had come sparkling resplendent and naked from the creek, Valentine Millimaki thought perhaps he did see John Gload's point. The cabin was still some miles south on the road. Too inhabited yet by Glenda, he avoided it. The jail, where once he found solace in its disconnectedness from the world, seemed now to be a stone bearing down on his neck. He stared unseeing out the streaked windshield. Grasshoppers sizzled in the brittle weeds and a chorus of meadowlark and red-winged blackbird filled the cab. It was comfortable here. If not for Tom he would have lived in the truck along the road and taken his meals there—cans of soup eaten cold, cheese cut from the block with his pocketknife and eaten on crackers, shaving in the dimming twilight before work beneath the dome light and sleeping across the seats through the warming brilliant days wrapped in his jacket like a bum and waking to the sound of passing traffic. He lurched red-eyed through his days in a purgatory described by home and the jail, content in neither place. A bird laboring in a hurricane wind, moving nowhere yet unable to alight. How different from the animated skeletons of Gload's old folks' home was he?

Among the papers on the dashboard that rose and fell with the breeze through the side window was the letter from his sister. He took it up and pulled it from the envelope and reread it and then refolded the pages carefully along their creases and put them back. On the dash it pulsed and fluttered against the window glass. As if the words within would escape to circle his head like carrion birds.

He'd been twelve years old. Should he have known his mother was living life out? For his paltry sins he'd had the kind alcoholic priest in his confessional to unburden himself to but the transgressions against his mother seemed too great to fit in that dim cubicle. He listed them instead in a notebook afterward, writing them out with a gnawed pencil in a mimicry of her elegant cursive: "Disrespect." "Sullenness" (she had called it). "Slamming the back door." "Didn't make my bed." Once he'd been caught stealing a fruit pie at the little market near the school and the proprietor had phoned. His mother related the conversation at the dinner table in a voice so flat and shamed that it burned his skin worse than the welts his father had later raised with the doubled belt. He had taken him by the arm wordlessly to the chicken shed so his sister couldn't hear the thwack of the leather across his back, or the cries. The entries in his ledger of sins became less frequent. "I pretended to be asleep so she would not kiss me goodnight." After six months, one or two others. He remembered the last: "The fucking slippers I knew she wouldn't ever wear." Two days later he had taken up the pencil and blacked out "fucking." That was the last time he'd opened the notebook.

The year he left for college, in the last month he'd ever stay on the ranch, he'd gone systematically from window to window to view her life and saw it reduced to four rectangles framing, whatever direction, intransigent weeds, thirsty fields lashed by wind. A barely discernible camber of earth under a sky that had yielded little but heartbreak. Scant barley, scant wheat. Pastures where their Angus browsed on knapweed and thistle. They were scabrous as dogs with mange, their ribs countable under the balding hides. The view—her life—did not change and, she knew, would not change. Even the greening of spring was to her nothing but false promise, brief April rains meted out by a prankster God for a smile. Millimaki realized then that her husband and children were no anodyne for the enormity of her despair. They had more than likely contributed to it—three more stones mortared into the wall of her private and inscrutable prison.

Without the analgesia that might have been offered by John Gload's irresistible hands, she had made one for herself with a lariat rope and a six-foot ladder.

For Glenda that same malevolent world of the outside had raised the latch and pushed open the door and had swarmed around her. Owls, snakes, coyotes. Insects leaked like sand through the door cracks to infest her hair. The wind came down from the trees to inhabit her. Did he want someday to find her, too, dangling from a collar tie or swimming in a tepid bath with her wrists blossoming gouts of red? He thought, once again, that somehow he'd become another stone in another wall.

Sweat plastered his shirt to the seatback. He looked at his watch, consulted the sun nearing its zenith to assure himself it had not spun wildly ahead in some cruel rift of time. The dog would be waiting in his kennel. He sat for a moment longer. The grass in the borrow ditch lay flat to the ground under the wind and rose again and fell and the colossal cottonwood yawed and groaned, sending down onto the truck's hood a clutch of tiny branches that clattered and skittered on the metal like juju bones.

As he rose finally to leave Gload that morning, taking his chair from the bars to the hallway, the old man had said, "Now you're the best part of my day, Valentine. I'm the same as those pitiful old sonsofbitches looking out the window at a man going to get the paper. That was a terrible thing to see and now it's me."

Gload sat watching him. Wexler leaned against the bars. The lights shone on his polished belt, his spit-shined Wellingtons. When Gload stood from his bunk Wexler pushed himself away from the bars and stood back.

"Hell, I don't bite, Weldon."

"Never said you did."

"Val, he sits right up here close."

"That's against policy. I could have him wrote up for that."

"I wish you wouldn't do that," Gload said. "As a personal favor. I kind of feel sorry for the kid."

"Any trouble he has he brings on himself. But I can let it go, sure."

"What sort of trouble?"

"Maybe 'trouble' ain't the right word. Laxadaisical is what

he is. Off hiking in the woods with that dog and one thing and another. Dirty boots like a farmer, wrinkled slacks. Thinks he has the old man's ear but he don't."

"I see what you mean."

"Dirty fingernails."

"He has let himself go, yes indeed."

"Anyways, that's what I want to talk to you about, John. I know you've got to like Millimaki but I want to say don't waste your time on him. It's time you don't have. He don't carry any whack around here. Seems like if you want to talk to somebody—for your own benefit—it ought to be me or one of the other ranking officers."

"Like Dobek maybe? He come in here with some pretty disturbing things to say, Weldon. Pretty gory stuff."

"He's a fucking animal, John."

"Kind of put the fear of God into me, I'll tell you that."

"A fucking caveman. Okay, forget Dobek." He took an incremental pace forward to illustrate his earnestness. "I'll be your man, John. If you can give me any information it might look good that you cooperated."

"I believe I have been cooperating, Weldon. What about the maps?"

Wexler sighed theatrically. "Maps didn't amount to shit, John. I think you know that."

"Them were good maps. I spent quite a little time on them."

"Didn't amount to nothing. Zero or less."

"I'm an old man, Weldon. My memory's not what it once was."

"You were fucking with me."

"Nosir." Gload rose and protested, approaching the bars with his hands extended in supplication and wearing an expression of wounded pride. "I wouldn't do any such thing."

Wexler took one step back.

"But I think I need to go on out there, Weldon. Got to walk the ground again myself. It wasn't exactly yesterday." He gripped the bars then and assumed a contemplative pose, his red-rimmed eyes to the ceiling. "What would really be best is if you were to get me a topo map of the place."

Wexler assumed his practiced pose. His hands atop his pistol butt and baton were very white. Gload watched his face. "You could do it with a topo?"

"I'm sure of it."

"A topo," he said. "Leave me think about it."

"Then we can go on out there and I could pretty well show you exactly where you want."

"Take you out? I don't believe I can do that," Wexler said.

"Right, right. The Old Man would probably want Val to take me out, if at all."

"I outrank Millimaki, time in grade."

"I'm just going by what I hear around here."

"Like what?"

"Like he was going to let Val take me out there in a set of leg chains, that's all." Gload chuckled, held out his hands, now in a gesture of helplessness. "As if a old sonofabitch like me could leg it out anyways."

FOURTEEN

He sat in his chair alone in the small garden reading the *Great Falls Tribune.* Francie that morning had gone to town as she had nearly every day for the past several days and after he'd read the single column about Sidney White, he laid aside the paper and sat looking at the crocuses she'd planted, unfurling their color around the base of a lilac tree. She'd planted tulip and daffodils there too and the crocus blooms stood among the deep green serpent's tongues of their emerging leaves like drops of paint. White had been arrested for rape and a separate charge of assault and battery in Miles City, where little more than a week ago Gload had left him with his money and had driven away with an abscess of misgiving festering in his stomach. The girl had been fifteen years old and White had gotten her drunk and taken her to the room and the next day the girl's father had come and White had beaten the man with a golf club from a set he'd apparently stolen from an unlocked car parked in the hotel lot. The article stated that he had also employed that implement in his assault on the girl, details withheld. He was awaiting trial in the Custer County jail.

Gload took up the paper once again and reread the article slowly and carefully and sat back against the chair shaking his head wearily. "Golf clubs," he said.

The countryside was still as a painting, the wind strangely becalmed and even the sky to the south where he gazed was without moving clouds and against the azure backdrop was not a starling, not a gull. Gload, undistracted before the motionlessness of his beloved view, in a very short time made his decision and as was his way, from that moment, he did not reconsider it or waver from its necessary course. He pushed himself up from his chair and laid aside the folded paper on the small table beside his cup and shambled through the dewy grass in his odd sailor's gait to the tool bin behind the house. When he returned with the proper implements thrown over his shoulder he paused briefly at the lilac and stood looking down at Francie's flowers and then continued on, past the chair and down the lane among the trees.

The evening before, he sat in the same chair at the same table. The dinner he had made for them warmed in the oven. A maelstrom of dust billowing redly in the sunset heralded her arrival and shortly the car pulled down the lane and stopped near the house. She came up the drive, slightly drunk and walking with great care as if negotiating a patch of ice. She smiled blearily at him. When she sat he could smell the smoke of the bar on her and she seemed to have applied more makeup since she'd left in the morning, more musky scent.

"Home is the hunter, home from the hills," she recited. "Home is the hunter, stoned to the gills."

"If you're talking about me, I'm not the one stoned to the gills," John Gload said. "At no six o'clock in the afternoon."

"Oh, Johnny. Be nice. I just had a nice afternoon."

"Doing what?"

"Visiting. A nice afternoon of visiting."

"Visiting in the bar, that would be."

"Yes. That would be."

"It just isn't dignified a woman your age in a bar."

"Oh, God," she said. "Dignity." She sat heavily, her legs thrust out. Her heels furrowed the dirt and in the rumpled hose the flesh of her legs seemed to sag from their bones.

"Why can't you just stay here? You got everything you need."

From the chair she gazed out vacantly, reached out without looking and patted the huge hand on the tabletop opposite her. "I care for you, Johnny, I do. But not everything. Not hardly."

"What do you need I haven't brought here for you? You tell me what it is and I'll try and get it."

"It's not things. I don't need things. You know that never meant nothing to me."

"What, then?"

"People, Johnny. The company of people. I'm not like you. You who could sit here alone in that chair for a week."

"I was people last time I checked."

"But you're your own world and I always have known that. You don't really need me and it's okay. I understand that and it's okay, it really is. I know you care about me, but I just need to see myself in other people."

"I do need you. I wisht you wouldn't say shit like that."

"Okay, you do."

"You say see yourself in other people. Good Christ, Francie. Let me tell you. People aren't mirrors. If they were, what you seen looking back at you would make your hair stand up. You don't want to see that."

Her hair had fallen in her eyes and she swept it back. Lipstick she had applied with a trembling hand earlier was blurred at the corner of her mouth.

"Just real people," she repeated.

"Bar people. Christ. They're not real people."

"They're real enough, John. And not all of them are drunks. Some people just go there for the socializing. Just to sit and gab."

"And to drink."

"A little bit of wine. Just because it's not something you do, because it's not Johnny's vice, doesn't make it bad necessarily. It makes me feel good. How can you not want that for me?"

"And who are they? A bunch of hayseeds and half-assed ranch hands. Dipshit farmers with their fat hands all over you."

"You used to be one. You told me so. You were a farmer yourself."

"I was a goddamn kid."

"And I don't need to be touched, Johnny. That's not it at all." She looked at him then and reached to stroke his dure cheek. John Gload stared at the ground.

"Yeah, well I'll tell you what *they* see. See a set of breasts and a vagina."

She laughed out loud. "Oh, God, you kill me, John. Vagina. In your way you are such a prude."

Looking long out over the trees and the sage flats, amber as an August wheat field beneath the dust of her earlier passing, she began to hum, a near imperceptible evocation of wind or of an infant mewing in a distant room. Gload leaned his ear toward her across the weather-checked tabletop to discern what air it was that had so quickly taken her and in so doing beheld for the first time the minute nodding affirmations of a palsy. He was reminded suddenly of a nun who'd been kind to him at the orphanage and the name they had given her affliction, St. Vitus' dance. Despite its name summoning images of whirling happiness, it was nonetheless for Gload ever after a sign of pitiful age. She had had a man's name, Bernard he thought, and she'd died one day nodding at her desk in front of a classroom of children, all horrified but one.

She hummed. Her eyes slowly closed as though by her own lullaby she slipped softly into sleep.

"What if I wasn't here?" he said.

She said dreamily, "Oh, let's not talk about that. You'll always be here to be my anchor."

"Dragging you down you mean."

"No, John. Holding me in place."

She turned in her chair and took his hand in both of hers atop the table. "We're okay now because I'm home to you and we'll have a nice dinner and we can sit and watch the sun go down if you want like two beautiful people in a movie. Can we do that, Johnny? I don't want to fight with you."

"Yeah. We can do that."

"Don't be mad at me. I can't take that."

"All right. I ain't mad at you."

"Did you make something? I smell something good."

"Just a roast. Nothing special."

"No, it sounds wonderful."

"And carrots and baby potatoes with the skin left on."

That night at her dressing table the woman John Gload would later call his wife sat massaging lotion onto her hands with a wringing motion and then with the backs of her hands patting the soft loose folds beneath her chin. All the while she stared at the image in the mirrors. From the bed Gload, feigning sleep, watched her. She tugged back the graying hair at her temples to dissolve for a moment the creases that swarmed about her eyes. Her hair was still thick as a horse's mane and Gload loved to lock his thick fingers in it. She touched at the corners of her lips, the cleft beneath her nose and then as if her arms could no longer support their weight, her hands collapsed to rest among the jars and tubes of ointments and balms, and the trembling that had recently befallen her set the tiny fluted vials of her perfumes with their jewel-like glass stoppers chittering softly. From the vanity's three mirrors three images stared out, each with red eyes brimming with the recognition of slow and irreversible decline.

After a time Gload hazarded a look and found her still sitting, and he watched with one burning eye the three images there until she rose from her stool stately and a little unsteady and came one last time to share their bed.

When he was done he stood back and it was a quaint agrarian pose he struck, the man stropping his face and neck with a bandana and leaning on the spud bar and behind him the slender black boles of the apple trees etched against a sky of splendrous color. He'd dug many such holes but none so fine or so deep. The sod and thin rich topsoil were laid aside in one pile, the stones and gravel he struggled through in another, and with a square-nosed shovel he'd skived the hole's edges sharp and plumb as though it might be entered in a county fair. It had taken him most of the day and at noon he'd walked back to the house to eat a pear and drink two glasses of water and then had returned to his work, clambering down into the hole with the leaned metal spud bar for support. He encountered rocks the size of men's heads as he went down and the roots of the apple trees like cables as the hole took its shape and he was forced to chop them away with the short-handled ax he'd brought. In doing so he feared for the life of the trees but he had little choice and hoped finally that the roots would take hold anew when the hole was filled.

He stopped frequently in the course of his endeavors, leaning on the polished shovel handle or on the long metal bar with its spaded end and shaking his head in amused resignation at the ravages of his advancing age. Still, he heaved obdurate stones from the hole that would have given trouble to much younger men and he drew satisfaction from that.

The sun he had welcomed early for its warmth on his face and that had scalded his neck later now threw his long shadow across the hole. He saw a large red stone in a corner of the hole that might cause discomfort to whoever rested there, so he clambered back down and with the long-handled bar prized the intransigent stone from its place where it had lain for ten thousand years and threw it out. Once again at the hole's edge he assessed it and checked its depth against the length of the bar and declared himself satisfied.

Had she been looking closely she might have seen the piles of fresh soil among the orchard trees but she wasn't. She had tilted down the car's rearview mirror as she drove down the lane and seemed to be studying herself in it. John Gload was once again in his chair. He had showered and changed out of his soaked and foul coveralls and shirt and his wet hair was plastered along his head. She swung open the door and stepped out and stood unsteadily before him.

"Now what'd you go and do?" he said.

"I thought it might make your old hag look a little younger."

"It's red."

"Auburn, Johnny." She pulled a strand of hair in front of her face and looked at it. "You don't like it," she said.

"I do like it. I like it quite a little bit." The chair creaked as he stood up and he took her by the hand. Like a child she allowed herself to be led inside, as she walked woodenly still examining a strand of hair. He said, "You look like a million bucks."

There was a small short lamp on the table in the modest dining room and in its pool of wan light they ate their dinner wordlessly. Her juice glass held her favorite sweet wine, the color of gasoline. She watched John Gload eat, the fork in his fist like a fork from a child's tea set. But he was neat and his manners were oddly courtly and she smiled at him over the rim of her glass. Afterward they sat in the chairs at the little table outside the door that Gload favored to read his newspaper. The river rolling in its primordial channel was invisible but clouds lay above it, a pale serpentine parody, kinetic and aswim with gulls. They spoke little and Francie seemed happy to listen to the conversations of small birds from the arbor, and from their cool holes the shrill piping of ground squirrels. The tops of the hills behind the house were softly aflame with scarlet sunset and they watched mule deer walk unalarmed through the conflagration like the prophets of Daniel.

She had refilled her glass after dinner and brought it with her, in her unstable state bearing it before her two-handed like a ciborium. When she drank the last of it and set the glass down her hand trembled. "Oh, my," she said. Gload had been watching and laid his hand over hers as though warming a young bird fallen from its nest.

"Why don't you go lay down for a while," he said. "I'll take care of that little bit of dishes."

"You wouldn't mind?"

"Go on. You look wore out."

"You're not supposed to say that to a lady."

He looked into her eyes and they were laced with red, her face with its faded makeup was ashen and the lines beneath her eyes and at the corners of her mouth seemed drawn with ink. "You look tired is all. How's that?"

"Oh, it doesn't matter."

He stood at the sink when he'd finished, watching a spring storm form up in the east, newly arrived birds roiling up before the verdigris clouds like autumn leaves. The water ran from the tap and after a long while he noticed it and screwed down the handles and stood once again looking out.

He came from the closet holding it, saying to her in a whisper, "I always liked this on you." The thin beige draperies rose and riffled on the breeze and the sky framed in the window sash was streaked with distant rain. The room had taken on an odd green cast. He sat in a chair by the bed for some time, watching her sleep and he held across his arms like an offering the green dress he had bought for her one year on a trip to Billings. Storm clouds drug their tentacles across the sageland ten miles to the east but he could smell the rain on the air. As if it grew in a window box he could smell the sage. Then he stood, still watching her, with the bed's other pillow in his hands.

Her movements under him he thought were not unlike those of their lovemaking, her squirming and bucking and even when she stopped and he pulled the pillow away her face was dreamy, her eyes half-closed as if on the verge of mere gratified sleep or rapture.

Gload removed her clothes and laid them aside—they smelled

of the bar, perhaps of other men—and he buttoned on the green dress that had been his favorite, his huge brutal hands fumbling at the buttons and impossible hooks and at an antique collar pin she had treasured. "This makes your eyes look greener," he said, but he spoke of an image of memory only, as in fact the light was gone from them and what he could see beneath the half-closed papery lids seemed leached of color.

From the bureau he selected one of her handkerchiefs, its edges trimmed in lace. He held it to his nose, folded it neatly, and put it in a rear pocket. He slid his hands beneath her, at neck and knees, and took her up. She weighed nothing. At the hole he bent and laid her in the grass gently as if to prevent waking her and went around to the opposite side and slid down into the cool of the earth. He lifted her once again and laid her down, arranging the folds of the dress around her legs modestly, and he crossed her arms on her chest, thought better of it and laid them beside her in the hole. Raindrops now, like falling coins, rattled through the sage south of the orchard. He touched her cheek, her hair newly red, laid the handkerchief over her face and climbed with difficulty out of the hole for the third time. With the spade he had left there leaned against a tree for that purpose he covered her over, not looking down but working at the two piles with an easy rhythm and listening to his own breathing, to the call of birds among the trees and the rain in earnest then hissing in the branches.

That night he lay on the selfsame bed and called on his dream of plowing, furrowing the ground over and over as the landscape reeled past and kits took his scent and the gulls came. Sleep, though, would not come and so he lay smoking in the dark. He strained to hear above the wind the pong of suspended harrow tines. Rain lashed the windowpanes and muddied the grassless square plot in the apple trees and John Gload imagined a voracious reticulum of roots beneath the orchard plot stirring, then writhing like a nest of snakes and finally, in the damp dark, winning purchase once again in earth, in bones.

The day following was warm and windy and he spent it putting the house in good order. He hosed off his digging tools and hung them in the shed. He aligned her shoes at the bottom of the closet and he washed and hung her clothes. Several times he went down the lane and from various points stood looking into the grove of greening fruit trees, the weave of their wild, untended branches astir with birds. He waited each time to hear the clash of his rustic windchime and then he went slewing back up the road.

He was standing so in the lane two days later with his hands in his rear pockets when he saw the dust of the approaching patrol cars and he went again unhurriedly to his garden chair to wait. Since the brief rains the twisted copse was furred with inchoate green, at his feet the crocuses and breaching tulips, nodding trumpets of the daffodils, yellow beyond yellow in the sun.

FIFTEEN

In later years, and at unexpected times, the thought came to him that it had been a ridiculous place for his life to come apart and it took little more than a linoleum pattern beneath his feet or the jangle of dropped silverware to dizzy him and make his mouth go dry.

He'd gone to the hospital shortly before noontime. In the ICU waiting room he sat across from an elderly woman who held in one sclerous hand a rosary of bloodred beads, covering her eyes with the other as though unable to bear the sight of the world beyond her memories. He'd fallen asleep in the plastic chair with his head lolling and his mouth ajar and he had nearly missed her as she swept through with one arm stuck in the sleeve of an overcoat as though she were going out somewhere. He'd not seen her in two weeks and his heart throbbed at the sight of her. She had grown thinner and her hair was cut in some new way. He asked her to lunch and she stood frozen looking at him with her arm in the coat and then looking for a long moment beyond him and she seemed to be making some kind of decision. She said she did not have much time but that they could eat in the cafeteria. They rode the elevator in silence, Val staring foolishly at her white shoes, at her perfect calves in their nurse's hose, white as bandages.

He had taken a tray and absently pointed at a stack of grilled cheese sandwiches. She would not eat anything and she chose a table in the center of the crowded cafeteria.

He set the tray down and when they sat he said, "How are things going?"

"They're going fine."

He pointed to the coat she had draped over the corner of the table. "Were you going out somewhere for lunch?"

"Not really."

"Not really? You were or you weren't."

"You don't need to talk to me like that, Val. I'm not one of your perps."

"That's not a word anybody says. That's a TV word."

"Well, Val, my point is I'm not an investigation."

"No, it's just that you were going somewhere because you had your coat so you were going out. I don't have to be a cop to figure that."

Her hands were in her lap hidden from him by the table and she stared into them.

"I am so tired of it, Val."

He looked at her. "If you could tell me what 'it' is, I would appreciate it."

"It," she said. At the serving line a metal tray was dropped and it clattered on the floor, the silverware skittering. "Struggling. Tired of struggling."

He studied her across the table. Her hair was a kind of short boy cut and there were streaks of lighter blond in it. In the hollow of her lovely slender neck rested a tiny silver dolphin on a strand of chain, a charm he had not given her and had never seen before and at the sight of it the blood drained from everywhere and seemed to pool cold in the bottom of his stomach. Her words after that fell on his head like blows, forcing his eyes to the floor where he beheld the linoleum's pattern swimming and blurred.

"We seem to struggle at everything," she said. "To find the energy to talk. To find time to be who we really are."

"Riddles. These are just crazy riddles, goddamn it, Glenda." He swung his eyes up to her face briefly. "I know who I am. But I look at you now and I think maybe you're finding out you're somebody else. That you're making yourself into somebody else."

"That's just it exactly, Val. You've always known who you were. But I was just a part of you. And I'm seeing that being part of you isn't enough. It's not fair to me."

He was close to weeping in frustration. "I never said anything ever, did I? Jesus. Fair? It wasn't like I ever said don't change anything. I wouldn't have cared about your hair."

"Christ, Val, it isn't about my hair."

With his head bowed he looked to be a man at prayer. His clasped hands as he sought to maintain some grasp on the world were white and the veins in his forearms stood out. But the world became in an instant nothing more than a sphere encompassing the two of them, a metal tray, a tabletop—all else beyond an indiscernible realm without meaning.

"No, not your hair," he said. "Not about your hair at all but about somebody else, about some other motherfucker." He stopped and breathed deeply. He stared at the floor. "It's a doctor, am I correct? And maybe he's the bwana with all the dead heads in his house and the fucking tasseled shoes. Is he here right now? I'll bet the fucker's here right now." He made a show of looking around the room, though he could have seen nothing at that moment beyond the end of his arm. "It's like a bad movie, like a movie you've seen a hundred times."

"I didn't say it was anyone." Her voice came at him flat and cold.

"But it is."

There seemed not the slightest bit of shame in her. She looked straight ahead at nothing. She took a breath. "I have been seeing someone."

He forced himself to raise his head and he wore a look of incredulity. "You're married to *me*. You can't be *seeing* someone."

"Nevertheless."

The security guard rose with some effort from behind a table where he'd been reading a newspaper. His shirt hung from his distended paunch and as he walked toward them he tucked the tails into the tops of his trousers. He stood beside the table with his hands crossed and resting atop his stomach. Indistinct tattoos on the back of one wrist and above each knuckle. He stood for some time looking from Millimaki to his wife and listening. Finally Millimaki looked up. The man was in his sixties and wore a utility belt hung with keys and a flashlight and a canister of mace.

"We're having a private conversation."

"Not all that private, Deputy, it turns out, because I could hear it over yonder."

"This is private."

"Maybe this ain't the place for this sort of business."

Millimaki ignored him. Glenda said, "We're just leaving."

"We're not just leaving."

"Deputy," the man said. "Conductation of this business to be done elsewhere."

Through the sudden diminishment of the world the man had become a vague and watery shape uttering words from far away. Millimaki glanced briefly to his left. "Fuck off. That's not even a word."

"Val, stop it."

"Fuck your conductation." He brought his hands up to the tabletop, his fists clenched. His ears rang strangely, as if he'd been clubbed.

"And it's a doctor," he said. "Couldn't it have been at least a fucking janitor?"

"It doesn't matter who it is."

"And he gave you that chain, is that not correct? That fish." He'd meant to point but as if they did not belong to him his hands rose toward her pale neck in a clutching gesture.

Her hand went reflexively to her throat. "Please please stop."

"A fucking doctor," he repeated. "All this mystery about doctors, all this, whatever, glorification." His voice was rising. People at the nearby tables had begun to stare. "All the fucking mystery. Cutting and sawing and rooting around. Christ, they're high-priced carpenters. They're nothing."

The guard said, "Deputy, I'm asking please."

Glenda buried her face in her hands, not crying, not ashamed, Val noted, but merely embarrassed.

Through her fingers she said wearily, "Oh, Val."

"I would cut every goddamn one of them from crotch to eyeball, I swear to Christ."

She took down her hands. Her perfect face was hard and

smooth as topaz. In a harsh whisper she said, "My God, Val. You're scaring people. You're wearing a gun. That scares people."

He leaned closer to her, the silver neck charm inches from his face. "Okay," he whispered. "Exactly. And how about if I take this gun and shove it up your doctor's ass? I could do that. I could do that just for a smile."

"That's enough, Val. This is a public place."

The security guard had been staring at Glenda's throat or perhaps trying to see down the front of her uniform. His left hand hovered near the mace canister at his belt. "Like the young lady says, pardner," he said. "Not here, not at this time."

"Yes," Millimaki said. "A public place. And it just now occurred to me why you decided to tell me all this here, because of your misguided idea that I would not do anything to embarrass you and this is the part where you're oh so very fucking wrong." He wiped a sleeve across his eyes and stood up. From the foggy periphery of his vision he noted the shape of the guard moving toward him. "Ladies and gentlemen, I am a Copper County sheriff's deputy officer can I have your attention I am a law enforcement officer and my wife has just informed me she is *seeing someone* and please remain calm. I assure all present that should he be here I will not at this time discharge my firearm into the anal region of the medical professional who is fucking my wife."

Two days later he sat lacing his boots on a long varnished bench in the locker room at the end of his shift, through the diamond mesh of the high windows a luminous light the color of wheat. He did not look up at the sound of boot heels coming down the row of lockers.

John Gload that night had been more reticent than usual and sat smoking quietly in his cell in the dark. The night wore on. Even the craziest of the men in their cages were subdued, as though the old man had cast a spell on them that he might have peace for his night's plowing and eventual sleep. Millimaki had himself barely slept since his seizure of grief and rage at the hospital and his shift beneath the tube lights had seemed without end.

Now Voyle Dobek stood over him. "I seen you in the park talking to Gload," he said. Against the bright backdrop of the morning's light, when Millimaki looked up, Dobek's figure was in shadow, his breath that close a nauseating admixture of coffee and Skoal. Millimaki's stomach lurched. The act of lacing his boots in his state of exhaustion seemed impossible work. He stared stupidly at hands suddenly as inept as a toddler's. Beside his scuffed boot toes Dobek's spit-shined Wellingtons were dazzling.

"How can you sit and talk to a piece of shit like that?" Dobek said.

"Which exactly piece of shit would we be talking about, Voyle? I thought they were all pieces of shit to you."

"Your old psycho." He effected a nasal sound of disgust. "The way you sit out there."

"You pretty much nailed it, Voyle. Two guys, a bench, the exchange of words. That's how it's done."

"No, that ain't the way you do it, asshole. Not out there."

"Out where?"

"Out in the public. Where the civilians can see you."

"Haven't noticed anybody watching."

"You'd be surprised. The fuckers see everything."

"I don't know what there is to see, Voyle. Two guys sitting on a bench."

"There's a right fucking way and a wrong fucking way is what I'm telling you and you don't sit out there with a psycho piece of shit for the citizens to see. If *you* don't give a shit." He waved a hand vaguely about the vacant room. "It looks bad on us."

"I'm very sorry, Officer Dobek," Millimaki said. "To make you look bad would just about ruin my whole entire day."

"I had you pegged as a smart-ass from the minute you come on. I was willing to give you the benefit of the doubt. But then I don't know." He straightened his back, looked around the room as if to address an audience. "Heard about your little performance up at the hospital. I guess if my wife was fucking some doctor, it might make me out to be a smart-ass too."

Because he was sitting down and had to come up off the bench as he swung, the uppercut caught Dobek squarely in the groin and Millimaki felt the soft give of the man's balls. His fist seemed to disappear and he had just enough time to pull back before the big man fell, clattering to the floor like a bagful of loose change as his billy, keys, cuffs and gun butt hit the tile. When from the other side of the lockers men came running, Val was astride the man's back with his nightstick under Dobek's chin and may well have choked him to death as he remembered nothing. He had heard the word "wife" come from Dobek's mouth, later remembered just that, as if like a cartoon voice balloon it hung in the air, or like a plume of winter breath, and after that there was nothing—a void washed in red.

As if drunk he arrived home with no memory either of the drive and he sat in his recliner staring out at the scarcely moving portraiture of the brilliant day—clouds, quavering branches heavy with leaf, a nervous sparrow on the windowsill. He became aware of a terrible odor and got up and walked about the room and sniffed at the dog, asleep on his bed. "You didn't puke somewhere, Tom, did you, bud?" He walked into the empty bedroom and found the smell there too and realized it was him, on him. He shucked his pants and saw the stain on his knees then, vomit he must have knelt in while riding Voyle Dobek like some giant tortoise in a crimson sea of oblivion.

Even as Millimaki closed the office door, the sheriff said, "I don't know what it is but we've got to get at this problem and solve it right fucking now."

"Yes, sir."

"My ass, 'Yes, sir.' Spit it out, Val. I cannot have my officers killing each other in the locker room."

"It was a difference of opinion."

"Yes, no shit." He called, "Raylene." Shortly the secretary's head appeared in the door. "Raylene, would you please do me the favor of going down to the dispensary and getting me some aspirin."

"There's some right there in front of you, in the drawer."

"I've been looking for it for fifteen minutes."

"Oh, all right. For goodness' sake, if your head wasn't attached."

He listened to her heels clack-clacking down the marble hallway.

"She is a wonderful woman but cursed with a lively curiosity and a certain lack of discretion in matters concerning interdepartmental conflict. If you understand. I don't have a headache, not counting, metaphorically, you and Dobek."

"I understand."

"And did you in fact blindside Officer Dobek in the locker room as he came around the corner?"

Millimaki stared at him.

"I didn't think so. And I might add that it speaks well for you that no one has come forward to corroborate his dim recollection of events."

"There wasn't anybody around at the time."

"That doesn't sometimes make a bit of difference."

"It was just me and him there."

"I imagine before the day is out Raylene will be able to tell me exactly what happened, but if you'd like to speed the process."

"It was a difference—"

"Of fucking opinion. Yes, I got that the first time."

"He said something about my wife."

The sheriff stood up then, raked a hand through his newly barbered hair, and called out, "Raylene." There was no answer. He said, "You know that I know what kind of a cop Dobek is, Val, do you not? What kind of man?"

"I have no way of knowing."

"Well, goddamn it, yes you do. You see these two round things on the front of my face?"

"Yes, sir."

"Voyle is just a guy who's been around too long and somewhere or other took the other course." He examined his nails. "He is a burdensome man."

Millimaki said, "It's not what started it but he seemed to object to me talking to Gload."

"Did you tell him I asked you to?"

"No, sir. I guess I figured that was between you and me."

"I'll talk to Voyle about that. In the meantime you're taking two days off. My suggestion, from the look of you, would be to try and sleep most of that time." He stood with his hands on the desktop, his pale eyes looking beyond Val's head to the door, and called out once again to his secretary. When he got no response he said, "Your behavior is not acceptable, Deputy Millimaki, and will not be tolerated. That being said, I would have done the same thing to that big prick and if a word of that last sentence leaves this room other than in your thick head you will be gone forever and I would not recommend you for a crossing guard." Into the ensuing quiet came the rapid clacking of Raylene's heels down the corridor and the sheriff said, "And now I'm going to on account of you have to take two aspirins I don't need because she'll sure as hell sit here and watch me. So I have you to blame also for the subsequent heartburn." He sat abruptly into his chair. "You'll not be seen here until your shift Thursday night." By way of augmenting his performance, as Raylene came into the room he said gruffly, "First and last warning, Deputy Millimaki. Now get your ass out of here."

That night he sat at his table once again and the fire of old lodgepole he had set in the fireplace veered and swayed with the wind that came down the old river rock chimney. The flames rose up suddenly, flaring high into the pipe as though like a sprite or comet they would escape out into the night and leave a cold jumble of blackened logs on the grate. The dog raised his head from his extended paws and stared at the fire. He looked at Millimaki and with a sigh lay back again with his square snout atop his forelegs and the fire moaned up the flue. In the brief silences lulls in the wind afforded Millimaki could hear coyotes in the hills calling across the dark.

He slept on the couch opposite the fire, wrapped in a quilt

his sister had given them for a wedding present and through his sleep low shapes prowled, only their slavering mouths visible, phosphorescent as seafoam, snuffling at the cupboard doors and running their rough tongues along the cutting board where he'd earlier trimmed a piece of meat, and in the dream the shapeless predators clawing at the walls and floorboards as if seeking something and not finding it turned their glowing muzzles toward him.

When he awoke the front door stood rocking open on its antique hinges, the trapezoid of milky light it admitted falling across the kitchen floor and illuminating a shirring flotsam of brittle box elder leaves. With his heart throbbing wildly against the planks of his ribs he latched the door and shot home the old-fashioned slidebolt and in his bare feet went about the house holding a pair of fire tongs like a baseball bat, throwing light switches and moving into the three small side rooms, looking behind doors and inside closets. He suddenly felt foolish, standing in his own bedroom with sooty hands around the tongs. His pistol hung in its belt from a chairback in the kitchen. "Tongs," he said aloud. "You're a dangerous man." He went to the outer room and added a split of pine to the coals, stirring them alive with the fire tongs, and curled once more in the goose down as the breathing embers provoked the dog's smoldering eyes from the dark.

Hours later his eyes opened to window light golden as grain dust and Tom sat staring into his face as though willing him awake for his breakfast.

SIXTEEN

The elms in full leaf shuddered above him and through the verdure he could make out an occasional star, a shard of moon. From their secret fissures in the courthouse dome, bats came afield, darting even beneath the trees for the legions of big moths so abundant there that night they blundered against Millimaki's face like the brush of an eyelash.

For his lunch he had an apple and a hard roll he had found in the bread drawer at home, having no idea of its age other than it was somewhere short of old enough to grow mold. He had a four-inch round of hard salami and on the bench under the elms he alternated bites of meat and bread and for dessert ate the apple, cold and hard, while stretched out on the bench like a vagrant, one hand behind his head and his eyes on the stars that sought him out beneath the green cupola.

When he used the bathroom on his return to the jail, the haggard face in the mirror above the sink wore on its forehead a smudge of moth soot like the ashes left from a priest's thumb long years ago.

When Millimaki returned to escort duty after his involuntary time off, the old killer had grown more fond and familiar, taking the deputy's hand in his between the bars and holding it there a long while. He seemed troubled by Millimaki's silences and stared at him with basset hound eyes. Wexler in Millimaki's absence had been Gload's escort and companion but the old man spoke little of him. "My pal Weldon," he would say. "My old buddy Weldon." Despite frequent inquiries Millimaki divulged little more than that his wife at the end of her day stayed with a girlfriend in town. It might be true, he thought. It might be true.

Gload, an inveterate reader of newspapers, had noted that county extension agents statewide were predicting record harvests and absurd per-bushel prices. Millimaki sat with a letter from his sister in his lap and Gload spoke of machinery and the cost of diesel fuel, in the slant of surgical light from the overhead fluorescents figuring and refiguring on his yellow legal pad the amount of money he and his father might have realized from harvesting the field of his dreams, imagining that sere and rocky plot an animated gilded drapery of ripe wheat. He seemed very much taken with the notion.

"Can that be right," he said incredulously, "five dollars a bushel?"

Millimaki glanced up briefly. "I guess it is, if that's what the paper says."

"You're in the wrong business, Valentine. You ought to of stayed on the farm. You'd have chains on your neck and a Coupe de Ville under your ass."

"I don't think it would look too good on me," Millimaki said distantly.

Gload returned to his calculations, his huge disembodied hands like cumbersome string puppets moving across the yellow page. It was near three in the morning and Millimaki sat with his legs crossed reading his sister's letter and eating a sandwich made of cheese and bread which he balanced on his knee. News of her daughter, her husband, news of a world that seemed of another universe. The world for these men was reduced to floor, ceiling, walls, and bars, and his own differed little—an unfixed cubicle of solitude that, like a carapace, went with him everywhere and was impervious to the warming sun or the wind in the trees or even the unconditional affections of a sister who seemed not to care he did not write in return and send his love, which she deserved.

He ate. The dry bread and questionable cheese turned to a clot of clay in his mouth. He read the letter to the end and considered the PS which again conveyed his sister's desire to solve the mystery of their mother. Of their abandonment. "PS," she wrote. "Do you think Daddy had someone else?" But no. He'd barely had enough affection for the three of them and Millimaki could not imagine the old man mustering the energy to lavish embraces and scalding forbidden kisses on some other, the flame he carried in his tight paunch barely sufficient to propel him through the days and seasons and years of numbing labor. Little but stone remained of him at the end of the day. The extent of his tenderness in all the years was an occasional squeeze of the shoulder or a tousle of the hair. He had seen his parents kiss only once.

From the shadowed recess of John Gload's cell the old man's voice came softly: "I have got one letter in my whole life," nearly a whisper, as if the presence of a man there reading a letter merely stirred a memory which he may have shared with the darkness, may not even have spoken aloud. "It was from the maid in the house where I spent some years as a kid. I can remember the whole thing, but only because it was short. The nigger gal's name was Vera Blue. She said, 'Dear John-Jee, Miss Goldie dead from a stomach sickness down here in Thermopolis. She asked about you at the end. I thought you would want to know she was dead. From a stomach cancer. Your friend, Vera Blue.' That's it, word for word." Gload made his chuckling noise. "Ain't that a kick? If I could get rid of old worthless shit like that out of my head I'd have room for more important stuff."

Millimaki said, "I'm sorry. What?" He stared blankly at the writing on the page and the old man's voice, so soft and distant, had barely registered. He'd only half heard. "What stuff?"

"Hell, kid, I don't know. Algebra maybe, or the business with triangles and shapes and all. That always interested me. What's that, geometry?"

"I believe it is."

"Those old Greeks or whatever they were and their geometry. Or Romans. And how about this while we're at it. Been stuck in my head for, hell, fifty, sixty years. I read it of all places off the back of a little fancy pillow: *Ex nihilo nihil fit.* Probably didn't say it right but I goddamn remember how it was spelled." Which he did, letter by letter for Millimaki's benefit, in the end rapping the smooth dome of his skull with his knuckles. "Now how did that stay in there? Don't even know what lingo that is."

"It's Latin," Millimaki said, "but I don't know what it means exactly."

"By God, you are a college boy."

"More because I was an altar boy."

"Sweet Jesus, an altar boy." Gload made the blowing noise that replicated a laugh. "I'm partnered up with a goddamn altar boy."

Val sat back, folded the letter carefully and returned it to its envelope. He sat tapping it on the heel of his boot. He picked up the sandwich and looked at what remained for a moment and threw it into the paper bag. From the tenebrous cages issued the snores and rustlings of his charges which in the previous long months had become as familiar to him as wind in the box elders around his home. After several minutes, from the near darkness, he heard John Gload say, "I can take it, Valentine. Nobody needs to be out there defending my honor."

Millimaki stared into the ink of the old man's cell. He could, as before, only see Gload's hands, now folded like a schoolboy's atop his writing desk.

"You've lost me," he said.

"I've dealt with cops would make him look like a goddamn fairy princess. He ain't nothing."

Millimaki thought the old man may have slipped off into his secret netherworld yet again, as he had after Sidney White had been brought in, so he merely sat and said nothing.

"You hear me, Val? Dobek's nothing but shit in a shirt. Don't be getting yourself strung out on account of me."

"What the hell are you talking about?"

"Heard about your little dust-up. And I do appreciate it, don't get me wrong."

"Somebody around here ought to have his lips riveted. And whatever you think, you think wrong. That had not one goddamn thing to do with you."

"All right, Deptee."

"Nothing to do with you and furthermore none of your goddamn business, either."

In his cage Gload was smiling, his brutal illuminated hands piously folded. "Yessir," he said.

Millimaki's sleeplessness worsened. No combination of the sheriff's beer elixir or Moon's organic pills provided relief. He shifted fitfully on the recliner or the couch beneath strangling sheets. He tried sleeping on an air mattress set in front of the fireplace and he tried the same arrangement on the open porch and was beset by mosquitoes. The one place he would not sleep or attempt to sleep was the bed he had shared with Glenda, where the most invidious ghost of all those that populated his hours, awake and asleep, resided.

In a snatch of sleep in his porch chair he dreamt his wife approaching in a strange bridal bedizenment of soiled bandages, a rope of intravenous tubes accoutering her neck. She walked up the lane in her gown of rags but seemed to come no nearer as though her small feet could find no purchase but her smile was as luminous as the sun. And so by the time he made his way from the porch chair to the jangling phone his heart hammered in his chest. It was not undone. Such portent in dream was not the stuff of mere wishing because what power do we have to shape our dreams? He could reason. He could even plead. Millimaki's hand above the phone trembled.

But it was not his wife and perhaps it was not her either in the dream but some other luminous creature meant to torment him with her apocryphal smile. He'd been home for less than three hours and had slept little of that time and so when he set out to search for the girl unaccountably lost among the blank tableland grain fields of Pondera County he was in sorry plight—burning eyes, the taste of ashes in his mouth. His heart chugged in his chest dull and distant and his veins seemed to pump lead to his sodden limbs. But awake, at least, he was not at the mercy of his dreams, a wilderness of guile where he wandered lost and powerless.

"You don't have to go," the sheriff said. "I could call over to Silver Bow and have them send someone."

Val looked down at his feet in the worn leather moccasins. He looked out the window at the cottonwoods far down along the creek, and the water glimpsed among the trunks and quavering leaves ran sleek and aluminum like the backs of the cutthroat in their secret holes. Another day, what seemed long ago, he and his wife might have gone there together.

"That's all right, Sheriff. Tom could use the work."

"You sure about this? I know you haven't had time for much sleep."

The skewed apparitional Glenda still lingered in his head. "Sleep," he said wistfully. "No, sir. I just figured out here recently it's overrated. I just need to get dressed and load my gear."

Wexler let himself in through the sally gate and went along the corridor with a martial air, looking neither left nor right and ignoring the sounds from behind the bars that followed him. His name sung in falsetto. Kissing noises. Moans of mock ecstasy. There would be time enough, he thought. And Dobek since his humiliation in the locker room would require little urging to exercise his rage on these animals in the blind hours of the night. In and out, a visitation as silent as a priest. At that hour bruises and broken teeth became mere figments sprung from the delirium of caged men. They may slip and fall. And who knew but that they might inflict such pain upon themselves?

Thus comforted he stood before John Gload's cell door. The old man looked up. The pencil he held was little more than three inches long, worn from his fevered doodling and geoponic tabulations and he held it up.

"I could use a new pencil, Weldon."

"I'll see about it."

"And where's our friend Deputy Millimaki?"

Wexler snorted. "Off with Rin Tin Tin on one of his wild-goose chases."

"Seems like he just got off shift. Didn't leave him much time at home."

"Ain't nobody there but that shepherd dog anyways."

"His missus?"

"Gone. Run off."

"My, my," Gload said. He wagged his great head sadly. "That's got to be tough on a young guy."

"I wouldn't spend any time feeling sorry for him. Women don't stray unless you're not getting the job done."

"So she's taken up with somebody?"

"That's the word. She's a good-looking little gal. She needs to be getting it somewheres." Wexler examined the backs of his hands. "I might take a run at her myself." He favored the old man with a vulpine leer. Gload forced a smile. He realized he was blunting the stub of pencil, wearing a deep black hole in his tablet.

Wexler took up Millimaki's chair and swung it around as if he might sit in it, then reconsidered. He affected a businesslike tone. "John, I'm taking you out today. I got your topo maps for north of the river and I want to see something come of 'em. No more dicking around."

"You're taking me out?"

"That's right. And on my own time."

"And you got maps?"

"I got maps and I want to see some fucking Xs and Os on the sonsofbitches."

"What about Millimaki? I more or less promised him I'd go on out there with him."

"Number one, he ain't here. Two, like I said before, John, I'm the ranking officer. Deputy Shitkicker made you promises he couldn't keep."

"So you're taking me out," Gload said.

"One o'clock. Have your lunch and we'll take a nice drive in the country and find some of your vics and put some poor people's minds to rest for once and for all."

"Val or no Val, I could sure use a little stretch of the legs." He pointed toward the streaked street level windows, golden with August light. "Get out in some natural sunshine."

"This ain't a picnic, John. And by the way, another snipe hunt and things might get unpleasant for you around here. Deputy Dobek has a kind of hard-on about you already. It's my fucking day off. I expect to come back with something."

"I'm just plumb grateful, Weldon," John Gload said. "I know once I get out there again it'll all come back to me."

When Wexler had gone, John Gload sat for a moment, his arm slung over the top slat of his chair. He rose and made a brief circuit of the cell, as it could only be brief, picking up in turn his accumulated wealth: a comb, a bar of soap, balled socks on a shelf. Pencil sharpener in the shape of a blue toad. He put his toothbrush in his shirt pocket, stood thinking, put it back on the shelf. Empty tablets. Magazines. Among them a John Deere dealership catalogue given him by Valentine Millimaki, which he transferred to the top of the pile. He smoothed the blanket atop his bed. Finally he sat once again. He tore loose several pages from the legal pad covered in his childish hand with smeared additions and subtractions and theoretical fields apportioned by theoretical acres, in the margins his doodlings of fabulous creatures and esoteric runes which occupied his hands while he considered perhaps the rich other-life of gentleman farmer, partnered with a father long ago frozen in the bull pines of Fergus County. He folded these neatly and buttoned them in his breast pocket and settled back to await his lunch.

SEVENTEEN

In the far west beyond the Teton Breaks, the Front Range marked the seeming edge of the world. Late August and the high cirques harbored yet crescents and stripes of snow, and in the summer haze they appeared to have been daubed on the purple-blue backcloth with a palette knife. Millimaki had arrived at the field and stood outside his sheriff's department Blazer looking out over the incalculable expanse of grain fields, much of it already cut to stubble, stretching away in all directions. They broke against the mountains like a blond sea. His father's rocky acreage had never looked like this. John Gload would have been agog.

Some small birds swarmed soundlessly in the distance. The dog sat erect in the backseat of the truck. Millimaki thought about the girl. And he remembered that ten years earlier, before he'd come on the force, a schoolteacher had been abducted and raped and left impaled on a duckfoot plow twelve miles to the east of where he stood. He wondered what in this beautiful country could inspire such evil. As if the wind that swept down from those bleak and frozen crags carried on it, like a microbe to infest the blood, the appetite of wolf and bear.

A cloud of dust appeared on the county road and he and the dog watched it approach. A sheriff's cruiser pulled in beside Millimaki's rig and a young deputy rolled down his window and said, "Just follow me. It's down the way a bit." He backed out and together they drove a half mile east and then north again and pulled through a wire gate and parked beside a small blue car.

The young man came toward Millimaki with his hand outstretched. He was taller than Millimaki and about his age. His hair beneath the Pondera County Sheriff's Department cap was an outrageous red, approaching orange, and every inch of visible skin was freckled.

"Malmberg," he said. "They call me Red."

"That's crazy," Millimaki said. "Where'd they come up with that?"

"Yeah. Go figure."

"What's with the tape?" Val said. "Must have taken about a half mile of it." The field was enclosed by yellow crime scene tape strung between cocked haphazard dowels pressed into the soil like a barrier erected by circus clowns and it snapped and fluttered and threatened to kite off on the wind.

"Yeah, no shit. I strung it myself." Malmberg pointed toward a rank of combines at the field's edge, new expensive machines with enclosed cabs, header blades with their rows of gleaming spring tines aligned. They seemed animate and rapacious and the sun turned their windshields to diamond.

"Old Farmer Brown wanted to roll in here and start to cutting. This was the only way I could keep him out. Says he's got something like a bazillion dollars sitting here and it's somebody's ass if it don't get cut more or less right away. I believe mine was the ass he was talking about. Anyways, I ain't too worried about it." He swung his arm east to west across the barley field in a papal gesture. "He ain't going to be too happy regardless." The grain was thoroughly trod, rows of parallel tracks where sheriffs and volunteers had ranged through and the ground was amber with grain as though it had been sown anew.

"We walked the whole shitteree, up and back. Nothing. Tracks go in and don't come out. Somebody thought she was picked up on that little bitty road at the end of this thing, but there ain't any tracks. Not a one. It's like she just flew away."

"What about over there?"

"It's a ditch. You got to be right on top of it to see it. There's no more than six inches of water in it now."

"Did you walk it?"

"Well, I didn't, personally, but it got walked. Like I said, it's nothing more'n a trickle. Not like you could have drownded in it."

"This her car?"

"We've been all through it."

They stood there looking. A gust came down off the Front Range and the field came alive, shuddering and undulant like a cat's back and issuing a long forlorn sigh.

"What do you think?" Millimaki said.

"I think if she'd wanted to disappear she'd had to of caught a bus and somebody or other would of seen her."

"True enough."

"If she'd wanted to disappear permanently for good she'd just as soon driven that piece of shit up there." Malmberg turned and pointed a milky and mottled hand toward the sawblade peaks. "And find a pile of brush the hell and gone. Way on up."

"That's what you'd think."

"Wouldn't you?"

"I guess most anybody with a lick of sense would."

The deputy stared long and longingly into the west. He gouged a hole in the ground with the toe of his boot, leaned and spat into it. "You know about her, right? Did they tell you?"

"Yeah, they told me," Val said. "I remember reading about it. But I didn't know all the fine points."

"She wasn't one of these bad kids. Just a kind of average girl. It was a hell of a thing. She'd grown up with every one of them kids."

"She might turn up yet, right as rain."

"A hell of a thing." The deputy went on as if he hadn't heard. "I got a twelve-year-old boy. Not much younger'n them boys that did that to her. Here after that happened for a week or so I looked at him like he might be some kind of different creature. I couldn't help it. We didn't raise him that way but still. He knew something was wrong, too. He finally just came up and got on my lap and started crying. Kids know a lot more than what you give them credit for, don't they?"

"I don't know."

"No kids?"

"No."

"You'll see," he said. "You just wait."

Malmberg's radio came to life and he went to his car. Millimaki opened the rear door of his truck and Tom jumped down and began running his nose on the ground. He went around to sniff Malmberg's knees and the deputy tousled the dog's ears while he spoke into his mike. Val had retrieved the dog's lead and stood holding it, surveying the barley field. The wind came down and like a ventriloquist's trick the field hissed and sighed from every quarter. Malmberg came to stand beside him.

"Sorry, I got to run to town. Got a domestic." He removed his cap and ran a hand through his tangerine hair. "This sonofabitch goes at his wife prit-near once a week. He's a first-class scumbag and so I ask myself, Why does she stay with him? He's tore hunks of hair off her head and then later in the week I see them sitting together in the café holding hands like teenagers. You ever figure that one out you let me know."

He did not wait for Millimaki to respond. He clapped one of his speckled hands on Val's shoulder, jumped into the cruiser's seat and backed onto the county road and was gone. Val stood watching the dust plume recede down the string-straight road until it disappeared beyond a low rise. All about him the barley slewed and rasped in the wind.

Because it's hard to be alone, Millimaki thought. That's what I've figured out, Red. In this country, it's just hard to be alone.

He went to the girl's car and stood looking in the window. He raised his head and looked out over the wide rolling country. Not a house or shed. Not a telephone pole. Finally he opened the door and sat in the driver's seat. He ran his hands lightly around the steering wheel. From the rearview mirror hung a tiny dream catcher and a plastic rosary. He inhaled the merest hint of perfume. "Penelope Ann Carnahan," he said. "Your name is a poem."

Reaching across he swung open the passenger side door. It squalled on a sprung hinge. He called the dog and he came and stuck his head into the car and began to snuffle at the floorboards, the seat. He nuzzled a hooded sweatshirt in the backseat. Millimaki held it up. On its chest, in sporadic spangles, it read ROCKSTAR. He laid it on the seat in front of the dog. "That's her, Tom-boy. That's our girl."

Beyond the ground search, the area had been flown over by a helicopter from the Air Force base at Great Falls and a stagnant reservoir had been dragged, exhuming from the murk nothing more sinister than a rotting angus heifer calf thought to have been rustled a month previous. As Malmberg had said, the girl seemed to have been lifted into the sky. It was not the first time he'd heard that or similar words when he'd shown up with the dog as the instrument of last resort, as though searchers in their desperation and despair imbued the victims with the power to rescue themselves. Changelings sprouting the wings of swallows or eagles. Angels. Transmutation by hope. He thought again of the holy card his Slovene grandmother had given him when he was a boy: The Assumption of the Virgin Mary into Heaven. He had kept it in his billfold for years, until the gilt edges were worn and the paper had become as pliable as cloth: angels with great immaculate wings escorting the Virgin toward Elysium on a stairway of feather clouds. Her face was awash with the sunlight of God. But Valentine Millimaki did not bring back angels. No, I did not, he thought. Souls did not aspire on his watch to safety or heaven but came trestled roughly from the dark woods, trapped in the alabaster statuary of rigid flesh.

The girl's track when they entered the barley was clear though some of the searchers had walked atop it. Tom surged at his lead the length of the field but then stood confused at its northernmost edge where it terminated at the narrow road Malmberg had spoken of. It was no more than parallel ruts and no vehicle had passed on it in months. Millimaki walked for a way in the weeds at its edge. Runic tracks of birds, tracks of fox. The dog plunged at his lead, urgent to return the way they'd come and Val let him go. At the car once again the dog veered toward the weedy strip beside the ditch.

"Hold on for a minute, goddamn it. Let me catch my breath." He tied the lead to the door handle of the girl's car and the dog whined and pawed at the dirt. Leaning against the warm quarterpanel he breathed the dusty smell of ripe grain, a scent from his childhood. An image of his father sprang unbidden into his head—a rare happy picture of an unhappy man, passing his hands over the ripened heads as he walked toward the waiting combines.

Millimaki went once again to the first tracks entering the field, knelt and studied them: tiny feet, antic whorls of the treads of her shoes. He got on his knees and took a long look at one of the prints. Then he shuffled ahead on hands and knees and studied another. And another. At last he knelt in the dirt, his hands resting on his thighs. She had entered the barley from the hard ground and then had carefully retraced her steps, one footprint atop another as she backstepped from the grain field. Now the barley tassels bowing under the wind brushed at the flesh of Millimaki's arms. "Bright girl," he said. "Bright girl." But he was not smiling.

Tom had torn up the ground at the limit of his lead and he bayed crazily when he saw Millimaki emerge from the barley. He untied the leather lead and the dog nearly pulled his arm out of the socket. "Okay, then, if you're so fucking sure." He unsnapped the leather lead and the dog vanished in the weeds.

A hundred yards along the ditch he came to the dog sitting, his ears pivoting as he registered some minute sounds—the burble of the ditch water, birdcalls, tiny things among the weed bines. Millimaki was about to speak when he saw the plastic straw. Later he would appreciate how very thorough she'd been. The straw approximated as well as possible the color of the barley and the August weed stems growing along the ditch—thistle and hemlock, volunteer wheat. He pulled but it seemed rooted there. He dug away at its base until the girl's lips emerged from the dirt and he realized with a start that he was kneeling on her chest. He stood up abruptly and backpedaled, nearly tripping over the dog. "Oh, Christ," he said. "Oh, Christ." He stood looking down for a long while. He realized the dog was waiting and he went to him and roughly stroked his head. He could hardly speak. He managed, "Good, Tom," and the dog stepped down the small incline to the ditch and lapped at the trickle of water. Millimaki sat among the dry weeds and he sat for a very long time. The dog came to lie at his feet. Finally with great effort Millimaki rose and began his routine. He did it all mechanically. He studied the ground, bent and snapped his pictures from several angles and he stood beside the grave turning to the four cardinal points and working the shutter—grain fields rolling endlessly to every horizon. Then at last he took a pair of latex gloves from his fanny pack and began to dig the girl out. The shepherd lay with his head on his extended forelegs, following the man's movements with his eyes.

The girl had cut away the turf in her small approximate shape and it came away in rough squares and rectangles and then she had dug the hole where she would lie. While breathing through the straw she must have covered her face with loose dirt before somehow pulling lengths of the sod over her arms, taking her last breaths through the straw as the drugs moved slowly down the long corridors of her veins. He was amazed at her strength and will to leave no trace upon the earth. It must have taken her hours. Beside her in the hole were the kitchen knife and the pill bottle and she lay in it rigid and symmetrical as if composed by the hands of reverent priests. He lifted her hands each in turn, examining the torn and broken nails and turned them with difficulty to look at her palms where blisters had formed and ruptured and bled like stigmata. Millimaki brushed as much of the soil from her face as he could and with his belt knife sawed away the straw from her clenched teeth. In the end he leaned over as if he might kiss those cold lips and blew the sand from her eyelids, from the corners of her mouth.

While he waited for the coroner to make the twenty-mile trip from town, he cut away some of the crime scene tape Malmberg had taken such pains to erect and planted some of the dowels in the dirt and strung the yellow tape, defining the plot the girl had chosen for herself from the enormity of the unbearable world. She'd wanted nothing but to disappear and Millimaki and his dog had taken that from her. Soon again she would be antiseptically probed on the coroner's tray when all she had wanted in the world was to not be touched again. He would not take her picture. When he'd lifted off the turf and stood looking at her so small and pale in her grave he realized what he'd taken, what he could not put back. If the coroner wanted those pictures he could take the sonsofbitches himself.

He sat at the edge of the ditch beside her watching the red sun fall slowly behind the western rim. A meadowlark sang. Pheasant and Hungarian partridge scuttled through the field, gorging on fallen grain. He could see them come gliding in in twos and threes and flare their wings against the paling sky. He stared at the tiny jackstraw figure at his feet. There had been no angel to bear her up. In the end only numbing chemical night falling on her eyes to damp the vision of the boys in the pickup bed with their bottles and shovel handles, in the plunder of her virginity not even the warmth of a human touch.

The birds picked among the furrows like barn fowl and the barley sawed hissing above them with the wind like a breath. It was a wonderful evening. He gazed down at Penelope Carnahan. He thought about taking her hand.

Together they went up the game trail and John Gload stopped periodically to turn and take in the country as if considering their solitude in the immensity, not assuring himself of it. Wexler beside him gloomily considered the new scuffs on his boots. He ran his finger along the looping lines of the topographic map, his tongue between his lips. The map popped and fluttered in the wind and they went on. They crossed a small divide, descended into a coulee, and presently the river disappeared as did Wexler's car beside it and there was no sign whatever of the world of men on the dusty path fresh tracks of mule deer and older sign baked into the gumbo-clay like the spoor of cloven-footed prehistoric kin. In that desolate hole the wind that had raised chop on the river was a whisper and overhead a hawk drifted among the thin clouds like a harbinger, keening high and shrill.

Gload stood and made a show of locating himself and he craned his neck once to study the map Wexler held. He was a fair actor and asked if they weren't about a mile from the river and wasn't the second dam perhaps a mile downstream and Wexler turned in that direction, where the old man with his shackled hands pointed and then the chain was around Wexler's throat. The folded map fell among the weeds and the old man for leverage had his knee in the small of the younger man's back and Wexler clawed at the hands wildly, wet sounds escaping his nose and from the white grimace of his mouth and very quickly his vision began to fail and fade and in that embrace, chest to back like prison lovers, John Gload could feel the muscles in the thin frame by degrees slacken toward tranquility. He walked two paces backward and laid Wexler's body down, turned it on its side that he might maintain his grip and he held him there yet, until the sound of breath was gone, until finally he could hear the thin high call of the hawk and he let go. He looked at Wexler and smiled at the mask of dumb amazement there regarding the empty heavens and he noted the dark stain on the man's pants front. He said to him, "You weren't no surprise, Deputy. I figured there was nothing to you and I was right."

After he retrieved the shackle keys from Wexler's pocket and the clasp knife from his belt and folded away the topo map carefully so that it would not be torn or bloodied, he set his capable hands to their task. The work was difficult and even in the cool air he was shortly sweating profusely and he noted how soft he had become in the months of confinement. It felt good to take long strides down the path, and going back up with the entrenching tool from the car trunk he began to feel alive. There were tire chains kept in a burlap sack in the car's trunk and he emptied them out and brought the sack with him. The digging was easy and he made several holes—some on the bald adjacent side hills, some deep in narrow defiles plowed out by the lashing rains of spring. Some in the coulee above, some below. One he stole from a badger, the bleak hollow socket gaping from beneath a rock the size and shape of a Stonehenge monolith.

He took his time, tamping down the small holes with the flat of the shovel and with his feet and with a sage branch he smoothed away the tread marks of his shoes. Then he stood back, appraising each site from different angles, different heights. Descending, he swept the trail assiduously with the sage, bent and shuffling like a peasant crone. By the time he reached the car it was dusk. At the riverbank he cast several things into the river and almost immediately the gulls began to swarm and screech. He stooped and put a round rock in the sack and threw it far out into the chop and then he washed his hands and arms and shoes as best he could in the silty water. The gulls splashed and dove and with his hands pressed against his ears John Gload stood on the rocky riverbank for several minutes watching. Though they were for him malign and detestable they were nonetheless a facet of his dream and they conjured for him the plowed fields of his youth. He was suddenly very tired. Oh how I could sleep right now, he thought. Oh how I could sleep.

The gulls came off the river and like the birds of his childhood memories began to home in on ground he had recently turned in the hills above. His thoughts of sleep were prurient and he turned his burning eyes toward the sun, low and molten in the west. Oh, yes, he would sleep. One errand and he would sleep indeed.

By the time the coroner had come and gone Millimaki was too tired to make the return drive, at the end of which was his empty cabin with its fire grate of cold ash and a refrigerator provisioned with little else but beer. He took a room in the town, ate his dinner at a truck stop where his companions were long-haul drivers sitting alone and catatonic in plastic booths, their harlequin eyes to the black window glass watching comets burn bleakly through the night on the interstate toward Canada. Wherever Millimaki looked he saw the girl's dirty face, the image like a photographic negative seared into the back of his eyeballs. He went back to lie on his sterile bed in a room that smelled of stale smoke. The dog when he came in rose to nuzzle his hand and returned to the bed he'd made in the worn brown shag.

Millimaki lay for half an hour squeezing his eyes against the shards of crimson neon penetrating the dusty draperies through lacerations that seemed to have been made with a knife. He got up, dressed, and went into the warm night and down the lone illuminated street of the deserted town. It was summer yet but soon the wind scouring the neglected asphalt and rustling the leaves in the infrequent box elder trees seemed to bear for him some message from the distant high snowfields. He turned up the collar of his coat. The swaying lamplights made a strange parade of jittering light pools through which Millimaki walked, encountering not a living creature afield.

He trudged numbly past near-identical single-room houses sided with asphalt brick and trailers set upon ill-aligned cinder blocks all but encased in snarls of hemlock and rampant lilacs and soon beneath his feet the pavement gave way to gravel. Coyotes bayed from the bluffs rising darkly to the west of town, the stream weaving beneath them at that time of year little but a series of tepid pools and brackish plaits burbling from the tangled willows with the sound of muffled voices. There was no moon and as he passed beyond the last town lights it was if he had passed through a portal, from the civilized world to one where darkness prevailed. He stopped in the road and held up his hands against the sky as if he might sift the stars in their billions through his fingers and make sense of the equivocal black like an ancient pyromancer. He walked for a long time. Trash fluttered along the right-of-way fence. Near a culvert where the creek went beneath the road he sat down in the wild ditch weeds. Small things scurried away and then he could hear nothing but a muted electric hum the wind elicited from the fence wires.

The girl's face again appeared before him and there were others, emancipated to float free and wide in that great black dome—porcelain masks of winter's victims, the drowned, sallow and bulbous, staring unperturbed from the stout embrace of submerged trees. Dismantled Picasso faces grinning crookedly from a bed of talus stones. There, too, was the blue-black mask his mother wore. The painted kewpie face of his recurrent dream was another lie, more deceit. Because it was not white and smooth but a bulging swollen thing above the rope with a half inch of black tongue that the flies had found. He put his face in his hands. After a few minutes he said the girl's name aloud—Penelope Ann Carnahan—like a prayer or a conjuring, the exquisite beauty of her resolve a searing indictment of his shitty pathetic loneliness and self-pity. At home, in a closet, Glenda's shirts and dresses hung like cartoon ghosts and only a day ago he had pressed his face into them, breathing her faint perfume and dampening the fabric like a child. He was ashamed.

Once they had hiked to the top of the eastern flank of the Big Snowies and they could see from there five mountain ranges, blue and isolate in seas of emerald spring grass. In the southeast, toward the Musselshell, antelope it seemed for sheer joy of speed coursed among the sagebrush and in the north a great cloud hove up, as white and substantive as a massif thrust up new from the prairie. She stood for several minutes turning, with her hand visoring her eyes, and finally put her arm around him and thanked him for all of it. As though it were a gift he had given her.

They ate their lunch atop a colossal lichened outcrop, which lay above the grass like the barnacled back of a whale and he told her about his uncle who had brought a Dutch woman home from the war and the marriage had lasted less than a year. When as a boy he'd asked about it his uncle had said simply, "It just didn't take."

"What, like it was a grapevine?" she asked.

"Those were the words. I don't know. I was something like ten years old."

"Well, to continue the metaphor, Valentine, he must not have made a good bed for it."

And he thought now, what bed had he made for his own wife? A four-room cabin at the end of a bad road. Twelve hundred a month and an eleven-year-old Datsun and lodgepole pine to heat her house. That was the bed he'd made. A red-hot oven and flies on the windowsill and a half-warped door drift-locked half the winter mornings and boots caked with impossible gumbo from an impassable road. Him, with his murderous companion and his lousy fucking twelve hundred a month and a graveyard shift. And his retinue of dead—like family, she had said. Or like lovers.

In his farmboy credulousness he had thought he could take her from the ivied trellises and green lawns of Dublin, Ohio, and make her happy with his mere fidelity. And she had starved on it, like a dog in a kennel with a bone alone for sustenance. Whatever there was left of himself he had given to the dead. She was right—the dead were easier. Like Penelope Carnahan, silent and beautiful in her eternal and seductive slumber.

The wind by the time he roused himself and began his walk back had come in earnest. Grit scoured from the bluffs stung his face like spoondrift, and tumbleweeds bowled past making clattering skeletal sounds in the blackness. He went before the gusts down the dark road with his arms outspread. His heart lay in his chest like a ballast stone and he thought that if not for that, he might kite away weightless and insubstantial as the feed sacks and bale-twine boxes pilloried to the fence wires.

She climbed the metal stairs in her practical shoes which, by shift's end, seemed cobbled from stone. The wind skirled weirdly in the stairwell and trash flew about like vile birds and flapped and lodged among the metal balusters. She paused on the landing to catch her breath and when he appeared the old man wore a look of mild surprise. The wind blew his thin hair forward and he swept it back with a huge hand. She didn't remember seeing him there before and wondered if he was someone's father or grandfather. The wind swept the thin strands of hair across his face again and he held them back, his hand at his forehead in a strange salute. He stood for a moment on the stairs two steps above her and she smiled at him but he only stared, cocking his head, his expression mildly thoughtful, and then he went past her and she could hear his heavy tread on the metal stairs, marking his descent by the pong pong pong of the treads. The sound stopped somewhere short of the ground floor and she stood listening as did he and then she could hear his tread again and she hurried to her door along the walkway dimly illuminated by the globed halogens in the adjacent parking lot. She was horrified she'd forgotten to lock the apartment's door and when she stepped inside she turned the thumb lock on the knob and threw home the deadbolt and slid the security chain into its track and for reasons she couldn't name stood breathless with her ear to the door for a full minute.

Through the parted blinds she watched the parking lot, weirdly blanched at that late hour beneath the buzzing lamps. Beyond the rows of cars she thought she saw the old man ambling slowly along the green boulevard or it may have been someone else or perhaps it was only her weary eyes at that late hour concocting from the windy shadows of the arborvitae a fairy-tale ogre shuffling his dirty brogans toward some far-off lair festooned with bones.

In the room again he lay with his fingers laced behind his head. Ribbons of ruby light shone through the rents in the curtains and lay across his legs like angry sutures. He'd been awake for nearly twenty-four hours and had walked nearly ten miles on the gravel in the dark and yet he could not sleep. He sat up on the edge of the bed. The television strobed. Women in scant clothing humped and churned to a manic Latin beat and there was much excited talk about abs and buns. He clicked it off.

He sat for several minutes immobile as a stone, the primary-color efflux of the television like a flashbulb still erupting in his vision. When he'd left that day after talking to the sheriff he'd stopped at the mailbox and gathered up the mail and put it on the dashboard of the truck. There'd been catalogues and bills and Glenda's magazines redolent of feminine scent. And there'd been a letter from his sister which now stood against the base of the bedside lamp. He picked it up and turned it over and over and in the end set it back. He could not take her PS tonight. It may not be this letter or the next but he felt eventually it would come: "PS—Why did you dawdle on the road?" "Why did you stand there and eat an apple?" "Why," at last, "did you not save her?"

Though the room seemed already warm, the wall heater unaccountably clicked on and stale air rolled across the room, conjuring out of the vile shag, with its smell of cigarettes and sweet perfumes, a desolate history of quick and forbidden couplings. Tom raised his head from his bed and looked at the heater and looked at the man and lay back. Nearby Millimaki's holstered .357 hung on a chairback, its bluing sultry and inviting. Suddenly he remembered what he'd heard about Ed Teagarden—thirty-two years in the department, happily married, had taken a shotgun to his garage and inhaled a load of #6 upland game shot, the sudden inutility of unwanted retirement harvesting fruit from the garden of his secret dystopia. It blossomed outlandishly on the wall above his workbench.

Millimaki fished through his wallet until he found the number written on the back of a receipt. A woman's voice came on an answering machine and began to talk. He hung up and called again. And again.

Finally a voice said, "Don't you not get it, asshole. It's three-fifteen in the morning. I'll get the cops on your ass."

"Jean, I'm sorry. It's Val."

"Oh, Val." He could hear her exhale, and the timbre of her voice when she spoke again was soft and sympathetic. "She's not here. I think she went out on a Life Flight. There was an accident in the Highwoods. I think the Highwoods. Somewhere out there. I thought she would be home by now."

"What was that about the cops? Is everything all right?"

"I'm fine. I can't sleep. I thought someone had been in the apartment."

"Lock the door."

"There was a man. It was nothing. The wind blowing and my imagination going crazy over nothing."

"I'm out of town. I could have someone come by."

"No, that's okay."

"I could get them to send a car by."

"How are you, Val?"

"I can't sleep, either. I haven't slept it seems like for a year."

"You can get something for that."

"I know. I hate taking anything."

"Val, that's not where she is."

"You mean the Life Flight."

"You could probably have checked on that. Checked if there was an accident."

"I'm really tired, Jean."

"I mean you could have that checked. With your department."

"Sure. I could. Why would I?"

"Val, that's not where she is."

"She's not out on the Life Flight."

"Yes. That's not right. I can't say anything more." She exhaled deeply into the receiver—a liquid sigh laden with weariness and all the heart-cracking mundane sorrow of her profession. "It just won't do any good anyway."

"Jean," he said. "Jean?"

EIGHTEEN

He'd made no attempt to hide the car though the uncut ditch weeds when he'd driven it off the road rose above the fenders and little could be seen of it but the roof and windows. There was much to do and the old man gathered pencil and paper and started in immediately, pacing deliberately down the narrow orchard lane that led to his house. He paced and stopped to scribble in a small wide-ruled notebook and paced again. To his right the scraggly orchard, where songbirds flitted and chirruped softly and on his left the old right-of-way fence whose strands of rusted wire hung in low bights or lay hopelessly garbled on the ground among the weeds. Beyond it acres of parched sage, running to the breaks of the river and into the low hills dotted in that arid place with random tortured junipers and bull pine. Pace, stop, write. Turn, pace. He consulted the sun, the shadows of the trees upon the ground. He noted the direction of the wind and with his head erect and eyes closed he appeared to be taking the scent of something. At last he stopped and turned in a circle, made a final notation with the stub of pencil and then, like a child who'd tired of a game, walked from the midst of tangled trees and through the weedy ditch toward the house.

At his table he transcribed his notes onto a larger sheet of paper, the pencil stub scraping slow and painfully along the page. He sat back and examined the work for a long moment then crumpled it and began again on a second sheet. By the fifth page he was satisfied. He held it at arm's length. He set it down and stood back and looked at it from a distance. He walked around the table and looked at it from several angles with a squinted eye.

Beneath the sink he found a coffee can Francie had used for compost waste. He took it to the back-door stoop and put in the note pad and the failed drawings and at last even the pencil and burned it all, the flames a comfortable orange in the velvet blue light of dusk. Nighthawks as he stood over the guttering can flared above the apple trees against a rose sky. A distant squall was prophesied on the breeze by the smell of wet sage. When the can had cooled he took it up and bore it like a monstrance before him down the lane where he trod the ashes into the dirt. He flattened the can under his heavy shoes and sailed it far out into the brush. The day's last sunrays gleamed on the rear window of Wexler's car, dangerously atilt in the borrow ditch of the county road. While the nighthawks veered and swooped above him he stood listening. If it was the end, and it almost certainly was, he had set things right. He felt a kind of peace he'd not known for years, since he was a boy. The day was done, the field plowed.

He turned then and went through the ditch and wove among the trees, no longer counting his steps now because they were counted and recorded and archived and he sat with his back against a tree under the dangling harrow tines in the mild evening air until it was quite dark.

"Some kid out sighting in his aught-6 found Wexler. Or his dog did. Part of him. The dog found part of Wexler. It was just a damn accident."

"Oh, God."

"God only knows where the rest of him is. Buried out there with his other bones. Or in the river. I don't know. We got the dogs out, boats in the water." The sheriff paused, swiveled his chair to the window. "He did his old best number on him."

Val sought a chair and sat unbidden. The sheriff swiveled back, considered him with weary eyes over the rim of his reading glasses.

"You know when they found him he was just sitting in a chair out at his place like he was waiting for a cab."

"I know."

"Just like the first time. Didn't make a bit of fuss. Put out his hands for the bracelets, said howdy boys."

Val looked into his palms. He could feel the sheriff's eyes on him.

"Then he asked where was Deputy Millimaki."

Val said nothing.

"Said he was expecting Millimaki. Said he'd like to talk to the deputy."

"I can't explain that."

"I'm not asking you to."

"He won't tell me where Wexler is, if that's what you mean."

"I'm sure he won't. That's another secret John Gload will take to his grave. And by Christ I hope he takes it there soon."

"Yessir. I hope so."

The sheriff removed his half-glasses and set them deliberately on his desk atop its chaos of papers. He passed his hands across his face in a washing motion. When he looked up, his eyes were fond and enormously sad. "Do you in point of fact, Val? Do you hope that?"

That question Millimaki considered as he drove home that afternoon and it occupied his thoughts all that evening as he sat on his porch watching the sky dim and the stars emerge from the void with their vanguard of bats and he even had the opportunity to discuss the difficult matter later with Weldon Wexler when he appeared in Millimaki's dream. But Wexler, carrying an armload of bloodless limbs like stovewood and wearing a vivid carmine scar on his neck, was disinclined to speak.

John Gload in the month of October was convicted of first-degree murder and was to spend the rest of his life in the Montana State Penitentiary in Deer Lodge. A casualty of the strenuous proceedings, his lawyer succumbed finally to the ravages of his vice and had been committed to a detoxification center in Billings. He'd shown up for trial in the suit he'd slept in, his bald dome white as an egg beneath the lights, and his tremors would not allow him to open his briefcase or lift a glass of water to his cracked and spluttering lips. John Gload accepted this as an inevitability and seemed hardly to notice.

Gruesome photographs and mock-ups of the young man disinterred from his unsatisfactory grave in the Breaks were set upon easels at the front of the courtroom and the heart surgeon for two long hours explicated them, in his thousand-dollar suit parading up and back like a university don, poking and slapping at the exploded images with a wooden pointer. He described the damage to the heart and how the chest must be accessed for its repair and at last setting aside the pointer and weaving his gracile fingers through the air like a tailor or shoemaker he illustrated his method for wiring together the sternum where it had been split. A technique unlike any other, he said. Unique. Proprietary. The prosecuting attorneys rolled their eyes at one another discreetly and Gload's young public defender stammered his objections. Even so, Gload had been intensely interested. He was at that time seventy-seven years old. Sidney White, in view of his cooperation, at an earlier date had been given forty years, ten suspended. His place of incarceration was yet to be determined. It was thought he should not inhabit the same institution as John Gload. White's trial for the Miles City rape and assault was pending. Regardless, he would be nearly the age of his mentor before he resumed his short and inglorious career in the world of free men.

NINETEEN

He went slowly along a long gray corridor, the redoubtable masonry of clammy stone on either side stacked and mortared against the penetration of hope. The familiar smell of disinfectant and floor wax was in his nostrils, the walls lined with scarred wooden benches with high backs that may have been pews rescued from a desanctified church. In passing he read names carved into the seats circumscribed with hearts or conjoined with chains and there were admonitions in crude calligraphy to fuck off, to eat shit. In one high seat back an optimistic vandal had inscribed his assurance that Millimaki would be reborn. The work of feral children, of wives and lovers mutely enraged by their celibacy, their infidelities. Mothers had dug their nails into the soft wood as they waited in the dank corridor to see the fruit of their wombs turned out so briefly from their cages.

The familiar fluorescents as he walked cast their antiseptic light. Another sally gate slid open with a rasp of metal and shortly, on his right, through the scratched and foggy Plexiglas he saw the face of John Gload, more equine now, the long jaw bones prominent, his eyes seemingly grown larger. All else save his hands seemed diminished and he sat with them flat on the table, sphinxlike, staring vacantly into the glass before him, heedless of the clamor of voices and the scrape of chairs. The terrible light turned his skin to marble. Several small round Band-Aids adorned his forehead and neck, the spurious flesh color like mismatched patches on a creased and faded shirt.

"My, my," he said. "Deptee." His smile revealed now a dead tooth the color of oak. "You're looking good."

"Hello, John. How they treating you?"

"Treat me like a goddamn convict, is what they do."

"If the shoe fits."

Gload stared frankly at the younger man's face for a long uncomfortable moment and then grinned once again, the awful canine like a grub clinging to his smile.

"Did I ever tell you that in the old days they used to put concrete shoes on these assholes who tried to escape? Weighed twenty pounds. Had to wear them shoes every waking hour, walking around clank clank clank. Like that."

"No, I guess you didn't."

"Well, it's a fact." He removed his cigarettes from a breast pocket and laid them in front of him, aligning the pack fastidiously with the table edge. He coughed. His voice had more gravel in it. "So you're a fed now, is that it?"

Millimaki shook his head in amazement. "Still tapped into your jailbird pipeline. You're a goddamn wonder."

The old man made motions as if to snatch feathers swirling around his head. "Words float around, Val, and you pick them up."

"Amazing. Any word out there regarding the color of my shorts?"

Gload effected a mirthless smile, the parchment skin of his horse's jaw tight. His tongue worried at the dead tooth. He said, "Please tell me you ain't FBI at least."

"ATF. About two years now."

"All Those Fuckers. If you'll pardon me. It's just a joke, Val."

"I hadn't heard that one," Millimaki lied. "That's not bad."

Gload removed a cigarette from his pack and tapped an end on his thumbnail. He said, "I appreciated that picture you sent."

"I took that on my last search. I was clearing out some stuff. Thought you might like it."

"Nice picture," he said. "Never did find the letter went with it, though."

"I'm not much of a letter writer."

The old man studied his hands and the burning cigarette between his fingers. "Kind of thought you might of stopped by and say good-bye before they shipped me out."

"They put me on two weeks' leave after that. You were gone by the time I got back. Then I got this gig and, well, on to other things."

"Well, anyways." Gload looked up. A weary smile, his lips thin and chapped. "They must treat you good. You're looking better'n the last time I seen you. Eating good, getting more sleep, am I right? Making good money?"

"I'm doing okay, John. And what about you? How you making it?"

The old man was terribly thin and bent. The signs of his chronic insomnia were very much in evidence—even through the hazy plastic barrier Millimaki noted the old man's eyes latticed with veins, the skin beneath them dark as war paint. His hand when he reached for his cigarettes exhibited a faint quaver.

"Oh, not what you might say thriving. I don't sleep much. You know how it is. Just living it out, like I told you once. Living it out." He struck his lighter to the end of a filterless Camel and blew smoke at the ceiling. "We're like two trains going different ways, Val."

"What about that farming dream?"

He snorted. "That gets harder and harder. Just like an old tattoo—the color has begun to fade and sometimes I can't hardly see it no more." He paused and wanly smiled. "Except for them gulls. Sonsofbitches are clear as ever."

He sat smoking. In the adjacent cubicle a man began to shout in Spanish and pound the tabletop and the glass in front of him with the flat of his hand. He jumped to his feet and his chair lurched backward to the floor. Two guards moved toward him. He was led away in cuffs weeping. Beside Millimaki, beyond the insubstantial privacy barrier, a young woman sat in the chair as rigid as an obelisk, her hands covering her face. John Gload seemed to notice nothing. He had lifted his ashtray with the cigarette in it from the tabletop that it not be disturbed and when the man was taken away set it down.

"You speak that lingo?" he said.

"Not much."

"He was asking her to save him. That's a good one. Oh save me." He did not look as the young man was drug away or at the girl beyond the glass but examined his cigarette or perhaps he considered the troubling phenomenon of its quivering end because he wore a wistful look. Finally the old man said, "So you were in the neighborhood?"

"Something like that," Millimaki said. "I got your letter. You understand I couldn't just come right away."

"I wasn't going nowheres." By way of illustrating this fact he half turned in his chair and nodded toward a uniformed guard who stood sleepily in front of a door with wire running through the glass. He turned back, shaking his head.

Millimaki said, "I always have wondered, John, why you didn't leg it out after Wexler. Why you waited out there."

"The damnedest thing you should ask that, Valentine." The old man wore a thin smile. "I'm just getting to that in a way."

"So what's on your mind, John?"

Gload adjusted the ashtray a half inch nearer, turned it on the tabletop which told in its gouges a hundred-year history of wrist chains. "I told you about a lot of things, Val, in those months we had together and I know you passed some of the shit on to the Bull and I do not hold that against you in the very least because I know it's your job. Was your job, anyways. But I'm going to tell you one last thing and I need your promise before I do. Your word that this is just between you and me."

"How in hell can you ask a promise of me after all that's happened?"

"Because we're friends, Val, aren't we? Can you sit there and deny that we're friends?"

"I don't know what we are."

"Friends, by God. Friends is what we are."

"John, I don't know if you can be friends with somebody who you think might cut your throat if the opportunity arose."

"Valentine," Gload said. He said the young man's name with a long exhalation, like a sigh. He passed one hand down his forehead and rubbed at his inflamed eyes. For a full minute, as Millimaki shifted on his chair, the old man sat with his hands cupped to his ears as if he would shut out further lies, further hurt.

Finally he rose up and spoke. "Think about this, Deputy. I want you to think about the times we were alone together and it was the same thing with that Wexler asshole. It was the same thing. It was nothing for me to get him. Think about how many times we stood out there in that park full of trees in the dark and there wasn't nobody around and you turned your back on me. Just like Wexler did. Many many times. Twenty or thirty. A hundred times. That many times I could of got hold of you. So, yes, friends is what I think we are."

"Is that how it happened? With Wexler?"

"I don't want to talk about that on account of I don't want you to be thinking about it for the rest of your life. I wouldn't do that to you. Val, I got a lot of feelings for you."

"Friendship, then, because you didn't kill me."

His tired eyes stared into Millimaki's. "It does not, Deputy, get truer than that."

"What's the promise, John? I can't promise you anything without hearing it."

"You won't have to do nothing for a while. I don't know how long but not for a while."

"What is it?"

"I want you to claim me when I cash in and to bury my ashes."

"For Christ sake, I can't do that. That's something your family does."

"Now you know good and goddamn well I don't have nobody. I told you all that."

"There's got to be somebody. Hell, Francie. Your wife. Francie."

"Gone."

"She'd come back for something like that."

"She's not coming back, Val, that's the thing. Or maybe I should say she never left. That's why I never kited out."

"I don't even know what the hell that means. In any case, when it does happen, the state takes care of that. Down on the prison farm I think. I could check on that."

"No."

"I can't do it."

"In my orchard with no stone or nothing. All's you need to do is to dig a hole."

"I can't."

"You can, too. A simple hole in the ground. And here's the deal. I can pay you for your troubles."

"You're not paying me because I can't do it."

"Val, I've checked into all this. I'm about a half jailhouse lawyer after all these years in and out of such places."

"Has to be next of kin or nobody."

"Well, yes. I done that."

"What?"

"You're my next of kin, Val."

"I am no such thing."

"Well, you're a few years behind the times, Deputy. They don't call it that anymore. They call it 'appointing a personal representative.' But it's the same thing. I prefer the sound of 'next of kin' because it's, you know, more familiar. But it's a what-you-call bygone term. And so I done that and I made a holographic will and a devisee. Which is you, Valentine."

Millimaki stared openmouthed at the old killer, who favored him through the Plexiglas with a smile so tranquil he seemed a different Gload altogether.

"This is crazy."

"Devisee is like an heir."

"This would take years."

"It's all set up and legal as God."

"I won't do it."

Gload turned his attention to the Camel on the ashtray, shaping its end with great care and nodding his head as though in affirmation of something. To Millimaki's left the young Mexican woman sat yet, ashen and immobile as a caryatid, her eyes reflecting an emptiness beyond the chair where her husband had so recently sat, in those black portals an unreckonable vacancy cold as far space where tears could neither form or fall. She was very small and seemed more waiflike still when she rose, passing a mesmerized Millimaki with steps so deliberate it was as if her bones were of frailest glass, and she left in her wake a scent of springtime blooms.

John Gload watched him watch. He waited for Millimaki to turn once more to the glass.

"Here it is then, Val. I was hoping I wouldn't have to play my hole card. That you'd do this for me out of pure friendship." He leaned toward the barrier and opened the collar of his workshirt, revealing among the sparse gray hairs a tiny silver chain, tight as a choker, girdling the leathery wattle of his neck. The silver dolphin nestled at the hollow of his throat.

Millimaki stared in disbelief.

"This was my other gift to you, Deputy Millimaki. I gave you your life in a manner of speaking and that's something. And I gave you hers, too. I could of took it but I chose to give it. Lots of times since I thought I should of took it because she caused you a lot of pain and it hurt me to see you thataway, it truly did. I thought about it for quite a long time, Val. I remember doing it real clear. I sat in that car for a long time, thinking about what would be the best thing to do for Valentine Millimaki, my friend. And I still do think about it. And then I ask this little tiny favor of you and you say you can't do it. You say you won't." His terrible eyes bore through the Plexiglas. "Tell me how that's right, Valentine. Tell me how that's anywheres near fair."

Millimaki could only stammer. "How?"

"How what?"

"Did you find her? Get that close?"

"A couple of phone calls, a couple of little white lies. It took nothing, Val. I got talents. You never really allowed that."

Millimaki could scarcely find his voice. "You went in her place? Her apartment?"

The old man's head drooped wearily, the years with their burden and the memories of difficult decisions settling at that instant like a great stone upon the knuckled bones of his neck. He ground out his cigarette, rolled his ravaged eyes up to Millimaki. He said, "I don't know that I have a thing you'd call a soul, Val, but I recanize it in other people. You have such a thing. I seen it smudged across your face the very first time I seen you. So I know you'll do this thing for me. Just put me up there next to Francie."

"Christ, it was Jean. It was Glenda's roommate you saw that night."

Gload stared blandly through the barrier. "It don't matter."

"I called that night. Christ, Jean saw you. It wasn't Glenda."

"All that don't matter, Val. I could of got her, one way or the other."

"And you got the chain then."

"Don't be a fucking cop now when I need you, Val. I'm asking you, just put me up there next to Francie."

"Where? Up where?"

"In the orchard. That's where she is. And that's where I'm going to be, too."

"Your wife's in the orchard?" Millimaki said. "On your place?"

But the old man did not hear, had retreated to his haven in the Breaks and his ears were filled with the sound of wind in the untended trees and the flutter of the songbirds that resided there. His eyes, gorged red blossoms dyed with the blood he had spilled on the world, stared beyond Millimaki's head and beyond the unassailable stones and wire and the desolate prison town.

"In the apple trees," he said.

TWENTY

John Cload had been in the state penitentiary for five and a half years and in that time his insomnia never left him. He was eighty-two years old. He accepted his age and that the elderly seldom slept well and considering that even as a younger man he had never slept, it was little surprise to him. But he had his trickery to fool it and at times it still worked. Perhaps this night. He lay on his narrow cot, the muted noises of the prison gallery in his ears—the snores and moans, the drone of the high suspended lights that were a curse in every joint he had ever been in, the maddening slow drip of the faulty showerheads down the corridor that seemed somehow as the night deepened to grow louder, at this desolate hour clanging like rivets on the concrete floor.

Beneath his bunk are two issues of *Successful Farming*. Taped to the cinder-block wall above his head the photograph of a field sent to him years ago by Valentine Millimaki—endless ripe grain and a slash of chalk sky adorned with a single bird of indeterminate species. In the photograph the bird is very small. In the uncertain enormity one could not tell its size in the actual world. It may have been vulture or crow or sparrow. In one corner of the picture is an unfocused yellow banner with black printed words which he cannot make out. On a paintless metal shelf in the cell a few swollen paperback books without covers, a comb and nail clippers, a yellow legal pad at a folding desk.

He lay on his narrow cot thinking about the field. And in the field are things as familiar to him as his own face—the red kits outside their den; far-off butte tops, phantasmal in the summer heat-haze; roiling grasshoppers spinning from under the tires; the gulls. He went around the field, once, twice. And then the bull Doogan came by and shone his light and he was forced to begin again. The guard's footfalls receded, the saffron light dimming, fading, gone. He took hold of the tractor's ladder rail once again and placed his foot on the first rung but he could not pull himself up. He lay thinking, Damn, boy, lift your foot, one two three. But he could not move. The summer sun bore down and he saw his boot on the rung and his hand on the rail and the gulls came planing in, circling down and down and down until like summer insects they swarmed about his head. He could not raise a hand to warn them off nor could he call out and the cries that had haunted him awake and asleep for over seventy years drown out everything.

Guard Gerald Doogan carries in his belly a constant pain which he thinks is surely an ulcer and he walks down the row with his hands on his tender stomach in the posture of women who are several months pregnant. He worries about his young daughter who spends her evening hours in her room alone with the Virgin Mother and he worries about his wife whose joints are swollen and tender to the touch. In these cages are boys little older than his only child who have settled with blood disputes over vials of powder made from cold medicine and fertilizer and he worries about a world where such things happen. His daughter's room is lit with candles and she prays on her knees in this dim place for hours. It wouldn't hurt you to say a rosary, thinks Doogan. It has been years.

He pauses outside a cell to remove an antacid tablet from his pocket where he carries them by the dozen like coins and he chews it woodenly while lighting a cigarette. He shines his light into the cell. John Gload lies on his side with his back to the hallway and he shifts slightly, as though the beam of light possesses substance—heat or cold or movement, like wind.

Guard Doogan goes down the row. He stops to throw his cigarette in one of the toilets. The water in the bowl runs without stopping and the showerheads weep and spatter on the concrete.

He lights another cigarette and smokes and thinks of his wife with her poisoned joints and of his daughter and then he turns to retrace his steps, a route he has walked five thousand nights. He imagines his Wellingtons have worn a trough in the concrete walkway and he tells his wife this as a matter of fact: I have worn a trough with my boots in the floor. He flashes his light into the old man's cell once again and the cone of light illuminates an empty bunk, a hanging blanket. He shines it toward the cell's toilet and sees nothing and thinks for an illogical instant that John Gload is gone. He swings the light back and then sees the old man beneath his bunk. He calls to him, says, "Gload, get up from there," but the old man does not move and does not move, says, "Get up, old man."

He sits high on the spring seat and the tractor churns through the dirt and the polished disks are small brilliant suns themselves, turning the soil in long slow serpents. The river in the distance is a shimmering knife blade and when he passes, the foxes raise their heads and follow with their anthracite eyes the young Gload on his perch and he feels the thrum of the engine in his bones, like the beat of the heart of the earth.

EPILOGUE

From the grassy side yard as he walked around the house a covey of Hungarian partridge flushed, sailing beyond the apple trees. Once above the leafy topmost branches they simply turned their compact bodies and set their wings and the wind took them out of sight in an eyeblink. Though he'd only been there once and that nearly eight years ago, from his many discussions with John Gload the place seemed familiar to him. He noted its disrepair, the slow decrepitude occasioned by the long vacancy since Gload's imprisonment. Clapboards hung loose from the walls and copper gutters sagged in perilous loops from the peeling fascia. All along the bellying soffit, hornets' nests hung like sinister fruit. Beside the back door a wooden chair, the dowels loose in their sockets, seat split and splintery from rain and sun and snow. He stood there and imagined the man whose ashes he carried biding the evening cool. The garden a tangle of weeds, strangled blooms throbbing with bees, and four enormous sunflowers leaned above the chaos, forlorn and druidical in their shabby attire.

The screen door stood ajar, badly warped and canted from Dobek's rough treatment when they'd first come for Gload those years ago and it made faint bird sounds as it rocked in the breeze. The door of the house was locked but he was able to push back the latch with his pocketknife blade so loose did it fit in the jamb. The door opened onto the kitchen, the linoleum there covered with a fine grit as if someone had recently sanded it for dancing. It displayed evidence of a brisk commerce of mice and packrats. Millimaki stooped to pick up a woman's handkerchief from the floor but it proved to be only a paper napkin, its edges made curious and asymmetrical lace by tiny teeth. Curtains shifted as the wind insinuated itself through the shrunken sash sides and the brass rings on their rods clattered softly. The house creaked and moaned. The loose clapboards made a strange fluttering sound beneath a gust of wind like a deck of riffled cards.

He went from room to room and found himself at last standing over the bed John Gload had shared with the woman he had called his wife. It was situated beneath a window and lay in a quadrangle of sallow light. He stared out the glass at the apple trees. An ashtray sat on the dusty sill. He set the metal canister down on the mattress and sat beside it and it toppled with a sound of shifting sand. A faint dust rose from the coverlet. He looked around the room. A chest of drawers, a calendar picturing a small yellow bird. In the gloom of a closet he could make out a row of paired and neatly aligned women's shoes that might have been a rank of elderly aunts hiding in that dim place in the moments before a surprise party, gloved hands pressed to their painted lips.

On a shelf in the garden shed as foretold he found the rusted Bag Balm can with its folded paper and he found the digging tools and he toted all down the road, so long unused it was now merely two paths separated by a windrow of wild wheat that sang on the undercarriage of his rented car when he'd arrived. He carried the spade and the spud bar over one shoulder and the canister cradled in his elbow and the dust rose beneath his feet like talcum. At the beginning of the inroad where he'd parked he stopped and leaned the tools against the car's quarterpanel and fished in his shirt pocket for the map. He unfolded it on the hood of the car, staring down at the old killer's rude cartography, his juvenile script. He felt like a child on a treasure hunt.

With his heels in the gravel at the edge of the county road he began pacing. And counting. He counted one hundred five steps ("normal steps, just regular walking steps") and stopped. There beside the road a great red stone stuck above the weeds. He had no idea of its size. It may well have had its roots in hell but what he could see of it would have weighed six or eight hundred pounds. It was cracked so perfectly in half it looked to have been cut with a band saw and it was here Millimaki was instructed to turn ninety degrees east and enter the orchard trees.

It was an awkward business, holding the childish map and the digging implements and the canister containing the ashes of the old killer. The fallen apples crushed beneath his feet gave off a winey smell as he counted his paces through the weft of branches and the knee-deep grass that grew thick among the gray boles of the trees. But Gload had been meticulous and had rehearsed the process many times against confusion and in ten minutes' time Millimaki nearly walked into the suspended harrow tines that marked where her bones were planted.

There was nothing there to indicate that a hole had been dug. The grass had grown up and the trees had dropped their leaves year upon year and the neglected apples moldered in the dirt. He began to dig and despite notations on the map's border assuring him that Francie's bones lay some six feet down, he feared with each shovelful that he would run the spade into a leg bone or dredge into the light instead of one of the innumerable rocks a grinning skull bewigged with auburn hair.

The day was mild and the wind found him even in that sheltered place but he was soon sweating nonetheless. Smooth round rocks from that ancient riverbed clanged under the spade's blade and roots as obdurate as reinforcing bar appeared and he chopped at them until his hands burned. He stopped once and laid his jacket aside in the grass and resumed digging. When the hole was three feet deep he stopped. It was less a grave than a posthole, like so many he had dug in the poor soil of his father's dryland operation under the buffalo jump. He leaned the spade and the metal bar in the crotch of a tree and ran a sleeve across his forehead. Above the faint rattle of dry leaves he thought he heard a cry but he stood listening and there was nothing. For an instant clear as crystal the far metronomic rofe rofe rofe of a dog. Then nothing. In the higher branches beyond the reach of deer a few small apples hung tenaciously on among the leaves, desiccated red gourds like Christmastime ornaments that seemed out of place among the gnarled phalanges of the feral trees—gray limbs, pale grass, pale sky.

When he tipped the can into the hole he was surprised at the rasping sound it made. He reversed the shovel and with the handle stirred among the ashes. He lay down and put his face close to be sure. Dust rose in the hole. A root cellar smell. Ashes, bits of charred bone. Finally he reached into the cool maw and sifted the mixture through his fingers but there were no teeth. He stood and wiped John Gload's ashes in a pale gray smear on his pants. It occurred to him that the old man would have approved of the exquisite anonymity of his own grave. Perhaps after all it was his plan—devout practitioner of his craft even at the end.

Millimaki stood looking down into the hole. After a while he removed Gload's last letter from the snap-button pocket of his shirt. He smiled grimly, remembering the brevity of Gload's summons, arriving six days into the old man's permanent and uninterruptible slumber: "Val, I'm ready for you now. In the tool shed in the Bag Balm can is everything you will need." It had come addressed simply to Deputy Valentine Millimaki, ATF, Cheyenne, Wyoming, and contained a check drawn on the Deer Lodge State Bank for $420.14. Note and check went into the hole. He had set the map aside in the long grass and now he took it up and threw it in. He stood for a long time with the wind cooling him and in the end he took the tiny silver charm on its silver chain from his pocket, weighed it in his palm and dropped it in.

Last he read the letter that had been written on yellow legal paper and folded and refolded until the page was small enough to fit through the hole in the top of the can:

> Thanks for coming, Valentine. If you didn't come whoevers reading this can go ahead and burn the whole deal cause it won't make no sense but I figure you would. I told you Wexler was ambitious he could of turned these in to the Bull and that would of been that but he wanted the glory if thats what youd call it. Like I said About him. But now there yours and you can find some bones and everybodys happy. None of these is Wexler

just so you know. I knew you were tired of finding bones and such so you can let the pogues at the Sheriffs take care of that part Just a little payback for putting up with an old man You were good to me Valentine. I hope you have a good life from here on in.

Your FRIEND John X Gload

PS I was yours even if you wasnt mine.

He put the letter in his breast pocket along with the topographical maps similarly folded, on them five clear Xs noting the location of graves in the breaks country north of the Missouri River and of the smelterworks and the city. Nameless bones—skulls without teeth, arms without hands—he knew would be dredged from their repose to occupy another hole under other stones, the plastic flowers planted there pale replicas of the wild blooms of prairie spring.

He began to throw dirt into the hole when he heard clearly then the high thin cry. He saw them drifting up from the river. At first they seemed mere wisps of smoke, like traces of fireworks in the flat white sky but they came on, riding thermals with infinitesimal movements of their chevron wings and soon enough they became clear, their breasts the color of dirty bandages. They came nearer and began to circle, two or three. A dozen. He dropped the shovel and moved into a clearing, his arms upheld and waving like the limbs of the orchard trees themselves. "Git," he called. He made shooing motions in the air and looked like a man trying to rid himself of something. He cried up at the birds. "Sonsofbitches. Git."

ACKNOWLEDGMENTS

My deep and lasting thanks to Dan Conaway, agent and friend; to Aaron Schlechter, for his intestinal fortitude; to Sarah Bowlin and her fine and talented colleagues at Holt. My gratitude extends miles in all directions for support and encouragement in the face of logic to Neil McMahon, Bill Kittredge, and friends and family who never stopped asking. I am grateful to my children for their sacrifice over the many years of my work. Thanks to Chuck Schuyler for legal insight and Jolanta Benal for her keen eye.

Special thanks to Mike Jaraczeski, ATF senior special agent, retired, for the many late-night, gin-fueled conversations that planted the seed.

And of course this book would not have happened without the enduring support, sensitive editing and beautiful poetic squint of my wife, Janet. It just flat wouldn't have.

WE COULD BE HEROES

BEN DIRS
TOM FORDYCE

MACMILLAN

First published 2009 by Pan Macmillan
an imprint of Pan Macmillan Ltd
Pan Macmillan, 20 New Wharf Road, London N1 9RR
Basingstoke and Oxford
Associated companies throughout the world
www.panmacmillan.com

ISBN 978-0-230-73615-3

1 3 5 7 9 8 6 4 2

A CIP catalogue record for this book is available from the British Library.

Typeset by SetSystems Ltd, Saffron Walden, Essex
Printed and bound in the UK by
CPI Mackays, Chatham, ME5 8TD

Tom Dedication
For Murf, my partner in excessive exercise, and for everyone I've ever annoyed, delayed or inconvenienced by disappearing off for a run/cycle/swim/catching contest.

Ben Dedication
For Mum, Dad, Nick and Oli

CONTENTS

PROLOGUE

CALAIS, OCTOBER 2007

TOM

I opened my eyes and looked around the inside of the campervan. It looked like a bomb had gone off in an underwear factory run by a pair of booze-soaked, sport-obsessed gadabouts. Everywhere you looked there were pants – hanging off cupboard-door handles, draped over the seats or stuffed into the half-closed cutlery drawer. Empty wine bottles were piled up on the dashboard. Salt-encrusted cycling shorts lay in a heap on the grill-pan. A rugby ball with eyes and a nose drawn on it in biro lay half-deflated on a pile of dusty flip-flops.

I climbed off my bunk and tugged the blinds open. Rain was going sideways past the window. The only colour for miles around came from a red neon sign blinking mournfully above the entrance of the hypermarché across the car park. We were alone in a sea of wet, grey concrete. I sighed and let the blinds drop back down.

From the bunk at the back of the van came the heavy, rhythmical rasping of a large asthmatic animal at sleep. Stepping over a 24-speed racing bike lying prone on the floor I rapped on the bulkhead. The rasping stopped.

'Already?' croaked a disappointed voice.

I rinsed out a pint glass, filled it with tap water and passed it to the shaking hand that reached out from underneath a pile of sleeping-bags and coats.

'Already,' I replied.

The greatest adventure of our lives had come to an end. After seven giddy, glorious weeks following the rugby World Cup around France, it was time for us to go home.

We had boozed in Bordeaux, tackled in Toulouse, partied in Paris and found nothing to do whatsoever in Saint Étienne. Our job had been to write a daily blog as we went along, lobbing in some video japes every few days and popping up for some chat on the radio, but to call it a job is to insinuate a degree of tedium and toil. There was none. The only task that was even vaguely shitty was emptying the campervan's chemical toilet, and that was nobody's fault but our own.

We'd thought beforehand that nothing could match the good fortune of our usual gig – watching cricket and writing live text commentary on the Beeb website as we went along. Staggeringly, that had proved to be wide of the mark. We would have pinched ourselves, but the risk of waking up was too great.

In the trusty Bloggernaut (the nickname our creaking van had been given by the blog users) we had cartwheeled from town to town in a haze of Calvados, up-and-unders and over-ripe soft cheese. In our wake lay epic sporting contests, never-closing bars, sun-baked beaches and appalling linguistic faux pas. We had danced nights away with bellowing Argentines, played invisible table tennis with tearful Australians and arm-wrestled Welsh women on campsites in Nantes. When there was no rugby to watch, I had recovered by cycling up mountains and swimming across lakes; Ben had eaten cold meats and smoked like a Russian soldier.

Now, it was over. In a few hours' time, a ferry would take us back to Blighty – back to a monochrome world of bad-news bank statements, soulless rented flats and towns where the most popular restaurant was a Dixie Fried Chicken.

Fantastique.

Ben fell out of his bunk, coughed like a backfiring tractor and scratched his stomach. Red-eyed and silenced by depression, he resembled an auditionee for an Ian Curtis biopic set in a pie shop.

'I'll buy you breakfast,' I said.

Inside the hypermarché's café, the menus were aimed with deadly precision at its booze-cruise clientele. So well-researched were the dishes that even the puddings came with a side portion of chips. We ordered omelettes and pushed the complimentary lagers to one side.

'My mum called me last night,' said Ben. 'She wanted to know if I wanted broccoli or cauliflower for dinner tonight. How depressing is that?'

He took a long suck on his fag and blew smoke at the life-size replica of Louis Blériot's plane which hung from the ceiling.

'How are we ever going to match the last two months? Things will never be this good again.'

It worried me to see him like this. The residual melancholy that must inevitably lie within a man whose parents have christened him Ben Dirs was in danger of overwhelming him.

At his lowest point on the trip so far – his mugging on the dark streets of Marseille in the insane aftermath of England's win over Australia – I had managed to put a smile back on his face by reminding him of the stadium manager we had met in Montpellier, a certain Monsieur Paul Bastard.

'Did I ever tell you about my mate Jon Pudding?' I said. 'His wife's just had twins, and they've named them Kate and Sidney.'

Ben took another drag and stared silently back.

'Yeah,' I said, 'and you know my mate Rob Ander, the one who got his girlfriend's sister pregnant? She had a little boy – they're calling him Phil.'

The waiter slammed two chip omelettes down on the table between us.

'Mahala Honeyballs,' I said desperately. 'Binky Pootwister. Herbert Lusty-Lusty.'

Ben shook his head sadly, picked up a chip and tapped it distractedly into the ashtray. 'Do you ever worry you'll die without having left a mark?' he asked despondently. 'I do. To be honest, in my bleaker moments, I sometimes wonder if I'll be one of those old blokes who sits in the pub, on his own, telling everyone he could have been a contender, yet no one even knows his name.'

He nodded at Blériot's plane. 'Take that bloke. He didn't sit on his backside, smoking and drinking his life away, did he? No. He went out there and he achieved something amazing. People doubted him – of course they did. They said he couldn't do it, that he was a madman. But that didn't stop him inventing penicillin, did it?'

I reached across and gently took the smouldering cigarette out of his omelette. 'Ben,' I said. 'How could anyone forget what you did in Montpellier? It was you and you alone who won that 3 a.m. break-dancing battle with the overweight

Australian girl. She thought her Funky Worm had won the day, but your Electric Boogaloo . . .'

'It's not enough,' he sniffed. 'I want to go down in history.'

I sat back and looked at him. He had tomato ketchup on his eyebrow. 'You're called Ben Dirs,' I said. 'You will.'

Rain splattered against the café windows. On the pavement, a man in leather trousers was arguing with a lady attempting to restrain a small yapping dog.

'Don't you feel the same?' he asked, his voice wobbling. 'We've spent our lives cheering from the sidelines, watching other people win things. Mainly Australian people too, with the exception of that fat girl.' He shook his head. 'I'm sick of being a watcher. Why shouldn't other people cheer us on from the sidelines, rather than the other way round? Just once, I'd like to be the hero.'

Outside, the lady was no longer restraining the dog. The man was still wearing leather trousers, but they now had a small dog attached to the left thigh.

'Of course you do,' I said softly. 'I'd like to be a hero too. Who wouldn't? But look at us. There's nothing special about us. I can do a passable Kevin Pietersen impression and you're good at smoking. That's it.'

There was a thud as the dog hit the window pane and slid down the glass, no longer yapping. 'They don't pick you to represent your country just because you fancy a go,' I said. 'Particularly if you are good at smoking. Whatever it is it takes, you and me haven't got it.'

'I'll tell you what we have got,' said Ben, pushing his plate away. 'We've got no kids, no mortgages and no prospect of getting either soon. So we can still do it – become the best at something. It's just a case of working out what that something might be.'

'You are the best at something,' I said. 'Montpellier has never seen a boogaloo like it.'

'I want more,' said Ben, jabbing his fork at my chest, 'and I know you do too. Why else would you cycle up all those mountains? And eat all that vegetarian shite? You love a pointless sporting challenge, so I know you'd love to be a champion.'

Pointless sporting challenge? He didn't know the half of it. My favourite moment in two years of going out with an ex-ex girlfriend had involved me accidentally dropping a crumb of toast, instinctively flicking out a foot, trapping the crumb on my instep, flicking it instantaneously back into the air, catching it back on the toast and then munching it with a delighted flourish. The ex-ex girlfriend hadn't even noticed.

'It's a beautiful idea,' I said, and I meant it. 'But it's also madness. What are we going to win? You might be a shoo-in for gold at the World Lateness Championships, but there isn't one. And if there was, you'd be late for it anyway.'

I paused for a moment to consider that one more closely. Could being late for the World Lateness Championships actually make you more worthy of the title than someone who'd turned up in time to take part? Did the organizers pretend the event started four hours earlier than it actually did, just to make sure the competitors got there on time? How late did you have to be until you were considered early for the following year's championship?

'There's got to be a sport somewhere we could be the best at,' said Ben, with a glint in his eye. 'We just need to find out what it is. Forget rugby or cricket or football or tennis. I tried all those years ago and it didn't happen.'

Another sporting memory surfaced. During a lull in proceedings in the office I had once taken part in a spontaneous game which involved trying to catch a golf ball on the end of a metal relay baton. The sense of pride and achievement in being able to do that pointless activity better than anyone else had been both significant and long-lasting.

Champions. I had to admit it – it had a lovely ring to it.

'There's some weird old sports out there,' I said, a tremor of excitement audible in my voice.

'Bloody weird sports that see far lesser men than you and me crowned world champions,' said Ben.

World champions! I tried to picture how it would feel to have a solid gold medal hanging round my neck. There'd be champagne, of course, and victory parades on open-top buses. Lucrative sponsorship deals. Giggling groupies, inevitably.

I stared out of the window, so caught up in the thought that I almost failed to notice that the man in leather trousers was now kissing the woman both passionately and publicly. The dog was nowhere to be seen.

'You got any major plans for the next twelve months?' I asked casually.

'Yup,' nodded Ben. 'I'm not getting married, I'm not buying a house and I'm not expecting my first child.'

'So – in theory – you could dedicate a year to something?'

'To travel the globe, jousting for glory in championship after championship? Oh yes.'

I scanned my own mental diary. I had things to do, but nothing that would give rise to open-top groupies and giggling buses. It would mean Ben and I spending the foreseeable future in each other's pockets, but we'd worked through any issues months ago. He didn't interrupt my exercise and I didn't complain about his smoking. I was careful not to wake him when I got up early; he was careful not to wake me when he went to bed late. He ate the meat, I ate the vegetables. I drove, he washed up. When the time came to celebrate, we matched each other drink for drink, and if every fourth one of mine was water and every third one of his was the filthiest local firewater he could find, that was fine.

'We'd need a new van,' I said. 'The BBC want this one back.'

'Let them have it!' shouted Ben. 'It ruddy stinks. We'll buy a new one!'

'A new second-hand one.'

'A new cheap second-hand one.'

'The Bloggernaut is dead. Long live the Bloggernaut!'

We were both standing up. Ben was waving and gesticulating like an orang-utan at a rave. There was omelette everywhere – on the table, on the floor, in his hair.

'I'll start the research tonight at my mum's house,' he said, eyes blazing.

'Don't make promises you can't keep. You won't get round to it. We both know that. Anyway – what about your mum's broccoli?'

'Forget my mum's broccoli. She's doing cauliflower.'

'Respect to Mama Dirs. I might stay over for tea.'

'This time next year, you and me could be world champions, Tommy!'

'We could be heroes, Benjamin – we could be heroes . . .'

I

COAL

BEN

So there I am, standing at the bottom of a hill in a small Yorkshire village called Gawthorpe. It's Easter Monday, it's snowing and I'm dressed like a proper wally in T-shirt and shorts. Then, to top it all, some clown goes and dumps 50 kilograms of coal on my back. And all I can think is: 'Life didn't have to be like this – if only I hadn't bollocksed up my Geography A-level.'

How did I let Tom, who I thought was one of the good guys, pull a stroke like this? When we made our glorious pledge, he was strangely reticent on the subject of lugging large sacks of coal up steep northern inclines. Stone skimming? Probably. Pipe smoking? Maybe. Coal humping? Not a ruddy peep. My nan had a name for people like him: 'Cunning little Stalins'. The key difference being that while Stalin wasn't, as far as I'm aware, big on his fitness, Tom just happens to be a seriously handy triathlete who could probably cycle up Ben Nevis with 50 kilos of coal in his shopping basket. My nan had another name for people like Tom: 'Bastards'.

In fairness to Tom (who, I must clarify, has never stuck

an ice-pick in anyone's head), he did tell me a full week before the event. Still, given my fitness levels, that's like telling Peter Andre that in a week he's going to take over as Governor of the Bank of England. Plus, trying to break into the world of coal-carrying in Essex is almost as difficult as getting a foot-up in tennis. Where does a man of modest means find a municipal court with a functioning net and a weed-free baseline nowadays? And where does a man purchase a giant bag of coal in 2008? I tried the local Esso garage, but I wasn't sure a couple of 4-kilogram bags of barbecue briquettes would accurately replicate the agony.

Luckily, my dad has a shed positively rammed with large sacks, containing everything from peat to potatoes to the very extensive collection of gentlemen's titles my mum found under my bed after I moved out. I plumped for the peat, although at 22 kilos it was hardly ideal. The fact that my mum and dad's garden is approximately 20 feet long was also a bit of a drawback, so the car park behind my flat in Romford was going to have to stand in for Yorkshire's rolling hills. What Mehmet, owner of the newsagent next door, made of my training sessions is difficult to say, but he did growl in my face one day and vigorously massage my biceps, which, seeing as the Turks know a thing or two about weightlifting, I took to be an encouraging sign.

Still, 22 kilos of peat, as even Peter Andre will tell you, is not 50 kilos of coal and I travelled up to Tom's brother's place in Leeds with a slightly nauseous feeling that started in the tips of my hair and stretched down to the pit of my stomach. Tom, unsurprisingly for one of the fittest men in the known world, seemed slightly more sanguine when he greeted me at the station. 'Ready to be a champ?' he said, with arms outstretched and a beaming smile on his suddenly eminently slappable face. My mood darkened further on discovering his brother Rob had also decided to take part, which meant I could look forward to being humiliated by two Fordyces in one day.

'Dunno about you, but I can't wait to get started,' said Tom as we tucked into tuna and pasta bake with frozen crinkle-cut chips sprinkled on top. ('The dinner of champions,' according to Rob. Champion of what? The Bedsit Olympics?)

'Yes and no,' I replied. 'Wasn't it the world marbles championship this weekend? Marbles, they're pretty light, I would have fancied myself at marbles.'

'Too much skill and tactics involved,' replied Tom, 'and anyway, you can't beat a tough physical challenge.'

That, in my mind at least, was a declaration of war. And I was sure, over the course of the year, that my light artillery of nettles, peas and eggs would be able to outwit even his heaviest guns.

TOM

Nerves. I'd seen Ben fearful before, not least when he and I had been caught doing poor South African accents by a group of five enormous Boers in a back-street café in Paris before the World Cup final. Back then we had got away with it by pretending to be French (even five enormous Boers hesitate at starting a fight with an entire country) but such tactics could only exacerbate our problems in West Yorkshire.

As always I tried to calm him with the trusty tools of cheap red wine and duty-free cigarettes. See it as a toe in the World Championship water, I told him. Sure, coal carrying might not be the ideal opener, but it would give us a decent indication of what it took to be a champ. And if any of the pre-race favourites took their eyes momentarily off the prize – why, there might just be a Dirs- or Fordyce-shaped hole we could sneak through to win.

By midnight his mood seemed positively chirpy. While he'd turned down the chance to practise his technique by carrying me piggy-back up three flights of steps, he'd allowed me to carry him. From my own point of view it was an ideal confidence-booster. No matter how uncomfortable the sack of coal turned out to be, at least it wouldn't be smoking or spilling cheap red wine down my back.

BEN

Live, as I do, in Romford and you get the distinct feeling that the apocalypse is just around the corner, probably drinking a bottle of WKD and getting ready to gob on your back. Whether it's the teenage mother tearing apart a Happy Meal for her baby in McDonald's ('I know she ain't got no teef, but she can chew it, can't she . . .') or the morbidly obese lady sharing doughnuts on the bus with her son ('Why are you having two?' 'BECAUSE I DIDN'T 'AV ANY FUCKIN' BREAKFAST!'), or indeed the friend whose mother gave her daughter a remote-controlled dildo for Christmas (come to think of it, his sister does have short arms . . .), not a day goes by when I don't momentarily turn into my dad and think aloud: 'I'm pretty sure it never used to be as bad as this.'

And so many a Romfordian (or is it Romforder?) clings to the hope that somewhere, out beyond the A12, are little reminders of what England used to be like: villages where people drink milk warm from the churn, young couples stepping out down lovers' lane on a summer evening, old men singing folk songs in the local tavern, people managing to chat to each other on public transport without using the words 'wanker' and 'bollocks'. My expectations aren't as high as all that – for me, just being able to walk through a town centre at night without stepping in a pool of vomit is the stuff of a madman's dreams.

Gawthorpe is situated on the A638 between Dewsbury and Wakefield, has got chocolate box Yorkshire written all over it and, the icing on the cake, a maypole on the village green. One of the organizers of the coal race, Brian Wilding, had been kind enough to send ahead some poems written by the event's founder, a Mr Fred Hirst, to give me a feel for the village and the history of the event. As a countryside-starved Essex man, I liked what I read:

It began in the Beehive a long time ago
The argument started as the beer began to flow.

Reggie Sedgewick, to Louis Hartley did say,
'I am a much better man than thee any day.

'At carrying coal, I am surely the best
All tha' wants to do is have a rest.'

Amos Clapham was there and this he said:
'I can beat both of you stood on my head.'

Horace Crouch said, 'For 10 pounds I will back
Reggie Sedgewick – to be first with the sack.'

Louis Hartley was not to be outdone:
'That 10 pounds is mine, it can easily be won.'

'O'wd on a minute,' is what I said,
Better introduce myself, my name is Fred.

'There must be something we can do with this,
It's a great opportunity, too good to miss.

'Let's have a coal-carrying race
On Easter Monday let it take place.'

It all started for a bit of fun
But, surely the hardest race to be run.

Proudly after thirty-four years we present
A truly great British Event.

But just as I was thinking of digging out the Harris Tweed from the boot, Brian went all melancholy on me and in the process shattered a few illusions.

'At one time, the village was a village, as opposed to being an extension of Wakefield as it is now,' says Brian. 'It's changed completely. There used to be three shops, a post office, a working men's club, community club, three pubs, and they were all supported quite well. Everyone knew everybody, but a lot of strangers have moved into the village and people keep themselves to themselves. Up to when I was nine or ten years old I could have named everyone in every house. Now, a lot of people don't even know their next door neighbours' names.' To be honest, that's not what I wanted to hear, although I tried to lighten Brian's mood by pointing out there are probably people in Romford who aren't on first-name terms with their flatmates.

Still, they're clinging on to the Maypole Feast and procession in Gawthorpe, which has been an annual event since 1875, so the community flame flickers. And it's comforting to

know there are still feasts in England that don't come in a cardboard bucket, washed down with a two-litre bottle of Coke. Although the pit has long since gone, the village retains its links with the coal industry and the 'coil race', as it is pronounced in Gawthorpe, was first run in 1964 to raise funds for the Maypole festivities.

'I was seventeen or thereabouts when the coal race first started,' says Brian. 'You couldn't say hello to Fred Hirst without him pulling a bunch of raffle tickets out of his pocket, and saying, "'av a shillings worth." And it was all for the maypole – he lived and breathed the maypole, it was his bread and butter. Anyway, he cottoned on to this idea of having a coal race to raise money for Maypole Feast day, because even at that time it was dwindling as far as money and everything else was concerned. A lot of people in the village have got no idea how much it costs to put May Day on. When I was on the committee, I was looking at something like £6,500 to £7,500 to put it on. Even the local band want paying to come and march for us.'

Brian's rather deflating words gave me the sudden urge to stroll off into a nearby field and crumble soil between my fingers while looking wistfully into the distance – but the arrival in the Royal Oak car park of a bastard great coal truck quickly focused my mind on the task ahead. As did the appearance of 'King Can', an anti-litter warrior from Scorton, Lancashire, and a man who can remember the year, date and exact time of day he started pumping iron.

'I bought my own free weights on 27 May 2006, 2 p.m.,' said King Can. 'And the bar bells. And I practise every day, alternating a snatch and jerk lift and also the dead lift. I did snatch and jerk last night and tonight's the dead lift. My personal best at the snatch and jerk is 195.5 lb and my dead

lift has reached 450 lb clean. I've improved a lot.' As I listened, I fingered my biceps, and it suddenly occurred to me they had the consistency of cream cheese.

King Can, it turned out, also competed in 1984 and 1986. So why, I asked him, the sudden urge to put his body through hell all over again at the age of 48?

'I was interested in coming up in 2006, because that would have been twenty years, but I didn't have enough money because someone had robbed my mother's inheritance,' he replied, with a candour that made this southerner wince. 'And I couldn't come last year because I picked up a food bug on the Maundy Thursday and was shitting through the eye of a needle.' Which reminded me, where did a hungry 'coil-humper' get a pre-race meal in Gawthorpe?

So off we trotted for a walk of the course, about ten of us in all, like jockeys running the rule over Aintree on the morning of the Grand National. On leaving the Royal Oak on Owl Lane, the competitors rise about 300 metres before turning left and winding up towards Benny Harrop Hill, a steep approach to the Shoulder of Mutton public house, in front of which stands the village maypole. It's a 1012.5-metre carry in all, and in 1991 and 1995 a certain Dave Jones of Meltham completed the course in an unfathomable 4 minutes 6 seconds.

'Any fell runners among you?' piped up a chap called Neil, who must have been about 9 stone and pushing 60. The question was met with much silent shoe-gazing and embarrassed tugging of jumpers, and even Tommy, a veteran of umpteen triathlons, looked a bit panicked when the wiry little sod added that (a) he was competing in his hundredth marathon in a week's time and (b) he delivered coal for a living – 300 bags a day. I also learned about local hero

George Crossland, who was still competing at the grand old age of 69 and who once ran there and back without dropping the sack – before helping load the sacks back on the coal lorry. The secret of his strength, according to Brian: 'He never smoked and ate two breakfasts every day.' As I am a man who smokes two cigarettes for breakfast every day, the omens weren't looking good.

Tommy, Rob and I broke from the pack and found a spot to eat in a village hall just down from the Shoulder of Mutton, lured in by a promise of corned beef hash for £1.80. After confirming with Tom that the A638 didn't double up as a time portal and it wasn't in fact 1978, Rob and I fell upon our gigantic portions like the ravenous coal-warriors we were about to become. Tommy, meanwhile, spent his time flipping through compilation disco LPs at the rear of the hall and sipping herbal tea, before pointing out there were only thirty minutes until kick-off.

Now, I'm no nutritionist, but I'm pretty sure you'll never catch Paula Radcliffe – or dear old George Crossland for that matter – falling upon a plate of corned-beef hash (served on a pancake mattress) half an hour before a marathon. So my late breakfast, allied with a bowel-cleansing Marlboro Light (am I the only southerner who feels unmanly sparking up a Marlboro Light Oop North?) had me fearing I might follow in Paula's footsteps and drop my guts on the side of Gawthorpe High Street.

It was when King Can informed me, on the way back down to the Royal Oak, that Arnold Schwarzenegger was popping over to Scorton in 2009 to back his anti-litter campaign that I really started getting jittery.

'He'll be coming over with lots of other celebrities,' said King Can. 'They're going to put King Can on every channel, although they'll keep Coronation Street and the other soaps on . . .' George Orwell, after a Sunday morning spent browsing for ceiling tiles at his local B&Q, could not have conjured anything bleaker. And then Ben Fogle rocked up out of the blue with a camera crew to really put the shits up me. Not only was I about to humiliate myself in front of the good burghers of Gawthorpe, I was about to humiliate myself in front of the good viewers of *Countryfile*, and you can't get a tougher crowd than those two. Disappointingly, Fogle seemed like even more of a bloody nice bloke in person than he does on the telly, and a healthier looking specimen I'd never laid eyes on: blond of locks, golden of skin and bulbous of thigh, he made Tom look like Frank Gallagher from *Shameless* and me like *Homo habilis*.

Back at the Royal Oak, Brian, perhaps sensing my alarm at the appearance of this otherworldly being, thrust a disclaimer into my hands with the words, 'Just so we're not liable for owt,' before asking how the training had gone.

'Good – I've been carrying my girlfriend's bags back from the shops for years,' quipped Tom, but Brian failed to see the funny side.

'Not many do it from down South,' said Brian, his eyes boring deep into Tom's soul. 'They think they know hills in Derbyshire, they haven't got a clue. These hills make grown men cry.'

The pre-race banter confirmed what I had heavily suspected all along, namely that I was coming into the event rather undercooked compared with the rest of the field. Eight-time champion John Hunter, 43, had spent the previous three months training with sandbags across the hills of his native Scarborough. John, who has been competing since 1990, has also completed the Billy The Kid Tombstone Race in New Mexico, which requires competitors to drag an 80-lb stone over a 100-yard course, complete with two 5-ft hurdles.

'That's what I do in my spare time, lift heavy stuff up and down things,' said John, who once covered the course in 4 minutes 19 seconds. I studied his face for a trace of irony, and either he possesses a sense of humour so dry you could use it as kindling, or he was telling the truth.

The training regime of Matthew Wainwright, competing for the fourth time, sounded even more masochistic, seemingly incorporating instruments of torture.

'This year I set aside three months to prepare specifically for it,' said Matthew, whose first love is cycling and who completed an 'ironman' in 2007 – a 2.4-mile swim and a 112-mile bike ride. Oh, yeh, and a marathon at the end. 'I did two months pulling Russian kettlebells – like a cannonball with a handle welded on – across a tennis court, starting with 16 kilos and moving up to 40 kilos, and then one month before the race I started running with a sack of coal on me back. I've also got a Garmin GPS [nope, me neither . . .] which I set to a race pace of 4 minutes 30. I also went up to the course and did it twice . . .' Twice. Impressive. '. . . with a ten-minute break between each one.' And there I was thinking the Gawthorpe coal race would be a bunch of pissed-up farmers, blacksmiths, miners and the like staggering up a hill for a bit of a giggle.

Mark from Wakefield seemed more like my kind of coal-humper. 'I was in the pub last night getting shit-faced and me mates told me about the race, so I thought I'd come down and give it a go,' said Mark. Now, some might consider it a fairly ignoble aim merely not to come last in anything, but I decided then and there that that was the extent of my ambition: 'Wait for Mark from Wakefield to collapse, as surely he would do, carry your sack past his prone body, and anything after that is a Brucie bloody bonus.'

As the race drew nearer, talk turned to technique. Defending champion Phil Ounsley, no doubt sensing that this rather doughy-looking southerner wasn't going to present much of a threat, was only too happy to share a few of his precious 'coil-humping' pearls.

'Drape the sack over your shoulders and use the back of your neck, take small strides and don't over-stretch,' said Phil, as Tom, Rob and I leaned in reverentially, as if Phil was talking about another kind of humping entirely. 'And don't grip the bag too hard, because your forearms will cramp up. Grip it lightly, as if you're cupping a budgie . . .' Did he just say what I thought he just said? A budgie? Seeing as a budgie weighs about 30 grams, I couldn't help thinking he'd been doing it wrong for all these years. That said, Matthew Wainwright was quick to agree that the grip was key.

'I dropped the sack a couple of years ago and I've had real trouble with my forearms,' said Matthew. 'But this time round, me kettlebells should have helped. And I'm also using a bit of chalk.' A nervous scan of the other competitors revealed that some were wearing weightlifting gloves; suddenly my own withered little hands on the end of my withered little arms appeared wholly inadequate.

Having logged these tips in the old memory bank – apart from the one about the budgie – the tarpaulin on the side of the coal lorry was whipped aside in dramatic fashion to reveal approximately three tonnes' worth of black gold. Tom and Rob were quick to test out the equipment and have a jog around the car park, but I declined a tune-up, mainly because I wasn't entirely sure I'd be able to take the weight and

didn't want to embarrass myself. The ladies' race prece
ours, and I couldn't help but feel a little pang of jealousy
when I clocked the 20-kg bags they had been asked to carry. 'No one complains,' explained the official programme, 'for they add a feminine touch where it is least expected.' I don't think I'd ever wanted to be a woman so badly. Now, with the ladies out of sight, it was my turn. OK, it was our turn, but rarely had I felt so lonely.

'No event in the Olympic Games could stimulate more enthusiasm than this annual contest of stamina and muscle,' stated the programme, and while there weren't exactly tens of thousands of screaming fans lining the course, there were probably more than you got at the 10 metre air pistol in Beijing. The starter ushered all thirty-six of us together for a little chat before the big push and warned us against any funny business, at which point I kicked myself for not slipping the lorry driver a few quid in return for 'liberating' a few lumps of coal from my bag. But it was too late now, and even a cry of 'trip that bastard Fogle' as we made our way to the lorry failed to raise the spirits. As for Fogle, a man who had rowed across the Atlantic just a few years earlier, he looked more than a little bit intimidated as, one by one, the competitors were loaded up like carthorses.

Realizing that the starting gun would only be triggered when everyone was saddled, and not wanting to stand around for too long with eight stones' worth of hard, lumpy stuff boring into my neck, I used some tactical nous and loitered at the rear of the pack. When it was my turn, I half expected the driver to pipe up with a cheery 'crucifixion?' as he heaved the sack on to my back, although I felt a surge of relief on finding that I was at least able to take the strain. Then, with my eyes focused on the tarmac about six inches in front of strange thoughts began to swirl round my was caught up in a natural disaster or had to carry 50 kg a kilometre up a hill to – or someone else's? Would I be able to do ordyce, I had to leave Tom behind in the fire because I'm a fat schmuck who smokes too much.' The shame of it. So I decided to role-play my way through it: the bag of coal was Tom and the Royal Oak was burning. Then I heard the crack of the starter pistol and we were off.

I didn't actually think many people 'ran' the coal race. I thought most people 'shuffled' or 'shambled' at best. So the sight of thirty-five pairs of feet disappearing at great pace into the distance will go down as one of the most demoralizing of my life. I was really letting my imagination run riot now: bollocks to saving Tommy from a blazing pub, I was now Jesus and this was bloody Calvary. It was Easter after all. Following a couple of abortive attempts to break into a trot I realized that while slow and steady was never going to win the race, it might prevent me from having a heart attack or snapping a fibula. So I shuffled. How long would it take to reach the top by shuffling? Ten minutes? Half an hour? Surely I could beat George Crossland's time of 16 minutes – he was 69 for God's sake, so he must have shuffled. The crowd quickly deserted me, trailing the main pack towards the finish, and I got my head down and concentrated on placing one foot in front of the other, a light flurry of snow and the chunter of the coal lorry my only companions from that point on.

It's not difficult to get your head down when you've got 50 kg of coal lying across the back of your neck. The really difficult part, as I had been warned, is keeping it there. The problem with lumps of coal is they're disobedient; they don't

sit still in their bag, but keep fighting each other, like frig
ened puppies, to get into the corners. And they're fucking
lumpy. So while I had been expecting my legs to fade first, in fact all my energy seemed to be taken up with repeatedly hauling the bag back into a manageable position. After a hundred metres or so my forearms were stiffening, my fingers felt like they were going to snap like twigs and my neck was so sore it felt as though I had been sleeping in the bath for a fortnight. If only Budgie Boy could have seen me, he would have been laughing his cods off. He was probably already on his third pint in the Shoulder of Mutton at that point.

The plight of Jesus slipped off the menu pretty early, to be replaced by rather more mundane questions. Such as: is it my imagination or is it easier to get a round of applause on Question Time than it used to be? Why have none of Dennis Waterman's loved ones told him that his new teeth make him look like Dick Emery's vicar? And will there ever come a point in my life when I actually like the taste of beer? Then I saw him: right there, wrestling with his bag about fifty metres ahead of me, a man who just might save me from total and utter humiliation.

Like a sailor in a storm, albeit an extremely calm one with not much wind and no waves to speak of, I remained focused on the big northern bugger ahead. 'Reel him in, Dirsy, just keep reeling him in,' I kept repeating to myself, forgetting I was travelling so slowly I was almost going backwards. And then it happened. His right hand came free, the bag twisted across his back and he could hold it no longer. He was out of the ruddy game! Now all I had to do was get a couple of steps beyond him, drop the sack and I'd won my own sad little victory. To my relief, he didn't even try to pick the bag

within the rules but nigh-on impossible, so
eth gritted and whimpering like a little girl.
d like an eternity, but what was probably
nds, I passed his sack and rewarded myself
k – not quite a weekend in Bath, but as pleasant in the circumstances – and looked for more signs of life ahead. I could only make out four or five distant figures, humping their way towards the bottom of Benny Harrop Hill, and so I decided my job was done for the day. I dropped the bag, sank to my knees and wondered about the fate of the brothers Fordyce up ahead.

TOM

'Don't lose to Dirs,' I kept saying to myself. 'As long as you don't lose to Dirs, you've avoided total humiliation.'

In my mind, it was all so unfair. I was coming off the back of a nasty twelve-week spell of post-viral fatigue – almost certainly brought on from having to chauffeur Ben around France for all those weeks in the Bloggernaut while trying to match his thirst-quencher intake. The only exercise I'd been able to manage for months was opening my eyelids when I woke up every morning, and even that had been so exhausting it had sent me straight back to sleep.

Still – all things are relative. At least I didn't have a liver as marinaded as a tikka chicken breast or lungs that had seen more smoke than a Northumberland kippery. Nor had I piled through a trough of corned-beef hash thirty minutes before kick-off. With a fag for dessert.

My pre-planned tactics were simple. Balance the coal evenly across the shoulders, keep the back straight and take the strain through the legs. Instead, as the sack landed on my neck with an audible cracking, there seemed to be a very real danger that my head might be forced clean through my shoulders, into my digestive tract and out of my own backside. I briefly wondered what it would feel like looking up at my own headless body, lurching around with a bag of coal across its back.

I staggered the first few metres with the tip of my nose grazing the asphalt and was aware of nothing but pairs of heels disappearing away from me. What shoes had Ben been wearing? Not those – they had clearly been used for running. Those? They were matched with clean socks – no chance. I was certain I was last. All I could hear was the rasp of my breath. The cold bit into my fingers. I felt snow on my face and tried to break into a run. It was almost impossible. I might as well have tried to tap-dance with an elephant on my back. Like a chubby toddler taking his first steps, I wasn't so much walking as just about not falling over.

At the foot of Benny Harrop Hill I was aware of other blue-shirted stumblers around me. None of them was wearing Ben's shorts. The crowd were leaning in from either side of the road, yelling and waving like Tour de France fanatics. The old triathlon fighting spirit kicked in and I picked up the pace. Where was Dirs?

As the Shoulder of Mutton came into view the adrenalin hit me like an espresso enema. I could see my rivals strung out in front of me. I can have you, I thought, latching on to one and passing him, and I can have you, I thought, closing on the next one – and you don't know I'm coming, and you look like you're almost dead, and you haven't got time to react if I come past . . .

Uh-oh. The sack was slipping. I was 20 metres from the finish line and the sack was slipping. I'd lost all feeling in my fingers, and the coal had started to shift. Fifteen metres to go, and I was taking two steps sideways for every one forwards. Thirteen metres – come on legs, remember the old days – 12 metres, and it was like gravity had trebled. Eleven metres – the pavement was looming up . . . 10 metres – 10 metres . . .

I hit the deck at the speed of a skydiving hippo. Limbs splayed, I raised my forehead from the concrete just in time to see two competitors trot past me. Panic forced me to my feet. I grabbed the sack and heaved. Nothing. I could get it about two inches off the ground, but as far as power-cleaning it back on to my shoulders again, I might as well have been lifting the Roly-Polys' tour bus. Two more rivals went past. It was heartbreaking. I could have sneezed on the finish line, so close was I, but I was stuck. Another man went past. The locals were shouting something at me. 'Draggeet!' they were screaming. 'Draggeet!'

Draggeet? Was he some local hero who'd just come past me? Charlie Draggeet, five times North Yorkshire cross-country champion? 'Draggeet, love!' cried an old lady. I stared back at her, my eyeballs out on stalks as I tried once again to hoist the bag. 'Drag. Eet!' she bellowed. Drag it. Of course! I seized the corners of the sack and pulled. It shifted three inches. I pulled again and picked up a little momentum. Another man staggered past. There was the finish line – five more paces. Another man passed me. Dirs? Fogle?

My virus-sapped legs felt like soggy Twiglets. Like a dung-beetle pushing a ball of hardened wildebeest shit up a mountain, I forced the bag over a wall onto the village green and collapsed onto my back. I felt a man slap me on the leg.

'Good lad,' he said. 'Eighteenth. You should ha' had tenth, but you fell apart like a reet girl.'

I lifted my head in time to see Fogle totter past, surrounded by cameramen and fawning local ladies. Hot on his heels was the younger Fordyce brother – twenty-second and twenty-fifth respectively. I looked around at the exhausted athletes, some lying on the snowy concrete, others in the arms of their support teams.

But where was Dirs?

BEN

I was getting a very cosy ride on the back of a coal lorry, thank you very much. I'd hitched a lift up to the Shoulder of Mutton and was mercilessly heckled by children along the way. 'Quitter!' shouted one young scamp, before chucking me a wristy, well-practised 'wanker' sign. It turned out I was one of only three people who didn't make it to the top and I now had a pretty good idea of what it was like to be in a travelling freak show: 'Roll up, roll up ladies and gentlemen! Behold, the weediest man in the whole of England!'

I made it in time to see the presentations, and was more than a little surprised to learn that the chap who'd been off his noggin in a pub in Wakefield a few hours earlier had come third. Mark, it turned out, was a professional boxer, and he was quick to point out that while carrying a bag of coal up a big hill had been tough, it didn't compare to getting punched in the face for six three-minute rounds. Defending champion Phil Ounsley had come second in 4 minutes 50 seconds, while Matthew Wainwright, he of the kettlebells and Garmin GPS, had romped home in first place with a time of 4 minutes 32 seconds.

Thirty-year old design engineer Matthew picked up a cup and a 'modest cash prize' provided by H. B. Clark & Co., a local brewery, but what are baubles and money when you've just proved yourself to be the greatest carrier of coal on the planet?

'Let's be honest, there's not many things I could be world champion at,' explained Matthew. 'I remember years ago me mates telling me about it and saying it were unbelievable, that all these blokes were sprinting with 50 kilos on their back, they couldn't comprehend it. So to be the world champion now, it don't seem right. I run me spuds off to get to the top of the hill and then once I was in the crowd, the roar got me to the finish. Obviously I was in absolute agony but the crowd pushed me on and I was thinking, "Bloody hell, I'm gonna be a world champion." That's what kept me going.'

Would Matthew be back to defend his crown? You bet he would, although he doubts Dave Jones's almost mythical world record will ever be broken.

'I've got a 4 minute 20 run in me but 4 minutes 6 seconds is absolutely ridiculous. That's like a six-minute mile, uphill, with that on your back. I can't get my head round it.' And that coming from a man who does ironman triathlons in his spare time. To me, a man for whom getting up in the middle of the night to go to the toilet is a bit of an effort, Dave Jones's mark is as incomprehensible as wormholes.

Tommy, meanwhile, was washing his so-called virus away with an isotonic drink that smelt like cat's urine. 'Did you realize that you, me, Rob and Fogle are the only competitors who aren't from north of Derby?' he said wonderingly. 'That makes me Southern Area World Coal-Carrying Champion. It's not a bad start.'

While supping on a welcome pint in the Royal Oak, I was collared once again by King Can. 'I came twenty-fourth,' said The King, beaming from ear to ear. 'In 1984 I was placed twenty-fourth, and that was twenty-four years ago, when I was aged twenty-four. Twenty-four years on, on the twenty-fourth of March, I also finished twenty-fourth. How's that, eh?' And we took that perfect note of symmetry as our cue to get the hell out of Gawthorpe. 'This time next year I'll be on the telly all the time, all over the world,' roared The King as we rolled out of the car park. 'Plus newspapers . . . make sure you call me after *Countryfile*!'

2

STILTON

TOM

I was trying to eat a bowl of cereal without crying when Ben phoned.

'Tommy!' he yelled, with the upbeat manner of a man who has pulled out of a coal-carrying contest before the course even started to go uphill. 'How you feeling?'

I winced. It was three days since the denouement on the snow-strewn streets of Gawthorpe, and I was still having trouble sitting down. Initially the pain had been restricted merely to my entire back, but in the last day it had spread down through the buttocks and begun to infiltrate my legs. Already I could feel my toes beginning to throb.

'It hurts when I brush my teeth,' I said.

'Don't worry about it,' said Ben dismissively. 'Fogle probably can't even walk straight, not after that spanking you gave him. Anyway – I've got some good news for you. I've found our next event.'

I could hear him scrabbling with some paper on the other end of the line. Knowing Dirs, he had written down the key details on the back of a receipt and then filed it somewhere safe like the butter drawer in his fridge.

'Hold up – I can't read my own writing,' he said. 'The burnt matchstick didn't work very well on the back of the fag packet.'

A poor impression of a trumpet fanfare gave way to a run of throat-ripping coughs. 'Right. Like cheese? Like rolls? Good. Because you, sunshine, will shortly be taking part in the forty-ninth running of the World Stilton-Rolling Championships.'

I shook my head. 'No no,' I said firmly. 'There's no way I'm chasing a cheese down a hill. I've seen it before. It's for maniacs. It's guaranteed broken bones. It's certain death.'

'Different cheese, different event,' said Dirs. 'You're thinking about all those Aussie and Kiwi clowns chasing a Double Gloucester down a hill and losing legs and ball bags and stuff. Forget about Gloucester, that's a demolition derby. This one's teams of four, racing each other along the main street in Stilton, winner goes through to the next round. Stilton-rolling is the cheese equivalent of the Monaco Grand Prix. You'll love it.'

'You mean "we",' I corrected.

'Nope,' said Ben. 'You and whoever else you fancy having in your team. I can't make it. I'm taking the Doris to Italy. Sorry son.' He coughed again. 'Booked the flights weeks ago, not a lot I can do.'

The line went dead.

I mulled the scenario over. In many ways Ben's absence would be no bad thing. If our trip around France was anything to go by, he'd be unable to get within arm's length of a cheese without stuffing the entire thing into his cavernous maw. I had visions of him wading wild-eyed through the village, crumbs of ripe Stilton in his stubble, brandishing a baguette over his head like a monstrous carbohydrate claymore.

It was also true that he owed his sweet lady Katie a substantial favour. For starters, she was actually going out with him, and had been for over six months. Secondly, she had proven herself willing to regularly leave her home town (Paris) to stay the weekend at his (Romford). The trip to Italy had to happen. At the same time, it would feel a little wrong going into such a big competition without any Dirs influence at all. This, after all, was a joint quest for glory. Even if he couldn't be present in person, I would have to ensure that his spirit ran through the very core of the team.

But first things first. I needed to recruit three team-mates capable of rolling Stilton faster than anyone else on the planet. What sort of physical attributes should I be searching for? Grainy pictures on the internet indicated that the cheese in question was cylindrical in shape and about 20 cm high and 40 cm long. 'It's very similar to a chunk of telegraph pole,' race organizer Olive Main told me.

'How similar?' I asked.

'Very similar,' she said. 'It is a chunk of telegraph pole.'

It made practical sense. As the competition had expanded down the years, so had the number of teams and the number of rolls a cheese had to go through in a day's hard racing. On warm spring afternoons, the issue of cheese fatigue had become unavoidable.

'It still looks like a cheese,' Olive assured me. 'And if you win, your prize is cheese too – an actual wheel of Stilton, as well as the Bell Cup.'

In a kitchen cupboard I found a biscuit tin of roughly correct proportions. I placed it on the floor, turned it on its side and gave it a push. Pain ripped through my buttocks and hamstrings. Even ignoring my post-coal injuries, it was clear that the ideal competitor would be low to the ground, with a powerful upper body and strong legs. Someone small. Someone squat. Someone almost dwarfish.

Sweet Jesus – that was it. A crack team of dwarves!

Where would I find them, I mused, chomping on a piece of broken biscuit. I didn't know any dwarfs. The smallest person I was in regular contact with was my nephew Ed, but since he was only three years old he didn't really count. My friend Phil Harlow was five foot five, but there was nothing medically dwarfish about him. He was merely very small.

I had once worked with a chap called Tiny Tim. Actually, that's not quite true; his real name was Tim Broom, but so compact was he that those people fortunate enough to be able to make him out with the naked eye had no real option but to call him Tiny. It wasn't so much a nickname as a scientific classification.

Tiny was so diminutive that he had never weighed more than eight stone eleven. He had tried everything – constant eating, a daily programme of weights in the BBC gym, snorting lines of protein powder – but nothing could get him through the magical nine-stone barrier. At one point he had walked up to ten-stone Phil Harlow, shaken his head admiringly and asked, 'Phil – what's your secret?'

Eventually, almost a year into an intensive weight-gain programme, he had made the breakthrough. At his morning weigh-in the scales swung all the way to nine stone one. Bunting was brought out and candles placed on a cake – only for celebrations to be cut short when he fell to the floor complaining of a severe pain in his lower back. Two hours later he was in hospital having a large kidney stone removed. When they weighed him post-op, he was back to eight stone eleven.

I'd lost contact with him shortly afterwards. And that was four years ago.

I sat down at the laptop and typed 'dwarves for hire' into Google. 'Dwarves4hire.com,' said the first link. 'The big place for little people.'

Bingo.

I clicked through. 'Search by height or talent,' it offered. I went for the second option. Up came a long list of names, each one cross-referenced with a range of skills. 'Actor. Stunt. Horse. Singer. Dancer. Acrobat. Roller-skates. Ice-skates. Motorcycle. Car. Mime. Swim.'

No mention of Stilton-rolling. The swimming would be useless, as would the ice-skating and miming – although the horse bit could be interesting, if mounts could be found. Imagine how intimidated potential rivals would be by a team of dwarves galloping into town on horseback.

I quickly scanned the names. Many were strangely familiar. There was Kenny Baker, famous for playing R2D2 in all six *Star Wars* films. A click on his name revealed that he had also been in *Time Bandits* and *Elephant Man*, not to mention a 1986 episode of *Casualty* called 'Act of Faith' when he had starred alongside Rula Lenska as a one-eyed knife-thrower.

A one-eyed knife-throwing dwarf? No wonder someone had ended up in A&E.

The trouble was, almost every person on the list was an established Hollywood star. In one sense at least, they were simply too high-profile. Every Ewok who had ever walked Endor was represented, as were most of the cast of *Willow* and all of Augustus Gloop's kidnappers in *Charlie And The*

Chocolate Factory. And while a team comprised of Oompa-Loompas would be a magnificent sight, it would almost certainly cripple Ben and me financially trying to put it together.

Think laterally, I told myself. Let's forget size for a moment. What about cheese-related friends? Did I know someone with a degree in milk coagulation? Anyone who worked at the British Cheese Board? A-ha, I thought. What about my lovely work colleague Caroline Cheese?

I know it seems unlikely. What sort of office was it where a Ben Dirs could work alongside a Tiny Tim and Caroline Cheese? Sadly for me, while Cheesey was very much a real person, she was also very much a real Caroline. Olive's rules stated that teams must be single sex. I would have to think again.

Who else, who else . . . What about Wales rugby legend Shane Williams? Not only was he small – five foot eight in his red socks – but he had the strength of a wrecking-ball and the speed of a hungry puma. I emailed my Welsh friend Tom Williams. While no relation to the sensational Shane, Tom had a mother who did aquarobics at the leisure centre where Shane's club side trained. His response was swift. 'Shane is your perfect recruit. My mum thinks nothing of sharing her opinions on team performance with any players she encounters, so I will ask her to pass the message on urgently. Pending Shane's acceptance, I am willing to step into the breach.' Either way we were a Williams up.

In Tiny Tim's absence, Phil Harlow would also have to get the nod. No one else I knew could match his dimensions. And if Phil was in the team, our mutual friend Ash would have to come on board too.

While at the upper age limit for a roller, Ash had recently

completed a Masters degree in sports psychology. Phil's well-deserved reputation for falling apart under pressure meant we needed someone on board who could keep him focused on the cheese in hand.

The Dirs connection was easier to establish. Before he left for Italy I took three photos of his face – one with him grinning like a chimp, one deadpan and one leering in a way that made him look uncannily like a white Mike Tyson. When blown up to 150 per cent life-size and attached to cardboard, they made masks so hideous that even the glue started sobbing.

Next stop was an online design-your-own T-shirt store. My thinking could be summarized in one word: Spartacus. Five minutes and sixty quid later, the deal was done – three dark blue T-shirts emblazoned with the stark message, 'I'm Ben Dirs'.

Now for a name. We needed something that reflected the cheesy nature of the event. 'Summer Bries' had a certain ring to it, as did 'Cheese Puffs', but they failed to incorporate either the influence of Ben or the relative leanness of the team in his absence.

Of course. Mini Cheddirs. Oh, how they would fear us!

The four of us assembled for a team bonding session the night before the big event. With Williams (Shane) having used his trademark side-step to avoid 60-year-old women smelling of chlorine, Williams (Tom) had got the nod. In a year Welsh sport could do no wrong (rugby team winning Grand Slam, Joe Calzaghe triumphing in the US, Nicole Cooke winning Olympic road-race gold) it made sense to have in our ranks a man who had been christened Thomas Geraint Williams.

Over a number of restorative beverages we worked out a

plan. Choosing the correct strategy, we reasoned, would be crucial. Each of us had to touch the cheese at least once – but who should roll when? Should we all frantically bash away at it together, blitzing our opponents in a frenzy of limbs and cheese with a move Tom W dubbed the Roll of Thunder? Or should we take a more measured approach, one grounded in sports science, operating with the slick, rehearsed precision of a Formula One pit crew?

When midnight struck we made our way out into the empty Cambridgeshire streets. I had brought the closest approximation to a section of telegraph pole that my local timber yard in Brixton could supply – a hollow cardboard tube. When stuffed with Tom's jumper it rolled in commendably accurate fashion. It was soon apparent that teamwork would be everything. Our first attempt, fuelled by a combustible mix of adrenalin and six pints of Hophead apiece, ended with Ash tripping over the cheese and Phil lying face-down in the gutter.

'That was an utter disgrace,' barked Tom's girlfriend Jo, who had taken on the role as touchline analyst. 'Where was the communication? Where were the tactics?'

Attempt number two went off slightly better. Adopting the team pursuit model used in track cycling – one man working the cheese hard at the front for a brief but intense period before peeling off to his right and being immediately replaced by the next man in line – we began to find our rhythm.

Phil was chosen as lead-off man, those power-packed legs of his giving us an explosive start. I was next, using a top-spin forehand technique to keep the cheese rolling fast and true. As I stepped away, wrist cramping, Ash took over – one push, two pushes, three pushes – before Tom W came in for the anchor leg. Only a malfunction from the cheese, which shed the jumper and then careered under a parked car, prevented us from completing the exchange at something approaching a decent lick.

'Smoother,' nodded Jo approvingly. 'Now let's go again.'

It was close to 1.30 a.m. before we called it a night. The next morning, however, there was a new purpose and togetherness about the quartet – which was just as well, bearing in mind the bear-pit we were shortly to find ourselves in.

BEN

My girlfriend had been asking me all night what was wrong. Was it the hotel? Was Lake Como too quiet? Was it something she'd done? I was unable to tell her the truth. The truth was a little bit embarrassing. My heart wasn't in my spaghetti carbonara. My heart was in Stilton.

Although you can never turn your nose up at a week lolling about the Italian Lakes, I'd felt a little bit guilty abandoning our journey at this early stage. And what if they ended up winning? Would that be a good thing? Or a bad thing? Surely a victory meant that mission was accomplished – and I wasn't even there! And what about these Ben Dirs masks and T-shirts that Tom had had knocked up? On the one hand, it would be nice for other people to understand the hell of being called Ben Dirs, if only for a day. But what if they ended up in the wrong hands? 'FOUR MEN DISGUISED AS BBC JOURNALIST ROB BANK.' Or in the grubby mitts of the Sun's headline writers: 'BANK BUSTED BY BENDIRS!' If only they knew my pain . . .

TOM

We breakfasted in near-silence on Stilton and crackers, hoping for some stinky magic to rub off on us. I looked around the team and tried to gauge each individual's mood. Tom Williams' demeanour inspired confidence. I had set him the task of coming up with a team song, and he had responded well. Already we had three excellent options to choose from.

1. The Commodores – 'Cheesy Like Sunday Morning'
2. Oasis – 'Roll With It'
3. Phil Collins and Phil Bailey – 'Cheesy Lover'

Only a half-arsed version of Shania Twain's 'Still The One', with the word Stilton replacing the first two words in the title, had failed to make the grade.

Next to him was Ash, struggling to open a bottle of orange juice. As he strained every sinew without any noticeable movement from the screw-top lid, an old lady reached over, took the bottle and ripped the cap off first time before handing it back without a bead of sweat breaking on her brow. On the betting exchanges, the odds on a Mini Cheddirs victory lengthened instantly.

Then there was Harlow. A single glance at his face was enough to confirm my pre-match fears. He was falling to pieces. All the classic signs were there – the white face, the sweating palms, the unpleasant odour. As I watched he grimaced, clutched his stomach and ran for the toilets.

'Ash,' I said gently. 'Go to work.'

Ash's credentials were – at first glance – impeccable. Despite opening his first psychology textbook less than a year before, he had already struck gold through his work with a professional snooker player.

Player X (who must remain nameless for legal reasons) had been in the midst of a dreadful career slump when Ash first contacted him; out of the world's top sixteen, without a big tournament win for years. Yet under Ash's tutelage, he had not only got through qualifying for the World Championships but battled right through to the later stages. Only an unfortunate double-kiss in the key frame of an epic contest had denied him the chance to do battle for the greatest prize in his sport.

However, there were strong rumours that X's renaissance had more to do with his new cue action and rediscovered zeal on the practice tables than Ash's mental trickery. That impression was only strengthened when Ash revealed the motivational slogan he had given the player to use at the Crucible.

'That's what you told him? "Smell the taste of victory"?'

'"Smell the taste of victory." Or, if he preferred, "Taste the smell of victory." I told him to go with whatever version he was more comfortable with.'

As for me, well, I had worries of my own. With Dirs (a) unable to drive, and (b) unwilling to learn, it had fallen to me to find us a new Bloggernaut. I had only ever owned one car in my life – a cream-coloured Austin Maestro that I had driven with dangerous glee for two weeks around my eighteenth birthday before a half-blind pensioner ploughed into the back on it on the A10 near Puckeridge and sent it in a crumpled ball to the wrecker's yard. Since then I had bought bicycles at roughly the same rate that Imelda Marcos bought sling-backs but had almost nothing to do with four-wheeled vehicles. In the land of the no-wheeled, however, the two-wheeled man is king. By default and seldom-used licence, I was the one responsible for our big campervan purchase.

Dirsy had stipulated that he wanted one with a stereo, beds enough for casual entertaining and a fridge that could keep beverages cold on hot afternoons. It sounded like his flat on wheels. I merely wanted one that I could park outside my house without local kids spray-painting it with the words, 'FUCK OFF GIPPO SKUM' before smashing the windscreen with bricks and setting light to the tyres. Either way, my head was a mess of eBay bids, insurance quotes and possible deals with panel-beaters from Bromsgrove. I needed to get my focus on the cheese and sharpish.

Out on Stilton High Street the atmosphere was intense. As the ceremonial roll-off drew closer so the crowds got bigger. There had been those doom-mongers who claimed that the simultaneous staging of Truckfest – 'the Crufts of trucks' – a mere five miles away at the East of England showground would hit attendances hard. They need not have worried. Under a perfect blue sky, roll-fans were gathering in their hundreds. Even the rival attraction of live ferret-racing in an adjacent field could do nothing to slow the arrivals.

For Phil it was the worst possible scenario. I could see him slumped on a kerb across the road, head in hands. Ash was crouched next to him, arm around his shoulders. 'Let fear be the fuel for your engine,' I could hear him saying. 'Release the hand-brake of negativity.'

Tom jogged across with some inside information. 'This could be priceless,' he said. 'I've just spoken to Doug, who's in charge of registration. He says that it's all about keeping the cheese in check. "Little and often", that was his tip. Imperfections in the cheese come out at speed. If we go too hard, we'll lose control.' I glanced back at Phil. One of us had lost control already. As I watched he rose unsteadily to his feet, holding on to Ash's arm like a pensioner on a windy seafront. At the same moment a man in a home-made zebra costume stopped in front of him. The outfit was clearly the work of many long Fen hours – a bed-sheet painted with vertical black-and-white stripes, a pair of tap-dancing shoes to provide a little clippedy-clop and a life-sized carved wooden head featuring maniacal eyes and a hinged, almost crocodilian jaw. Phil looked up and found himself staring at a Hieronymus Bosch painting made flesh. With a small cry of horror he slumped back down again.

Ash waved Tom and me over. 'Phil – boys – listen up,' he said. 'I want us to form a Huddle of Unity. Let's visualize what we're going to do out there.' Over the public address system I could hear the team names being announced to the public. 'The 2012 Hopefuls. Hairy Beavers. The Four Cheese-men of the Apocalypse.' We formed a tight circle with arms on each other's shoulders and shut our eyes.

'Phil,' said Ash. 'Calm, focused Phil. Talk me through it.'

Phil gulped. 'I crouch by the cheese and engage the clutch of concentration,' he said. Ash grunted with approval. 'On hearing the starter's whistle, I give the cheese a push which is firm but not aggressive.'

'I see your cheese,' I confirmed. 'It is rolling straight. Reaching down, I top-spin it in controlled fashion. Once. Twice. Three times a lady. With a loud shout of "Clear!" I step away to the side.'

Ash nodded. 'I brush past Tom's arse. Its proximity disturbs me, but I stay focused. The cheese is there in front of me. It is large and white. I smell the cheese. The cheese smells good. I like the cheese.'

Phil looked up. 'What's this – Peter and Jane?'

'Phil is nervous,' Ash continued. 'We do not blame him for his outbursts. I reach down for the cheese and tickle it onwards. The cheese is straight.'

'I can see the finishing boards,' murmured Tom. 'My hand is on the cheese. It is rolling at the optimum speed of between four and six miles an hour.'

The strains of 'Nessun Dorma' were floating over the speaker system. 'All teams to the arena,' came the shout. 'All teams to the arena.'

The crowd was three or four deep. As we waded through with the Dirs masks pulled down they recoiled to let us through. I looked around at the sea of faces. It was without doubt the biggest crowd any of us had ever performed in front of.

'Lager,' croaked Phil. 'I must have a lager.' Ash steered him onwards with a firm hand on the shoulders.

In my pocket I felt my mobile phone buzz. It was a text from Ben. '*Forza formaggi!*' it read. I sensed Katie's more sophisticated linguistic touch.

We stepped through the ropes and looked around. People were hanging out of the windows of the houses and pubs that lined the street. The course stretched down the street, the tarmac shimmering in the bright sunlight. At the far end, 50 metres from where we stood, we could make out the wooden boards of the finish line.

The Tannoy crackled into life. 'Mini Cheddirs – what's your team's name all about?'

I looked around. I had no idea where the voice was coming from. There was certainly no one with a microphone anywhere I could see.

'Who's Ben Dirs?' asked the same voice. Everyone seemed to be looking at me for some sort of response.

'Where are you?' I said, feeling deeply foolish.

I felt a tap on my knee. 'Down here,' said the voice. I jumped three feet in the air. It was a dwarf.

'Is Ben Dirs a celebrity?' he asked.

I felt my grip on sanity beginning to slip – surrounded by three men wearing giant Ben Dirs masks and 'I'm Ben Dirs' T-shirts, being interviewed by a dwarf MC leaning on a large cylinder of cheese.

The crowd had fallen ominously silent. I heard Ash clear his throat. 'Ben Dirs,' I said uncertainly. 'Is Ben Dirs a celebrity. Hmm. Well, ah, maybe a minor one. D-list. Or E-list. Somewhere between D and E.' Somewhere between D and E? Where was that, exactly?

'He's where the "Dirs" bit of Cheddirs comes from,' I stammered. 'And the "Ched" bit – that represents cheese. Ched and Dirs. Ben and cheese. Cheddirs.' In the circumstances I felt it best to avoid any mention of the Mini aspect. He nodded. 'Good luck,' he said, and gave me a wide grin. Only later did I discover the identity of our host. It was Warwick Davis, arguably Britain's biggest small actor – the star of Hollywood blockbusters like *Willow*, *Return Of The Jedi* and the Harry Potter series.

Perhaps my embarrassment explains our dreadful performance in the first heat. When we settled over the cheese, God knows we felt ready. The tactics seemed set. Phil's mask of concentration told me Ash had worked his voodoo. Tom had the faraway stare of a man ready to run on to enemy guns. As we touched fists, I repeated the famous words of the Blessed Martine of McCutcheon: 'This is our moment – this is our perfect moment.'

It was a disaster. Phil's start was solid enough, and my first touch kept us on line – but then the cheese veered crazily off-course as if gravity had gone sideways, and all hell broke loose. Ash was wrong-footed, Tom left going the opposite direction. Phil, thinking his job done, was nowhere to be seen. I pawed recklessly at the wrong end of the cheese and sent it tumbling back the other way. Ash dived in with a horribly ambitious swipe and the cheese bounced almost out of our lane. With half the race rolled, our opponents had a clear 10-metre lead. It was then that Tom produced a moment of genius, a piece of improvisation that his namesake Shane would have been proud of. Facing back towards the start-line, and with the cheese revolving in ever more pathetic circles, he grabbed it with both hands and hurled it backwards through his legs. The cheese fizzed down the lane like a guided missile, just at the moment when our rivals abruptly hit an invisible wall of their own. In a flash our hopes were reignited. Ash, showing all his experience, delivered a forehand clout that would have splintered lesser cheeses. Phil and I followed suit. Tom came from nowhere to thrash again, and as the crowd roared, Ash sent the cheese smashing into the boards.

Joy swept through us. We had been on the point of tasting the smell of defeat, yet suddenly we were smelling the taste of victory. And what a sweet-smelling taste it was!

We high-fived like giddy cheerleaders, we whooped like castrated jackals. We'd probably have embarked on a lap of honour had we not been brought back down to earth by two things: the expression on our team analyst's face, and the performance of a crack Polish team named Laconic in the following heat.

Jo was first. 'You completely fell apart! What happened to the drill? What happened to the discipline?' She shook her head. 'That was a massive let-off. Massive.'

It was the sobering assessment we needed. What had we done except bumble our way through like hapless Stilton virgins? Even as Jo was speaking the Poles were breasting the tape in a time that made a mockery of our shambolic effort. We had heard about this team – four-time champions, as ruthlessly efficient as robots from the future – but nothing had prepared us for the awesome sight of them in full flow.

'Learn from the masters,' advised Jo. 'Look at them. They weren't fighting the Stilton like you lot were – they let the cheese do the work. You must do the same. Let the cheese breathe.'

In the shadow of the Angel pub we convened an emergency team meeting. Harsh but fair words were exchanged. It was clear, we all agreed, that Phil's one-handed starting technique was hopelessly outmoded. Both the Poles and the reigning champions, Four Skins, had employed a two-handed shovel-style start. We had to do the same. We had to do more.

'Mini Cheddirs,' came the announcement, 'will now face the Lovejoys.'

Ash looked around at us. 'Brothers,' he said gravely, 'this is now. This is us.' He closed his eyes and licked his lips. 'Taste the moment.'

Phil looked up. 'Isn't that a Skittles advert?' he said suspiciously. Ash hushed him with a finger to his mouth.

We pushed through the throng and were face-to-face with our opponents. They wore false moustaches, berets and stripy blue jumpers. We nodded at them. They nodded back.

'On your cheeses,' said the dwarf. We leant in. My heart was thumping like a big bass drum. 'Un, deux, trois,' whispered Ash, 'smell my cheese.'

Great sportsmen sometimes talk about an almost holy state they experience once or twice in their careers, where everything suddenly feels supremely effortless. Tennis players see the ball in slow motion, seemingly twice its normal size. Runners feel as if they have a bottomless well of energy to draw on. Golfers know with absolute conviction that their 20-foot putt will roll straight into the middle of the hole. On that bright Bank Holiday afternoon, Mini Cheddirs reached their own nirvana.

The entire race had a dream-like quality. It was like watching ourselves on film. Phil's first ever two-handed start was straight from the coaching manual. I reached down in wonderment and gently touched the cheese onwards. Already we were aware that we would win. There was a strange, delightful certainty about the whole thing. Ash tickled one side, Tom tickled the other. The cheese seemed to glide onwards of its own accord, as if on a cushion of air, drawn towards the line by invisible, mysterious forces.

Clunk. Cheese hit finishing board. Wow.

It was a stunning victory. The crowd were going ripe bananas. At the front I could see Jo. 'Yes,' she mouthed at the four of us. 'Yes.' Somewhere up the course, the Lovejoys were in hundreds of tiny pieces.

This time we celebrated with a righteous elation. We were all yelling at once, shouting over each other in a glorious gabble. 'Did you feel . . .' '. . . just unbelievable . . .' '. . . amazing speed . . .' '. . . the look on their faces . . .' '. . . barely touched . . .' '. . . if my father could see me . . .' '. . . taste the moment, taste it . . .' Tom shook his head in disbelief. 'How can we improve on that?' he asked happily. His words hung in the air. How *could* we improve on that?

Could Michelangelo pull off a better job on the Sistine ceiling second time around, Da Vinci touch up Mona's smile, Betty Boo re-do the do?

Gradually, Tom's question seemed to morph from statement of celebration to ominous warning. How could we improve on that? We were only halfway through the competition. An awful prospect suddenly dawned on us. Had we peaked too soon?

We fell silent, just as the Poles cantered through their next contest with chilling ease and willing cheese. The fact that three of them were dressed as musketeers (breeches, flamboyant loose blousons, wide-brimmed floppy hats with gaudy plumes) and the other as a plumber (dirty stone-washed jeans, white trainers, sweaty polo shirt) only added to their other-worldly menace.

I thought of Ben, reclining in a Lombardy Travelodge with Katie at his side, ordering room service and wondering if he was allowed to smoke on the toilet. His face stared back at me from the back of Phil's head, where the mask had been twisted round in the post-win celebrations.

What would Dirsy do? I asked myself. Challenge them to a breakdance contest, probably, and then try to eat the cheese. It was no use. We would just have to hope we drew the Four Cheesemen of the Apocalypse in the last four instead.

BEN

I'd been caught texting in the Villa Carlotta, and caught again in the Villa Monastero, but I think I got away with it in the shithouse in Varenna. This holiday wasn't turning out to be the romantic leg-up I'd hoped for, and all because of a fake wheel of cheese.

They'd made it to the semi-finals, and I felt like a proper spare one. Maybe Tom would see sense and throw the contest. He wouldn't want to win it without me – would he? Don't be stupid Dirs, he's the most competitive man in England, he's been known to start flinging his marbles about when he loses to his niece at KerPlunk. There was only one thing for it: I'd have to head to San Giovanni Cathedral, light a couple of candles and pray for a fuck-up . . .

TOM

'It's the semi-finals!' Warwick chirped over the PA. 'First up: Mini Cheddirs!' I took a deep breath. 'Will play . . . Laconic!'

Christ. We'd drawn the bloody Poles.

Jo took us to one side. 'You'd have to meet them at some point,' she said. 'Why not now? Don't worry about what they're doing. Just go out there and repeat what you just did.'

I think, in retrospect, that it started to go wrong the moment we lost the toss and got given an unfamiliar lane. Both of our successes so far had come on the Angel side, but Laconic's D'Artagnanesque skipper called heads correctly and asked us to step across towards the Bell pub.

Next, Ash made a dreadful misjudgement. 'You done this before?' Warwick asked him jovially. 'Does it look like we have?' Ash replied. There was a pause. Warwick's smile died on his lips. An uneasy hush fell over the crowd. What had been intended as a cheeky comic riposte had come out as sarcasm of the meanest kind. Ash had dissed the dwarf. In an instant we felt the Fenland mood turn against us. 'Ash,' muttered Phil, shaking his head. Had Phil's faith in Ash's talismanic words been damaged beyond repair?

The starting whistle trilled and Laconic made their usual breathtaking start. Jo's wise words of advice disappeared from our collective memory, and suddenly – horribly – everything we did had nothing to do with our own form, and everything to do with their burgeoning lead. Around halfway we were still in with a shout – or we would have been against any other outfit. But up against the Poles, we felt like Harald Schmidt against Ed Moses, or indeed the ancient Egyptians against the biblical Moses. We were helpless in the face of their awesome onslaught. Horribly loud, we heard the death-knell crack of cheese hitting board.

I fell to my knees. Ash had his head in his hands. Tom looked aghast. Phil looked at his feet.

At least thirty seconds passed before any of us realized that the referee was repeatedly blowing his whistle. What was that he was saying? Shhhsh! What? Infringement? Infringement by Laconic? They had thrown the cheese. The Poles had thrown the cheese! 'Illegal move by Laconic,' boomed the referee. 'The race will be rerun.'

Phil was the first to respond. 'This is it!' he said excitedly. 'This is the bit of luck we needed. It's meant to be!'

'Phil's right,' said Tom. 'We're back in the game.'

'From the barren soil of despair can grow a great tree of hope,' intoned Ash. 'Let us harvest the fruits of good fortune and blend them into the smoothie of victory.'

We strode back up the course. I could feel the ghosts of great British leaders of the past stirring in my heart – Nelson, Churchill, Butcher (Terry).

'If we go down, we go down fighting,' I said fiercely. 'Let none of us fear the sting of defeat; let no one fear recrimination should we lose. Today, we must give it our all. Today, we become true men.'

I might as well have whistled the Top 40 out of my arse. They battered us. We didn't even get close.

'Humiliation for the Cheddirs!' cackled Warwick as Laconic cruised home. 'Beaten. Again! Twice!'

This time it really was over. There was to be no recount, no third chances. In some ways it was easier to take – we had been beaten so comprehensively, so roundly, that there could be no complaints.

'They were so good they would have beaten us eight times out of ten,' said Ash.

Tom nodded. 'Eighty per cent of the time we would lose, I'd say.' Phil was still down on one knee, staring blankly at the ground. 'Just give me a moment,' he said quietly. I sent Ben a text. 'Made the semis. Knocked out by the eventual winners.'

I'd like to say we left in that mood, content that we had gone as far as we could, happy with a top-four finish in our first attempt. I'd like to say that – but I can't. Because, in the final, the unbeatable Laconic were beaten. Twice.

We could barely believe our eyes. Up against Flik 66, a stumbling crew of guffawing teens who could only be described as shambolic, the mighty Poles disintegrated. Maybe we'd pushed them to their limits in the semis. Maybe they had nothing left in the tank. Or could it have been the fact that the Flik boys went out there with the facile arrogance of youth, too young to be intimidated, too young to know the meaning of fear. Either way, Laconic were unrecognizable. To be frank, they were dreadful. After being hammered in the first of three races, they were worse still in the second: 2–0, game over. We watched on, disgusted with ourselves. 'They were beatable, after all,' said Tom softly.

It physically hurt to watch the winners' presentation. In front of a cheering crowd, Warwick handed out gleaming medals, the majestic Bell Cup and a giant cylinder of genuine cheesy Stilton.

Flik 66 went red and sniggered behind their fringes. It was hard not to wonder whether they were fitting custodians of such a great trophy. Would the purists who set this event up in the late 1950s really have approved of a winning team who stepped off the podium and immediately tried to exchange their cheese for lager?

Now the semi-finals seemed like the cruellest place to lose. We could have beaten Flik 66. We all knew it. Instead, we were going home with nothing more than what ifs and badly sunburned noses.

'Remember this,' said Ash. 'Soak it up. These scenes will fuel us over the next fifty-one weeks of training.' A text arrived from Italy. 'Good effort son. Knew you couldn't win without me.'

As the crowds drifted away I took one last look back at the scene of our defeat. It was a poignant tableau. Warwick was standing on an upturned piece of telegraph pole, addressing a street that was now almost empty save for one old lady slumped in an electric wheelchair, clutching a grubby plastic bag.

'Ladies and gentlemen,' I could hear him saying. 'Welcome to our special charity auction. Now then – what am I bid for a night at Peterborough greyhound stadium? Starting at five pounds. Any takers? Five pounds only.' There was a heartbreaking silence. 'Four pounds, ladies and gentlemen, four pounds . . .'

'Right,' said Ben when he got home two days later. 'You ready to have your shins kicked?'

3
SHINS

TOM

'No, Ben,' I said decisively. 'I am not ready to have my shins kicked.'

If I'd known quite how awful it was going to be, I wouldn't have stopped there. I'd have changed my name, grown a face-obscuring set of whiskers and gone into hiding – anything to avoid the horrors that were to follow.

'Do me a favour,' said Ben. 'How bad can it be?'

In fairness to Dirsy, I'm not sure even he realized. How could he? We live in a country where casual violence is outlawed – except of course on television and in films, where it's enthusiastically encouraged. Bears are no longer baited. Cocks no longer wear spurs. Fox and foxhound form civil partnerships and raise strange vulpo-canine cross-breeds while enjoying the same tax benefits as any other married couple. The merest sniff of possible injury is enough to trigger a million-pound lawsuit. Why, just the other day a large sports equipment manufacturer had to pay out thousands after an amateur athlete slipped while attempting the high hurdles and shattered his personal best. In short, we live in a sanitized world. How nasty, then, could the British Shin-Kicking Championships really be?

I wish I'd known. I wish I'd been firmer. I wish we'd done more research.

'I don't want to do it,' was all I said. 'You know I suffer from shin-splints.' They were the reason why I swam and cycled rather than just ran everywhere any more; too much pounding of the pavements and I was reduced to limping like a man with Nik-Naks for legs. Only by sticking to an idiosyncratic regime of treatments – compression socks, cold baths, non-genital self-massage – could I continue to train and race like the obsessive exerciser I was.

I heard Ben snort down the other end of the phone line. 'Tommy,' he said impatiently. 'They don't hand out world titles willy-nilly. If you can't take a little pain, you're toast. We'll never become champions if we're not prepared to push ourselves.'

I snorted back. 'Like, for example, by dropping your sack of coal before you've got halfway up the course?' I said sarcastically. 'By allowing yourself to be beaten by a man who'd climbed off his sickbed to be there? As well as King Can?'

'Fame costs,' said Ben. 'And right here's where you start paying – in sweat.'

In retrospect, there were obvious clues that we should have picked up. In the official history of the Cotswold Olympicks, home of the shin-kicking championships, we found this description of a bout in the seventeenth century: 'Competitors, wearing boots tipped with metal, held each other by the shoulders or hands and attempted to kick each other. In this trial of skill, strength and courage, men sometimes padded their legs, but there are graphic tales of shins being hardened using planks and hammers.'

With hindsight it all seems so self-evident. How did we

fail to heed such obvious warnings? I think there were two main reasons: the lure of entering a sporting event that had been taking place for almost 400 years, and the following sentence on a website about the championships: 'Of course, these days no one is allowed to wear shoes, let alone boots.'

Looking back, doubts cloud my mind. Who exactly was responsible for that claim? Had a fellow competitor posted it with the aim of giving potential rivals a bum steer? Did we really read that line at all, or did we just hope we had?

Either way, it had the unfortunate effect of calming my nascent panic. Surely even the angriest man would struggle to do much damage to my shins with his bare feet. There was probably a good chance, I thought in a moment of insane bravado, that he would hurt his toes more than my legs. Doesn't the pub brawler often break his fingers punching his opponent on the chin?

There was another big something clouding my judgement too – the new Bloggernaut. Protracted research of the second-hand market had allowed me to pick up sufficient random phrases to be almost fluent in Campa, the unofficial language of the motor-home aficionado. So capable was I of casually dropping words like pop-top, hook-up and synchro-mesh into conversation, without any real understanding of what they meant, that I was considering renaming our eventual purchase the Blaggernaut.

A week before I had narrowed our choice down to three options: a Toyota Hiace Reimo conversion in beige, a 1988 Volkswagen Westfalia owned by a chap from Wellington named Brent and a 1981 Bedford CF van belonging to a Mr L. Simkiss of Bradford.

The Toyota looked a steal at a mere £4,000. Unfortunately

that's probably exactly what it was. The man who claimed to be the owner was strangely unwilling to give me the registration number, yet offered me a discount if I also bought a laptop and set of golf-clubs. He also insisted on payment in cash in the gents' toilet of a pub in Hammersmith. Having been warned against such convenience conduct by my old man before moving to London, I decided the deal had to be pooh-poohed.

The Westfalia looked more promising. According to Brent, it had 'sucks munths roadtecks', whatever that was, not to mention a gas hob so powerful that it took mere moments to fry up a portion of something he called fushenchupps. The only problem was that three of his mates were sleeping in it while they waited for a room to become free in the rented house Brent shared with eighteen other Kiwis in Southfields. As a result it had stained New Zealand flags for curtains, flip-flops in the disused fridge and the smell of a kennel at neutering time.

The Bedford, by contrast, was available almost immediately. What's more, it had a full year's MOT, two double-bunks and what appeared in the advert to be stained-glass windows running down each side. I wasn't quite sure what colour it was meant to be – either a very dirty cream, or a very faded brown – and it was so old that the previous model in the series came with a starter-handle and man waving a red flag to run in front of it, but there was something special about it – something which spoke of solid British craftsmanship, of the thrill of the open road, of glamorous fortnights away in Tenby or Whitley Bay.

'A lovely runner,' Mr Simkiss told me. 'I took her down to Abersoch and back last summer and she were magic. She don't go fast, like, and there's a bit of a knack to getting into first gear, but ah've had no complaints. For two grand she'll sort you out.'

'Stained-glass windows?' said Ben when I told him. 'They're probably worth two grand by themselves. Get involved.'

As a child I used to own a 'Supercars' version of popular card game Top Trumps. Each car was photographed against a stunning background; a vista of snowy Alpine peaks, a gleaming new architectural wonder, a surf-pounded beach. It's fair to say that my first glimpse of the Bloggernaut – alone in a near-derelict car park on an industrial estate in Runcorn, with sleet bouncing off the bodywork and the stench of the factories at Ellesmere Port filling the nostrils – was of a somewhat different vibe.

Mr Simkiss was an honest man. It didn't go fast. On the way back to Ben's I gambled on a short-cut across to the M1 via Snake Pass and topped out at 18 miles an hour. I parked up outside Sheffield to let a disgruntled milk-float past and decided to have a proper look round our new vehicle. The stained-glass windows were magnificent. Sure, the weight they added meant that our fuel consumption would never fall below a mile a litre, but with the way the daylight streamed through the multi-coloured panes, you could almost imagine you were in King's College chapel or Westminster Abbey. And in neither of those two buildings would you also be within arm's reach of a fold-out bed and fridgeful of lager. In front of the windows were curtains made from a thick, maroon fabric that looked like it had been torn from a Regency four-poster. There was a gaudy painting of the Yellow Brick Road nailed to the back wall. To the left of the rear door was a cupboard which had a shower-head hanging up in it. That would be the shower. Strangely, there was no toilet.

On second thoughts, there was no official toilet.

Up front, the Bedford engineers had developed a beautifully simple ventilation system for the driver and passenger. Whenever you moved the gear-stick, the rubber casing around its base shifted to reveal a gaping hole in the floor, through which you could reach down to touch the road beneath. As I inched back into my seat an icy blast of moorland air hit my ankles and blew the Regency curtains around behind me.

I wiggled the key into the ignition and looked up. Two kids in Sheffield United shirts and tracksuit bottoms were watching me from about ten feet away. One of them was smoking a cigarette like Alex Higgins while picking his nose with his spare hand.

'Gippo!' shouted the other one, hopefully. I turned the key and was rewarded with the sound of a man dropping a bag of spanners. I pulled the choke out to its fullest extent and tried again. The man dropped his spare bag of spanners. The kid with the cigarette started laughing while his mate started looking around for stones.

I rammed the accelerator to the floor and whipped the key round again. With a sound of a diplodocus breaking wind the engine fired and then burst into life. I threw the van into first, let off the handbrake and was thrown against the steering-wheel as the vehicle jumped five feet backwards. That would be reverse, then. I shoved the gear-stick forward. It was like I was forcing it through a wall. With a crunching sound it suddenly dropped into gear, and the van lurched forward. The two kids scattered and I bashed my fist against the horn in the middle of the steering-wheel in a triumphant gesture of defiance. 'Peeep,' it went sadly, like an orphaned penguin.

Perhaps it's a little clearer now why neither Ben nor I gave enough thought to our shins. It wasn't so much a question of what would happen to us at the championships as whether we would get there at all. To have driven out to Chipping Camden that Friday afternoon without serious mishap (and under 'serious mishap' I'm not including Ben being two hours late for our departure, the flat tyre we suffered at Hanger Lane, the way we almost crushed a stationary Toyota Yaris in a petrol station outside Moreton-on-the-Marsh or the time we drifted across a dual carriageway at three miles an hour after the engine cut out near Abingdon) felt like an achievement worthy of a medal in itself.

Even the bucolic scene that greeted us served only to lure us further into that false sense of calm. It was all so green, so lush, so early summer, that surely everything had to be right in the world. Families carrying picnics were walking happily up Dover's Hill to the arena, Golden Retrievers bounding alongside, children running ahead to make daisy-chains. Cheery toffs strode around in the full set of Barbour jacket, flat tweed cap and green wellies. Morris dancers were fluttering white hankies at each other like teary fiancées waving their sweethearts off to war.

There was a bouncy castle, well-marshalled by a middle-aged lady in a mauve cardigan and sensible flat shoes. Obedient young children sat still while having their faces painted to look like cats and tigers. A PA announcement reminded visitors that they should not miss out on the birds of prey enclosure or the static display of classic cars. So unthreatening was it that we could have been walking through the set of a Sunday evening ITV retro-drama. Even the local bored teenagers had a certain comedic charm.

'Bloimey,' said one, necking his pint of cider before lobbing the glass into a hedge. 'Oi am ferkin' ferked.'

'Yerr – so am oi,' said his mate, doing the same. 'That second E we done is mental. Oi'm coming up a treat.'

It was when we were handed a sheet of championship rules that we first sensed something might be horribly amiss. 'LEGAL DISCLAIMER' it said in large letters. 'Shin-kicking is inherently a full-contact, dangerous sport. Robert Dover's Games Society is not responsible for any loss or accident to you or to third parties including property damage, injury or death resulting from or to you or other third parties as a result of your participation in shin-kicking at the Robert Dover's Cotswold Olympicks.' Hold on a second. Death? Death?

'Footwear may be trainers, shoes or soft-toed (i.e. unreinforced) boots. This will be checked both before and after your bouts.'

Footwear? What footwear?

'Equipment,' it continued. 'Competitors must wear long trousers or tracksuits and may cushion their shins using straw (provided).'

'That's good of them,' snarled Ben.

'The contest will be started, finished and judged by an arbiter, known as a Stickler. The Stickler decides the fairness of the contest.' What you might call a Stickler for the rules, I thought, my old shin-splints injuries starting to throb. 'A contest is decided on the best of three throws.'

We looked at our fellow competitors. To a man, they were wearing heavy boots, most of which looked distinctly reinforced. Several had donned high-laced DMs. Others sported the sort of tan leather boots worn by adventurers in the Australian outback. Then we glanced down at our own feet. I was in lightweight trainers with a breathable mesh upper. Dirs was in battered white Nikes that looked like they'd featured in the 1997 JJB Sports summer sale. Nor were there any other options in the van, unless Ben wanted to wear an empty tube of Pringles or I wanted to force my feet into a half-eaten roasted-vegetable wrap.

Ben looked at me, aghast. 'Christ,' he whispered. 'We'd better find that fucking straw.'

BEN

The coal-carrying had been Tom's fault. This time, I only had myself to blame. Although in my defence, I'd been seriously misled. No boots, it had said on the internet. No sodding boots. And the offending article had glossed over death altogether.

This wasn't panning out as I'd imagined. I'd wanted to do crazy golf, but work commitments wouldn't allow it. I'd pencilled in the World Pipe-Smoking Championships, but it had been binned because of the ban on smoking indoors. Instead I'd almost snapped my neck attempting to carry a sack of coal through the snowy hills of Yorkshire and now I was about to have my shins rearranged by some massive galoot in army boots. No, this isn't what I'd envisaged at all . . .

TOM

Like drowning men grabbing at life-jackets we snatched handfuls of straw from the stack of bales and stuffed them desperately up our trouser-legs. The dry straw disintegrated with frightening ease. It would clearly offer as much protection as a custard flak jacket. We wedged up as much as we could and then bound each leg at the ankle with discarded twine from the bales.

Ben took a step back and lit up a nervous fag. In his stained polo shirt, grey tracksuit bottoms spilling straw from the ankles and grubby white trainers he looked like Worzel Gummidge off to do a painting and decorating job. He handed me his cigarette and grabbed another fistful of straw. 'No point in taking chances,' he said, shoving it down the front of his pants.

A flunky handed us the white coat that all kickers had to wear. It was supposed to represent the traditional shepherds' smocks worn in the contest for centuries, although to be honest it made us look more like Smithfield butchers at the start of their shift (or lab technicians from a pharmaceutical company).

'Tom Fordyce?' a man with a clipboard asked me. 'Good news – you've got a bye through the first round.' I let out a slow lungful of air. 'Ben Dirs? You'll fight Rory McGrath.' First Fogle, now McGrath. This was getting ridiculous. What next – Fern Britton at the World Nettle-Eating Championships? McGrath was already pacing the arena, a TV crew filming his every move. 'How am I supposed to knock that fat lump over?' gulped Ben. 'He's like a hairy fucking Weeble.'

'Don't worry about it,' I said. 'He's a big man, but he's out of shape. His ass is yours.'

BEN

I grabbed my celebrated opponent by the lapels and looked into his beady little eyes. At close quarters, they resembled piss-holes in blancmange.

'Have you done this before?' said a worried-looking McGrath as I considered his weapons of choice – a pair of dirty great Dr Martens – with justifiable suspicion. 'Not since 1987, and I got a week of detentions,' I replied, noticing the throng of cameramen closing in around us. I could make out a few chants of 'Ooh, aah, Rory McGrath!' as the Stickler explained the rules, and then, after a tap of his stick, we got down to business.

The first thing I noticed as I bored into the side of McGrath's bison-like head was how incredibly soft his hair was. For a second there I could have been nuzzling one of my mum's Angora sweaters, but a couple of robust right boots to my left leg reminded me exactly where I was: getting my shins smashed up by a 52-year-old comedian in a wet field in the Cotswolds.

After soaking up a few early howitzers, I noticed he was wheezing out of his arse and decided it was time for a spot of 'rope-a-dope': hold back for a while, let McGrath blow himself out, and then deliver the coup de grace when he least expects it, à la Muhammad Ali against George Foreman in the Rumble in the Jungle.

Only I hadn't accounted for my own decrepit state. Instead we lurched from side to side like a couple of tanked-up fishmongers play-fighting outside a Billingsgate boozer. The early flurries were soon replaced by the odd limp toe-poke and then no activity at all, forcing the Stickler to order us back into combat on more than one occasion.

'AIN'T GONNA BE NO REMATCH!' hollered Tom, in a desperate attempt to snap me from my lethargy, and I finally managed to kick McGrath off-balance and send him crashing to the turf in a hail of mud and camera flashes. McGrath rolled over and hauled himself back to his feet, but I could tell the fire had been doused.

'Please, just take me down,' he muttered wretchedly into my ear as we became reacquainted, and his legs soon buckled for a second time under a barrage of swingeing right foots. Victory was mine, although I'm convinced he took a dive. And the fact it took me more than five minutes to see off a man twenty years my senior, with the athletic make-up of a Glasgow tramp, was also cause for some serious soul-searching.

As I staggered from the combat area, ruddy-faced and drenched in sweat, I had a strange premonition. I was sitting in front of a TV thirty years hence and the newsreader announced that Rory McGrath – 'broadcaster, writer and humorist' – had died. One of my sons, who was sitting dutifully at my feet, turned to me and said, 'Dad, who's Rory McGrath?' And I said, 'Rory McGrath? I kicked his shins in a field in Gloucestershire.'

TOM

What a fight. What a win! No matter that, in McGrath, Dirs had been drawn against the only other contestant in worse shape than himself. He had ridden out that early McGrath hurricane to kick his way into contention for the British title, at a stroke wiping out the memory of his pitiful pull-out at the coal-carrying championships. It was a hugely impressive performance.

A local journalist came across to interview him. Ben had his hands on his knees, his chest heaving and his eyes half-closed with pain. 'I could see he was fucking fucked,' I heard him gasp, 'so I fucking booted him fucking hard and he fucking well went down.'

A red ball of a sun was sinking into the trees as I prepared for the second round. Over to my right I could see the Vale of Evesham stretching out into the hazy distance, our van glinting in the last of the light, with the bluish smudge of the Malvern Hills just visible on the skyline. In front of me rose a steepling grass bank which curved around the arena to form a natural grandstand for the hundreds of spectators. A local strode over. 'All set?' he asked. 'You'll be fighting that fellow over there – the one who's just beaten Rory McGrath.'

My intake of breath was completely misinterpreted. 'I know,' he said, shaking his head disbelievingly. 'Imagine knocking out the chap everyone's come to see. Does he think people would rather watch him than McGrath?' He shook his head again. 'What a twat.'

The twat in question was lying on the ground with his knees splayed, trying to smoke a cigarette and spit at the same time. I gave the draw a little more thought. In some ways it was a disaster – the very last thing I wanted. We were supposed to be comrades chasing glory together, not beating seven shades of shin out of each other. If we were going to meet, I'd wanted us to meet in the final, a championship title guaranteed for one of us at least.

On the other hand, it was quite brilliant news for me.

What little strength Ben possessed had already been sapped by the bout with McGrath. While I was nowhere near as fit as I had been before my spell of post-viral fatigue, Ben didn't understand that. To his mind I was a man who'd won triathlons before he'd got out of bed for breakfast. Nothing says 'victory' like an opponent who's flat on his back groaning like a beached whale.

I made a quick mental outline of the tale of the tape for our clash.

	Tom 'Fleet-Foot' Fordyce	**Ben 'Smasher' Dirs**
Age:	34	32
Height:	5′9″	5′10″
Weight:	11st 4lb	13st 7lb
Fight record:	Mainly against his sisters	Watched lots outside Romford kebab houses
Neck:	Sore	Brass
Chest:	42 inches	Wheezy
Resting heart-rate:	39bpm	What's 'resting heart-rate'?

With a nod from the Stickler we were called together in the centre of the muddy ring. I reached forward, grabbed Ben by the lapels and stared into his bloodshot eyes. 'Smell the taste of victory,' I said under my breath. 'You what?' said Dirs, and booted me on the knee.

My first surprise was how much it hurt to kick back. The lightweight upper of my trainers might as well have been made from muslin. Every blow I landed – and with Ben like a sweating statue, I was landing quite a few – jarred my toes and fizzed pain up my ankle. The second surprise was how much damage Dirsy could do with his occasional haymakers. Despite me opting for the defensive technique of a Lennox Lewis, dodging most of his left-footed jabs, he was still catching with the odd right-footed swinger. Already the middle of my left shin was going numb.

'Kick 'im!' screamed a bloodlust-consumed harpy in the crowd, a touch unnecessarily. 'Kick 'im in the 'ead!'

What made the difference, I think, was attitude. Physically we were evenly matched – my superior stamina against his big weight advantage. Mentally, however, Dirsy was beaten almost before we began. He knew he had very little more to give. I could see him working out what would happen if he shocked himself and managed to beat me – more pain, more being kicked, more exhaustion. He knew the end would come at some point; it was just a question of when.

Soon he began to take longer and longer between attempted kicks. There was a tell-tale shake of the head, an increase in the number of exhausted grunts and a noticeable slacking-off in how much resistance he put up to my attempted kicks and throws. Sensing a fading of the light, I stepped up my barrage of kicks. 'One-nil to Fordyce!' shouted the Stickler as I sent Dirs tumbling into the mud, falling on top of him to cushion my own landing.

Dirs looked up at me and I could see in his eyes that he was ready for the end. With McGrath back in the hutch, his big victory had already been won.

'Two-nil Fordyce,' came the shout, as a left-left-right combo put Ben on the canvas again. 'And that's the contest!'

I pulled him to his feet, and we embraced like Freddie

Flintoff and Brett Lee at Edgbaston '05. ''Played, son,' I said. 'Ugghhfffn,' he replied, collapsing on a bale of hay. I hobbled off to fetch him an isotonic lager and gather my thoughts for the battle ahead.

In the gloaming, the crowds were swelling with every moment that passed. A man dressed as the original seventeenth-century Robert Dover was riding round on horseback in front of a large two-dimensional cut-out of a wooden castle. A huge bonfire was blazing on top of the hill. In front of it I could make out the silhouettes of the teenage lads we'd spotted earlier, cavorting around in the light of the flames and waving their hands in the air. As I watched, one of them staggered to one side and threw up on a tree stump.

My own heart was thumping like Keith Moon's bass pedal. The evening air smelt sweet in my nostrils. My body felt loose and wired at the same time. I noted the adrenalin tingling through my fingertips and realized that my body had slipped into fight-or-flight mode. My shins simply felt numb.

Other pairs of fighters were battling for their own places in the last four, going at it hammer and toes in weird, locked-together dance. Beneath their feet the ground was churned up like Sunday at Glastonbury. The screams and roars of the crowd mingled with the thud and crack of boot on shin to create a primitive atmosphere underneath the darkening sky.

As bodies hit the mud with heavy slaps I tried to gauge which tactics were having the greatest success. Worryingly, each Stickler seemed to interpret the laws slightly differently. 'The aim is to weaken an opponent by kicking his or her shins,' read the official rules.

> Once the legs have been weakened, a competitor may throw an opponent to the ground off-balance over a leg. A

> successful throw involves unbalancing the opponent in the course of the kick. Shins must be kicked before a throw can be achieved. Contact must be made. A throw is not valid unless the thrower is in the process of kicking and has one foot off the ground. It the Stickler deems that the kicker has made an intentional trip, the throw goes to the opponent. The first person to hit the ground loses the throw.

The trouble was, it was almost impossible to work out the difference between legally unbalancing someone and illegally tripping them. What if you felled an opponent with a proper kick but slipped with him as he fell and hit the deck first? How could you throw someone over one leg if you had to keep the other one in the air?

'It's time for the semi-finals!' barked an official happily. I gulped down a mouthful of water and walked back into the Cotswold Coliseum to meet my fate.

It didn't look good. Waiting for me was a tall, curly-haired local with bulbous eyes and the sort of wild grin that suggested an untamed spirit and easy acquaintance with pain. 'Alroight babber?' he said, wiping his bleeding hands down the front of my smock.

BANG! His first right-footer smashed into my left shin. Anger and adrenalin sizzled round behind my eyes. I launched a combo at the bony inside of his legs, my left foot rat-tat-tatting his left shin, my right doing the same to his other leg. He lost his footing and we tumbled into the slime.

'Accidental fall!' shouted the Stickler. 'No submission. Reset!'

My opponent laughed and leaned in close to my ear.

'Tenacious lil' bugger, are you?' he growled, breathing heavily. The Stickler tapped us with his staff and we went again. Soon a pattern began to emerge. With his wildebeest-like legs and workman's boots, he would land one wrecking-ball kick every twenty seconds or so. Some of them I would hurdle; some I would take amidships with a horrible crack. With my better fitness but cottonwool trainers, I would then pepper him with a rapid but powder-puff series which would drive him backwards but otherwise appear to have little noticeable impact. There were two more slips, one apiece, both called as accidental falls by the Stickler. The minutes ticked by. Most of the preceding bouts had been over within four minutes, but we had been going for at least six already. Out in the gloom I could hear Dirs chanting my name.

I noticed that my rival was beginning to go red. Sweat was sliming his forehead and his breath starting to rasp in his throat. He was wrestling more and more, rather than kicking – shaking me so hard by the vice-like grip he had on my lapels that my chest was taking half the battering of my legs. I launched another left-right left-right left-right and forced him back towards the castle. Desperately he took aim with a big swinger, and as it whistled past my knee I stabbed a kick into the ankle bone of his standing leg. He yelped and collapsed into the mud.

'One-nil!' yelled the Stickler.

The fall seemed to inspire him. Like the tango partner from hell, he pulled me in close with a jerk of his arms before crashing the soles of his boots into my shins. I heard my shirt tear as he wrenched me sideways and landed a cross-kick into my left knee.

Weirdly, I could feel almost nothing at all in my shins. Like a disinterested observer I noted each blow, but was strangely unaware of the associated pain. Bang! 'Good one,' I would think, dispassionately. BANG! 'Very good one.'

The minutes ticked by and I began to lose all sense of time. All I could see were his shins and flying toecaps. The only sounds were the background roar of the crowd and his breath huffing in my ear.

With a huge effort he pulled me forward and sent me tumbling over his outstretched leg. I spat out a mouthful of mud and jumped to my feet, safe in the knowledge that, since I'd clearly been tripped, the fall would be ruled out. If the Stickler applied the rules properly, that could even be 2–0 – and the contest to me. 'Submission!' shouted the Stickler. 'It's one-all!' I was stunned. One-all? I'd been tripped – blatantly. Surely he must have seen that? The yokel grinned at me. 'You're moyn,' he said, and moved in to grab my smock again.

In retrospect, it was both the best and worst thing that could have happened to me. Before, I'd been determined not to lose without a fight, but equally ready to put the health of my shins before glory. Now, incensed by the miscarriage of justice, I was a shin-kicker reborn. There was now no way I was going to let this brute beat me – no way. I had no thought for my own shins anymore. If it took until dawn, I would keep going – keep kicking, keep absorbing kicks.

I crashed a succession of blows into his left shin. He was putting all his weight on his right leg, I noticed, keeping the left one withdrawn as if it was in some way weakening. I pushed hard from my right and he fell sideways into the mud.

'Slip!' yelled the Stickler. 'No submission. Reset!'

I hid my exhaustion behind an easy smile. 'Good this, isn't it?' I said to my adversary. For the first time he started to look uneasy. He took several seconds to get to his feet, several more to rejoin me in the middle of the ring. I went at him hard again, marching him backwards out of the arena and slamming him into the wooden castle. 'Woah woah woah!' said the Stickler. 'Back to the middle.' This time my opponent took even longer to retake his stance. He made a big show of rebuttoning his smock, taking every second of rest he could.

I winked at him. I didn't want to be there at that point – of course I didn't. Two hours earlier I could never have imagined putting myself through this sort of punishment. But in that moment, there was no way I was going to capitulate, nor show the slightest weakness.

I also knew with absolute certainty that he would give in before I did. It sounds daft, but it was a confidence born from years of triathlons – I was used to pushing myself so hard physically in training that I felt sick. I had yet to finish a race without puking up with sheer effort at the end. While that's nothing special for anyone who's taken sport to a semi-serious level, it gave me a huge advantage over him. I knew the pain wouldn't last for ever and that I could soak it up. I knew, too, that in these situations your mind starts offering up all sorts of perfectly reasonable excuses why you should give up. You've got to the semi-finals – that's enough. The other bloke's younger and fitter. Your shoes aren't right. You've already done better than anyone expected. The referee's against you. The other bloke is barely human.

The trick was to ignore this clamour in my own mind and to add more doubt to his. So every time I forced him out of the circle and we reset (which seemed to be happening again and again on the same nightmarish loop) I almost jogged back to the middle. I grabbed him before he was ready, gave him a little friendly smile, then told him how amusing and enjoyable this all was.

At the same time, I couldn't win a legal throw. Twice more I had him on the deck; twice more the Stickler refused to call it. I began to wonder how it would ever finish. We had now been slugging it out for over sixteen minutes. Could they not stop it on points?

The end, when it did come, was almost a surprise. Convinced that my kicks were too lightweight, I had been targeting the vulnerable spot just below his knee on his left leg, the point where the straw padding was thinnest. With a bellow he suddenly threw his arms in the air, limped backwards and waved his hand in front of his face. 'No more,' he croaked, 'that's it.'

We fell into each other's arms like drunken lovers. 'Brilliant,' I gasped, 'brilliant fight.'

'Too good,' he said. 'You had too much for me.'

BEN

When a sports hack doesn't want to call something 'boring', he'll have a rummage around in his big bag of euphemisms and pull out 'absorbing' instead. This fail-safe adjective could easily have been applied to Tom's semi-final, which had sections of the crowd streaming towards the beer tent long before the final throw. 'Congratulations, Tommy,' I thought to myself as he thrashed about before me, 'you've discovered Test match shin-kicking.'

TOM

I lurched away and almost collapsed on top of Dirs. 'Let's not fuck about, Tommy,' he said cheerfully. 'You're in the final.'

It was now almost pitch black. I turned back towards the middle of the arena and saw a giant lumbering into view. 'Christ,' I panted, 'we're going to need more straw.'

Ben held me by the shoulders and poured water over my head. 'You're one step away from being world champion,' he said. I felt him taping up my shins with Sellotape. 'Go to work,' he said, pushing me into the ring.

The bloke had seemed big enough from fifteen feet away. Close up he was enormous – 6 ft 4 ins and around 17 stone, with a face that looked as if it had been chiselled from granite. I tried not to think about the fact that he'd been sitting with his feet up for the last twenty minutes while I had been pushed to the very edge of my limits. The crowd were chanting something. 'Bulldog! Bulldog! Bulldog!' I glanced up at my opponent's chest, my breath coming in short rasps. On his T-shirt was a large print of a snarling dog. 'Good luck,' he said, smiling broadly.

I went for the win – I really did. As soon as the Stickler gave the command I threw myself forward, lashing out grimly with both feet, throwing kicks at those tree-trunk legs, leaning all my weight into his colossal frame. Like a grizzly bear toying with a salmon, he grabbed me with a massive paw and batted me effortlessly over his leg. One-nil.

It was at this stage that I understood the magnitude of the task in front of me. It wasn't that I didn't want to win, or that I looked defeat in the eye and welcomed it. I just realized how unlikely it was that I would come out on top. Maybe that's defeatist – maybe I should have pushed all those thoughts to one side and refused to admit the possibility of anything but victory. Maybe.

You can watch the final moments on YouTube – try searching under 'shin-kicking 2008'. You'll see us circling like enraged stags, me piling forward with straw pouring from my trousers, our kicks flying in, Bulldog's massive left leg coming out and me going down again like a snared rabbit. You'll see the Stickler point his staff towards Bulldog and then raise his hand, see me climb wearily to my feet and watch wordlessly as his supporters invade the arena and hoist the victor on to their shoulders.

It was chaos. TV crews were everywhere, hands slapping us on the back, camera-flashes going off. The winner – who I would later find out was a judo and taekwondo expert from Bedfordshire named Steve Williams – raised his trophy in the air. An official handed me my silver medal. Steve and I shook hands, laughing and limping. 'The better man won,' I told the TV crews. 'The better shin-kicker.'

Dirsy came over and we embraced. 'The final, Tommy,' he said. 'You made the final.'

He sat me down and began untaping my legs. My hands, grazed and bleeding, were shaking like twigs in a tornado. Fireworks were going off on the hill behind us. Locals were queuing up with long wooden torches and lighting them from the blazing bonfire.

'It's like the fucking *Wicker Man*,' muttered Ben. 'Let's get the fuck out of here.'

The days that followed were strange ones. The initial sense of exhilaration at making the final, at coming within two decent kicks of the world title, was soon replaced by a heavy exhaustion and remarkable level of pain from my battered body. The first night I couldn't sleep. The fight-or-flight hormones were whacking round my system, and Ben's nasal passages reacted badly to something in the mattress of the campervan. His snoring rattled the stained-glass windows like a gale.

Once I'd crashed off the adrenalin, everything hurt – my back, my shoulders, my ear where my earring had been ripped out. Ripe purple bruises flowered on my chest where my lapels had been gripped. And the shins . . . The pain was such that walking normally became a distant dream. The mere impact of my heels touching the ground sent searing pain up my legs.

'You've got bone bruising,' said a physio mate. 'Lots of spider-web fractures on the bones.' A fortnight later I was waking up at night with a howl whenever the bed-sheet brushed against them. After three weeks I was still unable to wear socks; the pressure of the material on my shins felt like fire.

Mentally I was struggling too. What sort of achievement was it to come second? Maybe that was the best shot we'd get at becoming a champion all year, and I'd failed to take it. I'd failed to win even a single submission in the final. Should I have done better? Could I have dug even deeper, pushed myself even harder? Was Bulldog truly the unbeatable man-mountain that I'd convinced myself he was? Twisted with self-doubt, I opened up Google and typed in the web address I'd seen printed on the T-shirts of his supporters that Friday night – *www.backswording.co.uk*.

'*Aisle O'var Backswording Clubbe*,' it said in large type on the main page. 'Welcome to the home of TE-MA – Traditional English Martial Arts.'

There were intimidating photos of serious-looking men holding wooden staffs and long, glinting swords. Several of the faces I recognized from Dover's Hill, not least a bandannaed bruiser who looked like Lincolnshire's answer to Hulk Hogan. I read on.

> We are scholars and practitioners of the Ancient and Noble Science of Defence and that most excellent of ancient country sports, English Country Backswording Circa 1600. Our main focus is in the study of the single-handed Backsword/Broadsword and the English Quarterstaff/Tipstaff which also involves the close study of English pugilism, indigenous wrestling styles and Strikes with the feet and the knees.

Strikes with the feet and knees? I gingerly touched the squishy swelling on my shin-bones and felt a wave of pain surge into my feet and knees.

> The Aisle O'var Backswording Clubbe, founded by Peter Holland, is currently one, if not the only, full-time Traditional English Martial Arts Clubs in the UK that specifically train in the art of Shin-Kicking. Steve 'Bulldog' Williams from Shefford, Bedfordshire, a long-standing member of the AOBC, decided to throw his hat in the ring and enter in for the shin-kicking tournament at the Cotswold games after viewing it at the 2007 event. Since then he has been training with his fellow TE-MA students and instructors running up to the 2008 games as well as spending time mentally preparing for the games, going over tactics and techniques and training at home.

Training? Tactics? Techniques? What foolishness, what naivety we'd shown! To think I had entered on nothing more than the whim of Dirs – ignorant of the rules, ill-prepared physically, armed with nothing but a calamitous campervan and a co-driver whose idea of exercise was ripping the cellophane off a fresh packet of fags.

Chastened, I decided to give Bulldog a call. Like the true champion he was, he was magnanimous in victory without downplaying the effort he'd put in to win his title.

'I remember watching your semi-final and feeling better and better the longer it went on,' he said kindly. 'It wasn't easy – I couldn't walk for two days afterwards. But I've done all the stick-fighting, things like cudgelling – full-contact stuff with ash and oak staffs. We wear helmets but anywhere that's open on the body is fair game.

'I was confident going down there. I'd learned the rules and taught it to my class, to the point that they told me to put up or shut up. A load of them came along to have a few beers and get stuck in – that's why it all went mad at the end.'

Steve's near-flawless performance, it transpired, had quite rightly brought him the plaudits he deserved. 'It's gone mad since I won,' he said. 'I've had them all on the phone – the *Biggleswade Chronicle*, Three Counties Radio . . . I was even on a radio station in Texas called KZNE. They'd had George Foreman on earlier in the week, and the interviewer said he couldn't believe it – Bulldog Williams and George Foreman on the same show in the same week.

'It's amazing, isn't it,' he said proudly. 'Something you do in a field in Gloucestershire makes you famous in Texas. We've had 130,000 hits on that YouTube clip. Mind you, some of the comments on there are quite nasty. I feel like saying, "Come on then – it's an open competition, why not come down and take us on? Just make yourself known to me . . ."'

Once a Bulldog, always a Bulldog, I reflected, scrolling down the YouTube page a few hours later to see what the wider world had said about our battle.

'man i wish i lived in england!' said the first comment.

'i think i would do good at one of these,' said the next. 'looks like it hurts like a bitch tho.'

'this is awesome i wanna party with these people,' read a third, 'but whats the deal with the lab coats?'

What indeed, I thought, reaching for an ice-pack.

'lol this is retarted but pretty funny. id expect the scotish to do something like this but not the brits.'

'scottish people ARE brits, faggot.'

'yo it would suck if you wore tight pants.'

'don't get it why would it suck if you wore tight pants?'

'because u cant stick any cusioning in the tight pants.'

'why cant they hit diks instead?'

The World Dik-Hitting Championships. Bingo. Now where could I get Dirs an entry-form for that?

4
NETTLES

BEN

Unlike most males, I didn't spend many of my teenage years daydreaming about what my first car might be. When I did give it some thought (and always being something of a realist) I probably imagined something no-frills, like a Renault Clio, or my old man's Hillman Avenger. A car that, as my dad always liked to say, got you from A to C and through B, however strange a motto that was for a man whose Avenger often blew up at A½.

One thing's for certain: never once did I fix any of my friends with a determined stare and whisper in portentous tones, 'You can shove your Ferrari Testarossa up your arse. You know what my first car's gonna be? A converted 1981 Bedford campervan.'

So when Tom first came clattering up my drive in said converted 1981 Bedford campervan, my natural reaction was, 'What in God's name is that sack of shit?' Still, the old cow had surprised me by getting us to the Cotswolds and back, and seeing as Tom was the poor sod having to wrestle with her all over Britain, I didn't really have any grounds for complaint. Even if it did smell like Tom had been airing his vests in it. And even if it did turn into a tumble dryer when you took her over 45 m.p.h. At a personal cost of around a grand. As Tom had reminded me, faux stained-glass windows don't come cheap.

Smarting from my humiliation at the World Coal-Carrying Championships, and having had my shins smashed to buggery by Fordyce in Gloucestershire, I'd decided to take athleticism out of the equation altogether for our next event and replace it with something much more up my alley: stuffing things into my cakehole. Although it had gone largely unsaid up until that point, it was clear a personal battle-within-a-battle was brewing between Tom and me (at least in my mind) and I was delighted to see Tom's agonized look when I told him where the Champervan would be taking us next.

'Nettle-eating?' said Tom, flashing me his best whisky face. 'As in stinging nettles? No, I'm not doing that. I could barely cycle to work after the shin-kicking – what are they going to say if I can't talk or type for a week?'

'Come on Tommy,' I replied, revelling in his obvious alarm, 'you bloody love leaves and stuff. I didn't see you eat anything else when we were in France for seven weeks, it was like sharing a van with a caterpillar.'

'A caterpillar with a driving licence,' replied Tom, his eyes narrowing. 'And lettuce and spinach leaves don't sting you when you eat them. Plus, what happens when stinging nettles come out the other end? It must be like passing razor wire.'

'Listen, mate,' I said, 'the way I see it, you stitched me up with the coal-carrying, now it's time to swallow some Dirsy medicine. Anyway, they give you gloves. And my nan used to eat nettle soup all the time, and she was pretty much allergic to breathing. Dorset, Saturday 21 June – let's have it.'

I'd been told about the nettle-eating competition by a mate's dad, who in turn remembered seeing it on a local news item when he was working down in Bristol a few years ago. A bit of digging on the internet had led me to the Bottle Inn, a sixteenth-century thatched pub eight miles from Lyme Regis on the B3165. Shane Pym took over as landlord in 1997, and he told me how what had begun as a quirky local event had quickly morphed into a prickly leaved monster of Triffid-like proportions.

'What happened was, two farmers were arguing at the bar over who had the longest nettles at the back of their silage tank,' said Shane. 'The then landlady, Frances Vincent, said, "What makes you two think you've got the longest nettles in Marshwood? I know, we'll have a competition to see." About three or four years into the competition, a guy called Alex Williams (an ex-Household Cavalryman) comes in with nettles 15 ft 6 in long, throws them down and says, "There, if anybody beats that, I'll eat it." You can guess what happened next. True to his word, Alex duly consumed the leaves from the offending nettle. After that it became tradition on Longest Nettle Night that if Alex didn't win, he would eat his own nettle.

'When I took over, for my launch party I wanted to have the theme of Midsummer Madness. It was on 21 June, which was summer solstice, and as part of it we challenged anyone to eat more nettles than Alex. I phoned the local paper to tell them what we'd got going on and they took some snaps of Alex seeing off the only two competitors with about eight feet of nettles. From there the Bristol papers got hold of it, and on Tuesday morning I had half of Fleet Street on the phone. I quite literally put my tongue in my cheek and said, "I thought everybody knew, we hold the World Nettle-

Eating Championships in Marshwood.' And from there it's gone from strength to strength. Nettle-eating is a true illustration of what it is to be British and in Britain in the summer.'

All of which sounded splendid, until Shane sounded a cautionary note for any other landlords tempted to let the world in on their eccentric little secret.

'To tell the truth, it's almost become a little too big for its boots,' said Shane. 'We used to do it out the front of the pub as a bit of fun for the locals, but now I have to hire a field at the back of the pub for camping and car parking, security, licensing, insurance. Then there's the entertainment budget, the advertising budget . . .'

Security? Insurance? Advertising budget? As Shane impressed upon me the magnitude of the event in its modern form, any faint dreams I'd been harbouring of glory began to fade. And just as I sometimes find myself watching ancient football footage on TV and saying to myself, 'This lot are shit, I could have played for England in the 1920s,' I couldn't help thinking I'd stumbled across this particular 'sport' a bit too late. But there was no pulling out now: I'd reeled Tom in, so I was just going to have to face the trichomes (that's the prickly things on nettle leaves to the rest of you).

If my travails at the World Coal-Carrying Championships had taught me anything it was that however ridiculous an event might sound, going into it with zero preparation is the behaviour of a bloody idiot. Plus, something had been nagging away at me ever since I'd persuaded Tom to take part. As I'd pointed out myself, Tom actually likes eating leaves, while the only leaves I usually eat come in the form of after-dinner mints. So recognizing that the World Nettle-Eating

Championships were by no means a Dirsy banker, and having neither enough time nor money to get some cow's teeth fitted and my stomach compartmentalized into four parts, I got hold of the defending champion's phone number a few weeks ahead of time and pumped him for tips.

'Ideally you should eat a few nettles beforehand,' said Paul Collins, a 29-year-old sign maker from Lyme Regis. 'But you should really start eating nettle soup a while before to get it into your system. That way you'll stand a better chance of not being sick.'

On hearing this, my immediate thought was: I wonder if Paul has any tips to ensure you're not sick while eating nettle soup while training not to be sick while eating raw nettles? But I quickly sensed that Paul was a man who took his nettle-eating very seriously indeed.

'Tennis players wouldn't turn up to Wimbledon without training,' he went on. 'Andy Murray will be training all the time so that when he gets there he can actually play some decent tennis. Also, the taste is pretty hardcore. What I find is that when you've still got a mouthful of nettles, swig a bottle of orange juice to add a bit of sweetness. I had a pint of bitter last year and really regretted it – an hour of nettles mixed with Bombardier is not a great combination.'

'Hang on a second,' I said, my throat tightening, 'did you just say "an hour"? An hour of eating nettles? How many nettles did you eat in an hour?'

'Well, last year, my debut, I did 56 ft, but that was still 20 ft short of the record, so I have to come back,' said Paul. 'I'd won the world championship, but I thought, I'm never going to be a world record holder at golf or tennis, so I might as well have another go at nettle-eating.'

My chat with Paul having further dented my victory

ambitions – 56 ft? Who or what had I been speaking to, a giraffe? – I got straight on the phone to my mum and demanded she whip up some nettle soup. 'Nettle soup?' replied my mum. 'What are you, a druid? I'll do you a nice madeira cake.'

Strangely, my mum was unable to grasp the seriousness of preparing for the World Nettle-Eating Championships, so I popped down to the local park with a pair of gardening gloves and some shears and had a go at knocking up some nettle soup myself. Now, I'm not sure if you've ever made nettle soup, but if you haven't, be warned – you need a shit load of nettles. About a carrier bag's worth in fact. Otherwise, it's not really nettle soup at all, more a saucepan of hot water with a few leaves floating about at the bottom. By the time I'd thrown in the carrots, onion, crème fraiche, chicken stock and herbs, it wasn't really nettle soup at all. Not that it would have mattered if it were, because my housemate staggered in from work that night with a couple of mates, saw it resting on the hob and between them they drank the lot. 'Kebabylon was closed,' shrugged Matt the next day, seemingly unconcerned that he'd sabotaged my entire world championship preparations.

The day of the event also began in catastrophic fashion with Tommy waking me from a deep slumber to inform me that one of the Champervan's front tyres was flat. For most people, this would be a minor blip. For a man as melodramatic as me, to whom every bunker on a golf course is a personal affront, specifically dug by the course designer to ruin my entire week, this was a disastrous situation. To make matters worse, while Tom is made of far sunnier stuff, he's as familiar with the workings of automobiles as a blind, armless Amish. Fortunately, Len from the Hangar Lane branch of Halfords did know a thing or two about motors – even motors made by companies that haven't existed for two decades. Unfortunately, Len was knocking off for lunch at twelve, so while he was happy to flog us a suspiciously expensive and inadequate-looking jack, we'd just have to fit the wheel ourselves.

'Have we got a spare wheel?' I said to Tom as we walked back to the Champervan.

'Course we have.'

'Where is it?'

'Not sure. But I wouldn't worry about it. We haven't got a boot, but it'll be there somewhere.'

After twenty minutes tearing the Champervan apart like a couple of narc cops at Calais, the spare wheel eventually turned up in the shower, looking like it had been salvaged from the wreck of a sunken car ferry. I started to think this Mr Simkiss bloke who'd sold us the thing wanted us dead. Maybe the Champervan itself had been salvaged from the wreck of a sunken car ferry? Were our ramblings on the BBC really that offensive? Was this Simkiss chap the front for that group I'd seen on Facebook – 'Benders and Fordyce are c@@ts'? Hardly Baader-Meinhof, but a little bit sinister nonetheless. Who knew? And who had time to ponder? There were nettles to be eaten, and a world championship to be won.

Over the years, I have transformed tactical smoking into something of an art form: wait until just before some important act has to be carried out before pulling out a fag and sparking up. For those who don't smoke, think of it as a more sophisticated version of the classic 'doing up your shoelaces when you don't actually need to in order to get out of doing something' trick. And so with the wheel ready to be heaved on to the axle, I deftly lit a Marlboro Light, leaving Tom scrabbling about on his back underneath a two-tonne motorhome with me in charge of the jack. What I didn't tell Tom was that this was my jack debut. Had I told him, I'm sure he would have objected more loudly. And if I had told him the jack nearly slipped a couple of times, I'm sure he would have been absolutely furious.

Muhammad Ali, when asked if he was any good at golf, replied: 'I'm the best. I just haven't played it yet.' I gave the great man's words plenty of thought as we clattered down the A303 towards the small village of Marshwood in Dorset, home to the Bottle Inn and the World Nettle-Eating Championships. For many is the time, frustrated by my failure to excel at mainstream sports and pastimes, that I've wondered to myself: 'Maybe, just maybe, I am the best at something – but like Ali and golf, I just haven't played it yet.' And as Tommy wrestled manfully with the gearstick beside me, like someone trying to throttle an angry rattlesnake, the thought occurred to me: 'Maybe, just maybe, that something is eating nettles . . .'

TOM

As the Champervan grunted its way past Stonehenge, I let Dirsy talk on. He seemed blissfully unaware of the irony of comparing himself, a man who had failed to carry a bag of coal up a short hill, to Muhammad Ali, Olympic and world heavyweight champion, civil rights icon and inspiration to millions around the world. I glanced across as he shadow-boxed at the windscreen with smoke billowing from between his lips. Maybe the chat would be good for his confidence. Maybe, over in Kentucky, Ali was telling his own mate how much of an affinity he felt for a balding smoker from Romford whose greatest sporting moment was a 3 a.m. breakdance victory over a fat Australian.

A large queue of traffic had built up behind us. There were sporadic outbreaks of angry beeping as drivers took it in turns to vent their frustration. You'd have thought people would have been happy to be passing one of the great historical sites of the world at a speed that allowed them to appreciate it fully, but a mood of impatience seemed to have settled over Wiltshire. With the summer solstice just gone, it was also clear that most drivers had written us off as hippy travellers, chugging round the country in a stolen campervan, stopping only to cover local beauty spots in extravagant amounts of litter.

'PIKEY CLOWNS!' roared a Clarkson-lite as he accelerated past in a sports car. I jabbed my hand on the horn. 'Eeek,' came the insipid noise, like a hungry baby owl. 'Eeek.'

On the sort of fantasy-driving television programmes that Clarkson frequents, motoring on country roads is portrayed as the ultimate in adrenalin-fuelled freedom. Low-slung super-sleek cars hammer round empty roads in dazzling bursts of titanium and sunlight. I mused on this as the Champervan groaned round corners at the speed of a grieving sloth and ploughed through overhanging trees like a penitent sinner intent on self-flagellation. I could have cycled to Dorset quicker. That at least would have worked up a decent appetite for the monstrous meal that lay in wait.

BEN

The field to the rear of the Bottle Inn looked more like Verdun after a few months of German shelling than a makeshift campsite, and we were more than a little concerned that it would become the Champervan's final resting place. Much more rain and we'd need a tugboat to tow her out the following morning. Despite the weather there were plenty of heads milling about, a folk band was in full swing and it was already a few deep at the bar by midday. Outside, a pig rotated on a spit, while a couple of washed-out clowns, make-up streaming down their faces, so that you weren't sure if they were happy or they'd had battery acid thrown over them, did a spot of juggling.

Tom and I found a cosy nook inside the pub, ordered a couple of pints of Poacher's Choice and got chatting to Stan and Ruby, a couple of pub sign enthusiasts from Market Bosworth.

'We're interested in all these English tribal customs so we travel round the country taking part in them and recording them on camera,' said Stan, while Ruby chewed absent-mindedly on a nettle leaf. 'I give talks to women's institutes and rotary clubs. It's our hobby really. That and pub signs. I give talks on them as well.'

Stan bridled at the suggestion that quaint tribal customs were dying out all over the country, slamming down his beer and taking a shrill intake of breath as if he'd just caught me snapping a pub sign over my knee.

'It's certainly not a case of cataloguing a disappearing England. All round the country these things are going on and it's extraordinary how many there are. Some have been revived after many years and others have been going since the middle ages and just keep going. I think it's a reaction to our plastic world.'

Stan, despite all his noise, would not be joining Ruby in battle that afternoon. 'When we were younger we went in for all of these, but since my knees gave way I've had to take on a supporting role. This is how we met. Morris Dancing, bonfire carnivals, worm-catching, snail-racing, conker championships, jumping into rivers – you never know, you might first lay eyes on the love of your life while you've got a face full of nettles.'

I'm not sure Stan had been paying attention, because if he had, he wouldn't have come out with a statement as wild as that. The only thing I was going to fall in love with at the Bottle Inn was Poacher's Choice, such was the rag-tag array of gnarled and rather salty men on display. All in all there were about six teeth between them.

Landlord Shane Pym also popped by, but he wasn't in the mood for chatting. Instead he stopped suddenly in the middle of the pub, looked out of the window and muttered under his breath, 'I'm going to be crying into my beer in a minute . . . you can really blow some money on a wet stinging nettle . . .'

I was just about to head off to the bar for another round when Ruby suddenly grabbed my hand and fixed me with an anxious look. For a second, I thought she was going to tell me she'd been cheating on Stan. Instead, she closed her eyes, tilted her head and started singing, her voice thin and reedy, like someone easing out a surreptitious fart.

Tender-handed stroke a nettle and it stings you for your pains,
Grasp it like a man with mettle and it soft as silk remains,
'Tis the same with common natures, use 'em kindly they rebel,
But be rough as nutmeg graters and the rogues obey your will.

This was some seriously spooky-arsed stuff. What with terrifying clowns and old crones singing songs about nettles, I half expected Stan to emerge from the shitter with his head under his arm and jangling some chains. We didn't wait to find out.

For a start, we needed a few more pointers, so we got mingling with our fellow competitors down by the temporary stage which had been erected for the event. According to Gary from Bridport, it was all down to 'optimum levels'. 'I'm a darts player, right, and I play a little bit of pool, right, and anyone who plays darts or pool knows about optimum levels.'

At this point Tommy rolled his eyes and made for the relatively safe haven of the Champervan for his traditional mid-afternoon kip, but I was like a sponge, ready to soak up all the tips my rivals had to offer.

'You know the way you're down the pub playing darts or pool and you start out pretty shit and then you have a few pints and you start playing well? Well, your optimum level is the point at which the booze has made you so loose and uninhibited, you're playing as well as you can possibly play.'

Gary stared straight at me and I stared over his shoulder, struggling to make the link between darts, pool, optimum levels and nettles. I'm not sure how long this stand-off lasted, but I do know it got a little bit embarrassing. I was just about to make my excuses and leave when, sensing his words of wisdom had fallen on stony ground, Gary sparked back into life.

'It's the same with nettle-eating. Eat a nettle stone cold sober, and it hurts like buggery. Get a few beers down your neck and it's like eating marshmallows. But it's a high-wire act. Go beyond your optimum level playing darts and you might miss the board. Go beyond your optimum level in nettle-eating and you end up with green shite all over your brand new trainers.'

While there seemed to be a scintilla of logic in Gary's technique, I thought I'd better just cross-reference it with a higher authority, namely the nettle-eating legend and three-time world champion that is Simon Sleigh. Simon's celebrity meant he wasn't an easy man to nail down, and when I eventually cornered him, I discovered a rather reluctant character somewhat burdened by his unusual talent.

'We were in the Bottle Inn one day and there just happened to be this competition taking place,' said Simon, who worked as a social work assistant in the area. 'Because it was a local event it caught my imagination and seemed rather extraordinary, so it seemed like a good idea to participate. I never knew I'd have a talent for it. I had no experience whatsoever, because it's not something one does, eat nettles raw generally speaking. But that first time I ate about 70 feet and came second. I set the record of 76 feet in 2000 and won it three years in succession. It was after that I thought, actually, this may appear a bit strange and I didn't want to be pigeonholed as the chap who eats nettles. That would sound a bit sad really. So I decided to retire and encourage other people to take it on.'

This was brilliant. Like Maradona and Gazza before him, like Higgins, like Best, here was a man constantly in the shadow of his former glories, struggling to escape, to forge a new life, but never able to do so. At this stage I should make clear that Simon does not, nor ever has had, a cocaine habit or a drink problem, and that the only reason he has never been able to break free is because he's such a bloody nice bloke.

'Every year I'm invited to go up and judge, so I do, and it's much more pleasant than taking part. And I'm willing people on because I'd like that record broken now. Then I can retire gracefully and disappear into obscurity, which is where I'd like to be. But here we are almost ten years later and nobody's managed to beat my record.

'I don't seek fame, although over the years I've been offered a remarkable amount of media events and TV and radio programmes to go on. It's been a bit of a circus for the last ten years. Back when I was still participating I did actually get a phone call from a guy over in New York who was running a beef burger-eating competition and he was prepared to pay for my flight. But I had to tell him I'm a vegetarian. He could not believe that someone who won eating championships was a vegetarian. He put down the phone and called back five minutes later just to make sure I wasn't joking.'

But surely there were upsides to being the greatest nettle eater that ever lived? Crumpet? Fast cars? Chapstick endorsements?

'It always raises a smile, and that's part of it because it's a rather wacky thing to do,' conceded Simon. 'My family are probably more proud than I am to be honest and it's something they mention to their friends and so on. And the majority of people I've spoken to about it over the years are genuinely interested because it is so bizarre.'

Why did Simon reckon we Brits were attracted to take part in so many weird and wonderful events?

'It reflects our character as British people. We're not very good nationally at other things – we may have invented a lot of sports over the years but ultimately we're not very good at most of them. So when it comes down to a local level people have a chance and go for glory.'

As it turned out, Simon's only tip was 'drink plenty of beer, they taste disgusting', but I wasn't short of pointers from other quarters. Some, like defending champion Paul Collins, preferred juice as an accompaniment. Others liked to actually dunk the leaves in their beer. Everyone seemed to agree that rolling the leaves into a ball before eating would lessen the sting. Mumbo Jumbo Ash even decided to stick his oar in, texting Tom the following message: 'Learn to love the nettle. See it as the leaf of a wondrous fruit. Forget the pain, focus on sucking its fine, lucky juices.' By the time I was sat on stage waiting to eat my first nettle my mind was all a-clutter, like a golfer who's sought advice from so many people that by the time he's on the first tee he's terrified to swing his club.

'Drugs in nettle-eating? What is happening to modern-day sport? They'll soon be jacking up on EPO before a kickabout in the park.' Tom could hardly contain his fury. Having already seen his beloved sport of athletics almost brought to its knees by dopers, he looked like a broken man when I told him a wired Scotsman had just offered me cocaine on the way to the stage. 'Just a few dabs on your lips, your tongue and the inside of the mouth and you're all numbed up. Never mind nettles, you'll be able to eat a fuckin' cactus.' I'd politely declined, and I was as baffled as Tom, but for different reasons. First, cocaine being a known appetite suppressant, dabbling just before an eating contest is as nonsensical as piling into a plate of pork pies while crouched in your blocks before a hurdles race. Second, why me? I hadn't spoken to him until that point. I hadn't even seen the bloke. Was he another one of 'them'? Was his plan for me to be sprung in the Bottle Inn's toilets with a tenner up my nose, thus bringing down the curtain on my BBC career?

As we made our way to the stage for the start of the event, I couldn't help feeling a little bit jumpy. This 'Benders and Fordyce are c@@ts' outfit seemed to have agents all over the country. Not that I could join Tom on the moral high ground, although I doubt Copydex would appear on most sport's list of banned substances. Once dry, however, you can barely see it and I was banking on it protecting my delicate fingertips from the savage stings of the nettles I was about to consume.

By the time Tom and I had climbed on to the scaffold it was chucking it down, but Shane needn't have worried. A good few hundred spectators had gathered in the marshy field at the back of the pub and Shane reckoned it may have been a record attendance.

'Whereabouts do you come from?' an onlooker asked as we settled into our chairs.

'Essex,' said Tom.

'Is that where all idiots come from?' came the reply, deadpan. That's a bit rich, I thought to myself, you're the soppy bastards standing in the rain watching people eat leaves. Didn't any of them have Sky?

One of the organizers threw a couple of bunches of nettles on the table in front of us and must have clocked the trepidation on our faces. 'They're really juicy this year, bang on, really tasty,' he said, laughing. Tom gagged. I didn't take that as a good sign.

Then we were off. I quickly settled into a routine, picking leaves off the stalk one at a time, rolling them up, dunking them in my pint before ramming them home, being careful to avoid the lips on entry. Tom didn't seem so comfortable next to me, gurning his way through his first few leaves while staring across at me pitifully, hood pulled over his head, rain dripping off the end of his nose, green nettle blood sliding down his chin.

'Only fifty-eight minutes to go,' I chirped. Tom gagged again.

TOM

Historically I've never been a puker. Nor has anyone in my family. Our genes have given us guts like industrial hoovers, capable of sucking in huge amounts of any food at pace and getting rid of it at the other end in double-quick time. When others who've eaten the same main course have been spraying the ceiling with vomit, we've been cheerfully tucking into pudding and a dessert wine. The family Achilles heel is mussels, but since the nettles were served sans marinière and about as al dente as could be, there should have been nothing to fear. It should have been a picnic in the park. Looking around at the grizzled faces of our fellow competitors, I even guessed I was the only vegetarian on the blocks. There was almost a sparkle in my eye and a jaunt to my jaw as the first nettle hit my throat.

Whoah. What was that unfamiliar trampoline feeling in my stomach? I rolled up another leaf, dipped it in my pint of Poacher's and shoved it home. Chomp chomp chomp. Sting sting sting. A big swallow, and it was gone to the . . . Aghfff. Or was it?

The Poacher's is probably off, I thought, clutching at straws and then some more stalks. That's why I feel a bit churny down below. That tectonic shift in my guts – just a little gas brought on by the Dirs-speed drinking. A little focus was needed; this was a world championship, after all. I just needed to get my head down and concentrate on the leaves. Those horrible wet leaves that tasted like lawnmower clippings dipped in chilli. Those leaves that were now somersaulting back up my throat like arsenic acrobats, up into my mouth, through my nose, down my chin . . .

Beforehand, I'd expected a little pain – something along the lines of the nettles hurting on the way in and hurting on the way out. I just hadn't expected the exit hole to be the same as the entrance. I shut my eyes and forced the emerald bile back down. You can't quit, I told myself. Victory might have gone, but dignity was still an option. Like Derek Redmond, I just had to get to the finish.

BEN

Twenty minutes in and I hit the wall. What stopped me in my tracks was the sight of defending champion Paul Collins dragging his fist down the length of a stalk, rolling the dislodged leaves into a tangerine-sized ball and throwing them into his mouth in one fluid movement like a ravenous ape. 'How many has he done?' I asked Shane. 'Thirty feet,' replied Shane. I looked at the shorn stems between my feet. I'd managed four. Plus, the rain had turned the Copydex on my fingers to goo, so that I now had to pick fragments of the rubbery adhesive from between my teeth after each mouthful. The rain seemed to have taken the edge off the nettle hairs so that they slid into the mouth quite comfortably. But – and this was something Tom and I, blinded by our fear of getting stung to high heaven, had rather foolishly overlooked – we were eating leaves. Leaves that were 'juicy' in the same way strips of bark might be juicy. Or lumps of charcoal. Every now and then Tom would shoot up out of his seat and wretch violently over the edge of the scaffold. And because we weren't allowed to leave the scaffold to use the toilet, both of us ended up pissing into pint glasses underneath our tables. Rain-lashed, eating leaves, urinating into pots, people gagging all around me. It was like some hyper-real historical re-enactment of the Mayflower's voyage to America. What next, a dose of scurvy?

Forty minutes in and most of the chairs around us had been vacated, which provided an interesting little psychological insight. We were sat facing away from the main throng of spectators, and with no crowd to cheer them on, the quitters couldn't find it within themselves to battle through. Tom, incredibly, was still hanging in there, although his leaf-to-minute ratio had tailed off to about a half.

The Geordie chap to my right spewed into his pint glass on about forty-five minutes, and eagle-eyed Shane moved in to disqualify him. 'That's it, mate, you're out.'

'What if I can get it back in?' said the Geordie, before tipping the glass to his lips. He made it about halfway, before bringing it all back up again. Tom and I spent the last ten minutes dipping each leaf into a pot of hummus Tom had secreted in his coat pocket. All in all it was one of the most miserable hours of my life, made barely tolerable by the tantalizing prospect of Tom spraying the ring-side spectators with a torrent of racing-green vomit.

'Cracking event,' said Shane as we made our way down from the scaffold. 'One of those uniquely British events. We don't get much of a summer, so we've got to make the best of it we can.'

Paul Collins had defended his title, but the retreat into

obscurity that Simon Sleigh so craved would have to wait. Despite consuming a phenomenal 64 ft of nettles – 58 ft more than me, 60 ft more than Tom – Paul was still 12 ft shy of the world record. As Simon's girlfriend Jenny put it, 'Oh no, we'll have to do this all again next year.' Next year? This record appeared Beamonesque to me and I feared Simon might have it hammered into his gravestone.

'I was close and I'll probably give it another go next year,' said Paul afterwards, his lips and tongue dyed almost black, as if he'd been licking a newly tarred road. 'I really think I can challenge that record with a bit of training. The pace I held at the start could have taken me there, but my stomach just couldn't cope, it was swelling up too quickly. But next year my stomach will be used to it.'

The next time I saw Paul he was leaving the toilet, blowing out his cheeks and making an 'I've eaten far too much rich food' face. 'Bit of diarrhoea, but I don't think it's got anything to do with the nettles. It must be a bug, surely?' That's right, old chap, absolutely nothing to do with the 64 ft of nettles fermenting in your guts . . . must be that bug . . .

Tom and I spent the rest of the day drying out in the Bottle Inn, sampling the array of ales on display before jigging the night away to the folk band in the marquee out back. I'm not sure what time we made it back to the Champervan, but I do remember being woken up at 4 a.m. by the chattering of my own teeth. It being June, I had been a little bit previous in my packing, deciding that a sleeping bag would be wholly unnecessary. My already foul mood was made worse by the discovery that the Champervan's wheels had sunk several inches into the mud. After three or four hours ploughing through a packet of Marlboro Lights in the back, I woke Tom and delivered the bad news.

Getting a converted 1981 Bedford campervan to move on flat tarmac is not the easiest of tasks. Getting a converted 1981 Bedford campervan to move in several inches of mud is bordering on the miraculous. After nailing down whose decision it was to park the Champervan overnight in a field in the midst of a monsoon (it was Tom's) we got to work extricating ourselves from the situation. Or rather we didn't. Tom was able to spark her into life, but his feathering of the accelerator only served to dig her further in, her wheels splattering nearby tents with mud as they clawed furiously at the ground. After half an hour of standing with hands on hips and sighing heavily, a musty, ruddy-nosed old cove in a wax jacket came yomping across the field to see what was what.

'Not the brightest place to park a campervan overnight,' he said. 'I s'pose you want towing out?'

'Oh, that would be fantastic,' I said, shaking Tom's hand. 'Have you got a Land Rover or something?'

'Nope, sold mine in March.' With that, he turned and yomped off into the distance, never to be seen again.

5
EGGS

TOM

The journey home from Dorset had been slow. The heavy defeat dragged in our wake like a sea anchor. Blasts of rain battered the windscreen; gusts of wind boffed the Champervan from side to side. The engine strained and bellowed as the road rose up towards the top of Salisbury Plain. Dirsy, with a stack of chocolate digestives in one hand and a fistful of Cool Lime-flavour Doritos in the other, was in his element. He had food, he had cigarettes and he had seven pints of Poacher's bitter sloshing around in his belly. He also had someone else driving him about again. 'Only two feet of nettles!' he crowed through a stuffed mouth, blowing fragments of crisp on to the dashboard. 'You can't be happy with that! Fifty per cent less than me! Fifty per cent!'

I was more than a little put out. For starters he'd apparently forgotten that we were supposed to be a team, chasing world titles and glory together, bound by the vision we'd had on that grey dawn in Boulogne. Secondly, if he wanted to make an issue out of relative placings, what about his succession of dismal failures so far? Which one of us had failed to complete the coal course in Gawthorpe? Who had been victorious in the clash of shins on that dreadful evening in Chipping Campden?

Another thought struck me. Was I looking at things the wrong way round? Perhaps the results so far had hurt Ben more than I'd realized. I recalled how quiet he'd been on the morning of the coal-carrying, how many fags he'd got through before the horror of the shin-kicking. He'd been genuinely scared by the physical tests we'd faced.

The nettles had been his best shot yet at a world title – eating, after all, was his forte. He'd even been allowed to smoke and drink heavily during competition. But despite all the things in his favour, he'd still finished way outside the top twenty. No wonder he was all hot air and digestive biscuit. Maybe what I was seeing in the van was less the big-headed boasting of a vainglorious braggart than a devastated man desperately seeking to re-establish a fraction of his self-respect.

In that moment, I resolved to find a championship where we could compete as a pair. No more would we see each other as rivals, vying for the same prize. We would go into battle together, as we had during the rugby World Cup. We had survived those two months by working as a team – I had done the driving, the French-speaking, all the organizing, and Ben had . . . Ben had . . . well, I forget the exact details, but he was definitely there. Together we would stand, divided we would bicker. The opportunity, when it arrived, came from an unexpected source.

'Clooney to attend egg-throwing championships,' read the headline in a celebrity gossip magazine my girlfriend had left in the bathroom. 'Hollywood A-lister George Clooney could be swapping Lake Como for Lincolnshire in June after being invited to the World Egg-Throwing Championships.' There was a large picture of Clooney laughing heartily while restraining a pig on a lead. 'The *Ocean's Eleven* and *Michael Clayton* star is known for his wacky ways and has already constructed a catapult to fling eggs at paparazzi outside his Italian home.'

World Egg-Throwing Championships? A minute's Googlage brought up the details – a contest involving pairs of contenders, one throwing a raw egg, the other trying to catch it with shell intact. The world champions were the ones who managed a clean catch over a longer distance than any of their rivals.

It sounded perfect in every way. Ben and I could enter as a duo. The Champervan's limited engine power would revel in Lincolnshire's pancake-like topography. Best of all, the championship would involve catching.

Catching things – mainly a ball, although anything vaguely aerodynamic (apple, conker, scrunched-up bank statement) would do – was possibly my favourite pastime in the world. As a child I'd spent endless hours lobbing tennis balls against walls around the house, diving full-length after cricket balls, begging my dad to boot footballs at me so I could throw myself about in the mud while making spectacular saves.

I loved catching the way some men love cars and others love computer games. As a teenager I'd spent every weekend and most weeknights keeping wicket for my school and the local club side, daydreaming about heroic catches when I should have been learning about quadratic equations and oxbow lakes. I used to lie in bed at night bouncing a squash ball off the wall at the foot of my bed, walk to the shops chucking a tennis ball at every surface I passed. Even now, as a grown man attempting to hold down a steady job and relationship, I could imagine few better ways of spending an afternoon than flinging a ball around with a pal on a nice soft patch of grass to cushion any dives.

If I'm honest, my catching obsession had actually got to the point where it was starting to interfere with other areas of my life. Before the advent of the internet, of course, it hadn't been such a problem. You had to make a real effort to get an eyeful of decent action – go down to the newsagents and buy a specialist magazine, or borrow a mate's how-to guide full of graphic photos. But now, however, you're only ever a click or two away from high-res images or actual video footage.

So many times I'd been at my laptop, trying to get some work done, when temptation would worm its way into my mind. I'd tell myself not to give in, to focus on what I was doing, but inevitably I'd cave in, fire up Internet Explorer and start searching. I knew exactly which websites to go to for the real hardcore stuff, too – big names like Colly, Twinny Waugh and Jonty Rhodes performing feats of athleticism which barely seemed physically possible. Like many men I found myself drawn to a particular genre – in my case, full-length stuff. I'm not proud to admit it, but there it is. Often, after watching the superstars do their thing, it would all get too much. I'd have to sneak off and have a quick session of solo catching, just to release the pressure that had built up. Of course, as soon as I'd released the final throw, I'd be overwhelmed by remorse and self-loathing, but the next day I would inevitably be at it again. Maybe, just maybe, the Egg-Throwing Championships might offer a positive outlet for my obsession.

And Ben? When we had talked before about catching, he had claimed to be a natural, to have what cricketers refer to as 'soft hands'. I wasn't entirely convinced. Whenever we'd thrown a rugby ball around in France, he'd struggled to take it cleanly, although that could equally be because he was often trying to hold a can of 1664 and a lit cigarette at the same time. I'd also seen those hands of his trying to steer a woman around a dance floor, and it was like watching a workman breaking concrete.

I waited until midday and gave him a call. 'Egg-throwing?' he said, a strange note in his voice.

'And catching,' I said quickly. 'You take it in turns.'

'I dunno,' he said.

'Come on,' I said. 'It's ideal for us. You don't need to be fit, like at the coal-carrying. It's not going to cripple us for weeks, like the shin-kicking. We won't have green vomit dribbling down our chins, like nettle-eating. What's not to like?'

'I've got a sore shoulder,' he mumbled.

'I'll give you a massage,' I said, 'as long as we never speak of it again.'

'There's something else,' he said quietly.

'What?'

'I – I can't tell you.'

'Why? What's the problem?'

There was a long pause.

'Look,' he said finally. 'I'll do it. I'll come along, but I'm not going to practise. I'm not going near an egg until the day itself.'

It didn't make any sense to me. In fact, it was worse than no sense. I didn't mind so much if Ben didn't have the same natural aptitude for throwing and catching as me – if he wanted to be the Garfunkel to my Simon, the Ridgeley to my Michael – but to refuse to train for a world championship seemed to invite failure. Did we want gold medals and glory or not?

Dirsy was still in a morose mood two weeks later, as we chugged northwards towards the friends' house where we would overnight en route to the big event. He was staring out of the window like a puppy snatched from its mother's kennel, taking his sad gaze off the horizon long enough only to bury his nose in another family-pack of Cool-Lime Doritos.

Music, I thought, I'll cheer him up with some music. I reached across to the in-van stereo and flicked the on/off switch, only to stumble across another endearing design feature of the Champervan: the radio only worked when the engine was turned off.

'Hey Ben!' I said, with the forced jollity of a children's entertainer. 'That sign back there said there's a farm shop up the road selling trays of free-range eggs. Fancy popping in and picking some up?'

He turned his face towards me, Dorito dust smeared through his stubble. 'Keep driving,' he said flatly.

At Rob and Jane's house he piled into the chilled lagers with relentless thirst, pacing the patio like a caged bear while lighting each fresh fag from the smouldering tip of the last. Worried sick, I dashed into the house, locked myself in the toilet and phoned the only man I knew who had the skills to turn around a situation like this: Ash.

'Classic performance anxiety,' came the murmur down the line, as I ran the taps to hide the noise of our conversation from the Dirs ears. 'Fascinating – absolutely fascinating.

'As so often before, the bathroom mirror of competition

serves only to reflect the acne of anxiety. How fragile we are – how fragile we are.'

'Are you quoting Sting lyrics?' I asked suspiciously.

'We must squeeze the pimple of pressure,' Ash continued. 'Only when the pus of panic has been wiped away can we go out into the world with self-belief restored. You must transport Ben to a happier time, take him to a better place. Where is he happiest?'

'The pub,' I said, with utter confidence.

'You must do something to remind him of the good times,' said Ash. 'Turn back the clock. Bring the wheels of time to a stop – back to the days when life was so much better.'

'Hold on,' I said. 'Isn't that Johnny Hates Jazz?' But the line was dead.

I walked back into the lounge. How could I remind Ben of the fun we'd shared in France? Pleasant though Rob and Jane's road was, suburban Solihull was nothing like Marseille. We were already sleeping in a van, and the chances of finding a fat Australian fan for him to breakdance against seemed slim.

I eyed Rob's record decks. Maybe I could find a tune in his collection that summed up those seven glorious weeks on the road. Over the course of the trip Ben and I had gradually whittled away at the artists on my iPod until only a few remained in the cross-hatched areas of our musical Venn diagram – Donny Hathaway, The Dubliners, Stevie Wonder, The Who and Bernard Cribbins.

Rob owned a lot of fine 1990s house. Of Hathaway and the Dubs there was precious little sign. What he did have was a magnificent stack of Stevie LPs, and – miraculously – the definitive Cribbins Best of. When the latter's 'Hole In

The Ground' followed Stevie's 'Hotter Than July', Dirsy smiled for the first time in weeks.

'The Cribbler,' he noted, nodding at Rob approvingly. 'What a voice. What a man.'

It was a timely intervention. Faced with another potential crisis the next morning when the Champervan refused to start, Ben stayed calm. 'My first car, this,' he told the subsequent AA man, patting the bird-muck-splattered bonnet proudly. The AA man was eyeing the van with a mixture of fear and disgust. 'Between you and me, mate,' Dirsy whispered to him, 'I think the fuel injection's gone. Or the traction control.' He coughed and nudged him in the ribs. 'Dorito?' It turned out the radio had been on all night, at a volume inaudible above the Dirs snoring. The AA man recharged our flat battery contemptuously and sent us on our way.

The flatlands of Lincolnshire rolled by under the Champervan's balding tyres. It was a land of fields, electricity pylons and scrubby hedges, but mainly it was sky, as if the ratio between earth and heavens had somehow got completely out of kilter. There was sky everywhere you looked, stretching from low-down horizon to low-down horizon with barely a bump to interrupt it. Global warming, you sensed, was very bad news indeed for fans of Lincolnshire.

Still – for the time being, the atmosphere in Swaton was celebratory. This was a world championship with something for everyone, particularly if you were into old farming equipment. Everywhere you looked were ancient threshing machines, rusting ploughs and seed-drills that didn't look like they'd been used since Cribbins's turn in *The Railway Children*. A running commentary was being given over the Tannoy. 'Is it a good tractor?' asked the compère, with the easy charm of a Howard Stableford or Mark Curry. 'Oh yes,' came the answer, 'it's a great tractor.'

A middle-aged chap in a smart blue polo shirt and roguish moustache came marching over. 'Fordyce!' he barked. 'Andy Dunlop, president of the World Egg-Throwing Federation. You've made it. Excellent. You're just in time for the egg roulette.'

He gestured at a table behind him covered in bits of egg. Two men in orange capes and white headbands were sat opposite each other, taking it in turns to pluck hard-boiled eggs from a large tray and smash them on their foreheads.

'Where's Dirs?' asked Andy. I turned round. Ben was cowering behind me, eyeing the egg-trays with ill-disguised fear.

'Where's Clooney?' I replied.

'He's not coming,' said Andy cheerfully. 'It's all a big wind-up. I sent out that press release to all the newspapers, but then someone actually got hold of his publicist and asked him about it.

'We had an even better one last year. I told them that John Prescott was coming along, what with his interest in egg-throwing. And I convinced one radio station that we only used cockerel eggs at the championships. They believed me, too.'

There was a cry of triumph from the egg roulette. One of the competitors had raw egg dribbling down his face. 'Six eggs per man, and they're all hard-boiled except one,' said Andy briskly. 'If you get the raw one, you've lost.'

'Tommy,' said Ben urgently. 'I need a word.' He grabbed my elbow and marched me out of Andy's earshot. 'Mate – there's something I have tell you. It's the eggs.'

'What do you mean?' I said suspiciously.

'I can't handle them,' he said, fumbling with his cigarette lighter. 'I mean, I properly can't handle them. They put the shits up me.' Over the PA system came the telltale squealing organ sound of Del Shannon's 'Runaway'. 'I'm serious,' said Ben. 'I've got a pathological fear of raw eggs.' I stared at him, stunned. I thought I knew all the Dirs quirks – that he claimed to dislike the taste of alcohol despite his heroic intake, that every film he had ever seen was 'rubbish', that he refused to eat any foodstuff that was small and round (beans, peas, sprouts, new potatoes) on the basis that it 'freaked him out' – but this topped the lot.

BEN

Are you the type of guy or gal who loves corn on the cob, but can't stand sweet corn? No? Didn't think so. No one has ever been able to work out why small round savoury things spook me out so much. Maybe Granddad Bill threw peas at me while I was lying in my cot. But then Mum probably would have discovered the evidence.

M&Ms, fine. Revels, big thumbs-up, even the coffee ones. Peas, beans and sweet corn, no way José. Put any of them anywhere near my plate and I'll stab you in the leg with my fork. Many is the fry-up that has gone back to the kitchen because of a rogue bean lurking under a sausage, while a fallen piece of corn from a solid, cylindrical (not round, you see?) cob is enough to put me off the rest of my meal.

As for my fear of raw eggs, no idea either. I can eat cooked eggs all day long: fried, boiled, poached, Cadbury Creme, but I could never knock something up in the first place. Evil little things, unnaturally smooth. As for the innards, don't get me started. Those long, glutinous strands that never seem to break, that hang like snot from a div kid's nose . . . just thinking about them makes me want to puke . . .

TOM

'Are you telling me,' I said, anger rising in my throat, 'that I've driven us all the way here for you to pull out minutes before kick-off?'

He shook his head. 'Listen,' he said. 'I'll do it. I just can't have an egg breaking in my hands – if that happens, I'll probably cry, and no one wants to see that.' He glanced at my face. 'Look, it's not a disaster. It might even help us. I'll have to catch the egg cleanly or I'm fucked. I'll just have to think of them as grenades.'

I shook my head wordlessly. It was classic Dirs – ignoring a problem in the naive hope that it might magically resolve itself behind his back. As a result of his blind-eyed optimism we were going into a world championship as undercooked as a plate of sushi. The way things were going, we were going to end up with egg on our faces. Literally.

I felt the pimples of pressure sprouting on my cheeks.

By the registration tent more of our rivals were pulling on the bright orange hooded capes. They looked like a Dutch version of the Ku Klux Klan. Andy had a piece of A4 in his hands and was reading out the championship rules.

'The organizers will supply all eggs used,' he shouted. 'They will be marked for security purposes and are required to be broken by the heat or final winner, to prove that it has not been tampered with, at the conclusion of the heat or final.

'Players are not permitted to use any physical, hand-held or worn aid when catching or throwing the egg. Aids include any kind of glove, net, propelling instrument, mechanical or otherwise, or any other object that gives an unfair advantage to the team.

'As a responsible governing body, we have banned the use of performance-enhancing drugs. Any competitor may be subject to drug-testing, and in case of refusal, the competitor will be disqualified. Swaton Brewery real ales are a permitted and indeed recommended substance.'

'Wallop,' said Ben, brightening visibly. 'Let's get involved.'

'Bribes are accepted in the form of money or refreshments,' Andy concluded. 'We do not accept credit cards.'

He handed us our capes and led us out into the egg-throwing arena. There must have been eighty-odd people, all in pairs, rustling their protective plastic ponchos as they walked, swinging their arms around and miming extravagant catching motions. The skeletons of what looked like four siege machines towered over us, the remnants of an earlier egg-trebuchet contest.

Broken egg-shells crunched under our feet. There were yellow stains of yolk spread in small slicks across the turf. Two middle-aged women watched from behind the safety-rope. 'I've seen nothing like this before,' said the first one, with a look of horrified fascination on her face. 'Well,' said the second, deadpan. 'Teks all sorts, dunnit?'

We lined up in two rows, ten metres apart. Ben stood opposite me, flexing his yellowed fingers. Andy came down the line holding a large tray of eggs, inviting each thrower to select their weapon.

I picked out a smallish white one and turned it over in my fingers. There was something about it that didn't feel quite right. I gave it the slightest squeeze and saw a film of gloop on the shell flex almost imperceptibly. Hairline fracture. It had to be.

Gently, ever so gently, I placed it back on the tray and casually picked up another. It was large, brown, and felt reassuringly robust to the touch. I nodded at Andy and he moved on. When each pair was armed, Andy gave the signal. The contestant on the extreme right threw his egg. Splosh – it landed in his partner's palms with a wet crack. One down. The next woman along took a deep breath and bowled hers to her team-mate. Clean catch.

As the throws moved down the line towards us I wiped my sweaty palms on the back of my shorts and swung my arm through experimentally. I'd decided to start underarm, on the basis that it would put less speed on the egg than a traditional overarm throw, and be more likely to produce a controlled arc through the air. Besides, the distance between us was small. The overarm fling could be kept in reserve for the monstrous distances we might require in later rounds.

It was our turn. I held the egg up so Dirsy could see it and watched him crouch low like a slip fielder. With heart banging under my ribs I drew back my arm, swung it forward and rolled the egg off my fingertips. The egg somersaulted through the air, dropped gracefully in front of Ben and plopped into his cupped hands. He held it aloft with a nervous grin. It was unbroken. He tossed it into the grass behind him, shuddered and mouthed the words 'soft hands' in my direction.

As expected at any world championship, standards were high. Only three couples fell at that first hurdle. When the last pair showed a clean egg, Andy nodded and paced out a much wider gap between the two lines. 'Twenty metres!' he shouted. It made an immediate and devastating difference. One by one, all five pairs before Ben and me crashed out – a mixture of poor throws, granite hands and substandard catching technique.

'Dirs to Fordyce!' bellowed Andy. This time it was Ben's turn to throw, mine to catch. The egg seemed to stick in Ben's right hand a fraction longer than it should have done. Rather than looping straight down my throat, it was spiralling away to my right. I took a couple of quick paces sideways and flung out my fingertips, trying to keep my wrists floppy and my palms loose. I felt the egg nestle into my hands. I opened my fingers. It was solid.

It wasn't the greatest technical catch I'd ever taken – that probably goes to a one-handed reflex wonder low to my right to see off an opening batsman in late June 1995 – but it was right up there in terms of importance. I lobbed the egg over my shoulder and gave Ben a clenched fist.

To my left, the carnage continued. Pair after pair bit the dust, yolks splattering on upturned palms, shells smashing with wonderful regularity. When the final couple prepared to throw, there were only two pairs through (us, and a pair of lean-limbed lads with a fluid technique two-thirds of the way along the ranks) and that last duo didn't even get close. The egg whistled metres over the catcher's head and shattered on the sun-baked grass.

'That's it!' yelled Andy. 'We have our finalists. George Wattam and Joe Spencer versus Fordyce and Dirs. We reconvene at 5 p.m!'

Ben and I stared delightedly at each other across the grassy divide. The final? Already? We were a mere catch – a single catch – away from being crowned world champions! We ran towards each other in our rustling capes and hugged clumsily, like mating tents. Already I was imagining how that gold medal would feel around the neck – the media interviews that would inevitably follow, the champagne, the egg-throwing groupies.

'Fucking hell,' said Dirs. 'I've got yolk on my laces. I think I'm gonna be sick.'

With a full hour and a half to go until our moment of truth, it was clear that we needed to decompress. I was finding it almost impossible to tear my gaze from the large silver trophy that sat gleaming in the sun a few feet away. Dirsy was finding it almost impossible to tear his from the Swaton Brewery marquee. We grabbed refrescos and wandered off to examine the other attractions the fete had to offer.

Snatches of commentary from the Tannoy drifted across the field as we strolled past rusting wrecks of farm machinery. There was a 'best hen in show' contest going on, a display of raw eggs on a line of trestle tables and a parade of classic cars slowly circling the cricket square.

'It's got a three-speed gearbox,' I heard Stableford/Curry announce. 'A lot of greengrocers had them. Marvellous workhorse.'

We paused by exhibit no.270, a Massey-Ferguson winch identified by its badge as an Eager Beaver. On its right was an abandoned motorized wheelchair. The owner was nowhere to be seen.

'. . . but unfortunately I forget to put the strap on,' said Stableford/Curry in the distance, 'so of course it slammed shut. I broke three of my toes.'

A pale, stroppy-faced teenage girl strode past the egg exhibition, followed by her tired-looking parents. 'Why should I care about a load of fucking chicken periods?' she screamed, storming off towards the car park.

'You know,' said Ben philosophically, easing himself into the motorized wheelchair, 'sometimes I think that the only reason I've got anywhere in life is because everyone else is shit.' He took a deep swallow of Swaton ale from his plastic pint-pot. 'School, work, birds – you name it. It always surprises me when I do well at anything. Luckily, it often turns out that everyone else is even more rubbish than I am.'

'The bathroom mirror of competition,' I said sagely, 'serves only to reflect the acne of anxiety.'

Ben gave me a funny look. 'This egg-throwing is a classic case in point. We've only caught two eggs and we're in the final. What have we done to deserve it?'

I thought back to all the hours I'd spent catching things. 'Plenty,' I said. 'Anyway – when was the last time you'd dared touch an egg before this afternoon?' He grunted. 'Come on,' I said. 'Let's go and talk tactics.'

All was quiet at the main egg-throwing arena. I picked up a tray of eggs and sat down on a bale of hay. This, I knew, was our big chance. In the shin-kicking final I had been the rank outsider, determined to give it my best shot but knowing deep down that the odds were stacked against me. This time, it was different. Where before I had sixteen stones' worth of Bulldog standing in my way, today we only had two callow youths. We might never again have such a golden shot at being crowned world champions. Our strategy would have to be spot-on. Which one of us should throw first? We'd have to take it in turns again, assuming the final went to more than one catch – so which way should we play it?

Ben had taken a lovely pouch in the first round and

thrown a touch ropily in the second, which suggested that I should throw on the key effort. But which one would that be? There was no use keeping our powder dry for later rounds if we failed to make a clean catch on our first attempt.

In the distance I could see our opponents warming up, capes flapping, eggs torpedoing through the air. 'Sure you don't want to practise?' I asked Ben, hopefully.

A dark cloud drifted in front of the sun. Ben sparked up a cigarette. Four scrawny kids slouched over and stood in front of us, staring at the eggs and Dirsy's cigarettes.

'Give us a fag,' said the biggest one.

'Piss off,' said Ben.

'We'll chuck eggs at you,' said the kid.

'I'll tell your mum,' said Ben.

The kid picked up an egg. Ben stood up.

'Fag,' said the kid.

'Your mum,' said Ben.

Smash. Egg hit Dirs. With a yelp he looked down. Slimy strings of white and yolk were hanging off his chest. He looked up in horror, just as another egg smacked into his chest.

'Aghh!' he screamed.

'Get him in the face!' shouted the kid.

Ben turned and ran. Snatching up handfuls of eggs, the kids sprinted after him.

Burgeoning smokers they might have been, but their youthful lungs were far superior to Dirsy's tar-sodden pipes. As Ben weaved desperately between corroded combine harvesters, orange cape flapping behind him, they closed in relentlessly like hounds hunting down an out-of-shape fox. Within seconds they had him cornered by the ice-cream van.

It was brutal.

BEN

If Noel Edmonds really wanted to mend Broken Britain, he'd stop making shit game shows aimed at people with IQs under fifty, but I still reckon he's got a point. Since when did refusing a seven-year-old child a fag warrant a full-scale egging? Maybe if they'd known, they wouldn't have done it. But how were they to know?

No one can know the horrors I went through that afternoon, jumping over tractors, hiding behind rusty ploughs, while all the time eggs rained down upon me. Fifty years ago I probably could have doled out a couple of solid right-handers and sent them off to their mums, but not in today's society, oh no. I had to cower behind a cooling unit like some terrified Marine hiding from the Viet Cong.

I saw the future of Britain at the Swaton agricultural show and I didn't like what I saw. I only thank God that they didn't make good on their promise and hit me in the face, or our world championship hopes would have lain shattered about me like so much eggshell . . .

TOM

Our preparations for the final hung by a thread. What worse scenario could there be for a man with a pathological fear of eggs than a ritual yolking at the hands of the local savages? The running alone had been bad enough. Ben hadn't moved that fast since the duty-free shop on the ferry home from France had announced last orders twenty minutes outside Dover. He was pale as a ghost and coughing so badly I feared his oesophagus might fly out and hit me in the face.

'Fordyce!' I heard Andy Dunlop bellow. 'It's time for the final!'

I dragged Dirsy to his feet. A heavy rain had begun to fall from a sky the colour of a London pavement. 'I've got egg in my stubble,' said Ben thickly. I put an arm round his shoulder and whistled Cribbins hits into his ear.

Our adversaries George and Joe were waiting for us in the arena, pinging eggs around with casual ease as the rain lashed down. 'Ladies and gentlemen!' roared Andy, to an audience of the two middle-aged women from earlier and an old boy loading an antique scooter on to a trailer. 'It's the final of the 2008 World Egg-Throwing Championships!'

He beckoned to George and me and marched us down the field away from Ben and Joe. 'Thirty-five metres!' he shouted. I squinted through the rain to where Ben stood, the hood of his cape pulled low over his face. The gap between us seemed enormous. My hands felt slippery with rain and sweat.

Andy produced a coin. 'Heads or tails?' he asked George. George called correctly. 'You boys can throw first,' he said.

I took the egg Andy proffered. It was lightly speckled and beautifully weighted. I freed my right arm from the cape, held the egg up for Ben to see, took a deep breath and sent it on its way.

It felt perfect off the fingers. The loop couldn't have looked better – spiralling gently upwards, then curving gracefully down. For one dreadful moment I thought I'd left it short, but there was Ben, hands outstretched, reaching forwards, closing his fingers . . . and opening them again to show a speckled egg lying intact on his palm.

Ben Dirs, I thought, I love you. Soft hands? They were like cotton wool. They were a silken cradle.

Against all the odds, despite his ovumphobia and the

terror of a yolking, Dirsy had come through. How could I ever have doubted him?

I stole a glance at George, holding his own egg a few metres away. He looked crestfallen and I could understand why. It was an impossible distance. Surely that was it – the trophy and glory ours to take back to the Champervan.

The rain thundered down on our ponchos. He stepped forward and bowled the egg into the distance – and instantly let out a shout of anger. The egg was going left. It was going long. Through the downpour I saw Joe leap backwards. His hands came together with a clap. He fell to the ground, turned back slowly towards Andy and held out the egg.

Unbroken.

It was an astonishing catch. Even as a cold slap of disappointment hit me, I realized I'd just seen something special, something worthy of top billing on any of the illegal catching websites I had bookmarked. The fact that Joe had done it at match point down in a world championship final made it even more remarkable.

'We move on!' yelled Andy, his waterlogged polo shirt plastered to his chest. He led us back another ten paces. 'Forty-five metres. We go again!'

The rain was now coming in horizontally. I tugged the hood back off my face and opened my eyes wide, letting the rain stream down my forehead and chin. I wanted nothing to come between me and the catch. This was my moment. This is what all the catching of tennis balls, cricket balls and acorns I'd ever done came down to – this single egg that Ben was about to send my way.

Here it came, fast and flat. It was going right – but I could still reach it. Blimey – it really was wide, but if I stretched and jumped . . .

I knew before I'd even opened my hands. There was nothing within but pieces of shell, gloopy yellow and stringy white. I wiped my hands on the soaking grass and turned, ashen, to face Ben. I'd blown it. I'd blown our big chance. If George caught Joe's next throw cleanly, it was all over. Ben looked me straight in the eye, made a fist with his right hand and tapped his chest in a gesture of solidarity.

I watched numbly as Joe took aim. Up went the egg – a touch high, but bang on target. George raised his hands to the sky and brought them back to his chest with a delicate recoil. There was an almost inaudible squish. A dribble of golden yolk ran down his wrist.

'It's a double breaker!' roared Andy. I let out a long, low lungful. On the other side of the arena, Dirsy was beaming like a Las Vegas showgirl. We were still alive.

Andy strode back to the other end with his head bowed against the rain. 'Reload!' he barked. 'New eggs, same distance, same order!'

I blinked the water out of my eyes and thought of my catching heroes. If Botham or Flintoff had spilt one at slip at a key point in an Ashes Test, how would they have reacted? With head-clutching remorse, despairing distraction and a knock-kneed descent into giddiness – or by stiffening their resolve, wiping the error from their mind and bagging the next chance that came along?

Even with the egg still sticky on my fingers from that last breakage, I knew what I had to do. All champions failed at some point. It was the true legends who came back from that to triumph afresh. I stood tall, nodded at Ben and clapped my hands. 'Let's go, Dirsaldo!' I shouted.

This time, it felt different. When the throw came spiralling through the deluge, I was aware of nothing but brown oval rotating towards me. Everything else – the rusting farm wrecks, Andy's twitching moustache, the lone press photographer – had faded into unnoticed background.

Ben had left it a touch shy again, but I picked up the trajectory early and was already sprinting forward, fingers spread gently, palms turned upwards. I could see nothing but egg, think of nothing but its hard shininess and my soft welcoming hands. Here it came, large as a rugby ball, revolving inwards, straight into my cushioned . . .

The sky and ground flipped sideways and swapped places. I had a dislocated sensation of looping the loop, and of something smashing on the tip of my left index finger. I was aware of a head-rattling bang and then wet turf in front of my eyes. There was empty air under my feet, blood all over one hand and, between my shaking palms, a mess of shell and egg. Pellets of water pinged off my cheeks as I pushed myself into a kneeling position. Streaked through the sodden grass behind me was the long muddy skidmark left by my slipping feet and somersaulted arse. Wordlessly I held my bleeding, egg-smeared hands out to Ben, pointed at the smooth, worn-down soles on my trainers and watched him grimace and kick the ground.

We both knew with absolute certainty what would happen when Joe and George threw. This was a world championship final. We'd already had our big let-off. You don't get third chances, not at this level. For the record, Joe's throw was the best of the day, a perfect parabola. George barely had to move. The egg sailed into his cupped hands and landed as lightly as a shuttlecock into bubblewrap. He waved it high for all to see, flung it skywards and dashed into Joe's delighted embrace.

Ben sat down heavily and stared at his feet. I stayed slumped on my heels. Dirs, the supposed weak link, had been faultless from start to finish. Me, a Botham or Flintoff? I wasn't even a Garfunkel or Ridgeley. At least Artie had come up with 'Bright Eyes', while Ridgeley had . . . well, he'd had the decency to leave quietly after one solo album. I'd had three chances and messed up two of them. I might as well have been catching for the first time in my life.

Andy pulled us to our feet and brought the four of us together. Hands were shaken, winners and runners-up trophies awarded, medals embossed with chickens hung round our necks. The storm raged around us with biblical intensity. If Ben hadn't taken my arm and led me back to the mildewed warmth of the Champervan, I might still be standing there today, staring into the distance, hands held out in front of me, my upturned face a mixture of pain and disbelief.

6
WIVES

BEN

If our experience at the World Egg-Throwing Championships had been the novelty sports equivalent of losing a Johnstone's Paint Trophy final, what did Tommy and I care? We had bigger dreams. Dreams of conquering Europe. We were off to Finland, the Mecca – the Bernabéu if you will – of novelty sports.

In truth, Tom had taken defeat in Swaton pretty hard. However many times I reminded him that he'd probably blown the best chance we'd ever have of winning a world championship by muffing that catch at a village fete in Lincolnshire (with only a couple of snotty teenagers to beat) he just couldn't extinguish the stench of defeat. A stench that hung over him like a putrefying omelette.

So I booked us up for the Wife-Carrying World Championships, once described (by Wonky Eyed Gary down the Golden Lion) as the Champions League of novelty sports. No more playing for paint pot trophies at agricultural shows. Tommy and I were going to be messing with the best on the biggest stage.

Plus, it would be a chance to leave the Champervan – and

the cursed English weather – behind for a few days. The Champervan, which had started out as our very own Mystery Machine, now had all the romantic allure of an Austin Princess with a dismembered corpse in the boot. Indeed, the only mystery was how anyone had persuaded Tom and me it was worth two and a half grand of our hard-earned money. As for the weather, it was beyond a joke. We'd had snow in Gawthorpe, rain in Chipping Campden and horizontal stuff in Marshwood and Swaton. There had been unbroken sunshine for the cheese-rolling in Stilton. Unfortunately, I was in Italy at the time.

The only thing standing between us and three days of potential perpetual sunshine in Finland was Tom's unquenchable Corinthian spirit.

'Wife-carrying? But neither of us is married.'

'Don't worry about that, I've checked up on the rules. It doesn't have to be your wife, in fact it doesn't have to be anyone's wife. She just has to be over 17 and more than 49 kilos. As long as you don't turn up in Finland with an underage stick insect, you're laughing.'

'You sure? That doesn't seem right. If it's the World Wife-Carrying Championships, surely you've got to carry a wife. If we're going to be true champions, we've got to do things properly.'

What his lovely, over-17, very slim girlfriend Sarah thought about him poring over the grubby pages of his little black book for a suitable 'wife' was anyone's guess, but I was straight on the blower to my woman in Paris. Katie was quick to sign up, to the bafflement of her friends and colleagues. Proof that while the French ask 'pourquoi?', Brits simply ask 'pourquoi pas?'.

It wasn't only Tom's deep-seated sense of fair play that

needed surmounting before we set off for Finland. There was also the matter of my atrocious fitness. When you feel like you're going to choke to death whenever you bend over to tie your shoelaces; when you get into a mild panic on discovering an escalator is out of order and you'll have to use the stairs; when a short jog for a bus leaves you with sweat trickling between your buttocks, you know the time has come to act. Also, I wasn't travelling all that way to repeat the humiliations of coal-carrying in Gawthorpe – I wanted to mix it. So I got Tom to draw me up a fitness regime.

In my salad days I was, believe it or not, a pretty fit young buck. But three years of university living had saddled me with the physique of a Victorian circus strong man and the lungs of Humphrey Bogart. However, I was fairly confident my natural fitness would begin to shine through after a month off the fags, and then Tom could begin to weave his magic.

I actually surprised myself on the fag front by managing to cut right down to one a day, taken on the balcony after the 10 o'clock news, like some ancient Hollywood actress of strict routine. I even started playing a bit of football again. Tom, a man permanently teetering on the edge of a ten-mile run, suddenly turned into Burgess 'Mickey Goldmill' Meredith, only in tighter, more lurid lycra. It was quite sweet really, yet a little bit frightening at the same time. He was infused with the zeal of a missionary who knows he's on the verge of making a conversion. The only problem was that he thought a few weeks of nicotine abstinence had transformed me from nuts and bolts into Usain Bolt.

It is a trait common in the ultra-fit to have very little comprehension of exactly how unfit others can be. Many was the time during our travels round France when Tom tried to persuade me to join him on a run, utterly failing to grasp that half a mile trying to keep up would have probably exploded my lungs. His exercise regime read accordingly, with abdominal crunches, commando sit-ups, concentration curls and something called 'jogging'. A concentration curl sounded like something you might do after a few weeks without passing a stool, but I was up for a bit of light running and some press-ups, and even a sit-up or two, just to keep old Angelo Dundee happy.

While I went about resculpting the Dirs physique, Tom continued his search for a suitable 'wife'.

TOM

It shouldn't have been a problem. I knew at least two actual, legally recognized wives who would be perfect – just a shade over seven stone, sufficiently sporty to be flung over the shoulder and with husbands either friendly or away on work, long enough to allow them to spend a weekend in Finland with Dirsy and me. The flaw in the plan was their selfish decisions to get pregnant at exactly the wrong time. Could they not have postponed something as trivial as having a child until the serious business of the Wife-Carrying World Championships was over?

Aunty Karen. Now she would be perfect. Not only did she have the lightweight physique of a jockey, but she also smoked and drank like a true child of the Sixties. In addition she hailed from deepest Essex, wanted no more children and was a PE teacher to boot. If it hadn't been for the PE teacher bit, I could imagine Dirs having a drunken pop. Aunty Karen was also one of the most competitive (and successful) relatives in the annual Fordyce sportathons that dominated every Christmas. At an idiosyncratic game called Puggles she was unbeaten since 1983, while you took her on at something called Up Jenkins at your peril.

For some mysterious reason, however, Karen feared she might be too old for the trials ahead, despite having been forty-nine for as long as any of us could remember. She suggested Becky, one of the sportiest of my thirty-one cousins and a fellow triathlete who'd already had the three kids she'd planned. Although initially keen, Becky was soon scuppered by a diary clash that couldn't be avoided. God knows what it was that was important enough to take precedence over the wife-carrying, but there you go. Inexorably, I was being forced in the direction that Ben had suggested all along: pretending my girlfriend was my wife.

'We'll have to wear rings and everything!' was Sarah's excited response. 'Shall we get some photos done in wedding gear too in case they ask for proof?'

The world championship campaign was causing problems I could never have imagined.

BEN

Tom finally had a wife, and I had a brand new body. No more jiggling man boobs when skipping up some steps, no more struggling for breath after taking off my socks. I imagined it was like falling asleep at the wheel of a Datsun Cherry and waking up a couple of minutes later at the wheel of an ex-rental Ford Mondeo. Well, I wasn't about to get too carried away.

Katie came to Romford the night before our flight to Finland, so we didn't have much time to get to grips with the 'Estonian style', the preferred technique of top-flight wife-carriers the world over. The Estonian style requires the wife to hang upside down with her legs around her husband's neck and her arms around his waist. It sounds slightly risqué, and if she was facing the other way, it would be.

It also sounds wilfully wacky, but the fact is it's by far the most efficient mode of conveyance. The head being the heaviest part of a human's body, you'd much rather have it hanging like a pendulum behind you than wobbling from side to side above you. The technique also frees up the husband's arms so he can run normally. You'd no sooner opt for piggyback at a wife-carrying event nowadays than turn up for a Ryder Cup clash against Tiger Woods with a set of hickory-shafted clubs. Katie took to the technique like a duck to water, although I was acutely aware that performing menial tasks such as making tea and knocking up a sandwich with a small woman draped round my neck was light years away from bombing round a 253-metre course, including a metre-deep water jump and a couple of hurdles. More importantly, for the first time in years, I felt like a contender.

Sonkajärvi lies about halfway between Tampere and the Arctic Circle, and the five-hour train journey north is the ideal way to drink in such a majestic – and spooky – country. Finland is almost one and a half times as large as the United Kingdom, but with less than a tenth of the population. It's no wonder Finns have a reputation for keeping schtum: you probably wouldn't say much if your nearest neighbours were a bear and a pack of wolves. About three-quarters of the surface of Finland is coniferous forest, while the rest is seemingly one unbroken lake, its smoking tentacles penetrating every corner of the land. In fact, there are almost 200,000 lakes, approximately one for every twenty-five Finns. As I drifted in and out of sleep, my seat fully reclined, the window wound down, I could only have been more relaxed if Katie had been basting me in butter. From time to time I'd spot a tumbledown cottage or a lakeside sauna – but rarely another human being. I might have been traversing a different planet, so far removed was it from the clutter of my own chaotic country. 'Visit Finland – clear your mind of clutter.' I thought that had a pretty good ring to it.

Katie and I had touched down in the southern city of Tampere at 11 o'clock on Thursday night (Tom and Sarah would be flying in late on Friday), although with the sun still high in the sky, it felt more like early afternoon. 'Bloody hot for night time,' I commented on leaving the airport, my addled mind forgetting that in Finland in July, night time doesn't really exist. After spending the night in Tampere (the Holiday Inn has a 'pillow menu' and I strongly recommend the Hungarian goose down) we took the train to Sonkajärvi, the town which has hosted the Wife-Carrying World Championships since 1996.

We were met at Iisalmi's old wooden train station by the lovely Anna, one of the event organizers, and she ferried us the twenty or so miles up the road to Sonkajärvi. Iisalmi felt remote, but as we travelled further north, it felt like we were being sucked into oblivion. This, Anna assured us, was genuine Moomin country.

Sonkajärvi has a church, a couple of pubs, a handful of shops and just 5,000 inhabitants. Champions League? It felt more like the Bristol and District League Division Six. On first seeing our lodgings I would have described them as police cell chic. On noticing they were attached to a police station, I realized they were probably just police cells. Had Sonkajärvi's mayor, like some mad African dictator, rubbed out all the prisoners ahead of the expected influx of foreigners? Probably not. I got the feeling no one had committed a serious crime in this town in a couple of hundred years. Whatever the case, I wasn't complaining: the sun was shining, the place was humming with anticipation, and we had the Wife-Carrying World Sprint Championship to look forward to.

The sprint acted as a taster ahead of Saturday's main event. Think the par-three competition the day before the US Masters and you're somewhere close. First, though, Katie and I went in search of a bit of tucker. We didn't have high hopes. Former French President Jacques Chirac famously described Finnish cuisine as being the worst in the world. Even, he added with glee, filthier than British cuisine. Italian Prime Minister Silvio Berlusconi twisted the stiletto, chiming in, 'The Finns don't even know what Parma ham is!' Fuck me, Silvio, where I come from, there are people who don't know what a pig is. For her part, Anna reckoned the defining foods of Finland were pea soup and pancakes. 'Hernekeitto and lätty, that's what people eat in Finland at elementary school, when they are soldiers and when they grow old.'

I would have liked to have come to my own conclusion, but of the four food stalls in the market place two were serving kebabs, another was serving up rather rude-looking jumbo frankfurters, while the fourth offered flying saucers, liquorice bootlaces and marshmallows. I opted for a chicken kebab and treated Katie to a bag of flumps before having a bit of a wander.

Now, far be it from me to comment on the quality of another nation's women, but I think I'm on pretty safe ground when I say that anyone wanting wall-to-wall blondes to make a bishop kick a hole in a stained-glass window, to paraphrase Raymond Chandler, should go no further than

Sweden. How to put it delicately? The Finns are a lumpy old bunch, and not just out in the sticks, but back in big-town Tampere too. However, any Finns feeling insulted on reading this should know that while your food might be the only cuisine in Europe worse than Britain's, British people are undoubtedly fatter than yours. Plus, your large-breasted men don't bowl about with their tops off at the first sign of sun, which is always a bonus.

After dinner, we headed down to the wife-carrying course to take a look at the sprint event. The first shock was the water obstacle, which wasn't so much a water jump as a sheep dip. The second shock was the two wooden hurdles on the home straight, both about three feet high. One chap, all 6 ft 3 in of him, was using one of the hurdles to stretch his hamstrings, while a husband and wife were deep in tactical conversation behind one of the stands that wrapped around the course. 'Jesus Christ,' said Katie, 'it's like an actual track meet.' Too true. Everywhere you looked were giant blond men in paint-on track pants so tight, you could decipher their religion. Tiny women loitered nervously by their 'husbands', occasionally offering words of encouragement, like jockeys whispering into their horses' ears ahead of a race. Katie looked worried. 'Those board shorts of yours aren't going to offer you much movement,' she said. 'Yep, my board shorts and the fact I'm going to be wearing a dripping wet woman as a necklace down the home straight. Damn those ruddy bloody board shorts . . .'

Katie didn't say much after that. The sight of muscle-bound husbands launching themselves into the water obstacle from about three feet out, their wives holding their noses in anticipation, put her into a state of open-mouthed shock. Most husbands disappeared briefly below the surface before emerging and clambering out the other side, meaning their wives were only submerged for a few seconds. Others didn't fare so well, losing their footing on the slippery banking and throwing their wives overboard. A dismount meant a 15-second penalty. Worse, it meant much panicked and undignified thrashing about in the drink.

The final was a stone-cold classic, but did nothing to wipe the disbelieving rictus from Katie's face. In a three-horse race, the two leading pairs left the water jump virtually neck-and-neck, only for both husbands' legs to buckle underneath them no more than ten feet from the finish line. Both teams went sprawling across the track, allowing local couple Joni and Jaana to tiptoe their way through the carnage and claim victory. While Joni and Jaana celebrated, the other two couples dragged themselves to their feet, traipsed across the line and raked over the ashes of defeat.

It turned out that Joni had been trying to win an event, any event, in Sonkajärvi for the last twelve years, so his elation was understandable. Jaana wasn't actually Joni's wife and I asked him afterwards why he hadn't used his own. Joni looked around shiftily, while his mates sniggered like schoolboys. It was then I noticed a rather robust woman lurking over my right shoulder. 'My wife is a bit . . . a bit . . . a bit too tall,' stuttered Joni. I hope he didn't get a kicking when they got back home.

On Friday night the event organizers gathered their foreign guests in the church hall for non-alcoholic beverages and nibbles. Forty-nine couples from fourteen countries had signed up for Saturday's main race, including Australian couple Lyneece and Jason. Lyneece and Jason had rocked up to a country show in the New South Wales boondocks at the start of the year and made off with the Australian title and a free trip to Finland. 'I just entered for a bit of a laugh,' explained Lyneece. 'I asked one of my brothers if any of his mates wanted to carry me and Jason was the only one who'd do it.'

'So you're not "together"?' I enquired.

'No, but he's been trying his fucking hardest.' To be fair to Jason, he can't have been the first man in the world to have misinterpreted the offer of a vertical reverse '69'.

We also met Janet, a 37-year-old biology teacher from Kerry and a woman determined to steamroller all in her path with an aggressive brand of zaniness. I had never thought wackiness in a person could be in any way menacing, but that was before I'd met Janet. The way she worked the room, jealously eyeing up potential rivals to her ker-razy crown and making nervous foreigners cower with her distinct brand of Oirishness like some giant, rogue leprechaun, made me feel quite queasy.

Weighing in just shy of 19 stones, Janet was wearing a T-shirt emblazoned in Finnish, 'Wanted – husband for the Wife-Carrying World Championships'. Somehow she didn't strike me as classic wife-carrying material, but she assured me she had form. 'I've been coming over for years and I've always found someone to carry me,' said Janet, which perhaps explained the preponderance of short, squat men with haunted expressions we'd noticed milling around the market place. Janet had also competed in the Australian championships earlier in the year, where she'd managed to persuade a local fireman and power-lifting champion to be her mount. Poor fella, he'd only turned up to play splat the rat. Jason later told me she'd stormed off a local radio show in Australia because the interviewer had introduced her as being from the UK. We were clearly in the company of an ego-zany-ac.

Later on, I had a chat with the event chairman, Veikko Tervonen, who claimed wife-carrying (which I thought had started some time in the early nineties) actually had a fair bit of history behind it.

'In the 1800s, a Finnish bandit called Ronkainen held competitions to see who could carry sacks of grain or pigs over obstacles in the forest,' explained the mayor. 'The strongest were allowed to join his band. After this, Finnish men would go into Russian villages and steal their wives.' The mayor leaned in, leered and gave me a wink. 'And you know what? I think the Russian ladies kind of liked it . . .'

Our little soirée in the church hall was all very nice, but I couldn't help wondering why we had been herded in there while there was a full-scale party going on in the town hall a couple of hundred yards away. I soon discovered what I thought was the answer. By the time Katie and I made it down there, the town hall was a seething, rubber-legged mass of crushed-looking, hollow-eyed locals, all getting stuck into the booze in that detached, joyless way we'd soon grow accustomed to. That smoky substance creeping across the stage might have been dry ice, or it might have been exhaust fumes. The karaoke, of the Finnish folk variety, was more Black Death than Black Lace, and the watery light streaming through the windows only added to the otherworldliness. Was this what the organizers had wanted to hide from foreign eyes?

We got chatting to a group of girls in Welsh rugby jerseys, who turned out to be Finnish nursing students from Cardiff University. 'The British are always laughing and joking,' said Maria, 'but we don't talk too much. There is an old Finnish joke: a couple of Finns walk into a pub and sit drinking for an hour without saying a word. Suddenly, one of them says,

"Cheers!" The other one turns to him and says, "I thought we came here to drink, not talk."'

How did it compare to the Welsh drinking culture?

'In Cardiff, everyone has a lot of fun and laughter, but then later on they all start fighting each other, sometimes even the women. So neither is great.'

Not being big on small talk myself, and hailing as I do from the 'Can't Unless I've had Ten Pints' school of dance, I could kind of empathize. But, as Katie kindly pointed out, a couple of hundred sober Ben Dirs crammed in a hall would make for a pretty shit party. Thankfully, the locals did eventually emerge from their shells, coaxed out by lashings of Lapin Kulta lager and Finnish pop phenomenon Isto Hiltunen. 'What's this bloke like?' I asked Maria, as Isto made his way on stage.

'Do you know Julio Iglesias? Do you know Garth Brooks? He's like a mixture of the two.'

Latin-country is clearly a popular genre in Sonkajärvi and all it took was a couple of Isto standards for the dance floor to start filling up. A brave few foreigners joined the fray, but it was only when Isto launched into Bryan Adams' 'Summer of '69' that the place really got going. Some of the younger Finns even decided to strap on their air guitars and, in the words of Maria's brother Teemu, 'go hunting for foreign pussy'. At one glorious point in the evening, I saw Teemu slide on his knees towards Lyneece and rev up his air axe with a vicious upwards thrash, before clambering to his feet and ramming his tongue down her throat. It was one of the most beautiful things I'd ever seen.

The drinking continued at a neighbouring pub, where a lad called Barry told me he'd been roped into carrying Janet the following day. Barry, a bricklayer from Nottingham, looked like a pretty strong lad, but I couldn't help thinking he'd bitten off more than he could chew. 'Too right I've bitten off more than I can chew,' said Barry. 'We had a practice earlier on and I gave her a little bit of a jiggle, you know, like you do, to get comfortable, and she farted on the back of my neck. That's fucking gratitude for you.'

TOM

There were two things that were freaking me out as I flew northwards with Sarah. The first was that I'd given up my slot in the Centre Court commentary box at Wimbledon to go to Finland, having been perched there lapping up a classic tournament and text-commentating for the entire fortnight thus far. Still, I reasoned, the Federer–Nadal final was sure to be a damp squib. The second was that the longer the journey went on, the lighter it got. Dusk had been gathering when we left Heathrow, but was nowhere to be seen in Helsinki. Three hundred miles further north in Kuopio it was positively hot.

'What time do the bars shut around here?' I asked the taxi driver as we coasted through Sonkajärvi at 2 a.m., the sun casting shadows from the fir trees all around.

'When you leave,' said the driver. He peered down the main street. 'Where you want to be dropped off?'

A hundred metres up the road, a portly figure who looked a little like a younger, scruffier Alan Sugar staggered into the road and attempted to breakdance across the street.

'By that Dirs up there,' I said.

'I am sorry,' muttered the driver. 'The Finns are not usually like this.'

'Don't worry about it,' I said breezily. 'He's probably Estonian.'

BEN

The next morning Tom and Sarah presented me and Katie with our race outfits, a couple of off-the-shoulder polyester caveman suits with matching headbands. Katie actually looked quite fetching in hers. Unsurprisingly, I looked like a complete bellend. Still, not as big a bellend as Tom, who'd somehow been persuaded to stick some paper flowers round his neck and don a grass skirt for the occasion. He looked like he should have been serving drinks in a Hawaiian theme bar. The appearance in the 'hotel' corridor of our Israeli nextdoor neighbours, both sporting gilt-edged flat-tops and sensible athletic attire, soon wiped the smiles off our faces. Some foreign guests, it seemed, would be taking the Wife-Carrying World Championships more seriously than others.

The opening ceremony was loosely modelled on the Olympic equivalent, with competitors from each nation led around the course by a flag-bearer. There were about a thousand spectators already in the stands and I began to feel quite nauseous as we strolled behind the Union Jack. Katie giggled skittishly beside me, and I could tell my nerves were contagious. After the pomp was over Katie went missing for an hour, and I thought she might have done a runner. Eventually I found her in the market place, and was slightly alarmed to see her tucking into a jumbo sausage about as thick as one of my arms. No jockey's breakfast of dry toast and milky tea for Katie, this horse was just going to have to put up with the extra poundage.

'Are you going to make it round?' said Katie.

'Oh, yeah, don't worry about that.'

'I'm a bit worried about the water jump. Are you sure you're not going to drop me?'

'Oh, no, no, no, I wouldn't do that. Look at me – would I do that? Nah, don't worry, Katie, I'm not going to drop you, I just wouldn't let that happen.'

Poor cow, she must have felt like she was about to tackle the Grand National on a pantomime horse. Of course she was going in the drink. Did I feel bad about lying to her? Not a bit of it. If I was a horse and I spotted my mount eating an eight-inch saveloy on the morning of a race, I'd do more than throw them off at the water jump, I'd back up and kick their railings in.

Having put Katie's mind at rest, we headed inside looking to quell our nerves with some Finnish folk music. Instead we met Rory, a bedraggled Aussie backpacker who 'just happened to be passing through'. Rory was in a state of high excitement because he'd been invited back to Maria and her mate Jaana's place for a sauna later on that evening. 'Two fuckin' blondes, mate, two fuckin' Finnish blondes in the fuckin' nuddy and I'm gonna be there in my fuckin' jocks, crackin' a fat, and there's only one way that's goin', mate. A few Lapin Kultas and they'll be fightin' over me old fella like a couple of dogs with a bone.' First Oirish Janet, and now Fair Dinkum Rory. Who next? A couple of castanet-wielding Spaniards in flamenco dresses?

The changing tent next to the start-line resembled a Seventies shindig in Studio 54. One couple in Ziggy Stardust spandex and make-up, another couple dressed as a bride and groom – the bloke suited and booted, the woman meringued to the max – one chap dressed up like Bjorn Borg, and a couple of castanet-wielding Spaniards in flamenco dresses. But the prize for the most ludicrous outfits had to go to James and Rachel, a genuine husband-and-wife team from the United States, who'd come dressed as a rabbit (James) and a carrot (Rachel). Rachel and James, a forces dentist with teeth that made the average American look like Wat Tyler, were celebrating their tenth wedding anniversary in Sonkajärvi. 'Ben, when you've been married as long as we have, you've got to start spicing things up a bit. So I said to Rach, dig out the carrot outfit, baby, we're headed to Finland.' You have to take your hat off to him, it trumps a Harvester mixed grill and a pair of Ann Summers undercrackers.

All wives were obliged to weigh in before the races got under way and any under the 49 kg (7 st 10 lb) limit had the weight made up with a rucksack containing rocks. Once again Finland's southern neighbour Estonia – whose athletes had walked away with the title for the previous ten years – was well represented, and every one of its wives needed handicapping, such were their waif-like frames. Last up was Janet, despite the fact that a blind man could have detected she weighed over 49 kilos just from her walk to the scales. Not since Cassius Clay fought Sonny Liston had a weigh-in caused such a hubbub, with the world's press – well, some woman from Reuters – scrabbling for a front-row seat. 'Well, I'll be damned,' whispered Bunny Boy James solemnly, as if he was witnessing the landing of an alien craft, 'someone's gonna carry that? Jeez, I'm guessing that's the first time anyone will have been between those hams for quite some time . . .'

Two couples went in each heat, and an English team made up of Ash and Aila, they of the Ziggy Stardust spandex, went in the first. Despite – or perhaps because of – their outfits, they looked mightily impressive, bombing round the course in 1 minute 11 seconds. You could tell that Tom's competitive porridge had been stirred. 'If they can clock that sort of time dressed as Bolan and Angie B, we've got to go close in our lightweight gear.' I thought that was pretty big chat from a man dressed like a float at a gay pride parade. Sarah, like Katie, had more modest ambitions and seemed to have spotted some basic flaws in Tom's plans. 'I'm not sure you're big enough,' she said. 'And I should know.'

First of the big guns were a German couple called Thomas and Anke. The shaven-headed Thomas, his huge 6 ft 5 in frame poured into what looked like a Lycra bobsleigh suit, looked like a Roger Moore-era Bond villain and skipped through the water obstacle as if it were nothing more than a foot spa. He dipped over the line in 1 minute 3 seconds to snatch the early lead. Even some of the Estonians looked rattled.

Boston's Keith Cardoza and Julia Stoner had qualified by virtue of winning the North American championships the previous year. They'd turned up in the town of Newry, Maine, to compete in a mountain-bike race, ended up being roped into the wife-carrying and, just like the Aussie champions, walked away with a free trip to Finland. Still, free or not, Keith hadn't come all that way to muck about, and he was the victim of much ribbing from the other nationalities as he put himself through a vigorous warm-up routine, as if he were preparing himself for an Olympic 1,500 metres final. To the amusement of the English contingent – why is it that the English like to see the over-keen fail so much? – Keith and Julia were well down on the German leaders, while the Australian champions finished a few seconds behind them. I think it's fair to say that theirs was one partnership that never quite gelled, with Jason tossing Lyneece head first into the sandpit beyond the finish line as if she'd jumped out of the forest and attacked him halfway round. 'He turns up shit-faced and fucking almost drowns me,' barked Lyneece when I bumped into her in the changing tent. 'That's a novel way of trying to get into someone's knickers.'

Katie and Sarah spent much of their time staring pensively at the water obstacle, as jockeys might look at Becher's Brook on the morning of a Grand National. While the more athletic competitors would leap in from a few feet out, legs shooting out in front of them like long jumpers, most were happy to 'ooh-aah' their way down the bank, like a child testing the icy water on Southend beach. A couple of husbands became separated from their mounts on entry, the impact of the water ripping their wives from their shoulders. But it was exiting that seemed to be causing the most problems, with both wives and husbands suddenly a few pounds heavier and husbands' legs turned to mush. Bunny Boy James – who had opted to hop all the way down the back straight – had another problem, namely his sheer white leggings and lack of pants. 'Jesus, that water must be cold,' said Katie as James stormed down the back straight, blissfully unaware that his crumpled member would be the highlight of many an onlooker's day.

Katie and I were drawn against the previous year's runners-up, Alar Voogla and Kirsti Viltrop of Estonia, who had taken a tumble in the sprint final the day before. As we lined up on the start-line, Katie and I decked out, in James's words, as cave dudes, Alar and Kirsti decked out as top-class athletes, my heart felt like it was going to smash a hole through my chest. I remembered getting a good start, although a photograph would later reveal our opponents to be out of shot while we were still rooted to the line. Still, I felt fresh as a daisy down the back straight, and it was only when we hit the drink that we began to be shorn of our dignity.

The bank was even more slippery than I'd imagined, but I managed to keep my footing as I waded in, while Katie arched her back behind me, desperately trying to keep her head above water. But she couldn't stay above the surface for long. At its deepest, the water was a metre deep, meaning Katie's head was a couple of feet under. I made it to the beginning of the bank on the other side, but was unable to get a grip, sliding repeatedly back into the mire while Katie floundered behind me. Imagine trying to haul a bulging net of angry piranhas from a muddy river, and you get some idea of what I might have looked like. After a few exit attempts, I was forced to flip Katie off and swallow a 15-second penalty along with a couple of litres of water. When we finally made it to the other side, I looked up to see Alar hurdling the final obstacle on the home straight – actually hurdling, as in Colin Jackson hurdling. It felt as if I'd been the victim of an underwater mugging and Alar was disappearing into the distance with my mojo.

Forgetting to ask Katie if she was OK, I managed to get her back over my shoulders, but I was pretty much spent. Although with her thighs wrapped around my neck and her teeth not too far away from my jaffers, it probably wasn't the best time to tell her that I could have done with her being a few pounds lighter. I trudged onwards, my fellow competitors roaring me on, Tommy and Sarah screaming encouragement as we turned into the home straight and Katie flicking me on the arse like a jockey. Only the wooden obstacles to tackle now, and I had a little sit down on both, giving Tommy a wry wink, as if to say 'your turn next sunshine', before tottering over the line and falling into a sorry heap. Katie gave me a big hug, but I wasn't happy. All those press-ups, all that jogging, all those fags I could have been smoking, and I end up coughing up a lung in a sandpit in front of a thousand Finns while dressed up as Captain Caveman.

TOM

On the bright side, I'd never seen Ben move so fast. Unfortunately, that move had been ditching Katie in the drink. Barely had the water reached his chest when he flipped her off his back and struck out for the far side, abandoning his wife in a manoeuvre so misogynistically mean even John McCririck would have blanched. The only reason she managed to remount was that he was on his knees within three strides of leaving the water, the effort of climbing the slippery bank exhausting his meagre energy reserves. If Ben had indeed been training hard, it was probably a good job – if he'd been any less fit, he'd have died on the start-line.

In some ways I tried to treat my heat like any other race I've ever done. I ate a small carbohydrate snack an hour before the gun, spent half an hour in solo contemplation on a Portaloo and then walked the course – on this occasion, outpacing Ben in his heat as I did so.

Some things, however, monkeyed with my head. Firstly there was the problem of running in a skirt. Not being in possession of a retractable undercarriage, I found that the acceleration from walk to jog shed light on issues which should really have been kept under wraps. My fear was that in the sprint for the line I would, to quote the famous line from David Coleman, open my legs and show my class. Next, the officials told me to pin my race-number to my chest. I pointed out it was bare and unlikely to keep a safety-pin honest. 'Then pin it to your skirt,' said the official sniffily. 'It might hide your salami and potatoes.'

On the line, with Sarah's legs forming a tight fleshy necklace round my throat, I shook hands with the Finnish brute alongside me. He looked like he had just returned from a spell in the special forces and enjoyed every second. Not only was he twice my size, but his wife was half as big as Sarah. He was wearing her on his back like a child's rucksack.

Until the water obstacle all was going well. I had the inside line and, once inertia had been sent packing on the gun, I kept my nose a fraction in front. I'd even agreed a plan with Sarah for dealing with the wet stuff – I would shout 'WATER!' as we entered it so she could hold her nose, and then slap her across the back of the leg when we were clear. The first part of the plan went fine, except for one of the Aussie contingent in the crowd yelling, 'Good spot, mate!' when I made the call and then cackling like a Woolloomooloo witch while his pals sniggered. The problem came in the timing. It took far longer to cross the tank than we'd imagined. I was only halfway across when Sarah ran out of air, took her fingers off her nose and inhaled two large nostrilsful of cold Finnish water.

It was like a reverse bucking bronco. The cowgirl bucked and flipped as if she'd been electrocuted while the mount underneath fought desperately to keep her on board. By the time I'd hauled us clear, the big unit in the lane alongside had disappeared at pace into the distance with his wife bouncing happily around his shoulders.

I dug in as best I could – head down, skirt up – but the gap was insurmountable. As we came into the home straight he was clearing his size 11s over the final hurdle. There was no hiding from it: unless he failed the mandatory post-race dope test, we were not going to be crowned world champions.

It was difficult keeping a smile on my face during the interview that followed. 'It was tough enough for you?' asked the MC, before translating her question to the crowd and sticking her microphone under my snout. 'Almost,' I said. 'Maybe you could put some crocodiles in the water jump.' There was a hush as she translated my answer, and then a small titter. By Finnish standards of public emotion, I felt, it counted as a standing ovation.

The truth was, I felt relatively fresh. At 253 metres, the course was 51,247 metres shorter than the distance I was used to racing over in a triathlon. I'd barely got going. Had there been some sort of marathon event, the podium might have been a possibility. At the same time, it wasn't like I'd been taken by surprise. The course had been 253 metres for years. I just hadn't trained for the right race. 'Not enough fast-twitch muscles,' I said to Dirsy sadly. 'Tell me about it,' he said, slowly lifting a beer to his lips.

Our time wasn't even good enough for us to be crowned British champions. Ash and Aila were worthy winners of that title, a clear fifteen seconds quicker. 'Never mind,' said Dirsy, who had only just managed to stand up again after his heat. 'Where did it go wrong?'

I looked across as Sarah. She was only an inch shorter than me, and despite a body fat ratio comparable to Paula Radcliffe's, only about two stone lighter. How could I put this tactfully? 'You know,' I said, 'if there was a version where wife and husband swapped places halfway round and had to run the remainder with her carrying him, I reckon we'd win it.'

BEN

Alar and Kirsti had posted a time of 1 minute 1 second and knocked the German couple off the top spot. But seven-time champion and world record holder Madis Uusorg and his mount Inga Klauson were still to go, and their clash with Finnish pair Taisto Miettneninen and Kristina Haapanen would prove to be another classic.

The cross-Baltic rivals had done battle many times, most recently at the Estonian championships, with Uusorg winning once again. On this occasion, both couples were bang on target to break the magic minute barrier when disaster struck at the final hurdle, Uusorg clipping it with his leading leg before careering sideways and falling in the path of the chasing Miettneninen no more than five yards from the finish. The Finnish pair pulled themselves together and plodded over the line disconsolately, their bid to bring the title back to the host country for the first time since 1997 in tatters. Uusorg remained prone for about half a minute before rising to his feet and, in an almost symbolic gesture, carrying his partner over the line as if it were a threshold. Afterwards, Uusorg's partner tried to console him, but he was having none of it, shoving her and a journalist's microphone aside before storming into the distance. To an Estonian, losing to Finland at wife-carrying must be like an Australian losing to England at cricket – bordering on the scandalous.

So it was Alar Voogla and Kirsti Viltrop's title – or was it? There was still Janet and her mount Barry to come. Janet weighed three stone more than Barry, and there was genuine concern among onlookers that one – or both – might do themselves some serious mischief.

'It will be the water jump that breaks her,' said Tom portentously.

'I think Janet's more likely to break the water jump,' chimed in Sarah as we watched Janet attach a little leprechaun hat to the top of her crash helmet.

'Oh, Jesus,' said Tom, 'on goes the waffer-theen mint . . .'

Sizing up Barry on the start-line, I was a little bit more upbeat. 'He'll be all right, look at him, he's built like a brick shithouse.'

'Don't be deceived,' said one of his mates. 'He's actually built like a shit brick house, in that he's liable to fall apart at any moment.'

The saddle-up was hairy enough, with Barry first lurching forward and then backwards as he struggled to distribute Janet's weight. After finally getting a handle on her, he managed to pull away from the start-line, with acceleration not dissimilar to the Champervan's. He actually managed to break into a trot down the back straight, but when he hit the water jump, what had started out as a bit of a giggle for all involved quickly turned into something of a car crash. The key difference being, people stop and stare at car crashes, while this proved far too grisly a spectacle for most.

After stepping rather daintily down the bank, roaring 'WATER! WATER! WATER!' as he went, Barry suddenly ground to a halt, his knees buckling beneath him as he struggled desperately to keep his head above water. Meanwhile, Janet thrashed around above him like an electrocuted seal. It was as if someone had dropped in a couple of toasters. This went on for about fifteen seconds, while officials and fellow competitors looked on, wondering whether one or more of them should dive in. Barry did manage to extricate himself and claw his way up the bank, leaving Janet flailing about behind him like a plump fly in a bowl of soup. Sensing genuine danger, a couple of officials eventually waded in and dragged Janet free, while one by one her fellow competitors filed away, shaking their heads and exchanging horrified looks.

'First she farts on his neck, then she tries to drown him,' said Tom, grimacing like a man eating stinging nettles. 'To be honest, I'm not sure what would have been worse.' But the show wasn't over yet. Janet was determined to finish the course, and Barry tried five times to haul her back over his shoulders, but to no avail. In the end, a chivalrous local came to Barry's aid, and the two of them (plus a couple of officials on either side making sure she didn't roll off) carried her over the finish line. Far from feeling humiliated, Janet lapped up the crowd's applause like a conquering hero, while Barry lay face down in the sand like a knackered horse.

Competition over, we all headed for the library for some post-race liveners. First, chairman Tervonen gave a touching speech explaining the ethos of the event: 'It's about providing more joy, more happiness and more fun between all the bombs and wars and economic disasters,' he said, before adding, without a trace of irony, 'I don't know where the man is who carried Janet, but he's a very brave man . . .'

The magnificently named Jacky Botty van den Bruele, a Flemish aristocrat and something of a local character, had a different take on the purpose of the Wife-Carrying World Championships. 'The winters are so long in Finland, you have to occupy yourself or your nervous system would break down, you'd commit suicide or you'd kill your wife.' Not that Jacky, nicknamed 'The Baron', thought killing your wife in Finland would be that easy. 'The women are stronger than the men in this country, because when they're six years old, they're out chopping wood. My friend went to a bar in Sonkajärvi and met a woman and she headbutted him – boom! He ended up with a broken nose and two broken ribs, but he was too ashamed to go to hospital. Finnish women shake your hands and they crush you.'

Magnificent though the hospitality was at the library (plenty of schnapps, plenty of fish, plenty of game – Chirac's got it all wrong), we were keen to get back to the town hall to sample a bit of Tapani Kansa, a cornerstone of Finnish pop music since the Sixties and Finland's answer to Elton John. Rory the Aussie was already there, sticking to Maria and Jaana like a limpet, and Tapani already had the locals up and jiving (the ones who could still stand that is). The Estonians threw their own party every year, which I couldn't help feeling was a bit off, but most of the foreign faces had opted to share in the desolation of a Finnish piss-up.

It's remarkable how quickly people bond when thrown together in bizarre circumstances, and Bunny Boy James was soon giving us all a lesson in male grooming, Stateside: 'It's all about the three-part programme: wax the thatch, clipper the thighs and blade the balls. You don't blade the balls? You Brits don't blade the balls?! That blows my mind! You've gotta blade the balls, baby, blowjobs go up 110 per cent . . .' Outside, newly crowned world champion Alar Voogla was carrying three women at once, including Katie and Sarah, while medics helped a string of locals off the premises, stumbling into the fading light like tanked-up zombies. All in all, it was bedlam, and it didn't stop being bedlam until the bar ran dry and the sun had finally retreated below the horizon.

On our way back to the lodgings we bumped into Rory, who by this stage was a shambling excuse for a man. 'Any luck with the blondes?' asked Tom. 'Nah, mate, turns out Finns aren't big on people vomming in their sauna.'

A few hours later and Tom was wearing the haunted expression of a man who could have been watching the greatest tennis match ever played but who was receiving a lesson in Finnish doll-making instead. I too had had a free pass for Rafa Nadal v Roger Federer in the Wimbledon men's final. But there we were, freezing our spuds off in a small wooden cottage, rain pitter-pattering off the roof, surrounded by a selection of the creepiest dolls outside of Dirty Barry's adult emporium. Particularly harrowing was the 13-year-old apprentice's dolls house, which to her eyes was a 'humorous' rendering of an early twentieth-century Finnish household, but to my eyes looked like Bergen-Belsen in miniature.

'Federer's taken it to a fifth set,' said Tom as he struggled to avoid the gaze of a porcelain clown, which looked like it wanted to rip his throat out and spit it back down his neck. He looked so utterly dejected at that moment he could have turned Yasser Arafat into a Jewish mother.

'Oh, well,' said Sarah, 'you can watch tennis whenever you want. But you'll never experience anything like this weekend again.' And you know what? Even Tom had to agree she had a point. The doll-maker's house was all part of the Sonkajärvi experience and the near culmination of a weird and wonderful few days: more characters than Doctor Zhivago, heart-warming Finnish hospitality and memories that would last a

Eight stone of coal + one virus-stricken Fordyce = world championship woe. At this point Ben was enjoying a cigarette and lager.

Mini Cheddirs at full pace. 'Let the cheese breathe,' we were told. Here, we strangle it.

A vision of hell: Dirs as rendered by Roald Dahl. Team psychologist Ash shows his concern in the background.

Fordyce vs Dirs, World Shin-Kicking quarter-finals. It wasn't meant to be like this.

'They hurt on the way in, and they hurt on the way out' – fear and loathing at the World Nettle-Eating Champs.

It might look like we've joined the Dutch wing of the Ku-Klux Klan, but we've actually just negotiated the semi-finals of the World Egg-Throwing Championships.

Dirsy attempts to recover from his egging in Swaton.
A glimpse into the future – the near future.

Preparing for the World Wife-Carrying Championships in Finland.
The Flintstones meets a Hawaiian-themed Gay Pride march.

The dreaded ice-cold, shoulder-deep water-jump at the World Wife-Carrying Championships. Note *de rigueur* spouse-lugging technique.

Love across the language barricades: Ben meets his groupie at the Wife-Carrying.

On your marks, get set, *slow* – the world's fastest snails crouch on their blocks. Note false start nearside left, and amorous advance nearside right.

Coach Dirs lets rip as Richmond IV blows his big chance at Congham. Note the penitent head of the sorry monopod.

Peashooting's easy, isn't it? Maybe we should have spent less time cocking about and more time practising.

The heat is on at the World Saunas. Ben begins to regret his pre-competition regime of lager and reindeer sausage.

'Rotate through the core, whip the arm through' –
Fordyce seeks the perfect angle at the World Stone-Skimming.

Semi-finals of the World Ubogus, and the oxygen deficit begins to bite.
Lungs scream, eyes bulge, crowd roars.

lifetime. Only my performance had been a disappointment. Yes, I could claim to be the 32nd best wife-carrier in the world. But the 39th best had been carrying a 19-stone woman.

From the doll-maker's house we headed for The Baron's lakeside residence, where we were treated to a traditional Finnish barbecue and sauna. As we sweated away the previous night's heroic intake of booze, we got chatting about me and Tommy's quest for glory with event organizer Anna. 'What about the World Sauna Championships?' said Anna. 'They're taking place in Finland in a couple of months' time.'

'Lounging about bollock-naked in a warm room? Where do I sign up?'

7
PEAS

BEN

There comes a time when all your pre-season hopes and dreams have long since faded, battered into submission in a wet field in Gloucestershire or washed away in a pub car park in Dorset. When the euphoria of embarking on a new journey has dimmed, so that you're operating on autopilot, posting in performances, doing little more than waiting for the journey to end. When you return from a big overseas adventure and find yourself the following weekend in a leaking campervan at a village fete in Cambridgeshire – they call that the mid-season blues, and Tom and I were about to be struck down hard.

In British sport, those blues are supposed to be the preserve of lily-livered foreigners, preening continentals with their Alice bands and hairless thighs. British sporting lore demands that when the weather turns bad and green fields turn brown, home-grown talent rolls up its sleeves, gets stuck in and elbows its way to the top. Surely Tom and I wouldn't melt like a couple of homesick Peruvians on a January night in Gretna – would we? Yet as we chuntered up towards Witcham for the World Peashooting Championship, it even felt like the Champervan had had enough, wheezing as she was like some clapped-out packhorse. To borrow another footballing cliché, we just didn't 'fancy it'.

Posterity will record that Donald Dirs helped his son in many ways, be it financially, emotionally or threatening to lay out a would-be assailant on his front lawn while wearing a pyjama top and no bottoms (don't ask). But when it came to peashooting, future generations will note he was about as much use as a pack of ball bag-flavoured crisps.

I had left it to Donny to build me a peashooter at the cutting edge, a high-spec instrument that I'd imagined would be the Smith & Wesson Model 29 .44 Magnum of the peashooting world. What he came up with after three weeks' ferreting about in his garage was a length of copper tubing.

'It's a length of copper tubing,' I said when he presented it, his face beaming, as if he was cradling a Fabergé egg.

'It's not copper tubing, it's copper plumbing pipe. You can't get truer.' Donny raised it to his eye and stared down the barrel at me, presumably to demonstrate its trueness.

'No laser sight then?'

'Naah, what do you want a laser sight for? Darts players don't have laser sights, golfers don't have laser sights. You don't see Tiger Woods with a laser sight strapped to his putter.'

'Nope, but he would have one strapped to his putter if the Royal & Ancient let him.'

I should have known. This was a man who had never upgraded from a wooden tennis racquet, a man who viewed the use of calculators as bordering on witchcraft and to whom remote controls were dangerous weapons. I once witnessed him throw himself to the living room floor when my brother was taking aim at the TV, and he is probably the only man alive who still gets up to change the channel. Hand him a tree trunk and he'll whip you up a sledge and a nest of tables in a couple of days. Throw a couple of microchips into the mix, and he hasn't got a bloody clue. So a length of copper tubing it was. And anyway, who in their right mind turns up to a peashooting competition at a village fete with a laser-sighted shooter?

'It's made up of part of a Nintendo games machine, a bike handle and a laser pen,' said defending champion George Hollis as I eyed his peashooter enviously. 'It's specially calibrated so wherever the laser is on the target, the pea should follow.' George, who must have been pushing 60, then swivelled on his heels and pumped out three bullseyes in quick succession. 'You're at the centre of the peashooting universe here in Witcham,' he added, 'and you're gonna get burnt up going into battle with a piece of tubing.'

'Copper plumbing pipe,' I said defensively.

'Whatever,' said George, before rattling off three more bullseyes.

The Hollis family were big beasts of the peashooting scene, with George winning in 1994, 1995 and 2007 and son David winning three times in a row from 1999. The event itself was first held back in 1971 and was the brainchild of village teacher John Tyson, whose crazy dream had been to transform a classroom jape beloved of schoolchildren across Britain into an event of global significance.

'Mr Tyson apparently caught some boys firing peas at each other in class and he came up with the peashooting competition to raise funds for the village hall,' explained Joy Walker, part of the event's organizing committee. 'The hall was eventually built and the Peashooting World Championship has been a focus of the village fair from then on. People have come from Scandinavia, France, New Zealand. An American chap even won it a couple of times back in the nineties.'

You might think the next thirty-seven years had meandered by in peaceful fashion, with not even the odd disputed effort in beat-the-goalie managing to ruffle the idyll of the village fair in Witcham, a settlement of 434 souls near Ely in the heart of the Fens. But you'd be wrong. In recent times the World Peashooting Championship has been beset by massive controversy, with the laser-sighted peashooter in the eye of an almighty shit storm.

'Some years back people started turning up with lasers and all sorts of paraphernalia attached to their shooters,' explained Terry, who was armed with nothing more high-tech than a translucent plastic tube. 'Where's the sportsmanship in that? It's like someone strapping a laser on top of his bloody snooker cue. Anyway, after some complaints, the committee banned laser and telescopic sights, but a few years later they brought them back again because the media lapped them up, these eccentric old fellas with their sci-fi peashooters they've knocked up in their sheds. I never thought I'd be able to compare peashooting to Formula One, but that's what it's like: nothing to do with the competitors any more, all about who's got the most jazzed-up peashooter or car. Not for me, though, I'll always be old school, whether I win the bloody thing or not.'

Back in the practice tent, an elderly gentleman called Fred was taking aim with an even more unsportsmanlike weapon than George's, a shooter with a laser, telescopic sight and more moving parts than an Uzi submachine gun. Luckily for his fellow competitors, Fred was pretty much blind. 'Is that you, George?' said Fred as Tom wandered into the tent, and

I didn't like to ask exactly how all his jiggery-pokery was going to help when he couldn't even find his own bollocks using both hands and a bollock map.

For a short while it appeared that the Witcham village fair would be blessed with uninterrupted sun for the day, but it wasn't to be, with sudden squalls sending people scurrying for cover every half an hour or so. I found Tom huddled in the trophy tent, absent-mindedly spooning couscous into his ever-willing gob.

'I'm a little tight through my right hip-flexor,' said Tom pensively. 'And my iliotibial band is playing havoc with my lateral knee inflammation. This peashooting couldn't have come at a worse time.'

Something was seriously amiss. Here was the most competitive man in England throwing in the towel before the contest had even begun. He was Churchill without his cigar, Montgomery without his beret, Ron Pickering without his whistle. But I could empathize. As someone once said – Julian Clary, actually – 'the English like eccentrics, they just don't like them living next door', and Tom and I had been living in their pockets for the last four months. We'd overloaded on wackiness, and we could take no more, for the time being at least. Perhaps if our zig-zagging across Britain in the Champervan had borne fruit we'd have felt differently. But sat in a tent in Cambridgeshire as rain swept across the village green, it felt as if our journey had run out of grunt.

TOM

What hurt most was that Ben had only bothered getting one bespoke peashooter made. Throughout our journeys together I'd always made sure I looked after his needs as much as mine – supplying him with his favourite Cool Lime-flavoured Doritos, wiping the egg out of his stubble in Swaton, buying him that fetching off-the-shoulder cavewoman outfit for the wife-carrying. You'd think after all that, plus thousands of miles of driving, he might get Donny to rattle off a decent shooter for me too.

But no. Instead, I was left to compete against the lasers and heat-seeking peas with a piece of plastic that had more kinks than the Marquis de Sade. Ben wasn't even using his copper tubing properly. Every time I looked across at him he was risking severe rust issues by dipping it in his pint and using it as a straw.

Mentally I was in the same sort of place as I had been at the nettle-eating. Without the prospect of a genuine physical test, and shorn of Ash's wise words of motivation, my hunger for battle was curiously absent. It was almost as if my subconscious mind had looked at the event, decided it lacking as a true sporting contest and removed my normal motivation as a result.

That in itself felt wrong. It was a genuine world championship, and as such was as valuable a trophy as any other I could claim. Reluctantly I began to realize that the flaw lay with me, not the event. Could I really aspire to being a true hero when my competitive spirit could be extinguished so easily?

BEN

I persuaded Tom to follow me to the practice tent for a few final pointers from George, but it was like dragging a drug smuggler along to a vigorous bum search. 'You're looking for uniformity,' explained George. 'The quality of the pea is key, the size is down to personal preference. I tend to go for smaller ones because I use a smaller bore. Roll the peas down the barrel and see how they roll. If they roll true, put it aside for the competition. Pop the pea in the mouth, put the peashooter to your lips, but don't blow – go "puh" with your tongue instead.' George raised his shooter and rattled off three more bullseyes.

Thankfully, my fear of the small and round didn't extend to dead things, so at least I was able to handle the ammunition and the odd stray bullet, unlike at the World Egg-Throwing Championships a few weeks earlier. I turned out to be pretty useful, nailing bullseyes with unerring regularity, much like a pre-dartitis Eric Bristow. George raised his eyebrows and nodded his head, such as a dad might on watching his son shave for the first time. Maybe this copper chappy my old man had knocked up wasn't as shit as I thought it might be. Alas, George's advice seemed to have fallen on stony ground where Tom was concerned. Every now and then I'd hear a dull 'phut' emanating from somewhere behind me, closely followed by spluttered expletives and banging as Tom attempted to extricate a trapped projectile from his standard issue shooter. When was Tommy going to learn that pea-to-bore ratio was key? Too late, I feared, much, much too late . . .

A round of beat-the-goalie only managed to drag Tom's

spirits even lower (how was I supposed to know the midget kid in goal fancied himself as Peter 'The Cat' Bonetti?), although the sight of a young boy shooting his dad in the face from point blank range and the ensuing kerfuffle ('ALEXANDER! I WARNED YOU . . .') did bring about the trace of a smile. The smile was fast erased by the onset of heavy rain as we queued to take our turn in the first round, with Tom's unique approach to 'layering' hardly helping matters. Only a very muddled man could think that three Lycra vests, one on top of the other, would keep the elements at bay.

First of the local favourites to shoot was Fred, he of the Uzi submachine shooter. Of his five shots, only one hit the putty target, scoring him one point out of a possible 25. The ripples of shock could be felt all the way from the prize vegetable tent to the second-hand book stall, although Tom and I seemed to be alone in wondering why. This Fred character was clearly an 'all the gear and no idea' merchant, the sort of man who'd turn up for a spot of fishing with a consignment of underwater grenades in an attempt to conceal his complete lack of angling nous. Were Tom and I really the only people to notice he couldn't see one of his best mates from a couple of yards away?

A burly rugger type dressed as a schoolgirl snuck into an early lead with a score of 24 and as Tom and I edged to the front of the queue, it became clear that we'd have to score above 15 to give ourselves a chance of finishing in the top sixteen and advancing to the knockout stages. Tom was up first, and the recognition of one of the officials seemed to give him a timely boost. 'You're Tom and whatsisname from the BBC,' said the chap with the clipboard. 'Where's that fat mate of yours . . . ?'

TOM

. . . In the beer tent, I wanted to say, or by the cake stand, or trying to fiddle the tombola. My resentment at going into battle armed with something you might drink a milkshake through was threatening to derail me before we'd even begun.

I licked my finger and held it up to gauge the wind direction. Said finger felt cold all the way round. The trees behind the target were thrashing about like the front row of an AC/DC gig. Great, I thought – even the elements are against me. My spirits sank a little closer to my flip-flops.

When we'd bought our bag of dried peas beforehand, Ben had been curiously keen to pass me my share. He'd even made a big deal of selecting me 'the best ones on offer'. Now, as I examined them in the palm of my hand, I saw why. All five were recognizably dried peas, but only just. At the very least they had been harvested at completely different stages in their life cycle. While a microscopic one looked like it had been plucked from the pod with the umbilical cord still attached, the monster alongside it had got all the way through puberty while being fed very large meals. Another was so misshapen it must have been raised on radioactive Rice Krispies.

I jammed one into the tube, took a snort of air through my nostrils and ppfffed at the clay target. The pea buried itself into the third ring. 'Three!' shouted the judge. My next felt slightly better – an improved balance between trajectory and strength of puff. 'Four!' came the shout.

Number three was a beauty. It was locked on the bullseye from start to finish. Five points in the bag, for a tally of 12 with two peas still parked in the chamber. At this rate I would cruise it.

At that rate, I would have done. Unfortunately that rate was over. My next pea fell out of the tube in a heavy ball of saliva and died just beyond my toes, while my final one dipped away as late and as viciously as a Waqar Younis in-swinger and just managed to clip the very edge of the outermost ring.

Thirteen. What sort of total was that? I couldn't even claim to be unlucky. I hadn't practised, I hadn't researched my rivals and I hadn't chosen my own peas. I'd been amateurish every step of the way, and an amateur's score was what I deserved. Hero? I wasn't fit to wipe the spit off a champion peashooter's chin.

BEN

I couldn't help wondering whether Tom already had one eye on the A10 and had therefore deliberately blown his last three peas. But I wasn't fucking about: I'd shown form in the practice tent and it was time to take Witcham by the jaffers. My first pea was bang on the money. Five points, thank you very much. But the second and third went awry, scoring only three points between them. My fourth effort arced right and scored three, leaving me on 11 with one shot remaining. I gathered myself, shuffling across the oche like a darts player looking for a route into the treble-twenty bed. I thought my final pea had hit the bullseye again, and one of the officials agreed. Unfortunately, the second official overruled him and I ended up with a four and a score of 15. For all my warm-up bravado, I'd wilted in competition conditions. I was in pea purgatory, desperately hoping it wasn't about to turn mushy.

Many others followed, with George signalling his intentions with a no-nonsense 23. Most of the other competitors favoured the standard-issue shooter, although a handful joined in the willy waving, with one bloke pulling what appeared to be a semi-automatic pistol from a mobile phone holster on his hip. If an off-duty police officer had happened to be passing, George and Co. might have found themselves involved in the most one-sided shootout since Portugal gunned down England at the 2006 World Cup. Terry managed just 12, but he seemed happy enough. 'Spears against cannons,' he kept on muttering to himself as he made his way from the oche, 'but at least my integrity's intact . . .'

Tom and I huddled in the village hall as we waited for the second round draw to be made – Tom tucking into a Greek salad, while I gorged on an almighty slab of lemon drizzle cake.

'I don't think we're going to make it,' said Tom, clutching the outside of his right arse-cheek and wincing at the same time. 'I'm a martyr to my tight glutes today.'

'Come on Tommy, chin up. What would the old man say if he could see you like this? "Tommy," he'd say, "you're a loser, a disgrace to the Fordyce handle." Fordyces never quit. He would have been smashing the granny out of the place, tearing the target a new arsehole. And he wouldn't have been eating a Greek bloody salad. He'd have been eating a man's salad, with big strips of steak on top. And bacon bits.'

'He doesn't eat salad. He's a war baby – he likes sugar sandwiches and beef dripping. He still gets excited if someone gives him a pineapple. And targets don't have arseholes, they have bullseyes. You never hear Sid Waddell going, "Now here's Phil Taylor, needing arsehole for the set."'

It was no use. Tommy was a goner, and so was I. News soon filtered through that the qualification mark was 16 – Tom had missed out by three, and I'd missed out by one.

That final call by the second official had been key. And he'd called me fat. I wanted to ram my copper tubing up his jacksie. Tom just wanted to go home.

As the Champervan coughed and spluttered its way past Ely Cathedral – the Ship of the Fens – I reckoned I knew what long-jumpers must feel like after early elimination at the Olympic Games. Four years' preparation for just three futile attempts. Except I'd been at a village fair. Shooting peas. And I'd done no preparation. Get a grip Dirs . . .

8

SNAILS

TOM

Until you've actually crashed out in the first round of a world championship, it's hard to appreciate just how useless it makes you feel.

First there's the denial – surely we scored enough to go through, the judges miscounted our peas, they must have lost our scorecard. Then there's the anger – our peas were doctored, our shooters were bandy. This is followed swiftly by an intense sense of shock – we're out, gone, fallers at the very first fence.

Later still comes the slow acceptance – the uncomfortable, ugly realization that, when push came to puff, we were failures, ill-prepared, devoid of skill, completely out of our depth.

What made it worse was the increasingly public nature of our pain. Friends, work colleagues and occasional acquaintances were all by now fully aware of our championship campaign. Every conversation began with a question about our progress. No sooner had an event finished than our mobiles would start vibrating with text messages asking how we'd got on.

When we were doing well that was fine. The longer we went without a world title, however, the heavier the burden of expectation became. Conversely, the near-misses at earlier championships – the semi-final in Stilton, the runners-up slots at the shin-kicking and egg-throwing – only seemed to make things worse. There was an unspoken expectation that we should be improving with each successive challenge. That our results had in fact started to nose-dive produced a mixture of surprise and disappointment which was hard to deal with.

It was difficult enough having to explain each fresh failure to the likes of Mini Cheddirs team-mates Tom Williams and Phil Harlow, both of whom still felt like compadres in our hunt for glory. The email I wrote to Tom trying to justify the disgraceful result at Witcham took several hours and three or four rewrites. Friends like Tom and Phil had invested heavily in our dream, yet the rate of return we offered was starting to resemble that of a Nigerian bank based in the Bermuda Triangle and specializing in sub-prime mortgages.

Harder still was relaying the bad news to our families. Donny Dirs was at least complicit in the peashooting debacle, but Papa Fordyce, for whom no exhortation of support had been too great, greeted each fresh ignominy with the pained confusion of a kindly sergeant-major shot in the arse by one of his own recruits.

Clearly he expected more from the fruit of his loins. This was a man who, in the late '70s and early '80s, had gone unbeaten for over 100 consecutive throwing-the-welly contests, rampaging through fetes across Essex and Hertfordshire in a whirlwind of muscular forearms, short-sleeved cheesecloth shirts and rotating rubber.

As a child I'd become blasé about his easy successes. You'd roll up to a summer fayre, locate the welly stall, wander off for a joust at bat-the-rat and then stroll back just in time to see Dad blow away the competition with a throw so long and fierce that the welly would still be rising when it crossed the Cambridgeshire border. He'd trouser the prize, splash out on a Mini-Milk for me and then wander triumphantly back to the Ford Cortina, fawning acolytes hanging off his C&A slacks and a celebratory Peter Stuyvesant glowing between his grinning lips.

Then there was his dominance of any contest based on general knowledge and mental dexterity. This reached its apogee one night in the mid-nineties when, up against a team made up of everyone else in the house (Mum, me, three sisters, one brother, brother's girlfriend, niece) he won a game of Trivial Pursuit without the rest of us getting a single turn. To spell that out, he correctly answered every question he was asked, on any topic, from initial roll of dice all the way through six triangles of cheese and then back to the middle of the board.

The only time anyone could remember him failing at anything was when Mum had been in hospital shelling the latest in an endless line-up of offspring, and he'd been given responsibility for doing my big sister's hair before she went to school. The pig-tails in themselves weren't a disaster. It was the fact that there were three of them (two of which jutted forward over her nose) in addition to a stubby French plait and a bun held in place by a masonry screw that ensured even the teachers joined in the playground mockery.

For those of us following in the old man's footsteps, his track record was something of a double-edged sword. It brought undoubted family pride but was awfully hard to live up to. At an age when Dad had gloried in the sobriquet 'The Duke of Wellington', I was being out-peashot by a man who couldn't see past the end of his own pursed lips. By mid-July, and the 36th staging of the World Snail-Racing Championships, the pressure had become almost unbearable. Failure was no longer an option. We needed a win.

We also needed a radical change of approach. If our experiences so far had taught us anything it was that mere enthusiasm and energy could only take you so far. From Gawthorpe to Chipping Campden, Marshwood to Sonkajärvi, the big prizes had gone to those who had dedicated their lives to the event. No more could we roll up and naively expect to win a world title through luck or desire alone. That laser-guided peashooter had to act as a symbol for our future efforts: in-depth preparation, assiduous practice and the unflinching pursuit of excellence were the only way forward.

At the coal-carrying we had been caught out by the brutal nature of the course. This time, I began the research early: our snails would be required to race from the centre of a circular table to a red line drawn around the circumference, 13 inches away.

At the shin-kicking we had been scuppered by a fatal misreading of the rules, doing battle in lightweight trainers while our rivals sported workmen's boots. Never again. I studied the snail-racing regulations in detail. All snails had to be indigenous to the British Isles. My plan to borrow a Ghanaian tiger snail (length: 30 cm) from London Zoo and win the championship with a mere inclination of its antennae was therefore a no-goer. The more background reading I did, the clearer it became. To succeed in the battle ahead, we would have to come up with something truly special.

Phil Collins's consumption of 64 feet of stinging nettles had been impressive. So had the finishing time of spouse-lugging superhero Alar Voogla. But the world snail-racing record of legendary mollusc Archie almost defied belief.

In the unforgettable final of 1995, Archie had blazed down the course in a staggering two minutes flat – the equivalent of averaging 9.25 seconds for each inch. With that single, glorious burst, he had redefined the boundaries of what was believed to be biologically possible. Just pause for a moment to let the enormity of those numbers sink in:

- it was the first time that any British snail had ever broken the magical 10-second barrier for the inch
- the winning margin was almost 3 centimetres – a staggering distance in such a high-profile race
- had Archie run through the finishing-line, rather than taking his foot off the gas and waving to the crowd, he'd almost certainly have gone close to 1 min 55 secs
- at his top speed, somewhere between the 8- and 9-inch mark, he was estimated to have been travelling at close to 0.15 inches per second.

It was all hugely intimidating. Apart from anything else, there was a good chance we'd come up against a snail who could outrun Ben. Seeking solace and some priceless pearls of inside information, I phoned championship organizer Hilary Scase.

'The competition will be fierce,' she confirmed. 'We've got a very high water table here in Norfolk, and that produces a particularly fast snail. As you've probably heard, Congham is to snail-racing what Newmarket is to horse-racing.'

I thought back to Dad's success with the wellies. Much of

it came down to pure technique. He would roll the boot up inside itself so that only the foot part was visible. Thus shrunken, the more aerodynamic boot would cut through the air like a harpoon through custard. Were there any similarly cunning strategies that Hilary might be able to recommend when it came to the dark arts of snail-racing?

'Well, the smaller ones are often quicker, aren't they?' she said briskly. 'It stands to reason – they have less to carry.'

She paused, as if weighing up the consequences of passing on years of accumulated wisdom to a debutant born outside the county boundary. 'Make friends with your snails,' she said finally. 'Let them crawl up your arms, round your face, up your nose. Respect the snail, and in turn the snail will respect you.

'Show your snail that you care. They're much more likely to do well if you've built up a relationship with them. Show it love. That's why children make such wonderful trainers – if they're on the touchline shouting, "Go Speedy!" it's obviously going to make a difference.'

What if our debutant snails were intimidated by the atmosphere? What if they got stage-fright, going into their shells both metaphorically and physically? 'Well, that's what us locals want,' said Hilary, matter-of-factly. 'You have to train them to deal with it. If they don't start, they don't start – it's a World Championships, after all.

'You should also know that we don't allow any betting. It might encourage jiggery-pokery. And we test for drugs, so watch out.' Inevitable, I mused, after the big doping scandals of recent years. Part of our remit would be to prove that it was still possible to win clean. 'One last thing,' added Hilary. 'It's strictly forbidden to eat any of the competitors. We had a French trainer come over one year, and we were shocked when we saw him looking at the champion and saying, "Ooh, what a lovely supper . . ." '

I put the phone down and began fleshing out my plan.

Nothing could be left to chance. I would hand-pick the cream of south-east England's snails, create the perfect training environment and then work them harder than they'd ever been worked before. Weekly speed and strength targets would be set, strict nutritional regimes and nightly curfews imposed. Those who failed to meet our exacting standards would be thrown off the programme, possibly into a hedge. At the same time, my snails would want for nothing. Those good enough to win central contracts would have access to state-of-the-art training facilities and the very latest in coaching techniques. Dietary supplements and deep-tissue massage would be an integral part of their daily routine. Money would be set aside for warm-weather training camps. One by one, the excuses for failure would be removed. Feeling inspired, I met Dirsy in a backstreet boozer in Shepherd's Bush to bring him up to speed.

BEN

State-of-the-art training facilities? Dietary supplements? Who did Tommy think he had living in his flower pots – Ivan Drago? Brian Clough had it right. If they're fucking about too much, punch them in the stomach. If they're not pulling their weight in training, make them crawl through some nettles. And if they're showing signs of nerves, take them down the pub and get them shit-faced.

I call my training regime the Smoke and Sambuca Method. First dip the snails in a saucer of Sambuca, just to give them a bit of a livener. Then place them on the training circuit, preferably something a few feet off the ground, so that if they run the wrong way and fall off, the shock will prevent them from doing it again. Next, gently blow smoke over their shell. They think a hedge is on fire behind them and run like buggery. And if they don't like it? Paint their shell luminous green and give them a dirty great toe-poke into next door's garden. Any self-respecting crow will be able to see them from 100 feet up.

As for living quarters, we all live together, like in an old-school boxing gym. They eat what I eat, they drink what I drink, and they watch what I watch. So if I'm having a Pukka Pie, they have a Pukka Pie. If I'm drinking Rioja, they drink Rioja, and if I'm watching Gordon Ramsay cooking snails, they can either watch it with me or hide in their shells like the drama queens they are. Do it my way, and they'll find I'm a very reasonable individual. Err from the script, and I'll come down on them so hard they'll wish they lived in France . . .

TOM

First things first. Where would we find lean, hungry snails with the raw materials necessary to one day become great racers? I had vowed to leave no stone unturned in my search, yet soon came across a problem: there were no snails hiding under any of them.

Frances had recommended dark, damp places, except there I found only earwigs, ripped-up gentlemen's magazines and partying Goths. Someone else suggested Brixton market and a pet-stall under the railway arches, but the only snails for sale were of the aquatic persuasion – and while the notion of snails donning tiny individual sets of breathing apparatus was a charming one, the microscopic reverse-Cousteau was probably beyond my engineering capabilities.

I never found out what exactly had hit the snail population of the south-east so hard that summer. Some pointed the finger at a plague of hungry starlings, others an outbreak of the Great Shell Blight of 1963. What I do know is that with just a fortnight to go until race-day, contenders were so rare on the ground that I was seriously toying with the idea of sticking hollowed-out eggshells on to the back of a few nippy-looking slugs and telling them to keep their mouths shut.

To the rescue came a wise old woman from my past, the lady who in her younger days had run the playgroup I'd gone to at the age of four. Now well into her late eighties, Barbara still maintained a large garden, if not the memory of me sneezing all over her freshly baked gingerbread men and accidentally gluing my coat to her kitchen table. Over the course of three nights she crept out into her garden after dark and plucked snail after snail from the long wet grass. By the time I popped over to examine her haul, her collecting bucket resembled a cross between a horror film and a hungry Parisian's wet dream – a seething, slimy mass of muscular monopods. They were perfect: strong, perky and big on mucus trails. We had our squad.

Next, the moulding of these raw recruits into a crack unit capable of storming the Congham keep. I read voraciously on the most successful sports in Britain and the free-thinking management gurus behind their triumphs.

From track cycling's Dave Brailsford (head of the GB team which would win eight Olympic gold medals in Beijing a few weeks later) came the idea of grouping my athletes at a single high-performance centre – or, in my case, a high-performance bucket. By keeping the boys together, I hoped I would foster the same collaborative yet competitive environment that had also worked so well for Jamaica's world-beating sprinters. I wanted them to eat, sleep and breathe speed.

From Clive Woodward, the eccentric coach who'd led England to the rugby World Cup in 2003, came a mantra: 'You can't improve anything by 100 per cent, but you can improve 100 things by 1 per cent.'

Instead of grass, I fed them organic lettuce. Instead of rainwater, they drank bottled mineral water poured into a china saucer, although an unnamed rebel in the camp frequently spoiled things for everyone by curling out worm-like shits into the watercourse under the cover of darkness. The bucket itself was the best Homebase could offer: deep, with a rim for shelter and a surface so smooth that sliding along it was like gliding across wet silk. Set at an angle, the sides provided the perfect location for strength-building hill reps.

I'll make no bones about it – it was a tough regime. There were casualties. Some snails cracked under the pressure. Others cracked when I dropped the bucket and they fell on to the concrete patio, which was unfortunate for them but good news for the local starlings.

Woodward had often warned about 'energy-sappers', those members of a squad whose negative attitude could spread like mould through the entire team unless they were weeded out. With this in mind, I noted which of my charges was the last out of their shell each morning, plucked them from their beds and drop-kicked them into sporting oblivion.

I remembered a great line I'd heard from cycling legend Chris Boardman. 'Some athletes want Olympic gold medals,' he'd told me, 'but the true greats need them.' I watched my slimy squad closely for signs of the requisite hunger and desire, struggling only with the question: what exactly was positive body language for a snail?

There were also problems with getting them to follow Linford Christie's famous dictum of going on the 'b' of the bang. On the 'h' of a hint of any loud noise, they'd shoot back inside their shells and not emerge until the 'w' of way too late. Still – race strategy was simpler. With the course just 13 inches long, the athletes would have to go flat out from start to finish. I needed racers with raw pace, their single foot loaded with fast-twitch fibres. Luckily for me, I found one.

I named him Fernando, in a nod to Spain's sporting successes that summer (Euro 2008 champions, Rafa Nadal the new king of Wimbledon). From the very beginning he was head and shell above the rest. He had the bulging muscles of a Chris Hoy, the languid stride of a Usain Bolt and a running style that was pure monopod poetry. Crucially, he was also peaking at exactly the right time. While his out-and-out speed was still devastating, the nicks and dents on his black and tan-swirled shell were testament to the big contests he'd already fought and won. The respect he was given by the other snails in the high-performance bucket was palpable.

I called Ben to see how Team Dirs was getting on and found him at a mate's barbecue.

'Red meat so rare it's still bleeding,' he said with satisfaction. 'I love it, my boys love it.'

'Aren't snails vegetarian?' I asked, puzzled.

'Not the Romford ones,' he said.

Woodward had used visual awareness coaches to get the most out his England players. Brailsford already had psychologist Dr Steve Peters helping his cyclists out. It was time for me to bring my own master of the mind into play.

'Ah, yes,' whispered Ash. 'It was Carl Jung, of course, who first noted that the snail is representative of the self in dreams.'

'But I've never dreamt of myself as a snail,' I said.

'How do you know?' murmured Ash. 'You were asleep.'

I told him about my preparations and the championship ahead.

'The key will be hypnosis,' said Ash. 'I will give you a message to read to Fernando in the moments before competition. Using mesmeric visualization techniques, we will take him into an enhanced state of awareness – transforming him into a happier, more confident, and thus faster athlete.'

On the eve of the championship I sat alone in the back garden with my team. The stars overhead were bright yet my brain was fogged with self-doubt and fear. Had I done enough? Was there something vital I'd neglected? Somewhere else in the country, was there another snail even fitter, even better prepared, than Fernando?

The occasional urban frog emerged from the bushes and flopped optimistically over to the high-performance bucket (HPB). They could sense the mollusc morsels close by. I gently picked up the pail, carried it to the garden shed and opened the door. On the shelf directly in front of me stood a large packet. 'SLUGGITS' read a large label on the front. 'The market-leading slug and snail killer.' Inside were hundreds of tiny pellets. With a lurch I realized the shortcut that fate was offering me. I could wreak utter havoc among my fellow title challengers. I pushed the packet away quickly and strode back into the garden. A frog looked up at me from a paving-stone and blinked its moist eyes nervously. It would only need a handful of pellets, sprinkled casually among my rivals' snails. That would be enough. The world championship would be mine. No one need ever know.

I walked slowly back to the shed and picked up the box. At my feet Fernando and the team lay resting in the bucket, sleeping off the high-carb pre-race meal of wholegrain oatcakes and hummus I'd given them earlier. I put my hand into the packet and let the pellets roll through my fingers. I thought back to that wet morning in Boulogne, when the whole world championship adventure had begun. I thought of my old man hurling wellington boots into summer skies, and of the hours of book-reading and learning that must have gone into the Trivial Pursuits victory. With a shudder I let the pellets drop and ran for the house, wiping my hands as feverishly as Lady Macbeth.

That night I slept badly, and not only because Dirsy kept phoning me accidentally from his trouser pocket. From the noises in the background it sounded like he was playing darts in a tapas bar in South Central LA, which at least explained why he was an hour late arriving at my house the next morning.

The Champervan did its best to take my mind off things. The heavy rain of the previous weeks had come straight through the hole in the roof above the shower unit and collected in large puddles on the laminate flooring. The punctured tyre we'd forgotten to get mended lay rusting against the sideboard. A half-eaten Mini Battenberg was disintegrating on the greasy table.

For a change, it started first time. The AA man's work on the battery had really paid off. There was the usual problem of the mysterious Invisible Brake (hand-brake off, accelerator pressed down, engine screams, van refuses to move) but some vigorous rocking from Dirs at the rear bumper sorted that out.

The odour inside was bad. It smelt like an abandoned bomb shelter that a family of badgers had been using as an outhouse. The most worrying issue was that the replacement front offside tyre was also misbehaving, or at least having an argument with the brake pads. Whenever I tried to slow down (a process that already involved stamping on the pedal so hard I was in need of a hip replacement) the van would veer suddenly to the right like a startled shire horse. To decelerate without killing us I had to simultaneously stamp down and wrench the steering-wheel violently to the left like a panicking rally-driver. It wasn't the sort of journey I wanted for Fernando and the boys. Worse still, with me on driving duties, Ben was suddenly in charge of the HPB.

On the slow road up to Norfolk we stopped three times for fuel. Driving a 2.3-litre high-fronted steel brick across East Anglia tends to have that effect. At the first petrol station I spotted the battered shoe-box Dirsy was keeping his snails in and laughed my socks off. At the second one I saw that the box was empty and laughed even harder. At the third one I realized that was because he'd chucked his fat-arsed snails into the HPB, and almost threw a wobbler.

'Relax,' he said, blowing cigarette smoke into the carefully arranged fronds of organic watercress. 'Richmond and the boys won't do anything. They're sleeping off their hangovers.'

'Why's he called Richmond?' I asked, momentarily thrown.

''Cos he looks like a Richmond,' said Ben, and tipped a packet of Cool-Lime Doritos into the bucket.

On Congham village playing-fields the competitors were already loosening up as I skidded the Champervan to a halt behind the cricket pavilion. There was a tall man in a T-shirt emblazoned with the logo 'Speed Not Feed', wiping water across a white circular table and taking down entrants' names. It was Neil, snail-trainer par excellence and official referee of the championships.

'There'll be some good times today,' he said, looking up at the fluffy clouds scudding overhead. 'It's not too warm. It's a little draughty – but they like it draughty, as long as it's up their back ends rather than their noses.'

The dry weather came as a relief to all; the 2007 championships had had to be cancelled after a prolonged period of heavy rain left the course waterlogged. Poetically, the near-biblical downpour had coincided with the passing away of Tom Elwes, the man who founded the World Snail-Racing Championships thirty-five years before.

'Looks like a big turn-out today,' Neil told us. 'The sport continues to go from strength to strength.'

'No slugs, then?' I joked, thinking back to my earlier problems finding enough recruits for my squad.

'Nope,' said Neil. 'We did have some calls for topless snail-racing, but this is a family occasion.'

At 20p per entrant it was a fan-friendly event. It also reflected the average age of the snail trainers. Not only was Ben the only one smoking, he was the only one who could legally do so.

In the queue for registration I talked preparation with 8-year-old local lad Regan. 'I've got three racers – Ronaldo, Speedy and Gonzalez,' he said proudly. 'They're all born and raised in my granddad's garden.' Congham snails, I thought anxiously. Those boys would be seriously rapid.

'Confident?' I asked offhandedly.

Regan grimaced. 'I'm a bit worried about Speedy,' he said. 'He did a bit too much yesterday.'

Our own charges were showing the effects of their long journey eastwards. Most of mine were worryingly soporific. I sliced a sun-blushed nectarine into the HPB and perched Fernando's massive bulk on the choicest piece. It wasn't ideal – there was a good chance the fructose could send his blood-sugar levels haywire – but he needed a lift from somewhere.

Ben was lying on his back on the Champervan's fold-out bed. Richmond was edging slowly across his stomach, twitching in the steady breeze of fag smoke that Ben was blowing over him. Behind him lay a treacly path of glistening slime.

'What a beauty,' purred Ben. 'He's got a neck like a swan.' He peered down his nose. 'Mind you, he's got almost no tail at all. It's as if someone stuck his shell on too far back'.

With ten minutes to go until the first heat, I took Fernando out for his warm-up. Around him his team-mates also went through their drills.

'Lovely stable of snails you got there,' said a man walking past clutching an ice-cream cornet. 'You interested in selling one?'

'Not till they've raced,' I said.

He licked an avalanche of chocolate sauce off his cone. 'What about for stud fees afterwards? I'll give you a cut of future winnings . . .'

On the other side of the pavilion a brass band began to play. The tombola stall was doing a roaring trade. Small boys were attempting to kick footballs through old tractor tyres hanging off ropes. It was almost time.

I reached into my pocket and took out the print-out of the email Ash had sent me the night before. I lay down next to Fernando. 'READ IN A HUSHED YET FIRM TONE' it said in large letters at the top of the page. I cleared my throat and began.

'Fernando,' I read out loud. 'Glory beckons. Let your subconscious mind flow. Listen to my voice. Be empowered. See yourself standing on the track. Feel the sun on your back. Taste the sweat dripping from your brow. These feelings generate within you and your shell. They flow through you from your bottom to the outer tips of your tentacles. See who is standing next to you in the starting blocks. Hear the crowd. You hear spectators shouting your name. You feel exhilarated, this is your opportunity. You want to run. The thought of running excites you. Breathe slowly. Stretch your shoulders back. Flex your tentacles. Hear the gun bang. See yourself flying away. Your body tingles with excitement. It flows. Your body wiggles vigorously and you are flying down the track.'

Inside the Champervan I could hear Ben slamming cupboard doors. 'Tommy – we got any more Doritos?' he shouted.

I focused my attention back on Fernando.

'You are excited to be running so smoothly,' I whispered. 'Your muscles are loose. They are smooth. You are smooth. You feel strong. The finish line is there. Your opponents are nowhere. They don't concern you. You breathe. You are relaxed. The pain in your body is nothing. It is normal. The juices inside you are flowing. Be smooth. Enjoy the race. Force your tentacles forward.

'You cross the line ahead of the others. Turn around and you have won. You wave your tentacles to the crowd. They roar your name. Relax. Breathe. Smile. Look around you. There is laughter. There is delight. You are the greatest. You are the finest racing snail in the land. Your tentacles are a thing of beauty. It is wonderful – you are unique. And you love thinking these things.

'When I click my fingers, open your eyes, stretch, relax and you are still smooth. You are now off to the race track to enjoy the race.'

For those of you who have ever questioned the worth of sports psychologists, I only wish you had been there for Fernando's heat. I guarantee that you'd never have seen a snail so utterly focused, so up for the fight. Lined up with fourteen others inside the red inner ring on the dampened table-top, he was a coiled spring as we waited for the gun.

'Ready!' shouted Neil. 'Steady! SLOW!'

Fernando exploded from his blocks like a dragster. He was off to a flyer. Antennae thrust forward, rippling chest low to the track, he began to eat up the ground with his effortless stride. At the four-inch mark he was half a shell clear of the pursuing pack.

In stark contrast Richmond appeared to be in a world of his own. He had yet to cross the start-line. His only contribution so far had been to attract the attention of his rivals on either side, one of whom was now attempting to enter his shell from the rear.

'Richmond!' yelled Ben. 'He's trying to bum you!'

At six inches another snail made a break from the pack and began to close the gap on Fernando. It was the right tactics – you couldn't afford to be a full inch down at halfway and still hope to win – but Fernando was in the magic zone. Despite a slight headwind wafting the orange race-number stuck on top of his shell, he still had a lead of around a centimetre.

The good news for Richmond was that he was no longer

being shagged by one snail. The bad news was that two others had also joined in. Only his beleaguered head was now visible under the writhing mass of humping grey flesh.

Fernando, meanwhile, was dominant. Even with photographers' flashes exploding in his face and the lactic in his foot screaming after that blistering start, he was maintaining his pace. The other snail gave it everything – and against any other snail, would surely have come careering past – but Fernando kept his form to the end.

'Number six wins!' bellowed Neil.

It was an emotional moment. Even as I threw a protective finger over Fernando's heaving shoulders, I felt a warm surge of pride. This was what all those painful training sessions had been for, all those dawn runs and weekly weigh-ins. He was the first snail into the final, and in the process had laid down a marker that would strike fear into any of his rivals. The high-performance bucket approach was utterly vindicated.

Ben, meanwhile, was trying to extricate Richmond from snail Gomorrah. 'Gang-raped on the start-line!' he bellowed, outraged. 'That's surely a yellow card at least.'

An onlooker shook his head. 'How do you know he didn't ask for it?'

Ben almost swallowed his cigarette. 'Ask for it? Ask for it? What's this, the Middle Ages?'

The man shrugged. 'Looked to me like he was enjoying it.'

'Yeah?' said Ben angrily. 'You think it's fun being gang-raped by a bunch of snails?' He shook his head in disbelief. 'I tell you one thing – don't come running to me for help next time you've got three of them burrowing up your arse.'

Richmond had his antennae tucked away in penitence. There were ghastly slime-trails all over his back. Ben flicked him angrily into the bottom of the bucket. He lay slumped in a pile of Dorito crumbs, gorging himself despondently. All he needed was a fag and a polo shirt and the look would have been complete.

Fernando, meanwhile, was surfing a wave of adrenalin. I placed him gently back under the rim of the HPB, where he started doing ostentatious pull-ups. You old showboater, I thought fondly.

Ben strode past me with his hands cupped in front of him. 'I'm having another go,' he said. 'Forget Richmond. It's all about Richmond the Second now.'

It was the start of a pattern that would repeat itself again and again over the next two hours. Ben would hand over his 20p to Neil, barge his way to the front of the spectator section and then watch in dismay as Richmond after Richmond found new and fresh ways to be knocked out of their heats.

Richmond II made a solid start but completely lost focus four inches in, essaying a slow U-turn and ending the race an inch and a half behind his own blocks.

Richmond III tried to get away quickly but was hauled back by a posse of five rivals. 'Like a flanker trying to escape from a ruck,' noted Ben sadly.

Richmond IV panicked in the spotlight and refused to emerge from his shell. 'Wake up, you little twat!' roared Ben, to disapproving looks from the parents nearby.

Richmond V – well, Richmond V looked so suspiciously like Richmond I that it was a miracle he was allowed to enter in the first place. His subsequent thrashing was nothing more than he deserved.

By mid-afternoon the cake stall was offering half-price on slices of Victoria sponge. I took a jammy piece back to the Champervan and sat down in the shade of the cab.

Sunlight refracted through the stained-glass windows. Shouts of encouragement from snail-trainers – 'Come on, my son!' – 'Go on, Dash!' – drifted across the greensward. To my right, a tiny child in a baggy Chelsea kit was desperately trying to boot a football through the tractor tyres. He was so small that the ball came up to his knees. No matter how hard he tried, he couldn't get it airborne.

A spectator walked past, barking into his mobile. 'What? Have you tried turning the valves? What? It's still leaking? Look, I can't do a lot – I'm at the World Snail-Racing Championships. Yeah. Nah – tenth. Fucking rubbish.'

I lifted up the protective lid of the HPB to see how the boys were doing. Fernando was celebrating his progression to the final with a leisurely boning of one of the younger squad members. He raised an imperious antenna in my direction, and I let the lid fall gently back. As long as he had a kip afterwards, the rumble would only do him good.

I strolled over to the arena. Ben was in conversation with a serious-looking man holding a small yellow snail. 'I didn't realise you were allowed to enter exotic snails,' I heard Ben say. The bloke looked at him with contempt.

'You what?' he sneered. 'Ernest is a common brown-lipped snail. Obviously.'

It was the last of the thirteen heats. Some 185 brave competitors had already been eliminated. Only the dregs were left – and a Richmond.

'Which one is he?' I whispered to Ben.

'Richmond the Second,' said Ben. 'Or the Sixth. I'm not sure. His race number fell off when I took him out of the bucket.'

Maybe it was the familiarity of his surroundings. Maybe it was the denuded field – only ten snails had made it to the start-line. Maybe it was the Sambuca that Ben had dipped him in a few moments beforehand.

Whatever it was, Richmond the Something stormed off his blocks like a snail with a lit cigarette up his arse. As with a doomed solo breakaway at the Tour de France, the other snails initially let him go. Perhaps they'd heard all about the Richmonds.

At halfway he looked to be strolling it – only for trouble to rear its head in the shape of a rapidly closing Ernest. Richmond was tiring. He was slowing up. Ernest was hauling him in like Red Rum running down Crisp in the 1973 Grand National.

With three inches to go, Ernest breezed past. The serious-looking owner was now clapping his hands and whooping. An inch from the end it was as good as over. Then something strange happened. Ernest started to cruise. He turned his head to the crowd and began waving his antennae in celebratory fashion. It was like watching Steve Ovett at his peak. The difference was, Ernest didn't have Ovett's awesome stamina, nor his unmatchable racing brain. For all the while, Richmond was doggedly closing in.

Ernest seemed to realize something might be up when his trainer started shouting obscenities. By then it was too late. Richmond had sneaked through on his blind-side. He was into the final.

'Can I ask the name of your snail?' Neil said to a cavorting Ben. 'He seems to have lost his number.'

'No problem,' said Ben. 'It's Richmond the Seventh.'

BEN

Want to know the definition of humiliation? Standing in the rain at the World Snail-Racing Championships watching your entire stable get trounced by a bunch of children. The stench of desperation hung over me like a serving of escargots de Bourgogne. *I'm a grown man, for Christ's sake, I should have been dropping the kids off to footy training or mulching some twigs in the back garden. But then I haven't got kids. Or a back garden. Still, I got one through to the final in the end, and against a common brown-lipped to boot. That reinflated the old ego a bit.*

But I couldn't help feeling a little bit chastened. Maybe my training methods had no place in modern sport. Try blowing cigarette smoke in Cristiano Ronaldo's face, see where that gets you. A mooey full of Portuguese phlegm and a transfer to Madrid, that's where. It's all nicely-nicely nowadays, arm around the shell and 'How's the wife?' Snail-racing had changed and I'd failed to change with it. But where were the characters in snail-racing today? What stories did Fernando have to tell? None. Other than the time he had cress for dinner and was allowed to stay up until 10.

Still, Richmond VII hadn't let me down, and I had a little feeling he might provide me with a fairytale send-off. But another part of me wanted Richmond to lose. There's no glory in beating a bunch of kids at anything. Is there?

TOM

In the half-hour we had before the final, the nerves began to clang. I'd stored the HPB back in the Champervan to keep the troops safe from marauding squirrels, birds and rivals armed with Sluggits, but now I worried that I'd done the wrong thing. The stench in the van after a long afternoon baking in the sun was enough to make even a cockroach queasy.

Should I have given them more air? Had they had too much rest or not enough? Were they hydrated enough for such a hot day? At least two of them appeared a little bloated. Had that nectarine pushed them over the edge? It was the classic coach's conundrum, repeated ad infinitum down the years: do you keep your stars under strict curfew, knowing full well they might get cabin fever – or do you leave them to their own devices and risk them being eaten by a crow?

With twenty minutes to go we brought Fernando and Richmond VII out of the bucket and into the grass. Fernando was moving ominously slowly. For some reason he didn't seem to be sliding as smoothly as before. Like an old man going up the stairs to bed, he hauled himself gingerly up under the lip of the bucket and sank back on his haunches, spurning my offer of a frond of organic rocket.

'He looks a bit sluggish,' says Ben. 'Sorry.'

Richmond VII was in even worse shape. While his energy levels were buoyant, his radar had gone completely. He seemed unable to move in straight line, turning this way and that in a bizarre sequence of loops and jerks.

'Maybe he's writing you a message with his slime,' I suggested, '"M-Y N-A-M-E I-S N-O-T R-I-C-H-M-O-N-D."'

Fernando appeared confused. There were bubbles of foam coming from underneath his shell. I tried to prise him gently from the bucket's rim, but he was hanging on for dear life. With a plop he finally came away, squirming with obvious pain.

'Christ,' I said. 'What if I've hurt him pulling him off?'

'Then it'll teach you not to go around pulling off snails,' said Ben.

At the championship table the contenders were lining up. All the big names were there – Ronaldo, the Congham Concorde (owned by Ben Elwes, son of founder Tom) and a glistening brute named Heikki Kovalainen. As Neil smeared a fresh layer of water across the course, the snails swaggered around the perimeter, parading their muscled physiques to the camera crews in the media seats. If there'd been any doubt about it, there wasn't any more. This was no place for ingénues or tyros. This was massive.

We handed Fernando and Richmond VII over to Neil and watched him place them delicately on the table. I took a deep breath and patted Ben on the back. He shook my hand. A few feet away, a large chocolate Labrador was licking his lips. I gave its owner a stern look. Overhead, a cloud sped across the face of the sun.

Those last few moments were probably the hardest of all. As a coach, there's not much more you can do at that stage. You've trained your athletes, fed them, done the drills and the tactics – but once they cross that line, your work is done. It's up to them now.

Fernando was very still. He appeared to be concentrating hard. Ash's words, I realized – he's going into his hypnotic trance. His body shuddered, and he shifted to one side. From under his body curled out a long sausage of shit, on and on, until it stretched half the length of his body.

'Is he all right?' I asked Neil.

Neil looked at me reproachfully. 'Talk to him,' he said. 'He's not a machine.'

I leaned across the ropes to give Fernando the final pep. As I did so the snail to his right slid across and started sniffing his mucus trail. With a start Fernando shrunk back into his shell. The other snail seemed to take this as a coquettish come-on. With obvious enthusiasm he crawled onto Fernando's shell and began grinding away like a man trying to sate a dreadful itch. 'Less of that,' warned Neil. He pulled them apart. 'Let's concentrate on this year's race, not on producing entries for next year.'

Fernando emerged from his shell and looked sheepish. A funny look had come over him. He turned towards his assailant and started flicking his antennae around in flirty fashion.

'Ready!' shouted Neil. 'Steady! SLOW!'

Heikki Kovalainen fizzed off into the distance. The Congham Concorde was hot on his heels. Fernando was rooted to the spot, still staring at the snail to his right.

'Come on, son,' I muttered under my breath. 'Come on . . .'

As if in a stupor, he looked slowly around and then finally began to move – straight at the backside of his suitor.

'Oh, dear,' sighed Ben. 'The downside of his Latin temperament. He's got the raging horn.'

Kovalainen had his foot down and was speeding down the course as if on rollers. A minute in he had a lead of three snail-lengths over the Concorde. I glanced around to see how the others were getting on. Two snails appeared to have died on the start-line. Either that or they were playing musical statues. Another had disappeared so far into his shell it would take him weeks to get back out.

Richmond VII was still to leave the central ring. He was careering round in endless circles like a rudderless speedboat. Ben was waving a cigarette across the table. 'Richmond,' he cooed. 'Follow the fag. Richmond?'

Fernando, meanwhile, was lost in a world of lust. With Kovalainen halfway to the line, he finally looked up from his neighbour's arse and switched into race mode – but the damage had been done. Kovalainen was pushing on with relentless energy. Fernando was now sprinting flat-out, travelling way quicker than any other snail on the table, but it was too much too late. To screams of delight from his two-man training team, Kovalainen crossed the line. Twenty-odd seconds later, Fernando did the same. Fifth place. It wasn't what we'd come for.

What made it worse was the winning time I had showing on my stopwatch – a relatively pedestrian 3 minutes 2 seconds. Fernando had clocked 2 minutes 40 seconds in his heat alone, and the plan had always been to use that as a sharpener for the final. If he'd gone even close to his personal best, he would have run away with it. At the same time, as I watched him warm down by trying to bash in Richmond VII's back door, I felt strangely philosophical. There wasn't much more I could have done. Like other sporting greats before him – George Best, Muhammad Ali, James Hunt – Fernando was a red-blooded rascal. Take that passion out of him and you'd be left with half a snail.

Of all the barriers between us and a world title, there was one which was insurmountable: sex. It was the lust in Fernando's loins that had derailed him, not any flaw in his training regime. You could as likely stop him shagging as you could make the Earth rotate around the moon.

Neil held the panting Heikki up to the crowd, laid him on a bed of curly lettuce springing from a silver tankard and called over his beaming owners, 13-year-old Georgie Brown and her aunt Carolyn Hancock, for the trophy presentation.

'Wow!' exclaimed an excited kid watching in the crowd. 'They've won a snail!'

Neil gave him a withering stare. 'That's the winner, you idiot,' he growled.

I shook hands with Carolyn and congratulated her on Heikki's performance. 'We did feel confident going into the final,' she admitted. 'He was on the same side of the table as in his heat, and that boded well. He's young and hungry, so we expect he'll be back next year. We'll put him back with his mates, then get him back into training.'

The mobile in my pocket buzzed. I took it out and saw a text from Mum's number. 'Grttings FROM YRDAD,' it read. 'RUWLDHCHAMPSORWLDCHUMPS?? OHNO-WHYALLCAPITALSoopsthere.'

Text messages. There was something he couldn't do, after all.

Neil handed the live snail-porn that was Fernando and Richmond VII back to us. 'It wasn't a classic, that final,' he said. 'Archie's display in 1995 was the classic. But it's been a good day's racing. It's been a little bit sporadic – we've had a fast heat, a slow heat, a fast heat, a slow heat – but there's been some good snails on display.'

Ben and I put a hand each on the HPB and carried it over to the long grass round the back of the cricket pavilion. Each of us took a moment to say a private farewell to our brave soldiers. We placed them tenderly on the ground and pointed them into the distance. As Fernando slipped away, he looked over his shoulder at me one final time. I could have sworn he winked.

'Born free,' sang Ben softly, 'as free as the wind blows.'

'As free as the grass grows,' I harmonized. 'Born free, to follow your heart.'

The silence in the Champervan was unbroken until we chugged through Thetford an hour and a half later.

'Good job we took those orange race-stickers off their shells, isn't it?' I said to Ben. 'The birds would be able to spot them from miles away.'

He turned to me, his face split with a beaming smile.

'Take the stickers off?' said Ben. 'I stuck a few extra on the back of mine . . .'

9
SAUNA

BEN

Some might think training for the Sauna World Championships would be a straightforward proposition: get yourself down the local hot box, strip down to your swimming cozzy, crank up the thermometer to 11, park yourself on the bench and start paying (in sweat).

Unfortunately, the thermometers at the World Sauna Championships don't go up to 11. They go up to 111. Degrees. Celsius. As Tom was only too happy to point out, 'That's not a sauna, that's a fan-assisted oven.' In addition, most people in Romford (many of whom travel to London and back in a sauna every day for work) don't want to spend their leisure time sitting in an oven, fan-assisted or otherwise. Including the chap I shared a sauna with at Fitness First, who, when I asked him if I could turn the temperature up to 80°C, replied, 'Do I look like a Christmas fucking turkey? Here, I'll bend over so you can stick some parsley up my arse . . .' Which gave me an idea . . .

While in Finland the sauna is often regarded as the most sacred place after the church, to many in Britain the word 'sauna' means one thing and one thing only: knocking shop.

So a couple of weeks into my training I realized there was only one thing for it: if the gym-goers of Romford were unable to cope with my elite sauna regime, I was just going to have to hit the town's foremost rub and tug. After all, who actually uses the sauna in those places?

This time I was going it alone. Tommy's August would be spent covering the Olympic Games in Beijing for the BBC, a rum gig and (he assured me) the only gig that would have stopped him joining me in Finland for the most prestigious event on the sauna calendar. Still, he was his usual supportive self when I told him I'd decided to take part: 'If there's one world championship you might win given a little bit of training, sitting still in a room and sweating like a dyslexic on Countdown might just be it.'

Though his words stung me, he had a point. Only the training didn't exactly go to plan. On the surface, Operation Rub and Tug seemed like a very clever idea. In practice, it turned out to be an expensive and humiliating one. Having achieved my first goal (namely getting through the front door without being spotted by someone's mum) I asked the old girl at the front desk (who looked disarmingly like Freddie Starr) if I could use her sauna. A simple question, many would think.

'What, you just want a sauna?' said the old bird, eyeing me as though I'd burst in off the street and asked for her hand in marriage.

'Yep, just a sauna,' I replied, as businesslike as it was possible to be while, behind Freddie Starr's head, a small Asian woman helpfully simulated oral sex to reinforce the point.

'You do know this isn't really a sauna?' said Freddie, her eyes flicking towards a security goon hovering by the door.

'Yes, but I don't want anything else, I just want a sauna.'

'GARY!' screamed Freddie, swivelling in her chair. 'This guy just wants a sauna, is that all right?' Quick as a flash, Gary appeared behind the desk.

'You don't want nothing else, just a sauna?' checked Gary, tugging on a thin panatella, in clear contravention of the smoking laws.

'That's it, just a sauna,' I said. 'It does say "sauna" on the door, doesn't it?'

'Yeah, but you do know this isn't really a sauna?' said Gary, flicking ash off the front of his black roll-neck jumper.

'Yeah, but you do have a sauna?' I replied, the security goon now taking a closer interest.

'Yeah, but people don't normally just come in for a sauna, they do what they have to do and then have a sauna, or they have a sauna and then do what they have to do. Listen, you can have just the sauna if you want, but it'll cost you thirty knicker, that's our minimum charge.'

'Thirty quid?' I said, raising my eyebrows, as Freddie popped a boiled sweet into her mouth and started sucking insatiably, her eyes narrowing as she looked in my direction. 'Do me a favour mate, I just want to sit in your sauna for twenty minutes, how's that thirty quid?'

'Because that's what we say it is, pal,' said Gary, shrugging his shoulders.

'How hot does your sauna get?'

'It goes up to 120 Celsius if you want to give it the big man.'

'Is there anyone in there at the moment?'

'Nope, it's all yours, pal.'

'All right,' I sighed, 'where's this sauna then?'

'Follow me,' said Gary, adding, 'You're silly really, you could have had your tyres blown up for forty quid . . .'

After a few minutes in the sauna, I was sweating like a gimp in a fur coat, but I still felt comfortable enough. My head was clear, my skin wasn't burning and I was able to breathe without any trouble. So I decided to ratchet the heat up to 100°C. The extra ten degrees kicked in after a couple of minutes, but I was able to withstand it, and as I leaned back and closed my eyes, a strange sense of pride rushed over me. Here I was, putting in the hours, eschewing life's vices and training for a world championship like the elite sportsman I dreamed of being.

I must have been in there for about ten minutes when the door opened and the small Asian woman from behind the desk popped her head round the corner.

'You want handjob?' said the small Asian woman.

'No thanks, not for me,' I replied, as if I was turning down a slice of Battenberg from a vicar, before making my excuses, gathering my clothes together and getting the fuck out of Dodge. I bet Andy Murray doesn't get people offering him handjobs while he's knocking up on the outside courts at Wimbledon. Although, saying that, these blonde horsey types who follow tennis nowadays are a lot coarser than they used to be . . .

The night before I left for Finland, Tom called from Beijing for a bit of a pep talk.

'I hope you've been training, I've just whacked a fiver on you to win it,' said Tom.

'What do you mean you've whacked a fiver on me?'

'You're 101–1 with the bookies. Have a look at the website . . .'

Sure enough, there I was on the Australian online gambling site Centrebet – Ben Dirs (UK), 101–1, just below some chap called Ron Broekhuizen from Holland but above a

Ghanaian bloke called Saikou Marong. Proof, if proof were needed, that Aussies will bet on just about anything, including blokes they've never heard of sweating in a hot, wooden box on the other side of the world. That said, I suspect Tom's punt might have been enough to singlehandedly move the market.

'How good is that?' I said. 'No one's been able to bet on me in anything before.'

'What about the time you started crying when you did a best man's speech? One of your mates told me they won twenty quid on the back of that . . .'

'How many times do I have to tell people? I didn't cry, I had a fish bone caught in my throat . . .'

'Whatever,' said Tom. 'Are you feeling confident? I think it's time to rewrite the Olympic motto, Dirsy: Faster, Higher, Stronger, Sweatier. I reckon that's got a pretty good ring to it.'

'Yeah, I like it. Got any tips for me? How would Usain Bolt or Michael Phelps spend the night before an Olympic final?'

'Gallons of water, plenty of fruit, energy drinks – and they won't be going out and getting shit-faced in the Olympic Village, of that you can be certain.'

Twelve hours later, I was getting shit-faced in the Olympic Village. Well, not exactly the Olympic Village, but Bar Bulmer, the official drinking emporium of the World Sauna Championships in Heinola, a city of 21,000 inhabitants north-east of the capital, Helsinki.

I had been picked up from Helsinki airport by a chap called Samuli, whose first words to me were: 'You have the perfect build for sauna – just a little bit fat.' Still, Samuli had been good enough to travel 140 kilometres to pick me up, so

I wasn't about to get punchy, and he went on to tell me how the event had started back in 1999. You've guessed it, it involved some bored old men.

'Some of the old men from the town liked to have very hot saunas and they started having competitions against each other at the local swimming baths, to see who could stay in the sauna the longest,' explained Samuli. 'People came from all over Finland to take part. The problem was that some people would turn up to the sauna not knowing a contest was going on, and they obviously weren't very happy about the heat. So the men decided to organize an official sauna bathing competition instead.'

Since the event's inception no non-Finn had ever reached the final. This wasn't for want of trying, as contestants from as far afield as China, Japan and Australia had all chanced their arm and wilted like so much spinach in the preliminary stages. But still they come, with the 2008 event attracting a record number of entrants – 160 men and women from 23 different countries.

On arrival in Heinola, Samuli reckoned I could do with getting a feel for competition conditions, so it was straight to the venue for a tune-up. A semi-outdoor theatre with seating for up to 1,000 spectators, the Summer Theatre is hardly Beijing's Bird's Nest Stadium, but it is a significant step up from Witcham village green, and imposing enough to give a man making his top-level sauna debut a serious dose of guts ache.

Ominously, all entrants had been asked to provide a doctor's certificate. Dr Watts, a no-nonsense practitioner of the old school, eyed me like a particularly grotesque haemorrhoid when I told him why I needed mine, and only when I'd presented it was I granted admission to the changing tent (or pukuhuone) which was buzzing with Speedo-clad men of every age and size. Samuli had told me that, according to Finnish lore, the human body is at its most beautiful 30 minutes after a sauna, so I assume that the chap with the weeping sores on his legs had had his 31 minutes or more before my arrival. Worryingly, Samuli was either unable or unwilling to confirm whether the injuries had been brought on by the sauna or not. Either way, it was not what a championship virgin wanted to see.

Up on stage were two hexagonal, glass-panelled saunas with cameras looking in. The cameras would beam live pictures of the action on to a giant screen. No bead of sweat, no burgeoning blister, no bubble of snot would be missed by the assembled fans.

Queuing up for a practice were a couple of brothers from Canada, Cory and Todd Ollikka, of Finnish descent and the proud owners of a wood-fired sauna back in Smoky Lake, Alberta. 'I learnt as a small child to make my mouth as small a hole as possible, breathe in and wiggle my tongue to protect the lungs from the steam,' said Cory. And with that, the talk of tactics had begun.

Håkan, an intense Swede who spoke about his training regime as Buddha might have spoken of his path to enlightenment, pitched in: 'At home I have my sauna turned up to 150 Celsius at all times and I train two hours a day, six days a week. Only the other week I had blisters in my mouth and my ear cracked and started bleeding.' Any tips? 'Don't do it. After last year, bacteria was eating my cornea for weeks . . .'

On that note, it was time to get acclimatized, and I was pleasantly surprised with how I coped. Along with my five companions I was able to remain in the sauna for the full ten minutes and, far from feeling drained on my release, I had a veritable spring in my step. Right up until the point I bumped into Samuli, who told me that the organizers had failed to turn the stoves on in time. 'How much hotter will it be tomorrow?' I asked. 'Oh, only 20 degrees hotter,' replied Samuli, with just the trace of a smile.

TOM

It was hot in Beijing, very hot – like a giant, smoggy, open-air sauna, in fact. Despite that, very few of the competitors were employing what we might term the Dirs Method – i.e. rehydrating on Lapin lager and salted nuts, and watching dawn break each day from a prone position just outside a pub's front door. Still – the last thing you want to do before a big final is suddenly change your approach. Ben had his method, his routine, and while it flew in the face of everything an Olympian might hold dear, no amount of reasoned scientific argument was going to shift him at this point. I had more worries about his fellow competitors. I had seen Dirsy in his pants almost every morning during the rugby World Cup, and the mental scars had yet to heal. How would the pick of Finland's perspirers manage to deal with a double serving of Romford pink pancake?

BEN

From the Summer Theatre, I headed straight to Bar Bulmer, where event organizer Ossi Arvela was already plumbed in for the night. Something of a Renaissance man, Ossi would appear to hold down half the jobs in Heinola. Ironic when you consider that one of his jobs is helping the unemployed find work. As well as careers adviser, the thrusting Ossi runs a travel agency specializing in trips to Central Europe and also writes for a regional newspaper, so how he finds time to organize the World Sauna Championships is anyone's guess.

'It's a serious operation, an all-year-round job,' explained Ossi over a Lapin Kulta or two. 'We have so many enquiries from competitors from all round the world, plus the media. This year we've had Reuters, the BBC and RTE, and last year a Japanese crew wanted to film me and my family having a sauna. Last year we also had Rick Reilly, eleven-time Sportswriter of the Year in America. He's seen Super Bowls, World Series and Olympics. But I was with him in a sauna by a lake when he said it was the best place he'd ever been. We don't have many things we can be proud of as Finns, but sauna sure is one. Even now, when Finnish UN troops arrive in another country, the first thing they do is build a sauna.'

Sauna, therefore, seems to be the fundamental expression of what it is to be Finnish. Yank GIs knock up KFCs, Finnish soldiers knock up saunas, a revealing little snapshot of two contrasting cultures. And Ossi soon provided another one. 'Last year, a guy from New York made the mistake of wearing moisturizer. After his heat, he was in trouble and the doctor said he shouldn't compete in the next round. But he said, "I've come all this way, I have to go on." He ended up in hospital with blisters all over his face . . .'

With shenanigans like this going on, it's not difficult to see why the Finnish Sauna Society (the self-appointed guardian of traditional sauna culture) had raised objections in the past. 'Do you think there might be a sauna in heaven?' asks a character in Maiju Lassila's novel *Borrowing Matches*, and it's clear that, to some Finns, a sauna is not just somewhere to relax and hang out with family and friends. It is sacrosanct, a place of ritual, a place in which to purify both body and mind. Finnish babies are born in saunas even today, and the dead are spruced up in there for their trip to the afterlife. In between, the sauna is the 'Finnish Cure', or the 'poor man's pharmacy', where people go to alleviate stress, relieve aches and niggles, even smooth out wrinkled faces. If booze, tar, or the sauna won't help, goes another Finnish saying, then it must be fatal.

'The Sauna Society was very pissed when they heard about this competition,' admitted Ossi. 'They thought our competition gave out the wrong kind of sauna culture and I can understand their worry. But I have said here and there that this is not the right way to take a sauna, and now I think they're OK. I think we have done a big job for Finnish sauna culture as well.'

Much of the chat in Bar Bulmer centred on the eagerly anticipated clash between Timo Kaukonen and Leo Pusa – the Muhammad Ali and Joe Frazier of the Finnish sauna scene. Both four-time winners, they had been engaged in a sauna ding-dong of epic proportions ever since the thrusting Kaukonen (a 38-year-old welder from Lahti) had rocked up at the 2003 event and wrenched the world title from his rival, who had been targeting four wins in a row. In the process, Kaukonen set an unofficial world record of 16 minutes and 15 seconds, while the paunchy Pusa (56 at the time) had to be dragged from the sauna by medics and revived on stage. As Kaukonen may or may not have said in the build-up: 'It will be a killer and a thriller when I get the gorilla in Heinola.'

The feeling among the locals was that Pusa was on the slide, a one-time sauna great railing against the passage of time. Although he regained his title in 2004, Kaukonen proceeded to win the next three, and victory in 2008 would cement his place as the greatest sauna sitter of all time.

Despite Timo's hero status among some of the locals, there was a bigger star in town: Matti Nykänen, the greatest ski-jumper ever and a man who makes Paul Gascoigne look about as controversial as Sebastian Coe. Nykänen was scheduled to appear with his band on the Friday night, but the sheepish smile that appeared on Ossi's face at the mere mention of his name (the same sheepish smile that appears on any Englishman's face when a foreigner mentions Gazza's name) suggested it wasn't a given that he'd show. As Nykänen once said, 'The odds are 50–60 . . .'

Here was a man who has been banged up for stabbing a family friend, been married five times (twice to the same woman, the heiress to a sausage empire) and who was, for a short time after his retirement from ski-jumping, a stripper. He has also posed for a hardcore porn magazine (Google it for yourself, you'll get to see his flaccid cock . . .), flogged his entire medal collection, bought it back, found God, appeared on a Finnish stamp and perhaps most remarkably in light of everything else, given his name to a brand of Finnish cider. Gazza Artois? That's about the strength of it.

'There are two types of people,' Nykänen has been quoted as saying. 'Some who take drugs, some who do sports, some who burn out and some who just sleep. I'm one of those people who does sports, makes love, sleeps and beats themselves up. It might be that sometimes one hits another person in the process.' To be fair, if you'd won four Olympic gold medals and five world titles and the most famous ski-jumper on the planet was Eddie 'The Eagle' Edwards, you'd probably go round clumping people as well.

Also in Bar Bulmer was Sauna Team Belgium, fifteen lads from the country's tiny German-speaking community who went by the alternative name of 'Les Hottest Belgian Frites'.

'One of my friends lived in Finland for a year and when he got back he built a sauna at his house,' explained Andreas, the de facto group leader. 'I saw a programme on Belgian TV last year and thought, 'Why not?' And to be honest, it wasn't difficult to find fourteen other madmen where I live. We've been training regularly since last December and we've been here since last Sunday, staying in two villas with a couple of saunas.'

Did Andreas and his buddies have high hopes of breaking the Finnish monopoly on the title – or at least getting a foreigner into the final for the first time? 'Our aim is to bring the title back to Belgium,' said Andreas, yanking his head back and clenching his jaw defiantly. 'We're going to push ourselves as far as possible . . .'

At which point Ossi appeared over my shoulder and muttered, 'They've got no chance, they've been drunk for the last five days. If only one of them dies, they'll have done well.'

The next morning it was clattering down with rain. Was there no escaping this cursed weather? I felt like an insect being urinated on by a drunk. It didn't matter which way I scuttled, even across the sea to Finland, he'd adjust his aim and soak me. Still, it gave me an excuse for a much needed lie-in. While most competitors had been happy to stay off the turps ahead of the first day of competition, I had been persuaded by an 18-year-old Irish-Finn who called himself Kristo O'Mikkonen that 6,000 miles was rather a long way to come for a few pints of water. When I did finally emerge, it was clattering down even harder than before and it would continue to do so for the next twelve hours. I checked my phone. I'd missed a couple of texts from Tom. 'Keep away from salt and alcohol. Plenty of water and fruit juice. Or Lucozade Sport. Avoid taking E.' One out of six ain't bad.

My heat wasn't until 2 p.m., so I had an hour or so to sit up in the stand and assess some of the competition. One of my new Canadian friends Todd went in heat one, and although he lasted more than five minutes, he came fourth out of six and with only two men going through to round two, that was his competition over. Heat two was done and dusted in under three minutes, while Belgium skipper Andreas went crashing out of heat three, which was won with a time of almost four minutes. A couple of things soon became clear: first, the early stages were a bit of a lottery. Second, someone had remembered to turn the stoves on in time today. I'd sat next to Todd in practice the evening before, and he'd still looked comfortable after the full ten minutes. Plus, I didn't like the way the competitors were literally running for the exit, their mangled expressions writ large on the giant screen. The way their bodies flinched and contorted as they hit fresh air, it was like they were fleeing a particularly violent tickling.

As I pulled on my swimming shorts in the backstage pukuhuone, in that coy way that Brits do, facing the wall so that no one could see my old fella, I was aware of someone moving rhythmically over my shoulder. I turned to see a small Asian man standing on a bench practising tai chi. This, I thought to myself, must be Jason. Everybody seemed to have decided that Jason was the championship dark horse. This was based, as far as I could tell, upon nothing other than the fact that he was from Hong Kong. That said, he had a translator in tow and judging by his pre-competition warm-up, he was taking no prisoners.

I left Jason to it and on my way to the stage I bumped into Håkan, who, as a previous competitor and former Swedish champion, had been handed a bye to the second round. 'Find the sisu within you,' Håkan whispered in my ear, like some sauna Jedi.

'Sisu? What's sisu?'

'Sisu – guts, determination, cojones. Or as you English might say, bollocks.' With that he was gone and the time had come to find out just how big my bollocks were.

There was an Englishman, a Norwegian, a Dutchman, a Belgian, a Dane and a Finn sitting in a sauna. It may sound like the start of a speech by Bernard Manning to the European Parliament, but there I was, in a small town in southern Finland, sat in a small box on a theatre stage, wearing nothing but a pair of swimming trunks and being studied on a big screen by a few hundred sauna fanatics. At that exact moment in time, Tom was witnessing Sarah Brightman floating above men with giant paint brushes on their heads at Beijing's Bird's Nest Stadium – but I still reckoned I would have come out top in a head-to-head weird-off.

The heat as I entered the sauna was a relief – toasty, but nothing I hadn't experienced before. As I settled into the optimum position – leant slightly forward on the bench, arms crossed and hands tucked underneath my armpits like Timo Kaukonen himself – I allowed myself to wonder what all the fuss had been about. Clear the mind of clutter, focus on a specific object (your big toe, a panel on the door) remember not to breathe through your nose (it's like singeing your nostril hairs with a blow torch) and pick off the lesser nations one by one. Before emerging, arms aloft, alongside your fellow Finnish qualifier. Five minutes, Dirsy, that's all it will take to get through . . .

The combined minds of Joseph Stalin, Adolf Hitler and Jeremy Beadle could not have thought up a more effective instrument of torture. Only if Beadle had been trapped in there with me could it have been any worse. The first dastardly deed on the part of the organizers was making sure the large digital timer on the stage remained tantalizingly out of sight of the competitors. So, unless you counted up each second in your head, a form of mental torment in itself given the circumstances, you had only a rough idea how long you'd been in there – and one minute feels very much like ten once the water starts raining down on 'The Terminator', the 18 kW stove that forms the centrepiece of this modern-day Iron Maiden.

Every thirty seconds the shower head above The Terminator did its damnable deed, and I soon became transfixed, the hissing of the coals proving to be far more hypnotic than my wiggling left big toe. After a few short, stabbing showers, the Dutchman to my left began to twitch wildly, as if he was locked in a room with a swarm of angry wasps, his arms tied behind his back and his head smothered in marmalade. His obvious discomfort encouraged me. True, I was sweating so much I was worried all six of us might drown, but I was still breathing regularly and my skin was free of pain.

Suddenly, the Dutchman shot up and lunged for the exit. The officials flung the doors open and the remaining five competitors basked in the cool air that came flooding in. After a brief glimpse of heaven, we were soon back in hell as the doors slammed shut behind him. The next dose of devil's dribble felt particularly cruel, The Terminator spewing out what felt more like iron filings than steam. The filings began to settle all over my shoulders and on the top of my ears, pricking and grinding away at the skin. The Finns call this sauna steam löyly, meaning 'spirit' or 'life'. Ironic really, as it felt as though both were being sucked out of me with every breath.

One dose later and the air turned to leak and potato soup, so dense you could almost chew it. I don't care what Tommy said, the smog in Beijing had nothing on this. Each breath became shorter and choppier. Dainty little hiccups replaced proper manly breaths. One dose later and it felt like my ears were turning to crackling and someone was flambéing my shoulders. Why was no one moving? Maybe they had more sisu than me? Surely not. 'Show them how big your bollocks are, Dirsy, dig deep and rummage around for the sisu . . .'

The Norwegian was next to go walkabout, almost staggering sideways into the coals as he reached for the door handle. He was closely followed by the Belgian, who let out an unearthly, guttural wail as he was gobbed out of the exit like a blob of lava. And then we were three.

'Where's this bloody sisu,' I thought to myself as the Dane and the Finn sat in silence next to me like a couple of stone Buddhas. 'Think, man, when was the last time you saw it? Jesus, it was quite a while ago now. I looked for it during the coal-carrying and couldn't find it then. Come to think of it, I haven't seen my sisu for fucking years . . . I'm not even sure I ever had any . . . IT FEELS LIKE SOMEONE'S HOLDING MY FACE NEXT TO A BOILING KETTLE! STOP THE RIDE! I WANT TO GET OFF!' With that, I was out the door, my world championship dreams a puddle of sweat next to where my feet had been.

It felt as if I'd been in for six or seven minutes, and I was a little bit disappointed to discover I'd lasted barely three. I bumped into Håkan again up in the stand. 'Sorry, Håkan, couldn't find that sisu anywhere.'

'Did you try looking in your handbag?' Håkan barked back. Damn these Swedes and their impeccable English.

My embarrassment grew as the heats wore on. Jason actually turned out to be pretty useful, but his time of six minutes wasn't enough to see him through. He suffered the ignominy of being disqualified for 'leaning forward too far', and I imagined the scene on his return to his apartment in Hong Kong: 'Oh, hello darling, how did you get on?' 'Bollocks, the bastards DQd me in the first round for "hunching" . . .'

Canadian Cory had to stay in for more than seven minutes to advance to the second round. That boy clearly had sisu in ladles. He told me afterwards that the insides of both nostrils were burnt from where his snot had been boiling. Is there no end to the glamour of this event, I thought to myself as the rain continued to come down like stair rods. The weather was so grotty, half of me wanted to climb back in.

One of the first-round heats lasted more than eleven minutes, and Håkan became convinced the coals were cooling down as the day wore on. This didn't seem to help Team Belgium much, and by the end of the first round, only two of the fifteen remained. The sole American competitor, who played for the local ice-hockey team, turned up sporting a Mohawk. 'The gel on your hair will cook, roll down your face and boil your eyeballs,' said a panic-stricken official. I never saw him again.

The only other Brit also bit the dust early. Andy, a turkey farmer from Colchester, had previously trained with the great

Timo Kaukonen and talked a good game, although he was unable to explain how exactly you 'train' someone at sauna-sitting – 'NO ANDY, YOUR LEGS ARE SWEATING FAR TOO MUCH!' . . . Andy had been spotted in the puku-huone in a contemplative state, plumbed into his iPod, as if preparing for the Olympic 100 metres final. But when the going got tough, Andy got out.

'I was sat there and thought, What the fuck am I doing here?' explained Andy. 'And I fancied a beer, so I scarpered . . .' Håkan, his sisu clearly piqued, looked like he wanted to force-feed Andy hot coals. Still, Andy had lasted longer than me, which meant that not only could I not claim to be the British champion, I wasn't even the best in Essex.

The big guns entered in the second round, and Timo Kaukonen was cheered into the arena like a conquering emperor. Timo doesn't wear his fame well, responding to the Belgians' chants of 'Timo! Timo!' with a look that said, 'I'm only the world sauna champion, not the fucking Pope.' Timo, his missus and other members of his entourage all sported cascading shoulder-length peroxide perms. Andy assured me it was more of a practical decision than an aesthetic one, the hair acting as a heat-shield for the tops of the ears. The hairdos provided food for thought: could Rick Parfitt have been one of the world's great sauna-sitters, one wondered, instead of wasting his life away playing rhythm axe with The Quo?

Timo and great rival Leo Pusa coasted through their second-round heats with the minimum of fuss, both exiting the sauna with all the urgency of men padding to the kitchen for a beer. Later, Canadian Cory battled his way through another brutal encounter, staying in for more than seven minutes and outlasting three Finns for a place in the quarter-finals. Håkan scraped through as a lucky loser. However, the two remaining Belgians went crashing out, and by the end of the second round only ten foreigners were left.

By the time the quarter-finals were through, only one foreigner remained. 'I didn't feel too bad to be honest,' explained Marcel from Switzerland. 'Although I started to lose the feeling in both my arms and I thought I was going to collapse.' Cory had made the fateful mistake of getting stuck into the beers too early and lasted barely three minutes in his quarter-final. Håkan hung on grimly for six minutes, all the while squirming and appearing to shrivel in the heat like burning paper. 'Swedes,' the Finn next to me said with a wry smile, 'such homosexuals.'

'How can you tell a Finnish extrovert?' goes the popular Swedish joke. 'When he's talking to you, he looks at your feet instead of his own.' As I had already discovered on my visit to Sonkajärvi for the Wife-Carrying World Championships, the Finns are a shy bunch, even after thirty-eight pints of pear cider. All except one young woman and her mum, both of whom tried to grab my cock as I queued for a round of Lapin Kultas. Aware of the Finns' normal reserve, I was initially quite chuffed, until I found out that she and her mum had also tried to grab the knobs of Cory, Andy and Håkan.

While the daughter could at least string a sentence together, her mother and stepdad were both utterly banjaxed in the way only Finns can be: joylessly, hollow-eyedly, incapable of speechedly. The old man, it turned out, was a local quack who spoke perfect English. When he could speak, that is. As we got stuck into our beers, the mum kept on grabbing my arm and muttering something under her breath. 'What's she saying?' I asked the girl. 'I think she likes you,' she replied with an entirely inappropriate smile. Her mum must have been pushing 70. I wished Tom was there – he's much better looking than me.

By the time Matti Nykänen had hit the stage, the drinking area resembled a coven of meth drinkers in a dilapidated railway yard. I'm pretty sure Matti would have approved. I can vaguely remember watching a young blonde lady providing the actions to Matti's seminal hit 'Give Me Sex', for the benefit of his deaf fans. And as I watched her enthusiastic pelvic thrusting on the side of the stage, I thought to myself, not for the first time that weekend, life simply doesn't get any stranger than this.

The next morning I awoke to the shuffling of feet and the clinking of glasses. I peeled my sweaty face from the seat of the faux leather sofa that had been my bed for the night and surveyed the scene through cloudy eyes. This wasn't my hotel room. Where in Matti Nykänen's name was I? Wherever I was, it had been the scene of much merriment the night before. A middle-aged chap in just his Y-fronts and tartan slippers was tip-toeing his way through the carnage, sweeping beer cans into a bin bag while nursing a cigarette. He gave me a weak smile as he bent down to pick up an ashtray by my head, before shuffling out of the room.

He returned a couple of minutes later, accompanied by a bald man in a mauve silk dressing gown and a woman dressed in a rather cheeky little negligee. Jesus, Mary and Joseph, I thought to myself, I think I might be witnessing the last knockings of a swingers' party.

It all began to come back to me. After Matti's quite humbling performance, most of the competitors (plus some of the locals) had transferred en masse to Nightlife, Heinola's premier night club. I vaguely remembered seeing a few of the Belgian lads taking it in turns to straddle the rampant mum, who was slumped and giggling in a chair by the cloakroom, and thrust their groins in her face. I could just about remember one of the Belgians licking her daughter's face like a 99, and her saying to him, 'I like you – you're different.' And I definitely remember seeing Håkan and a leather-clad Finnish bloke trading blows at the bar. No sane man should get in the way of a spot of Swedish–Finnish knuckles, so I'd decided enough was enough and headed home.

Only I couldn't find home. After an hour or so traipsing the streets of Heinola, I'd bumped into a guy smoking in a doorway and asked if I could crash for the night. He very kindly offered me his sofa. What he didn't tell me was that there were couples rumping all over his house. It hadn't been a dream. I had seen that bald fella walk past my sofa clutching his irate member. Like a wounded soldier in no-man's land I'd played dead, for fear that he'd turn his weapon on me.

It's famously difficult to make small talk with Finns. It's even more difficult to make small talk with a Finnish man who is vigorously goosing a Finnish woman. So I passed on a can of Woodpecker cider and staggered into the morning gloom, before almost running down the street, like a man escaping from a high security prison.

The next day – Saturday – I rocked up to the Summer Theatre at around four, looking forward to the titanic clash between Kaukonen and Pusa. Ossi saw me approaching and gave me a mischievous smile and a double thumbs up. 'All ready for the wildcard final?'

'What wildcard final?'

'I told you in Nightlife, you're in the wildcard final. Six o'clock sharp . . . I hope you didn't overdo it last night . . .'

Ah yes, the wildcard final, I remembered now. Six foreigners who had bombed out in the early rounds paraded like freaks for the locals, the World Sauna Championships equivalent of the school 'progress' prize. I already felt like death warmed up and was genuinely worried a few minutes in the company of The Terminator might kill me.

Before the wildcard final were the semi-finals proper, both men's and women's. Unlike in the men's competition, foreign women had had some success in previous years, Natallia Tryfanava of Belarus having won three years in a row between 2003 and 2005. Tryfanava was leading another crack Belarusian team on this occasion, with three going through to the final to join two-time champion Leila Kulin and two other Finns.

In the first of the men's semi-finals, Marcel was bidding to become the first non-Finn in the history of the event to make the last six, but he failed to get through the most savage encounter so far, the Swiss bailing out just before the fourteen-minute mark. Timo Kaukonen, as expected, coasted through to the final. Leo Pusa's semi lasted less than six minutes and the crowd had the final they had hoped for: Kaukonen, the young, flame-haired punk, against Pusa, the gnarled veteran of a thousand saunas. Who knew what might happen when these two colossal sisus clashed? Muhammad Ali said after his fight with Joe Frazier in Manila: 'It was like death. Closest thing to dying that I know of.' At least Ali was never in danger of being turned into crackling.

Bizarrely, the wildcard final was the most hyped event of the weekend, with dry ice, entrance music and a spot of Finnish hip-hop to get the punters in the mood. Infektio looked as if they'd come straight outta double science and I got the feeling it would have taken no more than an avuncular schoolmaster to hold them back. Rival crew Få

Flow had all the pent-up aggression of a couple of Mormon missionaries. Still, the crowd were all over it, and by the time I was introduced, the place was hopping.

TOM

Something must have got lost in translation. Absorbed in the action at the Laoshan velodrome, where the lean, muscled Team GB cyclists were handing out a majestic spanking to all and sundry, I had failed to hear my mobile phone ringing. It had been answered by a kindly colleague, and the message from Finland passed on as Dirsy had requested.

'It was your friend the bender,' said the colleague, eyeing my bleached blond hair and silver ear-hoop with a look of fresh understanding. 'He says to tell you that it's good news from the sauna – he's into a wild final showdown. He said it doesn't hurt as much as you'd think, although breathing is a nightmare, and the Belgians are a disgrace.'

'Ben Dirs, not bender,' I said, laughing.

My colleague blanched. 'I don't care how many of them there were,' she said. 'I thought you had a girlfriend, too. Some people . . .'

BEN

Me, Canadian Todd, Hong Kong Jason, Andreas the Belgian, Nemo the Serb and a corpulent German chappie whose name I didn't catch were given strict instructions to entertain the crowd after emerging through twin blasts of dry ice. I had planned to treat the crowd to a spot of breakdancing, but then I noticed the 'King of Swing' in the front row. He wasn't goosing his wife on this occasion, but he was nudging her, pointing at me and laughing. Knocked off my stride, I settled for some self-conscious waving.

The Terminator had been ratcheted up to 130°C ahead of the finals and it told. The bench was like a three-bar gas fire and when I sat down it felt like the back of my thighs were being barbecued. Once again unable to locate my sisu, I called it a day after less than a minute. Still, I felt I'd played my part to perfection: the lily-livered Brit demonstrating to the locals just how double-hard their compatriots were in comparison.

In the women's final, Finland's Leila Kulin outlasted arch rival Natallia Tryfanava of Belarus to win her third successive crown. Given that The Terminator was in a particularly spiteful mood, the time of 5 minutes 21 seconds seemed pretty respectable. But the men's final would make it look about as hardcore as a couple of minutes watering the plants in the greenhouse.

Who knew that watching six middle-aged men poach in a sauna could be so gruesomely compelling? Anyone who has witnessed a savage boxing match first hand will know the emotional response it can elicit. This wasn't much different. Their fortitude was unfathomable, the theatre only heightened by the very real possibility of physical damage. It was war in Speedos, and as close to martial arts as it was possible to get while sitting as still as possible in a small sweaty box. At the same time, it was probably the most absurd thing I'd seen since I caught my 87-year-old nan drinking a can of Pepsi Max.

The first thing you noticed as the finalists were introduced to the crowd was that top-flight sauna-sitting is neither a young nor a slim man's game. At 38, Timo looked to be the youngest by some distance, while five of the six were carrying plenty of excess baggage. As Andy the turkey farmer archly observed, 'The bigger they are, the slower they cook.' I half expected him to jump on stage and sprinkle them with parsley. Timo was clearly the fans' favourite and you wondered how some of his more lubricated fans might react were he not to triumph. Furthermore, such was the flag-waving patriotism on display, I decided it was probably a good job a foreigner's never come close to winning the thing. You suspect the locals would barricade the doors, tip the sauna over and turn him into toast.

The first finalist to buckle did so after 7 minutes 30 seconds. The second man out lasted just shy of 10. He very nearly toppled off the front of the stage on his release, his legs snaking beneath him like two overcooked strands of spaghetti. It was another three minutes before the next competitor came tottering out, bright pink and glistening like a leg of honey-glazed pork. And then there were three.

Both Timo and Leo remained on target for a fifth title, while they were joined in the shake-up by Bjarne Hermansson, the mysterious 'thin man' from the southern city of Turku. This really was gripping stuff. As the large digital clock ticked by, Timo began giving out tell-tale distress signals – clutching for breaths, wringing his hands and occasionally glancing across at his rivals. Pusa was unmoved, balled up in one corner like a hibernating bear. Hermansson, too, looked unflustered, his only movement an occasional dab of the forehead.

Sauna veterans tell of cans of beer boiling at 110-plus degrees, and I had to marvel at the mechanics of the human body as I watched these three maniacs go about their business, pumped up to the eyeballs with sisu, their innards cooled mainly by the torrents of sweat that spewed from every pore. But even the hardiest of Finns run out of sisu eventually.

It was Timo who cracked first, emerging after 16 minutes and 49 seconds. He was greeted in the outside world by a wall of stunned silence and head-clutching fans. He looked more bewildered than usual, staring into the near distance and blinking wildly, his scarlet nose and forehead bubbling, as if he'd had hot Bovril dashed in his face. Pusa and Hermansson sucked in the cool air that momentarily filled the sauna before settling in for the final push.

Not long after Timo's exit, Pusa, now leaking like some flesh and blubber colander, stopped acknowledging the officials. Of course, it had happened before, back in 2003 when officials, suspecting Pusa was slipping into unconsciousness, burst into the hot box and brandished a red card. A nonplussed Pusa said he was simply 'lost in thought'. Asked what he had been thinking about, Pusa replied, 'Whether I'd get back home in time for a sauna.'

At about the 18-minute mark, Pusa's body began quaking wildly and the officials had seen enough. Like SAS men storming an enemy base, they ripped the doors open, rushed in and hauled the burly Pusa up by his armpits. Pusa resisted, his arms flailing while his legs melted from under him. Seconds later Pusa was on the deck and surrounded by medical staff. Few in the crowd seemed to notice Bjarne Hermansson make his exit. He smiled sheepishly and gave a rather limp-wristed wave. The organizers continued to fluster over the stricken Pusa, while most of the crowd continued to chant Timo's name. Only if Pusa had burst into flames could poor old Bjarne have been more spectacularly upstaged.

When interviewed afterwards, Hermansson said the final

had been 'slightly more pain than pleasure'. Only by knowing some Finnish history – about its centuries of wars, invasions and foreign occupation – can you begin to understand such an outlook. If Hermansson had been around 100 years ago and captured by the Russians, he probably would have complained that his mattress was too soft. Mind you, it's a good job Bjarne didn't extend himself too much: all he got for his troubles was a few quid, a medal and a stove. Something tells me he already had one of those.

Six hours later and I was being serenaded by Hong Kong Jason in Heinola's main square. Jason had been adopted as Team Belgium's mascot – by turns dancing, busting Kung Fu moves and crooning Simon and Garfunkel standards. There were Belgians everywhere – necking cider, dancing on tables, hitting on blondes. One blond in particular. Despite being dethroned as world sauna champion, Timo was still the man in most people's eyes. His face looked like a chewed-up ball of strawberry Bubblicious, which made the adulation that much more remarkable.

As I made my way back to my hotel, I turned to see Timo having a piss in a bush, surrounded by fifteen Belgians in matching team kit all chanting his name. Timo smiled shyly and shook his head. If history's greatest ever sauna champion couldn't get his head round the weekend, what chance did I have?

10
STONES

TOM

Ben's garbled midnight messages from the World Saunas had an unexpected impact over in Beijing.

While temperatures in the Bird's Nest were certainly close to the ones that had defeated him in Finland, it should have been near-impossible for me to mentally transport myself from the greatest sporting event and stadium on the planet to a wooden shed full of sweating Scandinavians 4,000 miles away. Then again, modern technology can make the world a very small place. Mere moments before I watched Usain Bolt destroy the world record in the 100 metres final, my laptop pinged with an email which turned out to contain a video clip of Ben perched on a stage wearing nothing but his badly fatigued boxer-shorts. As a result, I'll forever associate one of the most sensational moments in sporting history with a half-naked Dirs sitting on a pink plastic stool while being ogled by drunk Belgians.

That wasn't my only headache. The next event in our own sporting calendar – the World Stone-Skimming Championships – was due to follow hot on the heels of the XXIX Olympiad. The time and facilities available to prepare for it were horribly limited. Did a stone-skimming culture exist in modern Beijing? Was there a lake in the area that wasn't being used to host Olympic rowing and kayaking events? What would the People's Liberation Army do if I started throwing stones at it?

For Ben a lack of training opportunities made very little difference. So partial was he to getting battered on the local brew the night before competition that he considered his preparations to have gone well if he arrived on the start-line still in possession of his credit card and shoes.

For me the opposite was true. Who cared about the start-line? It was the podium I was fixated on. The humiliation of the peashooting still kept me awake at night, while the egg-throwing – well, even looking at an egg-fried rice made me want to weep.

Bitter indeed was the irony of watching athletes in China who had spent their entire lives training, often Lottery-funded, for their own moment in the spotlight. The solution came after a chat with Chris Boardman about Britain's cycling success. Most pundits had struggled to understand how a team could go from laughing-stock to the best in the world so quickly, but Boardman, a former Olympic champion, had the inside knowledge to explain the process perfectly. From that moment, the logic was simple: the fast-track to stone-skimming expertise would be to bring in the experts. Just as it took an authority in track cycling to spell out what was needed in the velodrome, so only an authority in stone-skimming could reveal the secrets of skimming success. Bingo.

Surprisingly (particularly considering that the championships were being held in the Inner Hebrides) my first port of call would be the Laboratoire Physique de la Matière

Condensée et Nanostructures à la Université Claude-Bernard, Lyon. I was fairly sure Dirs wouldn't have thought of it first.

It was at Le Lab that renowned physicist Lydéric Bocquet had teamed up with Professor Christophe Clanet of the Institute of Research on Non-Equilibrium Phenomena in Marseille and, as a little light relief from studying matière condensée et nanostructures, rattled off a scientific paper entitled 'Secrets of Successful Stone-Skipping'.

My concern was that the secrets would remain exactly that. So tenuous is my grasp of even the most basic scientific principles that I struggle to understand how ships made of metal can float, or why the sky is blue. When I read the paper online, I hit problems as early as the very first paragraph. 'A stone-skipping throw involves four parameters; U and V are the translational and spin velocities, respectively, A is the "attack" angle of the stone in relation to the water's surface, and B is the impact angle of the translational velocity.' Even more opaque was the foot-long equation that followed. There were characters and symbols being used that I'd only seen before on the walls of Tutankhamen's tomb. Every now and then the words 'therefore' and 'thus' would appear, as if an explanation was in progress, but none ever came.

Lydéric's carefree use of complicated theory left me as dizzy as a discus. The only pearl I could pluck nestled in the very final sentence. 'The "magic" angle of 20 degrees is accordingly expected to maximize the number of bounces because the amount of energy dissipated during a collision is directly proportional to the collision time.'

I texted Dirsy. 'Practise at 20 degrees,' I wrote.

A text came back. 'You what?' it said. 'It's fucking freezing in Romford.'

In a break between watching Michael Phelps rip up records at the Water Cube, I called the next name on my list – planetary scientist Ralph Lorenz, formerly of the Lunar Laboratory, Department of Planetary Sciences, University of Arizona, and now resident at the Space Department of the Planetary Exploration Group at John Hopkins University.

Ralph knows how to spin things with precision. It was his expertise and calculations that allowed the Huygens space probe to land safely on Saturn's moon Titan. Probably because of that, there were exactly the same issues of comprehension that I'd suffered with les professeurs. At one stage I looked down at my notepad and saw that I'd only written down two things that Ralph had said: 'lakes of liquid hydrocarbon' and 'destroying a column of tanks'. Unlike his French counterpart, however, Ralph had a pragmatic side to his character.

'I'm well aware of Lydéric's work, but stone-skipping in the real world isn't the same as in a laboratory experiment,' he advised. 'You could tell a thrower the given angle and spin rate, but getting them to do that isn't trivial – our motor-control isn't done in an algorithmical way.'

I thought back to Ben's 3 a.m. breakdancing in France. Had that been algorithmical? Could that explain why the Australian girl had been unable to match his moves?

'Go on,' I murmured.

'In the real world, Bocquet's theoretical optimum of 20 degrees might not be the ideal throw. You won't be dealing with a perfect liquid surface. It might be that a slightly less optimal angle will be more forgiving if the surface is rippled. A 5-degree ripple on the water's surface might knock a 20-degree stone to 15 or 25 degrees, where anything above 22 degrees is disastrous for its flight. You might be better throwing it at 15 degrees so it will always bounce between 10 and 20 degrees. Then you need to consider the wind. That can make stones veer through the air, so they may not hit at 20 degrees anyway.'

I mentioned something I'd come across in my research – that the best stones for skimming were seldom the perfectly smooth round ones.

'Correct,' said Ralph. 'The ideal shape is oval or hexagonal, with a weight of between 100 and 200 grams. The heavier the stone, the more it will skip, but the harder it is to throw. A very thin stone is easier to throw, but it will fly in the same way as a paper plate – the lift will act forward of the centre, causing it to veer left.'

'Forget the 20 degrees,' I texted Ben. 'It's all about weight and wind.'

'That's what Katie said when me and her split up,' he replied.

The science, I felt, had been taken care of. What was missing now was the hands-on practical stuff. As the rest of Beijing slept, I nailed a green tea and got on the phone to the legendary Russ 'Rock-Bottom' Byars. By day Russ was an unassuming 45-year-old test engineer from Franklin, Pittsburgh. By weekend he was the greatest stone-skimmer the world had ever seen. On a bright autumn day in October 2007, Russ had skimmed a stone a staggering 51 times – a new world record, and a performance that had quite rightly made him a star in his home country.

'The secret's in the grip and stone,' he told me. 'The thumb sits on top, and I hook my middle finger under the bottom. You gotta concentrate on keeping the index finger on it and ripping it all the way through.

'You want a stone that's real flat on one side, but with a

chip on the edge so you can get a grip with your index finger. The more spin you have, the better it'll fly. And it needs to be about the size of a baseball.'

What about the throwing technique itself? What about Lydéric's 'magic angle' in Ralph's real world conditions?

'You know, it's weird,' he said. 'The Discovery Channel filmed me, and they slowed down the footage to show how I throw. Turns out my elbow goes out first, then my hand comes down and under. I don't use my shoulder hardly at all. I don't take a run-up either. Most people get lower to the ground than me, but I'm too lazy – I just lift my front leg and step forward real hard. I used to get quite low, but as I get more round I stay higher. It's hard for anyone else to duplicate. But as soon as a good throw hits the water, you know. You can tell.'

In an ideal world, I mused, I would go out to Franklin and immerse myself in Russ's world – skim with him every morning, be the Ralph Macchio to his Mr Miyagi. As it was, I would have to settle for studying his world record on YouTube. I would also need to work on my throwing arm. While direction wasn't a concern (the accuracy of my deliveries had been the only plus point in the egg-throwing nightmare), the world championships were about more than simply the number of skims you could notch up. Under the competition rules, a stone had to bounce at least three times to register; but the winning throw was the one that went the furthest – provided of course it had those three skims behind it. Neither were the distances to be sniffed at. It had taken 63 metres to win last year's title, and that in a play-off, after three men had all skimmed their stones to the back wall of the ancient slate quarry where the championships took place.

Even with my stunted numerical abilities I knew that 63

metres was a long way. It was the equivalent of throwing a cricket ball from the long-off boundary to the wicketkeeper, or the distance I would beat Dirsy by if we had a 100 metres race. It was big.

Who could help me build up my throwing strength, I wondered, as I watched the men's javelin final in the Bird's Nest a few seats along from four-time European champion Steve Backley. I needed someone who understood what it took to fling things huge distances – someone who had won medals and smashed records in a throwing event, someone whose reputation for innovation in training was almost unparalleled.

'Steve,' I whispered down the row, 'you haven't got a number for Fatima Whitbread, have you?'

If there's a nicer man in sport than Steve Backley, I've yet to meet him. Within hours he'd emailed me a detailed gym-based training plan. The drills included:

Over-weight throwing ('To build power')
Under-weight throwing ('To really speed things up')
General upper body exercises with dumbbells ('Incorporate as much rotation as you can')
Rotator cuff exercises for the shoulder ('Help to avoid injury')
Lots of torso work ('Especially with rotation')

There was also a very amusing tale about a hirsute Russian female athlete and a device called The Whizzinator, but I'll have to keep that under my hat (a little bit like she did).

'Dirsy,' I texted home. 'Backley's on board. Practise over-weight throwing.'

'Like I've got a choice,' he replied.

For the next two weeks, whenever I got the chance, I would hit the gym and work through the Backleycises. I won't pretend it was easy – you try going to a backstreets Beijing muscle-shop in a vest and bleached blond hair and throwing weights around without incident – but it did at least compensate in some small way for the lack of actual skimming practice.

By the time I got back to Blighty I felt confident enough to demonstrate my beefed-up technique round at Ben's flat. The standing effort I tried in his kitchen felt great, to the extent that I decided to incorporate a run-up as well. Unfortunately my approach was longer than I remembered. Either that or Ben's kitchen had got shorter. At the point of maximum hand-speed, my fingers made direct contact with the sharp edge of the washing-machine. The washing-machine failed to yield. My fingers didn't.

'Try texting me now, Tommy,' said Dirsy, with a certain satisfaction, as the blood gushed from two enormous flaps of flesh on my index finger and thumb.

At least he had remembered to book our flights to Glasgow. For this trip, sadly, the Champervan would have to stay at home. Wonderful though it would have been to test its alopecia tyres on Hebridean coastal curves, the RAC website was estimating a drive-time of something around twenty-five hours each way. That was assuming we didn't once stop, hit traffic or break down. Such was the cost of petrol and inefficiency of the Champervan's 2.3-litre engine that it would also almost be cheaper to start our own airline than to drive there and back. Even if Easdale Island was both downwind and downhill from Romford the journey could still end up costing more than the old warhorse was worth. Nope – early-morning budget flights it was.

At around eight o'clock on the night before our dawn departure, I gave Dirsy a call to remind him to bring directions to the B&B he'd reserved for us. The twelve bottles of Beck's he'd drunk meant he couldn't remember booking one. The good news was that he was on his way home and aiming to be asleep by 9 p.m. With thoughts of magic angles and rotator cuffs flitting around my brain, I went to bed a relaxed man.

In retrospect, I can't believe I ever thought it would be so simple. God knows I'd heard such promises before. So many times in France did Dirsy have 'one for the road' that the highway in question was surely now lying behind some dustbins with vomit on its shoes and bits of kebab in its hair.

I can only assume that the pain from my fingers wonked my thinking, or the heady sense of optimism that the Bocquet/Lorenz/Byars/Backley input had instilled in me. Either way it was only when Ben hadn't turned up at Stansted an hour before the scheduled departure time that I began to feel a little uneasy. I tried his mobile. It rang, but there was no answer. That was ominous. If it had gone straight to voicemail, it would at least mean he'd been sober enough to turn it off. The fact that it was ringing and not being answered suggested either it was lost or he was. With half an hour to go, I went through to the gate and gave him another call. No answer.

I practised my rotational exercises as an air stewardess with orange lipstick stood on a chair and looked out over the waiting passengers. 'Departure of easyJet flight 207 to Glasgow is delayed by fog,' she shouted. 'We hope to start boarding in forty-five minutes.'

Happy days, I thought. Fortune favours the massively hungover. I left another message on his voicemail. 'For once, it's worth you running. You'll still make it.' How wrong I was. When the plane roared northwards a full hour later, it did so with just one stone-skimming hopeful on board. Against all logic, I was half-expecting to step on to the tarmac at Glasgow to find him waiting with a sheepish grin and a tale involving a drunken wager in a Chinese takeaway in Gidea Park and a midnight hitch-hike up the A1. Predictably, there was no one save four bored-looking baggage handlers in luminous green jackets with complexions the colour and texture of suet pudding.

I was signing for the hire car when he finally rang.

'What time is it?' he mumbled. He sounded like a man with a side of ham for a tongue.

'Where are you?' I asked.

'By the toilet,' he said.

'Is it a Scottish toilet?' I asked, hopefully.

'Armitage Shanks,' he said. 'What time's the flight?'

'Before now,' I said.

There was a noise like a vat of soup being poured on the floor, followed by a long pause.

'Fuckit,' he muttered, finally. 'Look – it's not my fault. I haven't been in work for days, so my body-clock's fucked.'

'You've been relaxing at home, so you're knackered?'

'Yeah. It's been a nightmare. There's barely been two nights in a row when I've got home from the pub at the same time. What time's the next flight?''

I thought back to Ralph Lorenz's comment about stone-skimming in the real world not being the same as in a laboratory experiment. Ralph, I thought, you're an even wiser man than I first thought.

BEN

The lesson is clear: never book morning flights, because you never know who might turn up down the pub the night before. What had started out as a couple of medicinal pints to help me sleep had turned into an impromptu version of This Is Your Life, *with old faces appearing in The Ship seemingly at ten-minute intervals. And, as anyone who's ever had a drink knows, it's the impromptu piss-ups which are the best – and by far the most dangerous.*

In the battle between my alarm and the alcohol-soaked recesses of sleep, there was only going to be one winner. The snooze button didn't even get a look-in. Most people will be aware of the mild panic that sets in on realizing you've overslept for an important appointment. The repeated 'bollocks' and 'fucks', the pounding of one's pillow, the carnal roars as one stomps up and down the hallway, the 'Dirsy, you're an absolute fuckwit'. Or perhaps that's just me.

Then there's the dreaded phone call. Teeth-grindingly excruciating. Agonizing. Degrading. The blank staring at the screen. The abortive attempts. The polishing of one's story in the mirror. The beating of the heart as the phone at the other end starts ringing ... AND YES! IT'S GONE STRAIGHT TO ANSWERPHONE! Glorious, glorious answerphone, the god of over-sleepers across the developed world. The chance to relay your story unchecked, to lay some groundwork for the grovelling apology to come.

I cranked up the laptop and got myself online. A flight from Luton to Glasgow at 1330. Two hundred pounds, but what's money when set against the wrath of Tom? And my stone-

skimming dream was still very much alive. All hail those orange gods of easyJet! Thanks to you, I've got another hour in bed . . .

TOM

A footballing friend of mine, Jon, was waiting outside the airport terminal. Keen to be part of the championship quest, and operating outside the nightmarish vortex that was Dirs-Time, he had caught a train over from Newcastle early enough to take account of any delays and arrived in Glasgow with time to spare.

'Where's Ben?' he asked.

'Don't worry – he's decided to get the later flight,' I said. 'But he'll definitely meet us this afternoon in Oban. He promised.'

'It's a shame he's not here yet,' said Jon, three hours later, as we sat inside a pub on the esplanade, drinking Guinness with whisky chasers and watching the rain lash down outside. 'This has got all-dayer written all over it.'

It had indeed. The spirit of Ben was with us, even if his body was still 530 miles south. The filthy weather had given us the excuse to ignore the lure of the tourist attractions en route – Cruachan, 'the power-station in a mountain', and Inverary, 'Scotland's favourite prison' – in favour of a run-through of the twenty-four single malts on offer behind the bar.

There was no mistaking the fact that we were in prime stone-skimming territory. Everything in town was made of slabs of slate – the walls, the roofs, the urinals. It may have been the way they carried themselves against the stiff wind, but the local people also all seemed to sport unusually muscular right arms and shoulders. The only concern was that the three local hard-men at the bar, two of whom had oven-fresh black eyes, would kill us before Ben arrived. Jon had already raised hackles by loudly slagging off the Scottish weather, and there had been an uncomfortable sense when we first walked into the pub that our clothes and haircuts instantly marked us out as book-reading homosexuals from the big city.

For a moment I had considered affecting a Glaswegian accent in an attempt to pacify them until Ben arrived as back-up. Then I recalled with a shudder what had happened to my old pal Tony when he'd done the same once on a train home from work. Tony's idea had been to use a fierce burst of Govan-speak to scare away a drunkard who was pestering him in the buffet car. Unfortunately the accent had reminded the bloke of his dead father. As a result he had clung to Tony for the rest of the journey like a drowning sailor to the wreckage of his sinking ship. In addition, it turned out that the bloke caught that same train every single day. He sought out his new friend with enthusiasm on every possible occasion, thus forcing Tony to keep doing the accent, day after day, even when phoning his wife from his mobile or being met by his young kids at the station.

Soon the booze-hound was introducing him to other passengers as 'Tony the Jock'. A back-story had to be invented, involving support of Celtic, a tough upbringing on a windswept estate and a curious lack of knowledge about both the geography and history of his home city. After a while Tony found himself accidentally slipping into Glaswegian around the house or when out shopping. Old friends started looking at him strangely. His kids started crying when he absentmindedly read them bedtime stories of Winnie the Pooh in the style of Billy Bremner. Only when his wife gave him an ultimatum – buy a car and drive to work or move house and job entirely – was he able to realize how entrapped in this make-believe personality he'd become. It had taken months for him to feel truly himself again.

That salutary tale forced my hand. Spotting a brief gap in the weather, with no sign of Dirsy and the bar becoming as safe as a lion enclosure for a man wearing steak trousers, I grabbed Jon by the arm and dragged him over the road to the beach to practise our skimming.

'Good work, Tom,' said Jon. 'Now they've seen us holding hands.'

'Quick,' I urged. 'Skim some stones.'

'I tell you what,' said Jon. 'Why don't I recite some Oscar Wilde while we're at it?'

I glanced back at the pub. Three swollen-eyed faces were staring out of the window, watching us with expressions of dark, brooding menace. It made concentrating on the skimming rather hard. When I found a decent throwing stone there was a temptation to hold it back, rather than flinging it into the sea, in case it was needed in the pitched battle that might follow. Even when utilizing both the magic angle and my bulked-up arm I could still only reach the 25-metre mark, albeit with an average of eight or nine skips. Still worse was when I tried a speculative effort with my left arm. I managed to miss the sea.

Let's put that into context. For starters it was two metres away. Not only that, it was probably the biggest target anyone had ever missed. Forget slicing a shot over the crossbar from the six-yard box, or failing to throw down the stumps from a few feet off. I had missed a target that covers 70 per cent of the Earth's surface.

It didn't bode well.

I checked my mobile for messages. Where the hell was Ben?

BEN

A favourite saying of my father growing up was 'do it now!', usually roared into my face from point-blank range while I was cowering under my duvet. In hindsight, maybe I shouldn't have gone back to bed. But I am a man who works within very tight parameters – if I have to be somewhere at 1230, I like to time it so I get there at 1231. And as long as no one has thrown themselves on the tracks at Stratford, it usually comes off.

This time, someone had thrown themselves on the tracks at Stratford. And as I crawled past the magnificent-sounding places that straddle the Essex–East London border, such as Seven Kings, Manor Park, Forest Gate (the only magnificent thing about them being the sheer number of fried chicken takeaways in and around their stations), it slowly began to sink in that I wasn't going to make it for the second time that day.

I arrived at Luton airport about thirty minutes before my flight was due to take off and presented myself at check-in ten minutes later, sweat trickling down the small of my back, sambuca oozing from every pore. 'You're twenty minutes too late, sir, passengers are already boarding,' said the orange lady behind the desk.

Then I said it. That thing I never thought I'd say. 'But you've got to let me on. I've got the World Stone-Skimming Champion-

ships in Scotland.' The orange lady started sniggering, and I couldn't really blame her.

Maybe I could still make it. I commandeered a public computer and worked on the logistics. Planes were out – I'd already handed over £300 to those robbing bastards at easyJet and how had they repaid me? With a plane that had left on time. But surely there were trains? 'Start stirring my porridge,' I roared down the phone half an hour later. 'I'm on my way!'

TOM

Opinions were mixed in Oban that night on whether Ben could still make it in time for Sunday's showdown. A nice lady in the fish and chip shop was as optimistic as you can be when you've got chip sweat running down your arms; the old boy closing up at the tourist office less so. If Ben could get to Glasgow by 7.30 a.m., he said, there was an 8.20 bus to Oban. Trouble was, there were no seats left on the remaining flights, and the rail network was crippled by weekend engineering work.

Could a hungover Ben deal with a journey which involved three trains, a replacement bus from Doncaster to Carlisle and a night spent sleeping in the disabled toilets at Waverley station? The last text he had sent me left it open to doubt. 'Battery almost dead,' it said. 'So am I. Lost my credit card too. 'Mare.'

There was no sign of him at breakfast the following morning and no new texts. I pushed my kippers round my plate and tried to read a lucky omen into the fact that the milk on our cereal was skimmed. We left a message with the waitress to keep an eye out for blokes who looked like Alan

Sugar played by a homeless man, and jumped in the car for the winding drive south to Easdale.

As so many times before – at Chipping Campden, Swaton, Witcham, Sonkajärvi – the nerves began to grow as we got closer to the championship venue. Any other time I would have been cooing at the dramatic greens and browns of the scenery, the swooping, rain-soaked valleys, squat whitewashed cottages and humpbacked stone bridges, but now I gave them no more than a passing glance. At the small coastal village of Seil we parked up in the lee of a towering crag and joined the steady flow of people walking down to the harbour and the tiny ferry across to the island.

I looked around at our fellow passengers as we ploughed across the narrow, choppy straits, the weather flicking from bright golden autumn sunshine to splattering rain and back again in strange twenty-second bursts. All around were the lean faces and muscular frames of men forged in the white heat of high-class competition. It was an intimidating sight.

We stepped ashore and I glanced at my mobile. There was no signal at all. From now on, Ben was on his own.

The barbecue was already doing a brisk trade when we joined the line for registration outside a beautiful little hall made from slate and rose-coloured wood. A middle-aged man with close-cropped greying hair was buying a T-shirt bearing the logo 'Skim It To The Limit'. 'Got your stones yet, lads?' he asked with a wink. It was John Birch-Hurst, the reigning Welsh champion. John was one of the bookmakers' favourites for the world title. Short of stature but with hands like wrenches and forearms as wiry as industrial cable, he had thrown a phenomenal 75 metres just a few months earlier. 'I've got a fast arm,' he said matter-of-factly, 'too fast in fact to allow a stone to skim. I have to slow it down to get the spins in.'

I handed my £4 registration fee to the lady behind the desk and put in a request to keep a place open for Ben. 'You know my secret?' confided John. 'Javelin. I've thrown for Wales in the past. I once threw against Steve Backley. I couldn't get close to his marks, mind.' I nodded slowly, trying to keep my excitement hidden. Was fate handing me a huge psychological advantage over one of the big hitters? 'The man's a legend,' said John, with wonderment in his voice. 'When I threw 54 metres, it pulled my arm out of place – yet he went to 90. However fast I think my arm is, his is twice as fast. He could throw a stone a thousand times further than me.' He strolled over to the barbecue, bending his arms back behind his head. His back, even through his coat, looked like it had gone through years of over-weight and under-weight training, not to mention rotator cuff exercises. Would my three weeks of hot-housing be enough against that?

By the harbour, championship founder Bert Baker was watching on as the contenders drew up in boat after boat. What the Marquess of Queensberry had been to boxing, Bert was to stone-skimming. Although hailing originally from Islington, the septuagenarian had married a woman from Easdale and lived on the island for thirty-six years. Having started the championships in 1983, he had codified the sport and watched participation go through the roof. Fittingly, the trophy for the best local skimmer – the Bertie – was named in his honour. Alongside him stood event organizer Donald Melville.

'Call me Melon,' said Donald, shaking my hand. 'It's my nickname.'

'He's got one giant testicle,' said Bert sagely.

The pair of them explained the rules. All stones had to come from Easdale itself. They could be no bigger than three inches at any point. Every contestant was allowed three throws. Each effort had to stay within a lane marked out with buoys to count as a score. Donald would call the thrower forward, Bert would count the number of skims and judges positioned on the slopes above the flooded quarry would gauge the distance thrown.

'This is way, way tougher than in Pembroke,' whispered John. 'You could have as many throws as you liked there.' He frowned and then brightened. 'That was a good day, that one,' he said. 'As soon as I heard about it, I said to my wife – "I'll win that." And you know what? My first throw went twice as far as anyone else's. You should have seen the bloke who came second. He was standing there afterwards with his head hanging down. I went right up to him and said, "I beat you!" right there in his face, with his kids standing next to him.'

He paused and looked around at the burgeoning crowds. 'I do really want to win this,' he said. 'My mother's brother is already in the *Guinness Book of Records* for getting the longest hole-in-one ever – 390 yards, at St Helens. I thought I might do the record for how far you can walk just on your hands, because I was good at doing handstands when I was a kid. Then I found out it was five miles. Five miles!'

There was as yet no sign of current world champion Dougie Isaacs. Perhaps that was a good thing. There seemed to be a large number of people who wanted to see him beaten, and not just in the competition. As we walked across the island to the beaches to join an increasingly frantic search for suitable stones, there were dark mutterings about his demeanour in victory the year before. To hear industrial language like 'cock' and 'twatface' in those bucolic surroundings was strangely shocking.

Flame-haired children with pale faces watched on as people scrambled and slipped over wet rocks and flung practice stones into the deep blue-grey water of the quarry. I'd worried that the best stones might already have been taken, that the island had been denuded of decent skimmers by years of hosting the Worlds, but there were beauties lying everywhere. Within minutes I had a stash that met all of Ralph Lorenz's criteria – oval or hexagonal, with a notch for the index finger and a lovely weight in the palm.

The improvement over Saturday's efforts was immediate. The superior stones, flatter water and absence of staring local hard-men lifted me straight into the 15-skim/30-metre mark. Sure, the fingers hurt, and blood was starting to seep through the plasters wrapped around my thumb, but I felt my confidence growing.

John, meanwhile, was showing the sort of form you'd expect from a Welsh champion. He hadn't been lying when he'd said he had a fast arm. It was like watching a whip crack. Stone after stone shimmied across the water's silvery surface and splintered into the back wall 63 metres away. With a flourish he picked up a small boulder and flung it across the quarry like a missile. It hit the wall on the full with the sound of a cannon going off.

Throwing almost as far was a shaven-headed chap with a powerful build and pugnacious features. After coming seventh last year, Chaz Boshell had travelled up from Oxford after a winter of hard skimming, determined to go six better.

'I've been practising in the bath,' he said, sifting through a large pile of glistening stones. 'Start small and you never know what could happen. You've just got to feel comfortable with your stone.'

I looked again at my phone, hoping to see a message from Ben, but I still had no reception. Jon was the same. Ferries were shuttling people over from the mainland, but Dirsy was not among them. A brace of kayakers bobbed into view round the headland. Neither was towing a tired traveller behind them.

All around, people skimmed stones with the relentless regularity of wind-up toys. There was a serious danger you could stand up at the wrong time or place and get a snoutful of slate. All manner of idiosyncratic techniques were on display, not least from a serious-looking man in a sensible anorak who was experimenting with a backhand Frisbee-style throw. 'No, no, no,' I heard John say to himself. 'Where's the power storage? Where's the rotation?'

When the scrawny kid in a baggy blue T-shirt and white basketball shorts first sloped into view, most of us ignored him. He looked too young to be anything but an awkward teenager, maybe here to watch his dad compete. Then he started throwing.

It was like watching a fresh-faced Usain Bolt at the World Juniors in 2002, or Michael Phelps at his first Olympics in 2000. With no apparent effort, he flicked a random stone at the surface of the water and watched expressionless as it fizzed into the distance like a firecracker before exploding on the back wall. To gasps of astonishment, he did it again. And again. And again. It was effortless, incredible, breathtaking.

I'd heard rumours about The Kid, a reclusive local prodigy called Allan Laycock who'd been beating grown men since the age of 11 without ever practising, but I'd put it down to prittle-prattle and blather. Now here he was, skimming in front of us, shy and diffident but every bit as extravagantly gifted as a young Tiger Woods.

John was stunned. 'Look at his fulcrums! And those long levers! He's got the perfect throw.'

Chaz shook his head. 'He's not even trying. It's pure technique.'

'That stone was floating,' said John, awe-struck. 'Just floating.'

Allan picked up four fresh stones and casually pinged them halfway across the Irish Sea.

'I don't like him,' said John decisively.

'We'll have to get in his face,' agreed Chaz.

There was now just half an hour to go until the first male was called to throw. Skimmers were watching each other through narrowed eyes as they hefted stones from hand to hand. Spectators lined the high walls of the quarry, battling for prime viewing spots and tucking into doorstop crab sandwiches from the village hall. You could pick up an enormous plate of fresh lobster, bread and salad for the price of a Romford kebab. If I win, I thought, it's lobster all round.

A ripple of encouraging applause rang out to mark the start of the under-10s competition. First up was Emily Eyre, from Alstonville in New South Wales, whose father Brad had brought the family to Scotland specifically for the event. For once the Australian sporting hegemony cracked. Emily appeared to be intimidated by the raucous atmosphere and managed just 2 metres with no skims. 'Maybe stones rotate the other way round Down Under,' suggested Jon. A red-haired 4-year-old lad wearing a woolly knitted jumper and fierce face stepped forward to big cheers from the locals. 'And now,' announced Donald, 'Ranting Rory the roving fisherman!' With a scowl the youngster hurled a stone out to the 10-metre mark and stomped off in search of something to kick.

I turned away and walked across a narrow spit to the beach where the men were continuing to warm up. Like the finalists in the Olympic javelin event, we lined up behind each other and waited for the man in front to clear the runway before side-stepping over the pebbles and hurling away.

I could see John watching me intently. 'Let me give you a little mental tip,' he said. 'Whatever you threw then, throw it 20 yards further.' As pieces of advice go, I felt it was of limited use. It reminded me of the time I had interviewed Colin Montgomerie and asked him for the single tip that would most improve any amateur golfer's game. 'When you're holding your putter,' he had said, 'you should hold the shaft with exactly the same force that you would use to cup a small bird.' Only when I was passing the advice on to friends did its ridiculousness hit me. Which of us had ever touched a small bird, let alone cupped one? Going by his track record, certainly not Dirsy.

John himself had been hit by a bad bout of pre-match nerves. 'I felt confident before I saw The Kid,' he said. 'I don't feel confident at all now. The locals keep telling me they want me to beat this Dougie Isaacs bloke too. Everyone I've spoken to wants him taken down a peg. They keep saying to me, "I hope you fucking beat him."'

Chaz, meanwhile, seemed to be digging for buried treasure. 'I'm sure I hid a stone round here somewhere last year,' he grumbled, burrowing into the beach with his hands.

I climbed up on to the headland and looked out across the sea. Away to the north-east, plump grey clouds were swelling and rolling onwards in our direction. On the cliff immediately to my right, I could see the gangly figure of Allan Laycock sitting cross-legged on a rock, staring dreamily into the distance like a meditating monk. I closed my eyes and thought of magic angles and painful index fingers. Down below, Donald called the first man to the front.

The crowd was six or seven deep behind the safety rope around the throwing area. Bert stood on the quarry's edge, a red bat in one hand and a green one in the other, raising the former like an angry table tennis player when a stone failed to skim the requisite three times. Scores were patchy. While some threw out to the 30-metre mark, others pitched their stones wide of the lane of buoys, or saw their efforts nose-dive straight into the deep. Ralph Lorenz had been right again – if a stone was too light or thin, it sheared away like a paper plate. Cries of dismay or support from the spectators rang around the quarry's walls.

Tactics came to the fore. Some competitors went for the early bounce/lots of skims technique, aiming to use the water and negate the wind; others cleared as much water as possible before their first skim, reasoning that air would slow their stone down less than water. Increasingly, the wind was becoming a problem. Having been as flat as a tea-tray early on, the surface of the quarry water was gradually getting rougher and rougher. Decent throws were snagging on waves before they'd had a chance to get going. Up above there were still patches of blue sky, but an opaque curtain of rain was advancing menacingly across the bay.

'Don't worry about the weather,' shouted a steward as a powerful gust caught him amidships. 'Stones go faster in the rain – it flattens the water's surface.'

You could hear the rain coming across the water before it

hit. It sounded like sausages sizzling in a frying-pan. Coats and hoods went up hurriedly, children started crying, and umbrellas were starting to turn inside out. The effect on the throwing was immediate. Suddenly no one could get close to 40 metres. Stones were either blown sideways by the wind or hauled down by the watery green grasp of the waves. The one or two throwers who'd gone early and got a decent mark on the board were starting to look rather smug.

In our impractical big-city book-reading homosexual clothes, Jon and I were soon soaked and frozen. Chaz looked at the apocalyptic skies and shook his head. 'I wouldn't want to throw now,' he said. Donald peered at the list of names on his clipboard. 'Tom Fordyce!' he barked.

I sighed heavily, wiped the water from my eyes and strode to the front. In front of me, the throwing lane had been turned into a series of watery trenches. To the rear the crowd was packed tight. I scanned the faces for the perspiring visage of Dirs but saw nothing but ruddy-cheeked healthiness. I took out my three chosen stones, passed them through the wooden measuring device that Bert held out and raised them to the galleries to silence the suspicious hecklers.

The wind was buffeting my face. I rolled my fingers around my first stone, took a deep breath, rocked back and flung into the gale. The early shape looked good. It was heading down the middle of the lane, fast and flat – until suddenly it hawed away on the wind and sliced into the chilly depths like a plummeting sea-bird. Bert raised his red bat. No score.

I took another deep breath. The pressure sat on my shoulders like a sumo wrestler. Silhouetted against the skyline beyond the back wall I could see Allan, watching on, motionless. Come on, Fordyce, I thought. You're not just throwing for yourself here – you're throwing for Backley, for Russ Byars, for Dirs. Think angles. Think rotation. Think champion.

This time it felt good from the hand. Russ had been right. It flicked the water and leapt on like a flying fish, arrowing onwards. It skipped again, and again, and again. Bert waved his green bat. Donald looked up at the stewards on the slopes. 'Thirty-three metres!' he shouted.

I wanted more, I really did. I thought that was the start of something, that there was extra in the tank – but my arm was shot. The third stone wobbled out to 32 metres and sunk from sight with a small fizz. I grimaced, nodded at Donald and trudged back into the crowd.

'Here we go,' said a voice, and John stepped forward. It was immediately clear that something was wrong. He'd put his three stones down by the throwing platform a good ten minutes earlier, but now seemed to be scrabbling about in the bucket of cast-offs that the organizers provided for emergencies. A few whistles broke out from the crowd. There was a look of panic on John's face. He stood up, clearly distraught with the stones at his disposal.

'Thirty-five metres!' shouted Donald, as the first throw buried its nose in the water. The second was better – an angry 40 metres. The third flipped over after just three bounces and died even earlier than the first.

John was incandescent. 'Some bugger nicked my stones! I put 'em down for a minute, and he's gone and nicked them!' I tried to console him. Forty metres, I pointed out, had him in the top ten. He looked at me with eyes blazing. 'I didn't come here to throw 40 metres. Those stones were crap – crap!'

Conditions were getting worse. So many fancied throwers were failing to register a mark that Bert's red bat was raised almost permanently. A lad in a bright woolly hat and exotic beads had his head in his hands. 'Five thousand miles I've travelled, and I didn't even score.'

At the halfway stage, the lead was held by Eric Robertson, a short, stocky man from across on the mainland who had finished third on two previous occasions. After two no-throws he had hurled one out to 54 metres and been swamped by his delighted bunch of rowdy supporters.

Chaz stepped up, spitting on his hands. To jeers from the locals he asked for a towel to dry off his stones. The catcalls increased in volume when Bert called his first effort a no-throw. 'You're joking,' said Chaz, as the boos and whistles rang out. 'Could you not see the bounces?' The ire seemed to spur him on. His second throw was enormous, a stunning detonation that blew away anything else that had been seen all day. Tragically, it bounced just twice. Bert beamed and showed him the red. He may as well have kept the bat raised. The third stone went sideways on the wind and torpedoed into the briny. Three throws, three failures.

'Thanks for coming, pal!' yelled a gleeful local.

Chaz's girlfriend, who had given up her weekend to travel up from Oxford and support her man, did her best to comfort him. 'I'm choked,' I heard him say. 'That would have been 62 metres. Bastards.'

As I tried to work out where in the rankings I might be, I became aware of a low, angry grumbling. A wave of discontent rippled through the crowd. Spectators were shaking their heads and glowering towards the throwing zone. Dougie Isaacs. It had to be.

He had an aura, there was no doubt about it. He stood there behind the ropes like a prize-fighter, staring out over the onlookers with a nerveless belligerence.

'Bighead,' muttered the bloke next to me. 'Thinks he's Liam fucking Gallagher.'

Isaacs turned his back on the crowd and stretched his shoulders. Slowly, with great deliberation, he began to peel off layers of clothing.

'Get a fucking move on!' shouted someone from the back.

His first throw was big – 52 metres. It was no back wall-hitter, the 63 metres that he had thrown to win both the 2007 and 2005 titles, but it put him straight into second place. I held my breath and waited for more – but it never came. Whether it was the wind, the waves or the hatred, I don't know, but the most decorated stone-skimmer in British history simply fell apart. His next throw bounced just once; his third not even that. So loud was the cheering that I could have been back watching Usain Bolt in the Bird's Nest.

The rain lashed down with unremitting ferocity. There was one man still to go, and he wasn't even legally that. It was time for The Kid.

'Watch and learn, boys,' whispered John, 'watch and learn.'

Allan seemed nervous from the word go. Gone was the immense assurance of those earlier practice skims. Without removing his black hoodie, barely bothering to look at the stones on offer, he thrust his hand into the bucket, grabbed one at random and flung it skittishly into the quarry. Lacking speed and short of rotations, it skipped once and sank. A buzz of surprise went round the expectant crowd. 'Easy, lad,' came a voice.

Again his hand went into the bucket and closed around a stone indiscriminately. This time he at least looked down the lane before snaking his arm out and on. The throw was long – by God it was long – but, somewhere around the 50-metre point, and with plenty of kinetic energy still to burn, it hopped marginally outside the line of buoys.

A hush fell over the crowd. Both Donald and Bert were holding their breath. At last, Allan took his time selecting his weapon – maybe too long, for when he stood up, the wind had picked up still further. Out went the arm and away went the stone. Slap. It cannoned into the face of an oncoming wave and disappeared in an explosion of white spume.

There was a stunned silence. People stared, mouths agape. Five times The Kid had won the Bertie but now, in his first pop at the seniors, he had disintegrated. He pulled his hood back over his bowed head and, shoulders slumped, tramped away to the empty spaces of the headland up above.

'Well, well, well,' whispered Jon, shaking his head. 'All that raw talent, but he didn't have the maturity to convert it under pressure.'

'Not mentally ready for it, was he?' agreed Chaz.

Eric Robertson could barely disguise his delight. His 54 metres had been enough to take the crown, knocking Dougie Isaacs off his perch and making him a local hero in the process. No matter that it was the second-shortest winning distance in history, or that it would only have been good enough for fourth the year before. Conditions had been brutal, as the sixty-odd men who failed to score could testify. This weekend had been part of Eric's stag-do celebrations, and he had come away from it a world champion. Beat that.

'People might be saying the weather's too nasty for them, but that smacks of sour grapes,' he crowed. 'Mebbe I'll have to put the wedding on hold now, eh?' He winked at his prospective father-in-law. 'The wimmin will be all over me!'

The crowds began drifting away, bedraggled and cold. I stole a look at the final standings: joint thirteenth place for me, out of 160 men and 260 throwers overall. Three more metres and I'd have been in the top ten. I still wasn't a world champion, and that hurt, but in the circumstances I felt satisfied. I'd done as much as I could.

I walked back across the island with Jon. His own effort of 22 metres had been enough for seventieth, which put him in the top 50 per cent in the world. No matter that two of the under-10s had beaten him. His trip had not been wasted.

In the distance I could see the ferry coming across from the mainland to take people back to their cars. Unsurprisingly it was almost empty, with just the pilot at the rear and one chap standing up at the prow, arms outstretched *Titanic*-style, like a chubby, balding DiCaprio. Or, indeed, Alan Sugar played by a homeless man.

'Fucking hell,' said Jon. 'Is that Dirs?'

I sat down on the quayside and watched speechlessly as the boat docked. Ben leapt clear of the bows like a fawn and jogged over, his arms raised in celebration like a victorious goalscorer.

'Tommy!' he chortled. 'Told you I'd be here, didn't I? It's only taken me 45 hours and 389 quid, but I've made it. Now – where's the stones?'

II

SHOVE

BEN

'Lifes a bumwipe. And then you die.' So reads a graffito on a platform bench at Holton Heath station in Dorset. And as sheets of rain hurtled horizontally towards me, so that it felt as if they might scythe my head from my shoulders, I had to concur. Life at that particular moment wasn't just a bumwipe, it was a bumsuck, a bumsplash and a veritable bumstuffing.

It had taken me five hours to get from Romford to what appeared to be the remotest train station in England, only to discover I was about twenty miles from where I wanted to be. 'Oh, no, you've overshot,' said a curious local as I tramped past a nearby army barracks. 'You want to go back to Wareham. Cabs? We don't even get buses down here.' The internet can make pictures of naked ladies appear on your mobile phone, it can tell you the name of the little bald fella off the Benny Hill show (Jackie Wright, if you're interested), but it can't tell you the ideal way to get from Romford to Blandford Forum. Tim Berners-Lee can poke it. And if you don't know who he is, you can look him up on the internet. And when you discover who he is, I bet you'll ask yourself: why isn't he more famous?

The next train back to Wareham was in an hour's time, putting me in grave danger of missing my second event in a row. I'd sensed that Thomas wasn't very impressed by my late show in Scotland, and it was largely out of guilt that I'd made the trip at all. That and the sudden realization that our quest was coming to an end and I was about as champion as Charlton Athletic. But mainly my trip was a penance, and as a fellow Catholic, I was sure he'd appreciate my sacrifice. I'd let him down at the stone-skimming, but by travelling down to Blandford I was showing I shared his commitment to the cause. If I could surprise him on my return with a winner's trophy, then I was sure I'd be forgiven for my wrongdoings.

The problem being I was already half an hour late for my appointment and I seriously doubted the locals were going to delay the action for some mysterious out-of-towner from the wilds of Essex. 'I've been driving a cab round here for fifteen years and I've only ever taken one fare to Blandford,' said the bemused cab driver as we pootled up from Wareham. 'You wanted to get off at Poole.' Bit late now, but half an hour later and 40 quid lighter I was finally at my destination: The Railway Hotel, home of the 2008 Shove Ha'Penny World Championships. It had only taken me six and a half hours, about the same as it takes to fly to New York.

TOM

Ben's no-show at the stone-skimming had initially annoyed me significantly. I'd done all that research and training, yet he couldn't even be bothered to get there on time. As always, though, it was hard to stay angry with him for long. He'd been so obviously crestfallen at getting all the way to Easdale Island a few minutes too late to skim that I soon became more concerned about his lack of chirp and uncharacteristically unsociable behaviour.

His putative fitness regime had lasted as long as an Italian government, his on/off relationship was off again and he was back on the fags in a big way. Most damaging of all, he'd made almost no progress in our quest to become a world champion. As each day passed, his mood darkened further.

If I ever found myself in a similar slough of despond, I would go out for a long, 13–14-mile run, work everything out in my head and come back weary but revitalized. Dirsy would do the opposite. When Good Ben turned Bad, he'd lock himself in the flat, turn off his phone and bunker down with the black dog.

I decided to cycle across London and take him three of his favourite things to cheer him up: the complete Alan Partridge on DVD, a bottle of Calvados and a set of plastic false breasts. Unfortunately the plan hit snags – three of them.

The first was that the false breasts proved a nightmare to cycle in. Tucked under my top they drew wolf-whistles from passing builders; unleashed they created so much drag that I might as well have been wearing a tit parachute. Secondly, for some unknown reason, I couldn't find a single off-licence in Romford that stocked Calvados. Thirdly, Dirsy was neither opening his door nor answering his phone. Where was he? And what was he doing?

BEN

What I knew of shove ha'penny came largely from a handful of grainy clips I'd found on YouTube of classic seventies TV show Indoor League. For those, like me, too young to remember Indoor League, it consisted of legendary England fast bowler and professional Yorkshireman 'Fiery' Fred Trueman showcasing, in his inimitable words, 'the biggest sporting bonanza of sporting skill I've ever clapped eyes on' – namely 30-year-old men who looked about 60 playing darts, pool, bar billiards, skittles, table football – and shove ha'penny.

'I hear 'enry the Eighth used to knock the old shove 'a'pennies about a bit, when 'e weren't bashing missus,' says Fiery in one piece to camera, before quaffing on a pint of bitter and shoving his pipe in his mouth, just in case any viewers might have forgotten he was a Yorkshireman in the half a second since he stopped speaking. 'I don't know how Barry Stones and Alan Brown of Durham treat their missuses,' Fiery goes on, 'but they certainly can nudge a crafty 'a'penny.' Other nuggets include: 'If Maid Marian and Annie Oakley were alive today, there's no doubt where they'd be – 'ere' ('bollocks to Monte Carlo, Annie, I hear there's some top-class skittles going on in The Queen's Hotel in Leeds'!); 'We've got two of the cockiest blokes – students! – playing table football as though they were Giles and Bremner'; and a classic piece of Partridge-esque table football commentary from Dave Lanning: 'Having failed his degree, he's now working for a turf accountant's in Barnsley . . .' just before the bookie in question sticks an absolute corker in the bottom right-hand corner.

The shove ha'penny segments weren't really long enough for me to get a real feel for the game, but I did work out that it involved two players taking it in turns to 'shove' ha'pennies up a small wooden board with lines drawn across it using the heel of their hand. It appeared to be a game of gossamer touch, and Fiery agreed, telling the viewers that it 'matches the skill and dexterity of the miniature portrait painter'. To a man who struggles to keep within the lines in a colouring book, this was bad news.

I found the rules on the internet, a board and some old ha'pennies I tracked down on eBay, and I was up and practising a couple of days later. The only thing was, I had nobody to practise against. My housemate Matt had eyed the board suspiciously, not wanting to get too close, as if he expected the coins to start moving around of their own volition.

'What is it?' he said, shuffling towards it apprehensively.

'It's a shove ha'penny board.'

'Is that like a Ouija board? Are you gonna have a séance?'

'No, it's an old pub game. Wanna match?'

'An old pub game? Who are you, Fred Dibnah? Bore off, Dirs.'

The reaction had been pretty much the same from other mates, all of whom turned out to be strangely reluctant when asked whether they wanted to pop round for a match. 'Sounds like table-top curling,' said one, 'I'd rather glass myself in the face.' 'Shove ha'penny?' texted my ex-girlfriend Diane. 'Maybe you should think about getting help. I knew it had been for the best.' So I was on my own, and I soon discovered it was a strangely addictive game – and a bloody difficult one.

Each turn consists of a player 'shoving' five coins, each one positioned with the rear end protruding, up the board, which is approximately 14 inches wide and 24 inches long. The exception to this is the first turn, when only three are played. The areas between each pair of horizontal lines are called 'beds' and the object is to push the coins so that they land in the beds without touching the horizontal lines. To win, a player needs to land a coin in each of the nine beds three times. However, once three scores have been made in a bed, any further scores in that bed will be given to the opponent instead, unless the opponent already has three scores in the bed. As Fiery had pointed out, they have been playing versions of the game in English boozers for donkey's years – as far back as the fifteenth century a version was played using groats and thus called shoffe-grote – although shove ha'penny as we now know it is thought to have come into existence in about 1840.

A game for the Nintendo Wii generation it isn't, and I found myself becoming more and more frustrated as coin after coin landed on, and not between, the horizontal lines. This was clearly a game that required serious dedication, deftness and the repeated grooving of one's action. I improved to the extent that one in every few coins was 'floating' into a bed, but the dark arts of 'tickles' and 'cannons' proved depressingly elusive. My only hope was that shove ha'penny had become so unfashionable in recent years that the world championships consisted of me, the landlord of The Railway Hotel and a handful of regulars who could barely see the board. Maybe old Fred from the peashooting would be there?

Blandford Forum is a small market town in Dorset, about fifteen miles north-west of Poole. As always seems to be the way with English market towns, every second premises appears to be a pub, and The Railway Hotel is one of three in Blandford with a twenty-four-hour licence. Which is bizarre when you consider how difficult it is to find a late drink in London at times.

The first thing I noticed as I entered The Railway was that everyone seemed to be covered in chalk. The second thing I noticed was that everyone looked double hard. I had rather expected shove ha'penny's elite players to be of the chunky-cardigan-pipe-smoking persuasion (much like Fiery Fred) but there were more tattoos on display than on an eighteenth-century British galleon. Most of the action was taking place out back in the skittles alley, which is where I met Dale Wills, defending champion and event organizer.

'Where do they play shove ha'penny in Essex?' enquired Dale, who had more inkings than a Maori biker, including a Tottenham Hotspur cockerel on the back of his head. 'Erm, nowhere really,' I replied, 'except in my kitchen in Romford. Got any tips?'

'Yeah, don't wear black,' said Dale, before slapping me on the back and leaving behind a dirty great chalky handprint.

Not that I had much time to digest any pointers – I was immediately ushered towards a board and introduced to my opponent, landlord Nigel Jones. 'Got any tips?' I said to Nigel.

'Yeah, don't wear black,' said Nigel, before slapping me on the back and leaving behind another dirty great chalky handprint. It was clearly a shove ha'penny classic. Then I noticed that the board wasn't a board at all, rather a meaty slab of slate. And the ha'pennies weren't actually ha'pennies, they were metal discs with holes in the middle, polished on one side. I'd only been practising with the wrong bloody equipment. Furthermore, this chalky substance that everyone was covered in wasn't actually chalk, it was arrowroot, and they used it to dust the slates. Nope, I hadn't been doing that either.

Dale's wife Mandy, ladies champion in 1995 and 1997 ('not many kids can say both their parents are world champions,' a proud Dale told me later) was our designated 'marker' or 'chalker', and no more than five minutes after walking through the door, my first-round match was under way.

Nigel kicked off by floating his first three discs into the bottom bay (you only get three discs on your first turn) before turning to Mandy and churning out that old darts line, 'That's what I'm all about, three in a bed.'

'That's right Nige, that's why you're in here playing shove ha'penny,' Mandy shot back.

Then it was my turn, and oh my, this dusted slate was one slippery mother. A feather with the heel of the hand sent my first disc skating across the surface like a puck on ice, and my next two efforts sailed beyond the bottom bed only to land across lines. I managed to rein myself with my final two efforts, scoring two chalks, but slate is to wood in shove ha'penny what grass is to clay in tennis, and I wasn't sure I'd be able to adjust in time.

It soon became clear just how out of my depth I was, with Nigel quickly filling up the nearest beds and pulling off the subtlest of shots: the finest of cuts and ricochets, faint kisses that 'tickled' discs between beds, long 'draws' that glided directly into the furthest bed. It was quite hypnotic. I wasn't about to start messing around with 'tickles', 'draws' and 'cannons', and so I carried on hacking away in my own inimitable style, finding the beds with some shots, finding the lines with others, and sometimes failing to reach as far as the first line at all.

It didn't help that what seemed to me to be perfectly acceptable scoring shots weren't being chalked because, this being the world championships, the discs had to land slap bang in the middle of the beds to count. 'The only thing against the game is the marking,' admitted Dale. 'With darts or skittles it's either in the bed or it's not, or you knock them down or you don't. But with shove ha'penny there can be a discrepancy. Certain markers will mark the ha'penny a little bit closer to the lines than another marker. It's escalated into arguments over the years, and sometimes someone will ask for his marker to be changed.'

But the event's most shocking chapter took place in Leckhampton, Gloucestershire, in 1996, when Barnstaple's John Witcher was disqualified after being caught trying to apply sweat to the slate in order to get his coins to grip. The shameful episode made the national newspapers, Witcher was forced into hiding by outraged locals wielding flaming torches and he is no longer allowed to live within 400 yards of any establishment where shove ha'penny is being played. Not really, but Dale tells me he was a little bit embarrassed about the whole thing. As the organizer of the 1996 event Jeff Bird said at the time, 'You might cheat and get away with it in other sports – but not in shove ha'penny.'

Nigel quickly wrapped up the first leg before surging into an early lead in the next. This was horrific: six and a half hours' travel and I was about to be dumped out less than ten minutes after walking through the door. Surely Nige was going to ease up on the romantic outsider, the raider from Romford, this exotic creature in his midst? Well, no actually. Metaphorically speaking, he bent me over the slate, pulled my pants down and shoved it up me as if he was the Ha'penny King and I was his bitch.

Shellshocked, I limped to the bar for a pint. Part of me wanted to beat a silent retreat, but then it had taken me so long to get there. Plus, I was acutely aware I was walking among the embers of a dying culture. I felt like an anthropologist who had stumbled across some lost tribe, a tribe most people thought had died out years ago, and as such I felt almost duty-bound to record it. And besides, Nige and Dale refused to give me the number for a taxi, so I didn't really have much of a choice.

'It's definitely dying out, without a doubt,' said Dale wistfully as he supped on a Guinness, games going on all around us. 'At the first world championships in 1988, there were about eighty entrants. But the last two years we've been down to thirty-two. So in twenty years, fifty people have gone. There are no up-and-comers, the young kids prefer to play pool or on the fruit machines. It saddens me, of course it does. I love the sport. But you can't force kids to play it. I don't know, it's strange.'

Dale said his kids would probably take up the game, but doubted whether there would be leagues still around to play in. The Blandford League had simply ground to a halt in 2008 because Dale, a construction worker, hadn't been around to run it and nobody had stepped in. It had been very different when Dale was a kid, when almost every pub in the area had a slate and there were shove ha'penny hotspots dotted all over the country. And Newport's Steve Short, the 2005 champion, remembers when his family would gather down the local to play, and when his dad was a legend of the game.

'Those days were far simpler,' explained Steve, a rolled-up Racing Post shoved under his arm and his eyes flitting between me and the TV screen. 'The whole family would come round and play, and me and my brothers played from a very young age. My dad was the first to win the Newport singles three years on the trot. Talk about shove ha'penny in Newport and he'd be held in great esteem. But every town had players like him.'

Steve's dad John is considered to be one of the greats of

the game, a world champion in Durham in 1988 and again in Barnstaple in 2006 at the age of 70, when, in Steve's opinion, he was twenty-five years past his prime. What made his achievements even more remarkable was that both victories had come on 'away' boards.

'Conditions are different all over the country,' explained Steve. 'In Newport we use slate and halfpennies, but no powder. Barnstaple is on wood with halfpennies, but they don't dust the board, they clean it with methylated spirits and paraffin to get the coins to slide. In Radstock they use discs and potato flour, but their beds are an inch and three-quarters, whereas a usual standard size is an inch and a half. Up in Durham it's wood and with old halfpennies. I don't know whether they use powder or what up there.' Jesus, these boys want to get together in a pub or something and do some standardization – if the man Dale considered the finest all-board player in modern shove ha'penny didn't have a firm handle on things, what chance did anyone else have? And there was more.

'Sometimes electric heaters are used to help the flight, and on the wooden boards, players have to read the grain. So it's fair to say that home advantage is key and it's a good effort to get to the semis in someone else's backyard. When my dad won a couple of years ago, he was the oldest bloke in the competition playing on a wooden board and a local bookie had him at 14–1, but no one bet on him. He won the final 3–0. I suppose you could say he's the Andre Agassi of the shove ha'penny world – good on all surfaces.'

Back in the skittles alley, the first-round doubles matches were under way and there was some serious ha'penny being played. Fiery Fred might have talked a load of old Yorkshire ballbags most of the time, but he was bang on with his 'miniature portrait painter' line. As Steve said, 'It's a game of real finesse, and it's the subtleties that separate the good from the average.'

Shove ha'penny, when played well, is a beautiful game to watch, full of deft cuts and deflections and ever-changing angles of attack, each player with his or her own peculiar rhythm. All against a backdrop of subtle gestures, sounds and conventions – the dusting of the discs before each turn, the marker's tapping of the chalk after each score – so deeply ingrained after all these years that perhaps I, as the sole outsider, was the only person in the room to fully appreciate them. The delicate nature of the game was thrown into greater relief by the tattoos and shaven heads of many of the competitors (as well as the amount of beer they were consuming).

Sid Waddell, the hatstand darts commentator responsible for bringing Fred Trueman's Indoor League to British screens, once lamented the fact that most of the games featured on the show had fallen by the wayside, adding, 'I'd love to be remembered as the first man to put shove ha'penny on the television.' And watching the action in The Railway, it occurred to me that the idea of shove ha'penny on TV wasn't actually as ludicrous as most modern minds would have it. For it is a more intriguing and intricate game than its pub cousin, darts, with its relentless shelling of the treble twenty, yet it was only darts that survived. Perhaps it was this intricacy – compared to darts' simplicity – that did for it in the modern age. In 2008, Giant Connect 4 probably had a better chance of getting airtime than shove ha'penny.

While the scene in The Railway's skittles alley was a beguiling one, there was no getting away from the fact it was also a little bit melancholic. For probably the first time on my travels, I was witnessing the best players in the world at a particular sport or game. These weren't men and women who'd turned up primarily for the crack or in the hope of triumphing at some cobbled together, wacky pastime. As impressive as Matthew Wainwright had been at carrying coal, was he really the best in the world, even in Yorkshire? Was Alar Voogla really the world's best wife-carrier? Or George Hollis the best at peashooting? Far more likely, they were just the best of those who happened to turn up on the day. The guys and girls at The Railway, who had been honing their art for years, were the cream, and the feeling that they were among the last bastions of a fading culture seasoned the scene with extra poignancy.

TOM

I finally managed to get hold of Dirsy's flat-mate Matt. 'Where is he?' I asked, seriously concerned.

'Dunno, but he left the house with his new Ouija board,' said Matt. Dear God – it was worse than I thought! He was trying to make contact with the dead, seek inspiration from his sporting heroes of the past – W. G. Grace, Muhammad Ali, his nan. I had to find him before Bad Ben took over for ever.

I did a whistle-stop tour of the major pubs in the Gidea Park/Seven Kings area. Nothing. There were more pubs in London than there were days of the year, and he could be in any of them. Maybe he'd gone further afield. Maybe he was trying to hitch back to Marseille, location of the greatest forty-eight hours of sporting mayhem either of us would ever see. Maybe he'd sold his golf clubs and set of five Fred Perry polo shirts (pastel pink, pastel green, pastel blue, pastel yellow, pastel grey) and used the proceeds to go crazy in Vegas – Bas Vegas, that is, or plain old Basildon to non-locals.

A text arrived from his number. 'Chest-deep in melancholy,' it said. 'The world is moving on, but not everyone is moving with it.' Oh no. I tried phoning but got no answer. Where was he? And could anyone get through to him in there?

BEN

Steve's second-round match against a fellow Newport 'shover' (I just made that up) was a cracker, with all elements of the game on display. 'Sometimes you might need to cut the ha'penny very fine to win a match,' Steve had told me beforehand, 'so you have to keep your nerves under control and your heart-rate down – temperament is as important as hand–eye co-ordination.' Sure enough, with the game still anyone's in the deciding leg, Steve pulled off a shot of excruciating delicacy, cutting a disc into one of the nearest beds and gliding the other into the furthest to seal the match. The competitors fell into each other's arms, and the relief on Steve's face was plain for everyone to see.

With play having started at 11 a.m., by the time the second-round matches had kicked off, pretty much everyone was alcoholically inconvenienced. 'How much booze is too much?' I asked Steve.

'Different players have different levels, it's all about finding your comfort zone,' said Steve.

'When you can't see the fucking lines,' said Dale.

Radstock's Andy Pike appeared to be about twelve pints and half a dozen gin and tonics beyond his comfort zone as he made his way out back to play Dale for their second-round match. But the transformation as he settled above the slate was quite stunning; a monkish calm falling upon him as he filled bed after bed with unerring accuracy. Dale took the first leg comfortably, but mistakes started creeping into his game and Andy came roaring back to take the second before pouring it on in the decider to clinch the match. Dale's reign as shove ha'penny world champion was over. And Andy was badly in need of another pint.

The quarter-finals, semis and final were to take place the following day, and sadly I had to be back in London that night. But before I jumped in a cab down to Poole (not Holton Heath, or Wareham), I had one last pint for the road with Dale, who was in a contemplative mood.

'When I was a small kid I wasn't allowed to play, but we used to sit behind the shove ha'penny board and watch all the adults play. The older people would often not let the youngsters touch their board. You had to show you had respect for the game and really wanted to play. Nowadays, you ask kids in the pubs if they want a game of shove ha'penny and they'll say, "Nah, it's an old man's game."'

Those days of kids huddling round slates in the local pub, hoping upon hope to be allowed to play a leg of shove ha'penny, are gone. Instead they're crouched over computers, dealing cyber drugs, gunning down cyber cops and beating up cyber whores. What would dear old Fiery Fred have said? 'I just don't know what's going off out there,' no doubt.

As I headed back up to London, I weighed up whether to tell Tom about my little excursion or not. On the one hand I'd paid my penance for missing out on stone-skimming a couple of weeks earlier. On the other, I'd had my arse handed to me by the locals. There had been no glory on the backstreets of Blandford Forum. Not for me anyway. A few days later I phoned Dale to find out who had ended up walking away with the £500 winner's cheque. 'Andy Pike,' said Dale. 'He couldn't really stand up, but he was playing some serious shove ha'penny.'

12
UBOGU

TOM

As autumn turned into winter and the Champervan's open-roofed shower filled up with dead leaves, empty crisp packets and roosting finches, Ben and I had a big decision to make. After eleven world championships, we could only make one more. Even if we hadn't been on the brink of the poorhouse after driving the world's least economical vehicle around Britain during a period when petrol cost more than gold, we were running out of weekends. With the chilly weather signalling the end of village fete season, potential events were also getting thin on the ground.

There were only two more world championships left on our original list. The first, something called the World's Greatest Liar, proved hard to locate. I phoned the chap I'd heard was in charge, only for him to tell me that I had the wrong number and should piss off. There followed a slightly awkward exchange where I jokily accused him of lying as part of his role running the World's Greatest Liar contest. He then told me to piss off again, whereupon I repeated my accusation with a little less laughter. It was only when he shouted a complete falsehood about my mother that I realized he might be telling the truth.

The other event was the World Gurning Championships. This had the advantage of an organizer who was both keen to help and reticent on the subject of my mother and chimpanzees. I also felt that we were in with a decent shout of winning. I could do a passable impression of a man with an inflatable face (think Dizzy Gillespie mid-parp crossed with Violet Beauregarde post-gum), while Dirsy on a hangover would be a sight to strike fear into any opponent.

Unfortunately the date was all wrong for us. Only by both pulling sickies from work could we make it, and that seemed pointless. If we bunked off and won, we'd be found out and sacked in seconds. If we didn't win, what was the point of bunking off in the first place?

At the back of our minds, meanwhile, there was an alternative. Gradually, over the months, as the miles and events had gone by, a fanciful idea had taken root. We'd taken part in more world championships than any other men on the planet, benefiting from the hard work, inspiration and enthusiasm of organizers from the Hebrides to the north of Finland. Wasn't it time we put something back? Wasn't it time we held our own world championships?

Admittedly at first glance it was a laughable notion. I was useless with numbers; Ben was so disorganized he was capable of missing two flights from different airports on the same morning. If you asked him to organize a piss-up in a brewery, not only would he fail to turn up in time to let everyone in, but when the doors were forced open they'd find he'd drunk the place dry the night before. Meanwhile I'd be out on a long bike ride having bought the brewery a delivery van that broke down on exposure to air. What sort of hellish shambles would the pair of us come up with?

Then again, Andy Dunlop in Swaton, Anna Huttunen in

Sonkajärvi, Donald 'Melon' Melville on Easdale Island – not to mention Hilary Scase in Congham, Shane Pym in Marshwood and Joy Walker in Witcham – had all managed it. None of them had been superhuman, unless Donald's nickname really did derive from the fact that he possessed one giant testicle.

What was really holding us back, except cold feet and a lack of experience? And time. And money. And a venue. And a sport.

With the sort of old-fashioned British pluck that saw Richard the Lionheart set out on the Crusades or Scott of the Antarctic journey across the, erm, Antarctic, we decided to push on regardless.

'If we're in the public eye, I won't have to give up fags, will I?' asked Ben.

'Relax,' I said. 'Captain Scott got through more tabs than your nan.'

'Makes sense,' said Ben reflectively. 'It's probably how he kept his face warm.'

Our most pressing consideration was to select an event. When we started giving it proper thought, it was both amazing and depressing how many sports had already been taken. Most things that involved hitting a ball with parts of the human body had gone, and those that hadn't were available for a good reason. Could the popularity of football and handball ever be threatened by arseball? You had to doubt it.

Likewise, the possibilities for bats and racquets had almost been exhausted. Short ones, thin ones, strung ones, solid ones – they'd all been thought of. We were reduced to coming up with hybrid sports of an increasingly extravagant nature.

'Golf on ice,' said Ben. 'Toboggans instead of trollies. Snowdrifts instead of bunkers. Whites instead of greens.'

'Nice,' I said, 'but Romford Ice Rink will never allow it. It would get in the way of the heavy petting and fighting.' I stroked my chin. 'Anyway, I'm sure some bloke in Greenland has beaten us to it. What about snookis? Tennis played with snooker balls. Twice as dangerous, half as fast.'

'I've got it,' said Ben. 'Rugbowls. You have to roll a rugby ball as close to the jack as you can, while a 19-stone bastard tries to put you off by punching you in the kidneys.'

Three hours later we were still struggling, although Ben had drawn three nice sketches of Rugbowls in action across the souvenir poster I'd brought back from the Olympics in Beijing. We thought we'd cracked it when we came up with the idea of combining our respective favourite activities, but disappointingly that only produced the World Cigarette-Smoking While Cycling Championships and something called the quadlushthon – a triathlon with a pub-crawl shoe-horned into the middle.

The breakthrough came when we started thinking about the daft games we'd played while at the rugby World Cup in France, parked up in the Bloggernaut in the middle of nowhere between matches. The first had been something we'd christened 'Pint-Glass Fez Bin'. As the name hints, it involved a pint glass, a fez and a bin. Each was upturned and placed on the floor equidistant from us. Players were armed with three scrunched-up balls of paper, and took it in turns taking pot-shots. Landing the ball of paper in the bin was worth one point, the fez three and the pint glass five, reflecting the relative size of each aperture.

It might sound simple, but the tactics that soon developed

were both brutal and labyrinthine. Did you play safe with an opening shot to the bin, knowing that you could be left behind if your opponent nailed a fez? If the other man binned, did you settle for matching him, or attempt to pile on the pressure by landing a hat-shot? And under what circumstances should you go for the riskiest, most lucrative shot of all – the pint-glass five-pointer? The game was so addictive that one Calvados-fuelled match lasted from 11 p.m. to 4 a.m. Only when the pint glass got smashed by some over-zealous dance-based taunting had a halt been called to proceedings.

Trouble was, we were the only people to have ever played the game. Converting enough new players in time to stage a world championship was going to be mighty hard. Then there was the problem with the name. In its existing form, Pint-Glass Fez Bin was far from catchy, and even Carole Vorderman would struggle to make a pronounceable acronym from four consonants.

The second option had none of those problems. Its name? Ubogu. The aim: to say the word 'Ubogu' as many times as you could on a single breath. The audience? Burgeoning. It had started when former England rugby player Victor Ubogu (a cult figure in the game in the 1990s) had posted some chat on our blog, inviting us to join him for drinks in Lens. Later that night, polishing off another few egg-cups of Calvados, Ben had broken a fuzzy silence by slowly repeating the Big Vee's surname in the manner of a priest incanting an ancient prayer. Soon we were both at it. The rules were formulated shortly after: each Ubogu had to be discrete, with no running-together to form an Ubogubogubogubogu. Only one breath could be taken. And that was it.

We'd put a throwaway line about it on the blog and thought nothing more of it. Mere hours later, users began posting their own Ubogu personal bests. Soon the blog was being deluged, and talk was of Ubogu world records. My initial mark of 52 was soon blown away; 60 was reached within a week, 70 a few days later. By the semi-finals in Paris, I'd gone as far as 92, forced upwards by the relentless pressure from Uboguists across the globe.

In the capital we had finally hooked up with Victor and, in an historic moment, taken him on at the sport he had unwittingly given his name to. We switched to the man-on-man version – two players saying alternate Ubogus, last man to say 'Ubogu' wins – and an epic battle had been fought. Victor's cunning use of front-row tactics (nose to nose, bellowing into my face) had helped him to a well-deserved victory, but only after both of us had almost passed out from oxygen depletion.

We had marked the occasion by creating WUF, the World Ubogu Federation, installing Victor as honorary life president and Dirsy and me as vice-presidents. And while neither Ben nor I had played the game much since, the more we thought about it, the more perfect for our current circumstances it seemed. The only argument against was that some naysayers might claim it wasn't a fitting sport for a championship. I had an answer to that: they'd said the same when Major Walter Clopton Wingfield invented something called 'Sphairistike' in 1874 – yet they're still playing lawn tennis, as it's now called, 135 years later.

Ben's answer was simpler. 'Wife-carrying,' he said. 'Egg-throwing. Shin-kicking. What more do these people want?' The Ubogu World Championships it would be.

Our first task was to let the masses know. There was no official ruling on the numbers of participants needed to make something a bona fide world championship, but we felt that around forty was the absolute minimum required – the World Stone-Skimming Championships had begun with exactly that, before quadrupling in size over the next five years alone. One of those forty would also have to be The Big Vee himself. To stage the inaugural Ubogus sans Ubogu would be to admit defeat before we had even begun.

At the same time, Victor was Britain's busiest man. When he wasn't running his hospitality empire from Ubogu Towers he was entertaining high-profile clients at the biggest fixtures in sport. A large swathe of possible dates for the championship was therefore ruled out by clashes with major rugby internationals at Twickenham. While we hoped that one day the Ubogus would be classed in the same bracket as England v Australia (82,000 in the stadium, worldwide TV audience of millions), it was more a three-to-five-year target than an immediate one.

I put in a call to the Uboguphone. After a brisk conversation during which Victor's attention appeared distracted by the three other phone calls and two board meetings he was simultaneously hosting, he agreed a date. He did call me Sandra and ask me to bring through coffee and biscuits, but since it was his party, I decided to let it pass.

Next task was the venue. Wembley Stadium was already booked, Edinburgh Castle too expensive. Reasoning that everything was more exciting after five pints, we downgraded the search to a pub with compliant landlord. For a man who had spent so much time and money in so many boozers, Dirsy had mysteriously few friendly contacts in the business. Rather than open doors, his name seemed to padlock them shut. Three nationwide chains threatened legal injunctions before a friend of a friend came up with a potential solution – a high-ceilinged independent called The Arbiter, midway between Fulham and Hammersmith in west London. As championship venues go, it was an instant classic. Transport links were excellent. The toilets were clearly marked. Beer was quite literally on tap.

Owner Nick recognized the hand of history when he felt it on his shoulders. Even as I explained the concept he was offering to clear a large area for a stage, rig up a PA system and advertise the championships on large chalkboards outside the pub. He even embraced our fanciful idea for a special one-off cocktail to mark the occasion – the Ubogu Juice ('short, powerful and strong enough to bring a scrum to its knees').

Ben, meanwhile, offered to look after the guest-list. In an uncharacteristic burst of organization he created a World Ubogus group on Facebook. Invitations were sent out to anyone we'd ever met, plus a whole heap of punters who had become our Facebook friends through the rugby blog and cricket commentaries. Video footage of my clash with Victor in Paris was circulated on the internet; plans drawn up to sell advertising space on competitors' tonsils.

'It's all good,' said Ben one morning, 'but there's no way Victor's turning up.'

'Relax,' I said. 'He promised.'

'To get you off the phone he did,' said Ben. 'I guarantee he won't come. Sandra.'

'Listen,' I told him. 'If Victor was holding the World Dirs Championships, you'd go, wouldn't you?'

'Only because I'm scared of him,' said Ben. 'He's probably passed stools bigger than me.'

Like a pair of puritanical Victorians we set out to codify the competition. The format was designed to be both scrupulously fair and attractive to spectators: each entrant would do an individual round of Ubogu – competing against the lung, so to speak – with the eight highest scorers going through to the quarter-finals. We would then switch to the more aggressive man-on-man version, with the top qualifier meeting the eighth, the second the seventh and so on. Winners would progress through to the semis and then final.

When playing the game in France we had relied on the Corinthian spirit of those taking part and accepted all Ubogu totals at face value. The sorry example from other, more established sports, however, suggested that the increase in the sport's profile would lead to a concurrent rise in the temptation to cheat. Various options were discussed. I suggested that each competitor be forced to take a vow of honesty with their right hand resting on Victor's shaved pate. Ben preferred a vow of honesty with Victor's right hand fastened around their testicles.

We toyed with the idea of releasing a brightly coloured gas into the air, so that illicit breaths could be easily identified, or sellotaping thin sheets of tissue paper across the forehead and over the mouth, watching closely for any sign of in-suck. Draconian penalties were mooted – life bans from WUF events, peltings with spare stock from the World Egg-Throwing Championships. In the end we settled for something more austere: a single plastic clothes-peg fastened tightly over the nose. It might not have looked pretty, and on the larger-beaked it inflicted painful nostril abrasions, but it was mighty effective.

As far as the legal side of things was concerned, we were fully legit. Aware of the health and safety ramifications of hosting a Worlds, we had secured the services of Jacqui Fenton, one of London's premier respiratory nurses. Jacqui had a lifetime's experience in dealing with people with breathing difficulties. Should there be any repeat of the near-blackouts Victor and I had suffered in Paris, she would be on hand to step in and bring rapid relief. Should the pain all be mental, Ash was there to pour soothing words into troubled ears.

At times it felt great being on the other side of the fence, running the show, trying to incorporate all the best bits of the championships we'd been to and adding a few original touches of our own too. Did the football World Cup have its own lethal cocktail, for example, or the Olympics an Official Clothes-Peg?

Conversely, there were moments when we were both stricken with nerves and nightmares. Forget Victor – would any competitors bother turning up? Would Landlord Nick change his mind and turn us away at the last minute? Would the microphone fail as I took to the stage, the clothes-peg snap, the Ubogu Juice run dry?

Anyway, we couldn't forget Victor. We needed him there. I sent him a 500-word email, detailing again the venue, time and directions, emphasizing how many Uboguists would be there, how much fun it would be, how many Ubogu Juices Ben and I would buy him.

I received the following email back: 'Okay.'

'I told you,' said Dirsy. 'He's not coming. He's shitting himself.'

'He's not,' I said. 'He's just using his BlackBerry.'

'While shitting himself,' said Ben.

At this stage there was no sense that it was a championship which we could actually win. So busy were we organizing everyone else's fun that with a week to go I hadn't Ubogued in months. It was turning into the classic British sporting scenario – we invent the sport, take it to the world and then spend the next 100 years being beaten at it by the latecomers.

A few people looked at my world record and talked up my chances. I laughed them off. Apart from anything else, it seemed the height of bad manners to aim to win a world championships you were actually organizing. Would you allow a child to win the pass-the-parcel at his own birthday party? Of course not. Their present was the day itself, the attendance of all their friends. So it should be with us.

In my quiet moments, of course, I did think about it. After two second places, a semi-final, a fifth, a thirteenth and an eighteenth, I still hadn't been numero uno. I had one shot left. Would I be a bigger hero if I stood aside to let someone else win than if I somehow triumphed myself?

Dirsy stepped in to take my mind off things. It had come as a pleasant surprise when, with a fortnight to go until D-Day, he had offered to source the trophies. We'd thrown about some ideas and decided to follow the All-England Club's lead: a cup for the gentlemen's competition, a plate for the ladies. Thanks to an inspired suggestion from Mini Cheddirs team-mate Tom Williams, we also had a name for the cup – the Victor Ludorum.

The less pleasant surprise, or lack of surprise, was that thirteen days later Ben was yet to lift a nicotine-stained finger. He hadn't even located a shop that sold trophies. Feeling not for the first time like his mum, I found one on Google and printed him out directions. When I saw him next he was clutching a plastic bag.

'Da-da!' he said, pulling out two small wooden shields with shiny plastic crests glued on the front.

'Where's the ladies' plate?' I asked. 'Where's the Victor Ludorum?'

He shoved the shields back in the bag. 'Victor Ludorum?

Victor Ludorum? Where's Victor fucking Ubogu, that's what you want to be worrying about.'

I didn't want to tell him, but I was. A little earlier I'd received a troubling series of texts from the big man.

'How long is the gig tomorrow? Vic,' said the first. I sent something back that significantly underplayed it.

'Cheers,' came the response, lulling me into a brief false calm.

Ten minutes later came another. 'What road is the pub on and what part of London?'

Christ. He wasn't going to make it, was he?

BEN

Victor Ubogu attended Oxford University, drives a yellow Lotus and likes opera. He used to own a bar in Chelsea and now runs a successful travel and hospitality company. In amongst all that, he became a Bath rugby legend and won twenty-four caps for England. To achieve all this, you need plenty of trap. Which is why his monosyllabic emails and texts were making me very nervous. They were the messages of a man who had better things to do on a Saturday afternoon than listen to a bunch of inebriated men and women repeat his name over and over again while holding their breath. Like reading the paper. Or scouring his bath.

I was beginning to wonder if our little idea had been an enormous folly. It was one thing Victor not turning up, but what if no one else turned up either? And why would they? Half the friends on my Facebook page didn't even know who I was. A quarter of them I hadn't seen in more than ten years. And the other quarter were about as reliable as the Champervan. I remembered a time when you could gather fifty mates for a shindig at a few days' notice. But as I lay there under my duvet, staring at the ceiling, that seemed like a very long time ago. I blamed marriage mainly. And babies. Whatever the reasons, this had all the hallmarks of the biggest bastard flop since Heaven's Gate.

TOM

The morning of the championship I got up early, unable to sleep. Outside frost lay twinkling on the roads and gardens. Curtains were still closed along the street. This was it – the final few hours of our quest. I crept downstairs, pulled on my cycling gear and headed out on the bike.

As I pedalled, I thought back to how it had all started, sitting in the Bloggernaut in that sodden car park in Boulogne. It felt like a long time ago. We'd been to places I'd never heard of, carried coal, kicked shins, dropped eggs, skimmed stones. We'd also shaken hands with eleven world champions. By tonight it would be twelve. By tonight it would all be over.

Waiting for me in Richmond Park was Tom Williams, up in town for the big event, keen like me to clear head and lungs with an early-morning ride-out. With him were the four other members of Team Wales.

'You'll like this, Fordyce,' said Medz, one of the boys. 'We were in the pub last night, and there was a random bloke in there talking about the Ubogus. He didn't know we were going or anything, but he knew about the championship. I think it's gone viral.'

It had gone viral. Jesus. We were going to be swamped!

An awful vision filled my head: hundreds of clamouring Uboguists banging on the pub's walls, shattering the windows with bricks, smashing down the doors, rampaging through the bar and carrying a screaming Victor over their heads, out into the street and away to the hills. We were facing one of those internet horror-stories that made the ten o'clock news – two clowns inadvertently triggering a riot with an idiotic prank that goes terribly wrong.

What had we done? What had we been thinking?

It was with a heavy sense of dread that I walked down North End Road a few hours later and pushed fearfully at The Arbiter's main door. There were two people in there. One was the barman, and the other wasn't Victor.

I wasn't sure whether to be relieved or panicked. The invites had told people to arrive from midday onwards. It was 12.45 p.m. Excellent – we hadn't been overrun. Shit – where was everybody?

Still, I reasoned, we'd said that registration didn't open till 1 p.m., with the competition itself under way an hour later. There was plenty of time, and no reason to worry.

By 1.45 there were six of us. Three of them were my mates, another was my girlfriend and the sixth was Ben.

I was now on my third Guinness, Ben on his fourth. We'd both had Ubogu Juice chasers. I placed the trophies on the bar and tried not to let my panic show. Ben disappeared out of the door for his fourteenth fag of the hour. With that, his constant trips to the toilet and a ten-minute spell in the McDonald's next door, our numbers were effectively down to just five.

Jon, veteran of the stone-skimming, gave me a look. 'Feeling anxious?' he asked, as I repeatedly looked at my watch and then out at the empty pavement. I tried to sound ballsy and upbeat. 'Tube's probably up the spout,' I said. 'And the traffic's dreadful on a Saturday.' Ben came striding back in from a deserted street. 'We'll push the start back a touch, shall we Tommy?' he said. I bought another round of Guinness. What if Victor arrived now? What if he walked in and saw this?

BEN

This was a fucking disaster. Bollocks to Victor, what if my mates came in now and saw this? They'd think I didn't have any mates. I'd like to relate that my mobile phone was buzzing off the hook with friends informing me they wouldn't be able to make it. But most of them didn't even bother. And these weren't just passing friendships, these were people whose weddings I'd attended, people who I'd laughed and cried with.

Maybe it was my fault. Had I been too distant? Their girlfriends didn't like me? I hadn't laughed and cried enough? This wasn't right. I had 315 friends – it said so on Facebook.

TOM

My phone bleeped three times in quick succession. Three messages and three more drop-outs. It bleeped twice more. Someone had forgotten the name of the pub, another was running late, but at least they were on their way.

When I came back from the toilet, I had to step round a couple of new arrivals. There was no squeezing past to be done, but the pub was definitely a fraction fuller. There was a trio by the bar, a pair in the corner and a couple of chaps by themselves. All of them seemed interested in the trophies on display. If by some chance they weren't here for the Ubogus, they were about to find themselves press-ganged.

With a squeak of brakes three black cabs pulled up outside. A load of blokes in polo shirts piled out. It was Dirsy's Romford boys, hot-tailed over from Liverpool Street. A few steps further back were another group of familiar faces. It was my lot – eight, nine, ten of them. How many were in here now – thirty? Thirty-five?

The barman was busy. He'd had to call into the back room for assistance. There was a large printed notice on the bar. 'Ubogu Juice' it said. 'Just £4.20 a glass.' It seemed extortionate until you saw how much vodka was being thrown into the cocktail shaker. All around, people were wincing as they saw the price and wincing again as the fiery drink sizzled down their gullets and set light to their stomachs.

The numbers now coming through the doors should have calmed my nerves. They actually just made it worse. Shortly I would have to stand on stage and address this rabble for anything up to three hours. All of them would want to know where Victor was.

Victor. The name was flashing on my mobile. It was Victor!

'Victor!' I croaked into the phone, trying to exude a bonhomie and confidence I didn't feel. I waited for his big excuse. His car had broken down, or his alarm had failed to go off, or he'd been recalled to the England team at the age of 44. He was sacking us off.

'Tom?' said a reassuringly deep, well-educated voice. 'How far is the pub from McDonald's?'

'Adjacent,' I said, heart in mouth.

'Well, then,' said Victor. 'I'm at the door.'

I looked up. Blocking the entrance was the massive, unmistakable silhouette of a former international prop-forward.

'Shitting hell!' I heard Dirsy shout. 'It's the Big Vee!'

He'd come. Sweet chariots above, he'd made it! I signalled to the barman for a Guinness and Ubogu Juice and dashed over to sink my hand into the enormous Ubogu paw. The thick black roll-neck jumper he was wearing only served to emphasize his enormous physique. Mentally, however, he seemed a little edgy. He glanced around at the drinkers, as if to gauge whether he'd made the right decision turning up, or how quickly he could leave without appearing rude.

I attempted to steer him deeper into the pub with a firm hand on the elbow. I might as well have tried to manoeuvre a mountain. 'We'll start in five,' I told him, making desperate hurry-up gestures to Dirsy behind my back.

Jon had been going round with a pen and paper, taking down names of those who wanted to compete. With a surge of pride I saw that the list filled two sides of A4 paper. We'd gone way past the magical mark of forty. Beyond all doubt, we were a world championship.

I scanned the names. Five in particular stood out.

Big Al. 6 feet 7 inches tall, lungs the size of hot-air balloons. Winner of several spontaneous Ubogu-offs in preceding weeks.

Rob Murray. Mate of Dirsy, professional opera singer. Diaphragm control to die for. Able to sing entire arias without taking a breath.

Konkers Kirkwood. Pal of mine since age of two. Metabolism of a sparrow. Could swim underwater without snorkel for several miles.

Tom Williams. Semi-finalist in Stilton, accomplished amateur sportsman. Lungs trained since birth by regular singing of 'Land of My Fathers' in crowded rugby stadia.

Ben Dirs. Smoker since school years, lungs like rotten peas. Seemed to be holding three different drinks; already unsteady on feet.

BEN

And five that didn't stand out . . .

Kev O'Shea. *The most cynical man in England. No doubt thinks he's too cool to throw himself into Ubogu, despite the fact he's 5 feet 3 inches and prematurely bald.*

Steve Brooks. *Had his wedding in Las Vegas the previous week. Just happy to be alive.*

Matt Conti. *My housemate. Very large frame would suggest massive lungs, but he smokes even more than me. Bulbous nose, peg-fitting might prove a problem.*

Steve Rackham. *After several lagers, struggles to remember his own name, even if asked to say it over and over again.*

Random French Bloke. *Trying to work on his laptop in the corner. Tried to explain the rules to him, but he didn't have a ruddy clue what I was talking about.*

TOM

I forced my way through to the area that had been cleared for the stage. The microphone was waiting on a stand. Ben was standing next to it, pointing it out to me. I would be doing the talking, then. Hmmm.

The last time I had spoken in public had been an unmitigated disaster. Called upon to host a jokey quiz at an athletics club's Christmas dinner, I had misjudged both the atmosphere and the number of mulled wines I'd got through. When an old gent had read out the question, 'What do you call a bird that can lift heavy weights?' I'd jumped to my feet and, with an expression of delight on my face, shouted, 'Fatima Whitbread!' There had been a horrified silence before the old boy piped up again, his voice quavering with fury. 'No,' he had said. 'The answer is "a crane".'

I looked out at the sea of faces and cleared my throat. The Ubogu Juices I'd been nailing had come to my aid. While my legs had gone numb, so had my nerves.

'Ladies and gentlemen,' I began, 'today, a great man walks among us – a man who struck fear into evil men, who performed miracles on the sporting field, who gave his name to a craze that is taking over the world.' For fuck's sake, Fordyce, I thought. Where the hell are you going with this? Get a grip, man, get a grip . . . 'He is the reason we are all gathered here today. Let us welcome him into the room and into our hearts. I give you . . . VIIIICTOOOR. OOOOOBOOWGOOOOOO!'

A roar swept the room as Victor edged his way through to the front, shaking well-wishers' hands and being slapped on the back with boozy enthusiasm. A chant went up from the ranks. 'UBOGU! UBOGU! UBOGU! UBOGU! UBOGU!'

'Victor,' I said, shoving the microphone under his nose, 'twenty-four England caps, 14,000 appearances for Bath, representing your country in World Cups – where does today stand in that list?' He barely batted an eyelid. 'It's right up there,' he said, nodding. 'It doesn't get much bigger than this.' Bless you, I thought, and all who sail in you. An hour after the published start time, it was time to begin.

The tension was evident in the faces and performances of the first few called to the stage. Each went through the same ritual – a handshake from Victor, a brief pre-match interview from me and a clothes-peg on the nose from Ben. They then began their own idiosyncratic preparations, some working through deep-breathing exercises, others working through a fresh Ubogu Juice. When they were ready to go, they raised their thumb, a hush would fall, and they started to Ubogu. Ben counted silently as the faces turned purple and eyeballs rolled back into heads. When the contestant was on his knees, unable to give any more, Ben signalled the end and, like a darts official, announced their score.

Initial totals were markedly lower than most expected. The pressure of performing in front of so many people, let alone The Big Vee, sent pulse-rates through the roof. Numbers that people could do in their sleep suddenly became distant targets.

Kev O'Shea went out fast but ran out of gas at 17. Tom Lucas, a posher lookalike of Bob Hoskins in *The Long Good Friday*, collapsed on 5. Dom Tait, summoned to the stage halfway through his lunchtime steak, drew applause for a bloodstained 47. The first to break the half-century mark was

Bettsy. This was a man who loved to cycle but lived deep in the inner city. As a result he did most of his riding on rollers in his living room while watching *The World At War* on his DVD player. Having held his breath through most of episode twenty-three ('The Battle for the Pacific'), not to mention episode six ('Banzai! Japan'), his lung control was magnificent, and 56 was a fitting reward. Less impressive was Steve Rackham, disqualified by Referee Dirs for running his Ubogus together into an unintelligible and illegal monoword.

The range of different Uboguing styles was extraordinary. Some brought Eastern influences to play, murmuring their Ubogus like a mantra. Others went conversational, chirping away like sparrows. 'Ubogu? Ubogu? Ubogu?' Subdued applause greeted the lower scores, gasps of astonishment the biggies.

All the while, Victor sat nearby, perched on a bar-stool, accepting drinks and plaudits with grace and gratitude. Gone was the caution of earlier. Now he was fully involved, shouting out advice, taking photos, dishing out good-luck hugs. Even when Ben's flatmate Matt risked his ire by mistakenly referring to him as 'Hector Gububoo' he remained jovial. To be on the safe side, Dirsy disqualified Matt and banned him from all future WUF promotions.

Then the big cats came out of the jungle to play. Konkers Kirkwood breezed out a 58 and walked off announcing, 'There's more to come.' Opera singer Rob Murray saw that and raised it to 68, barely breaking sweat. Tom Williams confirmed his Stilton class with a 62, despite being confronted not only with someone who had scored his sole international try against Wales (Ubogu), but also with a man whose face he had been forced to don as a grotesque mask (Dirs).

Clear patterns started emerging. Something seemed to happen to people's lip control as they broke through the 30 barrier; perfectly enunciated Ubogus became Udogoobs and Boogoboos. The mentally strong could get it back, but others never recovered. I could see a steady stream of contestants queuing up for consultations with Ash.

'It's time for Ben Dirs!' announced Ben Dirs.

'Who's counting for him?' asked Kev O'Shea.

'I am,' boomed Victor.

For a man whose lungs contain more tar than the M1 motorway, he put in a decent effort. Forty was no disgrace – unlike many others, Ben produced one of his best-ever efforts when it mattered most. Unfortunately for him, his best-ever effort was still 30 per cent short of the anticipated quarter-final cut-off point. With a shrug of his shoulders he accepted a bear-hug from Victor and returned to his refereeing post. It was a mark of the man, I felt, that rather than wallow in the horrible fact that his own world championship crusade had come to an end, his thoughts were only for the event itself.

BEN

So that was that then – my odyssey was over. But there's nothing like an Ubogu Juice to numb the pain. Maybe it would sink in later, or more likely the following day. But, for now, there was a world championship to help run, and a world championship to be won. It just wouldn't be me who was winning it . . .

TOM

I was now feeling the effects of three hours on the Juice. My commentary was veering between the soporific ('He breathes in . . . and out again. Now in. And now the breath comes out . . .') and the suicidal ('Your first time? An Ubogu virgin, you say? Fancy a virgin, Victor?').

Big Al's deep bass rumble shook the room and put him in joint first with Rob on 68. 'Merely laying down a marker,' he boomed, as people clutched vibrating glasses and pictures fell off the walls. Two lads off Facebook – Roo Mower and Tom O'Connor, both clearly assiduous trainers – weighed in with big scores of their own to move comfortably into the top eight. Soon there were just two more competitors to go: me, and The Big Vee himself.

A hush fell as Victor stepped forward and unclipped the clothes-peg from the mic stand. He brought it to his nose and stopped. There was a gasp of horror from the rear of the room as someone realized what was about to happen. 'Ah,' said Vic calmly, 'I think we might need a bigger peg.'

Ben, to his credit, thought on his feet. 'Who wants to touch the Ubogu nose?' he yelled. 'Too late! I'm doing it!' Waving his forefinger and thumb in the air, he reached out with a flourish and pinched the nostrils shut.

I wouldn't have blamed Victor if he'd used that as an excuse for what followed. At his own world championship, with the eyes of the entire pub on him, he thundered out to 16 – and then suddenly, dramatically, broke down entirely.

The place was in uproar. Dirsy was reeling away with his head in his hands, his jaw slack. Betting slips were being ripped up all around. I grabbed the microphone and dived in. 'Victor – Christ, man – what happened? Where's the monster who destroyed me in Paris?'

He looked me in the eye. 'My time at the top is over,' he intoned gravely. 'The mantle must be passed on.'

'And what now?' I asked. 'Retirement? The seniors tour?'

'I shall sleep on it,' he said. 'Let the battle recommence.'

I handed the mic to Ben and emptied my lungs of air. This was the technique I had developed in France – get rid of everything, refill to the top, empty again and repeat. Ben handed me the peg. I anchored it tight and slowly raised my thumb.

'Ubogu. Ubogu. Ubogu. Ubogu.' The first 20 were easy – what I called the free ones. Nothing hurt, nothing worried me. 'Ubogu. Ubogu. Ubogu.' I kept my eyes on the floor and my body as still as possible. That must be 50, I thought, my chest tightening and my nostrils fighting the peg. 'Ubogu. Ubogu.' My lungs started burning and my lips fell out of sync. I stuttered. The crowd howled. 'Objection overruled!' shouted Ben. With a desperate effort I hauled myself back on track with my last few teaspoons of air. 'Ubogu. Oo-bo-gu. Oo-g- . . .' I was gone.

'Eighty-two!' yelled Ben. I was into the quarters.

BEN

Controversy. Where would any self-respecting world championship be without it? Some in the crowd thought Tom's 'Ubogus' had stopped being 'Ubogus' at around the 25 mark and started sounding more like 'Bogos'. But this was a sport of rare subtlety, and his 'Ubogus' had been good enough for me. Besides, I had to make sure at least one of us got through to the head-to-head stages . . .

TOM

It was just as tight in the ladies' plate competition. Although the number of entrants was lower than for the gentlemen's, the scores were just as impressive. Victor certainly seemed to be enthralled, not least when a pre-match lucky hug with my girlfriend extended past the one-minute mark, or when a peck on the cheek of my youngest sister Saranna became another peck, and another peck, and another.

'Victor,' I warned down the mic, emboldened by the booze, 'Hands off in the ruck . . .'

Two contestants were lung-and-tonsils above the rest and went straight into the final: the nerveless, blonde-haired Anna Lucuk, over from Geneva for the occasion, and the other representative from the Fordyce family, Saranna. 'I've been drilling her for years,' I announced with a tear in my eye, before being drowned out by the Romford crew's cackles. The Big Vee gave me a look. 'Foolish,' it said, 'very foolish.'

The hiatus before the quarter-finals was brief. The queue for both the toilets and bar was now long. Snatches of conversation buzzed around the pub. 'My lips went totally blue,' I heard someone say, wonderingly. 'I went dizzy,' said another. 'When I came back to the table I couldn't make out what was going on.' Thank God we'd had the foresight to get respiratory nurse Jacqui F on board.

Konkers was trying to console Bettsy over his first-round

elimination. 'That was tough up there,' he was saying. 'I was way out of my comfort zone.'

'Last time I felt this low was when I got to the end of my *World At War* DVD,' said Bettsy sadly. 'I just sat there in my sweaty cycling shorts, watching the bonus feature.' He shook his head at the memory. 'It turned out to be a series of German artists' portraits of Hitler. What I didn't realize was that my neighbour was on the path outside, looking through the window. There I was on the sofa, half-naked, staring at slowly rotating pictures of the Führer. He'd only popped round to return a spanner.'

Victor was standing on the pavement outside, talking into his BlackBerry. 'It's insane,' I heard him say, 'but it's rather good fun.'

Ben drained a cider and stepped forward unsteadily to announce the quarter-final draw. The line-up and first round rankings read as follows:

Tom Williams (5) v Tom O'Connor (4)
Al Herbert (2=) v Roo Mower (6)
Rob Murray (2=) v Konkers Kirkwood (7)
Alex Husk (8) v Tom Fordyce (1)

The tension ratcheted up a notch. No one quite knew which tactics would be employed now we'd switched to the man-on-man, 'alternate Ubogu' format. Was it better to respond as rapidly and aggressively as possible, or to linger over your reply and watch your opponent squirm? Should you stay stock still, preserving your precious oxygen supply, or aim to intimidate with the bullish front-row tactics Victor had debuted in Paris? If you won the toss, should you opt to lead out and take the first Ubogu, or sit back and let the other man go off at the front?

I brought The Big Vee back to the front for a quick interview. 'Which Uboguists have impressed you most?' I asked. He paused for thought. 'Opera Man, just ahead of Welsh Lad,' he declared, in the style of a particularly suave racing commentator. And the ladies? 'The blonde ones,' he said with relish, winking at the crowd.

Toms O'Connor and Williams took to the stage. Ireland v Wales was always one of the best rugby fixtures in the calendar, a boozy Celtic brotherhood eliminating the edge present when England were involved. So it proved in this match-up. The exchanges were clean and crisp, the pronunciations clear. There was no nasty business, none of the rough stuff that would mar later bouts. After a splendid ding-dong, every bit as close as the respective qualification scores suggested, Wales came out on top. 'A big shout out to Ash,' panted Tom W afterwards, raising his hand to his mentor at the back of the room. 'He's transformed my focus – transformed it.'

The second bout was an altogether darker affair. 'I'll be using some full-on front-row tactics,' warned Roo in his pre-match interview, drawing a nod of approval from Victor. 'Whatever,' said Big Al, deep and dismissive. 'If you muck around, you'll only use up your own energy.'

Credit to Roo for spotting the big man's weakness. He'd got his tactics absolutely spot-on. From the very first shout of 'LET'S UBOGU!' he was in his opponent's face, jabbing his peg up into Al's chops, going eyebrow-to-eyebrow, switching from quiet to loud with dizzying speed. Al was like a giraffe being attacked by a hyena, twisting this way and that, unable to work out where the next bite would come from. 'Ubogu?' he would occasionally bellow, only for Roo to smash him back down with an instant 'Ubogu!' of his own.

The end came in dramatic fashion. Al, weak of knee and empty of lung, let out a last, desperate Ubogu with a sound like a dying tuba. 'Ubogu,' said Roo, and raised his hands in celebration.

In the background a baby started screaming. The unmistakable smell of freshly filled nappy drifted across the room. 'Bloody hell,' said Bettsy, a look of wonder on his face. 'Al must have hit the brown note.' I'd read about this phenomenon – an infrasound frequency so low that it causes kids to shit themselves – but until this point had assumed it was an urban myth. No more. Truly we were witnessing history today.

More remarkable still was the Konkers Kirkwood v Rob Murray battle. Barely had two Ubogus been exchanged when Rob took matters into his own mouth. Snatching the mic, he leaned back and let rip with magnificent, soaring song. 'OOOOOoooOOO. Boe-wooooaaa. Gooo. HOOOO!'

From a pub in west London we were suddenly transported to the stage at La Scala. Passers-by pressed their noses against the window panes. Flunkies threw carnations at Rob's feet. Grown men wept. The only witness not wildly applauding and whooping was Konkers, his face a picture of Kirkwood kalm. 'Ubogu,' he murmured, utterly unmoved.

Rob still had hold of the mic. 'OOOOOoooOOO. Boe-wooooaaa. Gooo. HOOOOOOO!' he warbled again, even louder, longer and more lovingly.

'Ubogu,' repeated Konkers quietly.

It was too much for Rob. Ripping off his clothes-peg, he took a deep lungful, held his hand outstretched to Victor and fell gloriously on his own sword. 'Ooohoo-hooo-hooo, boohoo-hooo-hooo. Gooo-hooo. Gooo-hoooo . . .' The beautiful notes swelled and swooped, sailing high, dipping low, teetering at the top, carrying us all rapt with them. I don't know how long it lasted – a minute? two minutes? – because, like everyone else, I was lost in the wonder and beauty of it all. Never before had a world championship defeat been so sweet, so splendid.

'He scared the hell out of me,' admitted Konkers afterwards. 'I was on the verge of panic – but then I thought, let him sing. Let him blow himself out.'

After that, my own quarter-final could only be anti-climactic. With the pub still awash with wonder at Rob's display, concentrating was mighty hard. I fell back on my breathing drills, focusing on the basics and getting my heart-rate down. I knew from Alex's qualification score that a par performance should be enough to see me through, but it was a tougher tussle than his eighth place suggested.

Although he began with a light, chatty approach, he'd clearly been holding something back. Cunning, I thought, releasing small amounts of carbon dioxide with each Ubogu to prevent my lungs from exploding like over-filled inner-tubes. Taller by a couple of inches, and buoyed by the occasion, Alex took me to my outer limits. If it hadn't been for my Ubogu experience he'd probably have seen me off, but I'd been to those places before. I knew that, when it gets to the nitty-gritty, when you're out on your feet and start seeing stars, you have to keep pushing. If you're hurting, they're hurting too. As the room swam before me, he staggered sideways and was gone.

And then there were four. Roo Mower, Tom Williams,

Konkers Kirkwood and yours truly. Within the hour, one of us would be a world champion.

The pub was now rammed. People would have been on the edge of their seats, had there been any seats left. Empty glasses were piled high behind the bar. Fresh Ubogu Juices were being shaken, stirred and sunk in seconds. Victor, his excuses forgotten and his attention total, watched on engrossed as Roo and Tom went to war.

Once again, Roo used his peg as a nasal lance, jabbing Tom on his own peg, going in so close that at one stage their lips almost met. When Tom proved resolute, he switched tactics and sank lower on every Ubogu until he was kneeling on the floor, hands behind his back, face raised in supplication. Again, Tom stayed strong, and Roo was forced to his feet.

It was Uboguing of the highest quality. For the first time we saw the pause being utilized. Tom withheld his response for what seemed like an age; Roo squirmed as the lack of air bit hard. Both men were going pale, their lips draining of blood and their eyes closing. Ubogu by Ubogu, their air was running out.

It was Tom who broke first, but there could only have been molecules in it. Roo, just sixth in qualifying, had come storming through the ranks to stand within breathing distance of the title. For Tom there was only heartbreak and despair. For the second world championship in a row, he had fallen at the penultimate hurdle. While Roo hugged Tom O'Connor delightedly, his berth in the final secured, a distraught Tom stumbled away through the crowd.

Konkers. If I'd had a choice I'd have faced anyone but Konkers – my oldest friend in the world, compadre from a time when we'd just learned to walk all the way through the ensuing thirty-two years. We'd spent endless hours as kids playing every sport under the sun – running, swimming and cycling; football, cricket and table tennis; throwing, catching and diving. As we'd got older we'd incorporated the drinking, dancing and partying, but we always returned to sport. We were already looking forward to the games of bowls we'd be playing as pensioners.

It was like being drawn against my brother. I knew better than anyone else how long he could hold his breath. This was a man capable, while in a swimming pool, of performing a mushroom-float for upwards of two minutes. 'Is he dead?' a lifeguard had once memorably asked me.

For his part, there was the small matter of my numerous Ubogu world records and dominant scoring in the qualifiers. As we warmed up, Dirsy standing by to adjudicate, the intensity of the moment threatened to overwhelm us both. Maybe because of that, the start was slow. For the first 25 Ubogus you might have been watching a rehearsal, so lacking were the sort of showy tactical sallies seen earlier. Then, without warning, the pace suddenly picked up.

Konkers accelerated first, throwing a trademark raised eyebrow and two upturned palms. I responded with a questioning style of my own. 'Ubogu?' 'Ubogu?' Konkers went again, this time looking to the crowd, winking provocatively and turning back with a smile playing across his lips. 'Ubogu,' he said leisurely, like a man selecting a cigar. I held his gaze and my breath for what seemed like an age. 'Ubogu,' I said finally, shrugging my shoulders.

A rapid-fire exchange followed. From a stamina point of view it was suicidal, burning through our already-depleted reserves, but we were locked together, careering towards the edge of the cliff. I could see he was struggling, but so was I. I had about five Ubogus left in me, seven if I could force a fraction more air out with my diaphragm.

'Ubogu.' 'Ubogu.' I began to see black spots. 'Ubogu.' 'Ubogu.' We were both leaning forward, trying to squeeze the last drops from our lungs. 'Ubogu.' 'Ubogu.' His face swam in front of me.

I was on my very last Ubogu, staring into the abyss, when Konkers hit the deck. A moment later my legs went too and I collapsed to the ground. On the front row, Konkers' five-month-old son Finley burst into tears and began to howl inconsolably. Dirsy was shouting with excitement.

'Our finalists,' he was yelling. 'Roo Mower . . . and Tommy!'

BEN

Women's finals at Wimbledon are hardly ever as good as men's finals. That's just an uncomfortable fact. Unforced errors, collapses and grunting. That's what women's finals at Wimbledon mean to me, and that's why hardly anyone ever remembers them. And it's not much different with Ubogu. Call it the occasion, call it nerves, call it a fucking shambles.

Not that the final between Anna and Saranna was without drama, with the two resets caused by mispronunciation keeping the crowd oohing and aahing throughout. But just how two intelligent ladies could repeatedly forget a three-syllable name when that three-syllable name had been uttered upwards of 5,000 times in the previous couple of hours is beyond me. Oh, Saranna won by the way, just don't ask me the score . . .

TOM

Was Saranna's win a lucky omen? Or was it asking too much for two Fordyces to be crowned world champion on the same day?

I excused myself and went to the toilets. I found an empty cubicle, locked the door behind me and sat down to gather my thoughts. I had been here before – not in the cubicle, although the one next door had seen action after the nervous qualification round – but on the brink of a championship final. At the shin-kicking I'd barely had time to recover from my semi before I'd been thrust forward to face Bulldog; at the egg-throwing we'd had almost too long to wait. At the snail-racing – well, the chances of me being derailed today by a randy mollusc were hopefully slimmer.

I opened the door and glanced at my reflection as I washed my hands. Our last world championship, our last chance. I could hear the hubbub building outside. The memory of all those narrow misses came flooding back: the embarrassment of the thrashings at the nettle-eating and peashooting, the envy of watching Alar Voogla being awarded his trophy at the wife-carrying and George and Joe cavorting in their egg-stained capes at Swaton. I wiped my hands dry and walked back into the bear-pit.

It's the small details I'll always remember – Ben tossing the coin, Roo calling incorrectly, me giving him the honour, the shouts of 'Stay over him!' as he went down low and brought his peg up into my chest. Fixed in my mind is an image of him, beads of sweat on his forehead, cheeks losing their colour, staring at me wide-eyed as the suffocating shakes hit us both at exactly the same moment. Only briefly did doubt cross my mind, when he began smiling dreamily as we traded the final few blows.

I should have recognized the signs of imminent asphyxiation more easily. In slow motion I watched him reel away in agony. The peg was off his nose, his knees on the floor, his head shaking. Even as my legs buckled I was aware of Ben yelling, of Victor applauding, of the strange sense of relief that came flooding through me. Ben pulled me to my feet. 'Aarrghhhh,' he seemed to be shouting, 'aarrghhhh.'

Roo staggered over and we embraced. An enormous black hand grabbed me round the neck. 'Congrats, champ,' said Victor, and thrust a small wooden shield with a shiny plastic crest glued on the front into my grasp. I stared out at the crowd, and then back at Ben. In the distance I could hear Ash shouting. 'Smell the taste of victory! Smell the taste!'

Ben grinned at me. 'We're world champions, Tommy!' he whispered. 'We're world champions!'

EPILOGUE

BEN

What in Ubogu's name had that barman been putting in my Ubogu Juice? And where in Ubogu's name was I? It wasn't supposed to end like this, wedged under a radiator in a strange living room, rain splattering against the window, evening already drawing in. I wanted to cry. Then I remembered – Tommy had pulled it off, he'd won the Ubogu World Championships! And then I wanted to cry some more . . .

Not that I envied Tom his victory, although I won't deny there had been times in the preceding months when our marriage had been sorely tested (on discovering he'd enrolled us for coal-carrying, for example). But it signalled the end of our adventure. And the landing was going to be hard.

I grabbed the side of a sofa, hauled myself to my feet and found my way to the kitchen, where Tom was sat gazing at his trophy. 'All right champ?' I said. Tom didn't reply. Instead he breathed on his prize, pulled it towards him and gave it a polish with his vest.

'What a day,' I continued. 'Not that I remember a great deal of it. I've got a text from Konkers – he says something about prawn crackers. And what was I saying about Jesus?'

'Doesn't matter, son,' said Tom. 'Nothing else matters

today. We're world champions at last. And, despite what you said about Jesus, he wouldn't begrudge us that.'

I was about to point out that I wasn't actually a world champion at all, but I was quite touched by Tom's use of 'we'. While competition had sometimes crept in between us – will I ever witness anything more beautiful than Tom retching on nettles? – for the most part we'd managed not to be so vulgar. We'd been a team. Just me, Tom and the Champervan – the oddest trio since the Thompson Twins – chasing all over the country, and sometimes beyond, in our quest for glory.

TOM

It was peculiar waking up that Sunday morning, and not only because Ben's snores were somehow travelling through two closed doors and several thick walls. I thought I'd feel fantastic, but I actually felt a little bewildered.

I could handle the bellows of 'Fix!' from Big Al as Victor had handed me my trophy (when you reach the top, you're bound to awaken jealousy among those beaten on the way) and I could deal with Dirsy's rapid post-ceremony descent into Juiced-up madness. For one thing they hadn't been my prawn crackers that he had done that unmentionable thing to, and for another he'd apologized several times for what he attempted to do to my little sister.

No – it was something else. At the same time as feeling a huge sense of satisfaction and pride at being crowned world champion, there was something missing. Why wasn't I climbing the walls with joy, spraying champagne out of my bedroom window, getting a commemorative tattoo inked across my lower cheeks?

I thought back to Boulogne and the conversation in the hypermarché café that had started it all. I'd thought a world title would mean a victory parade on an open-top bus, but the only slow motor journey on the cards was driving Ben home in the open-roofed Champervan. It wasn't even much of a consolation when I subsequently got what appeared to be my first groupie. 'So, have u considered entering the slip n slide championships at the playboy mansion??' read the Facebook message from a blonde I'd never met called Sasha. 'I can get u an invite if u like?! xxx' What was the point? I had a girlfriend, I couldn't afford the airfare to Los Angeles and Sasha was probably Ash in disguise anyway.

I sat at the kitchen table, waiting for Ben to wake up. For about two hours, soundtracked by the industrial rasp of his sleeping breaths, I flicked through photos of the events and people who'd made up our year.

BEN

Like medieval explorers, we'd seen things few people had ever seen. Rory McGrath stuffing straw down his jeans in the Cotswolds. Seven-year-old dancers simulating sex at a village fete in Norfolk. Men being boiled alive, a twenty-stone woman being carried upside down. Imitation cheeses being rolled down a street, eggs being slammed against heads. Grown men shouting at snails, tattooed men covered in arrowroot. A plate of corned beef hash for £1.80. A stone-skimming prodigy breaking down in Scotland. A man drinking a pint of green vomit in Dorset. A Massey-Ferguson Eager Beaver. A Finn's erect cock.

Way back before our journey started, I genuinely thought

I'd finish the year a world champion. I still maintain that if the World Pipe-Smoking Championships hadn't been cancelled, I could have been. 'How hard can that be?' It was a refrain that had become familiar. But I had been hopelessly naive. Coal-carrying, shin-kicking and wife-carrying – I hadn't had a hope in hell. They had been Tom territory and I'd been chewed up alive. As for nettle-eating, sauna-sitting and shove ha'penny, what on earth had I been thinking? I hadn't reckoned on the hordes of people out there who'd be taking all these 'funny' little pastimes much more seriously than me. And the truth is, when I'd got over the pain of another crushing defeat (usually after about 10 seconds) I found this fact heart-warming. In what seems like an increasingly uniform world, where eccentricity is often frowned upon, you can still uncover plenty of nuts if you know where to squirrel.

Where was old King Can now, I wondered. Collecting litter with Arnie, no doubt. I never had phoned him back after *Countryfile*. I'd felt a bit bad about that. And what about Fred the peashooter? Or Allan, the mysterious stone-skimmer? Crazy characters ran through our story like multi-coloured thread. Before we'd set off on our journey, I'd been a little wary of eccentrics. In fact, I'd wondered if they still really existed. I'd met my fair share of wacky characters in the past, but their eccentricity usually seemed a little bit forced. A funny hat here, an amusing voice there. Most of them weren't fooling anyone, they were just everyday people looking for an angle. But a blind man entering a peashooting contest? That's eccentric. Men who collect winches? That's eccentric. As for King Can, he's probably still waiting for my call.

TOM

We'd done it – after ten long months, we'd done it – but now it was over. That was why I felt strangely hollow. I had a trophy that no one else in the world had, but nothing to look forward to except cleaning up the trail of destruction Dirsy had left behind as I'd carried him back from the pub.

Actually, I did have something else – a rusting wreck of a 1981 Bedford CF campervan. It sat outside the house, canted at a malevolent angle, the rain running patterns down the stained-glass windows. Sometimes when I looked at it I felt a mix of anger and fear – anger at the extravagant cost of keeping it running, fear at what might go wrong with it next. Today, however, its sorry appearance just added to the air of melancholy. We could at last truly call it the Champervan, but it had no more world championships to go to. What would happen to it now? Where would it go next? Where would we go next?

BEN

Back in my cold flat in Romford, I didn't feel much like a hero. There had been no welcome home party. No Champagne. No crumpet. Just a hand-written note on the kitchen table: 'UNLUCKY NOBHEAD – TRY BEING A HERO FOR ONCE AND DO THE FUCKING DISHES.' That was a low blow. I'd tried, God damn it, at least I'd tried . . .

ACKNOWLEDGEMENTS

We would like to extend our heartfelt thanks, in no particular order, to the following, without whose help 2008 would have been much like any other year: Brian Wilding, for filling us in on all things Gawthorpe; King Can (send Arnie our regards); the heroic Mini Cheddirs line-up and team analyst Jo; Shane Pym from the Bottle Inn (for your sake, we hope this book doesn't sell too many copies); the magnificent enthusiasm of Andy Dunlop at the World Egg-Throwing Federation; Simon Sleigh (don't worry son, one day someone will break that record); Anna Huttunen, 'The Baron' and the lovely people of Sonkajärvi, who made us feel incredibly welcome; Rory the Aussie (he knows why); George and Fred, peashooting legends; Hilary Scase and Neil the snail-trainer in Congham, plus Mrs B-B for the superb stable of snails; Gary and Freddie Starr down at the Romford Rub and Tug (no, I still don't want a blowy); Samuli, for picking up some bloke he'd never met from Helsinki airport; Ossi Arvela and the kind people of Heinola (Christ, those Finns can drink); stone-skimming experts Russ 'Rock-Bottom' Byars, Lydéric Bocquet, Ralph Lorenz, Donald 'Melon' Melville and Steve Backley; Dale Wills, for allowing us into his world; Victor Ubogu and Nick at The Arbiter, for the wonder of the inaugural World Ubogus; our colleagues at the BBC Sport website; book experts David Luxton, Richard Milner and Jon

Butler; Conti, for putting up with his housemate staring at a blank laptop screen for hours on end; Katie, for being a bloody good sport (it was a blast while it lasted); the faithful readers Jon T, Tom W, Jamie K and Brother Rob; Big Al for a germ of an idea; the Fordyce and Dirs clans, and to all the other competitors we met on our amazing adventure, especially those who triumphed and who can now call themselves heroes.